M000012196

INTO THE UNKNOWN

(1st Edition)

by Jasper T. Scott

JasperTscott.com
@JasperTscott

Cover Art by Tom Edwards
TomEdwardsDesign.com

AUTHOR'S CONTENT RATING: PG-13

Language: Moderate
Sexual Content: Mild/None
Violence: Moderate

Author's Guarantee: If you find anything you consider inappropriate for this rating, please e-mail me at JasperTscott@gmail.com and I will either remove the content or change the rating accordingly.

ACKNOWLEDGMENTS

This book went through more edits than usual in an effort to make it more pleasing to listen to, as well as to read. As usual there were plenty of people who helped with that process. A big thanks goes out to my editors, Aaron Sikes and Dave Cantrell, to my proofreader, Ian Jedlica, and to each of my beta readers. You guys never cease to amaze me! In particular, I'd like to thank William Schmidt, Davis Shellabarger, Ray Burt, Tim Runyan, Harry Huyler, Ryan Nelson, Karol Ross, Gerald Geddings, Ian Seccombe, Jackie Gartside, Dave Topan, Michael Madsen, Lisa Garber, and Mary Whitehead.

To those who dare,
And to those who dream.
To everyone who's stronger than they seem.
—Jasper Scott

*"Believe in me / I know you've waited for so long /
Believe in me / Sometimes the weak become the strong."*
—STAIND, Believe

CHAPTER 1

After passing through spaceport security, Liam Price and his family took a tram to the launch tower and piled into a dedicated elevator the size of a small house. More than a hundred people from the tram crowded in with them, and then the elevator began the long climb to the departure gates. Liam's wife, Aria, held his hand on one side, their seven-year-old daughter, Payton, on the other. Ten feet away, their son, Nikolai, stood with his eyes and palms glued to the twenty-foot wall of windows facing the view. Liam broke ranks with his wife and shouldered through the masses to stand beside Nikolai and watch as the gray urban sprawl of Philadelphia dropped away. They emerged from a forest of lesser skyscrapers to see the sun-speckled meeting of the Schuylkill and Delaware rivers. Giant, cloud-sized shadows roved slowly across the city.

"Excited?" Liam asked, gripping his son's shoulder.

Nikolai shrugged. "I guess." Teen-speak for—
Hell yeah!

Liam smiled. The elevator soared on, and the patchwork of skyscrapers lost all sense of depth and scale, becoming a flat gray grid. Liam's ears popped, and puffy walls of cumulus began drifting across the windows. Pea-sized jewels of moisture freckled the windows, growing to fat droplets and then streaking down in trembling rivulets.

Moments later, the clouds parted. Blazing sun and blue sky appeared, wrapped in cottony wisps and towering walls of vapor. Liam felt the elevator begin to slow down. The sensation reminded him of floating in water, not weightless, but much lighter than normal. That went on for about a minute, and then an automated voice crackled to life inside the elevator: "Now arriving on level four twenty. Departure gates three hundred to three hundred and eleven."

Liam gently turned his son away from the view and went to stand with his wife and daughter once more. A few seconds later, the elevator stopped. The doors dinged and rumbled open, and then everyone shuffled out into a vast, circular waiting area. Banks of seating surrounded the numbered departure gates around the vast circumference of the spaceport. In the center of the departure level holo-signs advertised everything from coffee to Johnnie Walker Scotch. A handful of gift shops, duty-free liquor stores, and convenience kiosks corresponded to those advertisements.

"Where's our gate?" Aria asked. Her long dark hair flared over her shoulders as she turned her head back and forth, searching the busy concourse.

Liam scanned the gate numbers within his line of sight. One through four. He nodded and pointed to the stores in the center, blocking their view of the gates on the other side. "That way. Number nine. Let's go." He grabbed Aria's and Payton's hands again and set a brisk pace across the crowded concourse.

Nikolai kept up beside them, but his pace quickly faltered as an ad for Coca Cola stole his attention. "I'm thirsty," he said.

Liam frowned. "Can't it wait? Drinks are free on the cruise."

"How long before we board?"

Liam consulted the time in the top right of his augmented reality lenses (ARLs). "Half an hour."

"Half an *hour?*" Nikolai moaned.

"I'm thirsty, too!" Payton added.

Aria's pace slowed, the battle already won. She looked to Liam. "It's just a few credits. I'll pay."

"No, no, that's okay," Liam sighed. "Go ahead and get them something. Take Niko. I'll take Paytie and meet you at the gate."

Aria flashed a heart-stopping smile and dropped a kiss on his cheek. "Such a good father," she whispered in his ear before spinning away.

Liam watched them head for the offending kiosk. Icy beads of moisture slipped down the sides of coca cola bottles in an endless loop, inciting a traitorous wave of thirst. But he wasn't going to buy any more five-credit sodas than he had to. Not when he was just half an hour away from an open bar.

"Come on, Paytie," Liam prompted, squeezing her hand to get her attention before setting off around the concourse once more. Gate nine swept into view, and Liam led his daughter past half a dozen rows of seats to the twenty-foot wall of windows running around the outer circumference of the building.

"Is that our spaceship?" Payton asked, pointing excitedly through the windows.

"It is," Liam confirmed. Shaped like a missile and gleaming silver in the sun, the fifteen-hundred-meter-long spaceship hovered beside the spaceport with its thrusters facing down and aimed at the distant city below. Clouds alternately concealed and veiled the ship as they whipped by the spaceport. Three ferris-wheel-like rings encircled the vessel along its length, their undersides glowing blue from the grav lifts that enabled the ship to hover in midair. The nose of the vessel extended several hundred stories above their already dizzying altitude on the four hundred and twentieth floor of the spaceport. It was as if someone had strapped engines and grav lifts to a mega-tall skyscraper and called it a spaceship.

"Wow..." Payton whispered.

Liam looked away from the windows to regard his daughter. She wore a rapt expression, her mouth agape, her green eyes bright and sparkling with wonder. Half the joy of being a parent was a vicarious one, and he wasn't about to miss out. He reached out and absently stroked his daughter's long, dark hair. She was the spitting image of her mother. Smiling fondly, he looked back to the view. They stood there like that for what must have been at least ten minutes, admiring the ship in silence.

"There you two are!"

Liam turned to see Aria striding over with Nikolai, each of them carrying a tall cup of soda.

"Hey, beautiful, what took you so long?" Liam asked. Aria passed her cup of soda to Payton, then looped her arm through his and leaned her head on his shoulder.

"Long lines," Aria explained. "There must be a thousand people on this level, and somehow all of them decided to go to the same kiosk."

"Such a good mother," he replied, returning her earlier compliment.

"Yes, I am, aren't I? Remember that, you urchins!"

Payton giggled, and Nikolai slurped noisily through his straw.

Liam leaned his head against Aria's and reveled in a moment of pure domestic bliss. Sometimes they forgot to slow down and appreciate moments like this one. Thankfully, there were plenty of them. Liam and Aria had won the lottery by finding each other, and after fifteen years of marriage, it still felt like they were in the honeymoon period. With so many people nowadays opting not to get married at all, and those who did experiencing an ever-increasing entropy of happiness, a part of Liam had been resigned to the same statistics when he got married. He'd expected to eventually see what everyone meant about marriage being a bankrupt institution, but he was still waiting.

"How can it hover like that?" Payton asked between sips of soda, still watching the cruise ship.

"Grav lifts," Nikolai explained.

"What do they do?"

"They hold it up..."

Payton flicked dark hair out of her eyes and shot him an annoyed look. *"No,* I mean how do they *work?"*

Liam chimed in, "They generate a force equal to that of gravity, but in the opposite direction." Since this was Payton's first trip to space, she'd never seen the technology in action before. "If it weren't for the grav lifts, that ship would plummet out of the sky."

"What if they break?" Payton asked in a shrinking voice.

"They won't."

"But if they did?"

Liam shook his head. "There are too many. Even if a few of them were to fail, the others would compensate. Don't worry; cruise ships never crash."

"Never...?" Nikolai trailed off in an ominous whisper. "Did you ever hear about the *Constellation of Bliss?"*

"No..." Payton replied.

"That's because it smashed into Sierra Four." He framed an explosion between his free hand and his soda cup.

Payton made huge eyes at him. "Really?"

"No," Liam said. "He's talking about a movie."

"Liar!" Payton punched her brother's arm, and he yelped.

"Hey!" He punched her back.

"Daddy!" Payton screamed.

"Cut it out! Both of you," Liam snapped. So much for domestic bliss.

The kids subsided, rubbing their arms and glaring sideways at each another.

Liam looked back out the windows to their ship, the *Starlit Dream*.

"I still can't believe you did this," Aria said. "This must have cost you a fortune!"

Liam flashed a grin at his wife. "We haven't taken a vacation in three years, and you always said you wanted to see the colonies some day."

Aria grinned back and slid her hand into his. Liam had surprised her with this trip on her fortieth birthday. Taking a month off was just what they needed right now.

A groaning noise started up somewhere beneath them, and then multiple boarding tunnels swept into view like giant robotic arms. Three tunnels for each of the ten departure levels assigned to their cruise. Liam nodded to the tunnel that corresponded to their gate as it came into line with an airlock in the side of the cruise ship. "Looks like we're about to start boarding."

"Already?" Aria asked. "What about our luggage?"

Liam shrugged. "Maybe one of the lower gates is reserved for loading luggage. It will probably be waiting for us in our suite by the time we get there."

"Our *suite?* You booked us a suite?" Aria asked.

Liam feigned innocence. "I didn't mention that?"

"No... Liam, how much *did* you spend on this trip?"

"A gentleman never spends and tells."

Aria took a quick step away from him and crossed her arms over her chest to fix him with an admonishing look. "What about paying off the house?"

"Relax, I got an amazing deal. Besides, you can't put a price on happiness."

"Now you sound like a booking agent."

A crackle of static issued from the ceiling, followed by: "The *Starlit Dream* is now boarding cabins two forty-one to three sixty at gates seven through nine."

"That's us," Liam said. He wrapped an arm around his wife's shoulders to turn her away from the windows. "Come on, kids," he said, keeping half an eye on Nikolai and Payton as he led the way to the gate.

The waiting area was suddenly a bustle of activity as everyone jumped up from their seats at the same time. When they reached the line to board the ship, at least a hundred people were already waiting there ahead of them.

"So what's it look like?" Aria asked.

Liam dragged his gaze away from the backs of the people in front of them. "What's what look like?"

"The suite!"

He smiled slyly at her. "You'll see."

"Oh, the suites are amazing!" a man standing behind them said.

Liam turned to see a tall, rakishly handsome man with dark hair and stubble. He was wearing designer clothes and grinning broadly with a perfect set of teeth. He looked vaguely familiar. *A client?* Liam wondered. The man had his arm around a dark-skinned beauty with lilac-colored eyes. She had a tiny waist and an impressive amount of body modifications for such a slender frame. Or maybe she was genetically engineered to grow into her parents' ideal of beauty. That might also explain her unusual eye color. That, or her augmented reality lenses were tinted purple.

"First time on an interstellar cruise?" the man asked, still grinning. "We go every year." He thrust out a hand to Liam. "Markus," he said.

The face might have been familiar, but the name was not. *Good.* Until just last year he'd worked as a criminal defense attorney for one of the biggest law firms in Philly. He'd had to defend plenty of wealthy criminals, and he'd got to meet even more. It was a dirty business that he was glad to have left behind now that he'd switched to family law and started his own firm.

"Liam Price," he said as he pumped Markus's hand. He turned to introduce the rest of his family. "This is my wife, Aria. And my kids, Payton and Nikolai."

Markus reached for Aria's hand. "A pleasure to meet you," he said, holding her hand between both of his in an overly friendly way. Liam frowned and pointedly eyed the other man. Just before the incident could go from awkward to inappropriate, Markus released Aria's hand and nodded to indicate the woman standing beside him. "This is my consort, Elisa Romero," he said.

"Pleased to meet you," Elisa said, and extended her hand to Aria.

"Consort?" Aria asked as she shook hands with the other woman.

Markus shrugged. "We don't like labels. Consort is suitably generic, don't you think?"

Liam nodded noncommittally and flashed a polite smile. He glanced back to the front and saw that the line was starting to move. "We'd better keep up," he said.

"For sure. We wouldn't want to miss our flight after all the money we spent on our rooms! Am I right, Liam?" Markus replied, slapping him on the back hard enough to make him stumble. Liam scowled. He hoped their suites were on opposite sides of the ring deck. But even as he was thinking that he overheard Aria and Elisa chatting excitedly about the trip. Aria wasn't one to make friends easily. It might be nice for her to socialize. Maybe he shouldn't be too quick to judge. Markus might grow on him.

Liam half-turned and forced another smile. "So, you've been on one of these cruises before?"

Markus's blue eyes lit up. "Oh yeah! Lots of times. It's fantastic! You're never going to forget this trip, I can promise you that."

CHAPTER 2

Aria shuffled down the line with the other passengers, walking hand-in-hand with her husband. Their footsteps made hollow thumps in the carpeted boarding tunnel. Aria tried not to notice how it bounced with their collective footfalls or think about the fact that they were suspended over a kilometer above the ground.

At the entrance of the cruise liner, Aria saw a pair of smiling stewards welcoming people aboard. They looked like they'd stepped right out of a brochure.

"Welcome aboard, Mr. and Mrs. Price!" the female steward said brightly.

"Thank you," Aria replied, nodding to them as she and Liam walked on board. She ushered the kids ahead of them while she and Liam brought up the rear, walking at a more leisurely pace. They passed down a short corridor and emerged in a large, circular concourse surrounded by cafes and shops on two levels.

A pair of winding staircases swept up to the second floor. Behind them, a backdrop of floor-to-ceiling windows gave a breathtaking view of gilded clouds and the gleaming spires of mega-tall skyscrapers. The interior of the ship was crisp and bright with muted gold lighting and softly-curving surfaces, all gleaming whites and silvers. The deck shone with faux marble tiles. A simulated blue sky with fiery clouds blazed on the ceiling. Aria's eyes tracked back down, and she saw palm trees standing between sitting areas, dividing them among the various eateries on the first floor. Leafy green fronds with purple blossoms draped the second-floor railings, the fronds drifting like willow branches on air currents from climate control vents. Appetizing smells and floral fragrances drifted to her nose.

Passengers fanned out as they came aboard, their collective voices rising as they went to look at the shops and restaurants. Others climbed the stairs to the second level or crowded into glass elevators on either side of the concourse.

"This is amazing!" Payton said.

"Can we get something to eat?" Nikolai added. "I'm starving!"

"Not yet," Aria replied. "We should check into our room first." She looked to Liam. "Do you know the way?"

"Mmmm?" Liam slowly dragged his eyes away from the view.

Not waiting for him to catch up, Aria mentally switched her Neuralink implant from the spaceport's network to the ship's network, so that she could ask for directions. As soon as she did that, a virtual assistant sprang to life in the form of a gray-haired man with warm brown eyes and a friendly face. He wore black pants and a black vest over a white shirt. A red tie peeked out just below his collar. His face wrinkled in all the right places as he smiled.

"Hello, Mrs. Price. Welcome aboard the *Starlit Dream!* My name is Jules. I will be your guide and personal assistant on this vacation." Jules' voice emerged from small speakers built into the sickle-shaped comm unit she wore around her right ear.

"Hello, Jules," Aria replied.

The assistant smiled crookedly at her. "It is not necessary for you to reply until the rest of your family can see me. I would not wish for you to look as though you've begun talking to yourself."

Aria smiled wryly. This AI had a sense of humor. She turned to Liam to see his eyebrows arched in question. "You'll have to connect to the ship's network to see him," she explained.

Liam nodded. Images began flickering over his eyes as he connected his ARLs.

"To see who?" Payton asked.

"Our virtual assistant," Aria explained.

"We have a virtual assistant?" Nikolai asked.

They all joined the network and Jules inclined his head to each of them in turn. "Hello, Mr. Price, Master Nikolai, Young Miss Payton. I am Jules, your personal assistant for this trip. Welcome aboard the *Starlit Dream!*"

"Thank you, Jules," Liam said.

"Do you know the way to our room?" Aria asked.

The AI's gaze returned to her. "Of course, madam. Your *suite* is located on ring deck three. Would you like me to lead the way? I am looking forward to meeting you face-to-face."

Aria's brow furrowed. "Face to face?"

"Yes, madam. My mobile unit is waiting in your suite."

Aria grimaced and shot her husband a sharp look. "We have a robot butler?" They'd recently had to sell Lilly, their domestic bot of ten years, to help finance Liam's family law practice. The kids still missed her, and having a robot butler for this trip would be an unpleasant reminder of that.

Liam flashed an apologetic look and shook his head. "Sorry, I didn't know."

"Is there a problem, madam?" Jules asked.

"No problem," Aria said, summoning a wan smile. "But you can drop the madam. I'm not that old."

"Of course. I meant no offense, Mrs. Price. If it makes you feel better, my facial recognition database suggests that you look nearly ten years younger than the average woman of your age."

Aria smiled. "I think I'm going to like you, Jules. Call me Aria."

"Of course, Aria." Jules gestured to one side of the concourse. "Your room will be most readily accessible from the elevators. When you are ready, I suggest you head there, and I will enter the appropriate deck number for you."

"Lead the way," Liam said.

"Yes, sir."

CHAPTER 3

Liam and his family exited a large elevator on deck thirty with at least twenty others, all of them speaking in hushed tones with their own virtual assistants. Liam wondered if the assistants were all the same or if they had different appearances and names.

Jules led the way down a gleaming white corridor. A pair of silver doors parted as they approached to reveal a set of tracks and a long glass corridor with two waiting trams. The tracks were guarded by glass railings on either side.

Jules gestured to the rearmost row of seats. "You may sit here."

Payton and Nikolai darted in one after another, followed by their mother. Liam entered last.

"Buckle up, kids," Aria said.

The other couples and families took their seats in the rows ahead of theirs. Liam absently scanned their faces, but none was familiar. They'd lost track of Markus and Elisa after coming aboard. *So much for socializing.*

"Please keep your hands and legs inside the tram at all times," Jules said as he went to stand at the front like a tour guide on a bus. A waist-high door slid shut beside Liam, followed by sliding gates in the glass railings. A split second later the vehicle began gliding forward, picking up speed.

Long windows separated by thin metal frames flashed by to either side and overhead, revealing stunning views of sky, clouds, the ring deck, and the spaceport.

"There are twelve spokes for each ring deck," Jules explained from the front of the tram. "You may use any of them to travel to and from your suite."

Liam noticed other travelers bobbing their heads as Jules spoke, but they were probably listening to their own virtual assistants.

"It is only a few hundred meters from one end of the tracks to the other. Some time when you're not in a hurry, I recommend you try a leisurely stroll along the spokes. The view is worth every step."

The tram slowed, then stopped, and the doors and gates slid open. Jules stepped off the tram, and everyone followed him to another pair of broad silver doors. Everyone walked through into a wide, gently curving white corridor with dark blue carpets and a transparent ceiling that gave a clear view of sky and the soaring bulk of the *Starlit Dream.* The grav lifts from the other two ring decks glowed bright blue above theirs.

Liam dragged his eyes down, focusing back on his immediate surroundings. Passengers trickled down the corridor to their rooms. A familiar couple stood before a golden door with the number 250 on it, glowing white. It was Markus and Elisa. Liam wondered how they'd gotten there. He hadn't seen them board the tram. Maybe they'd taken a different spoke. Liam was about to call out to them, but then their door slid open, and they stepped inside.

"Mr. and Mrs. Price, please follow me to your suite," Jules said.

Aria nodded. "Come on, kids."

Payton went skipping ahead of them, following so closely behind Jules that she was actually stepping on his virtual heels. Nikolai trailed between her and his parents at a more reserved pace.

Before long Jules stepped up to one of the doors on their left, along the outer circumference of the ring-deck. The number 258 glowed brightly there.

"Welcome to your suite," Jules said. He gestured grandly to the door. It swished open to reveal a short foyer with their luggage sitting beside a second doorway, already standing open to reveal a large, open living space with a bank of curving picture windows along the far wall. A floral fragrance wafted out, drawing them in. Payton and Nikolai rushed inside, and Liam heard their muffled exclamations a moment later. He and Aria walked through the door at a more leisurely pace. The opening was wide enough for them to pass through side-by-side. Liam wondered about that, and about the second set of doors. He suspected it might be an airlock, but he struggled to fathom the purpose of an airlock between their suite and the rest of the ship.

Aria's jaw dropped as they entered the living area, and her emerald eyes grew round as they flashed around the space, taking it all in. Liam had already seen their suite when he'd booked the trip, so he wasn't as surprised as she. Still, it was one thing to see the photos on his AR lenses, another thing entirely to see the accommodations firsthand.

Liam walked up to the curving windows on the far side of the living area. The windows were gilded with a misty golden vapor, but as Liam watched, that veil parted to reveal scraps of park-greens and city-grays below. Looking up, Liam counted the hazy spires of three different skyscrapers, all over four hundred stories, just like the spaceport.

"This is incredible," Aria whispered, stepping up to the window beside him.

Softly-thunking footsteps approached. "It is indeed," a familiar voice said as Jules appeared beside Liam.

The bot regarded them with a crinkly smile and inclined his head. "Mr. and Mrs. Price. It is good to finally meet you in the flesh."

Liam briefly deactivated his ARLs, but Jules didn't disappear. He was, however, slightly different from his virtual counterpart. His skin and face looked ever-so-slightly artificial, despite an impressive attention to detail that had faithfully included every freckle and every pore of the real human model he'd likely been based upon.

Liam nodded slowly, and Jules smiled, revealing straight white teeth. "How do you like your accommodations?"

Most bots were not so faithfully and carefully crafted. Their beloved Lilly, for example, had possessed a virtual face and skin projected on a flexible screen beneath her transparent skin. She had literally glowed in the dark.

Payton and Nikolai came bounding over.

"He's a real person?" Nikolai asked.

"According to some advocates I am both real and a person, but I am not human if that is what you mean," Jules replied.

Payton reached out to poke Jules in his slightly-protruding belly. Her finger sank into a convincing imitation of belly fat.

"Amazing," Liam said, shaking his head.

"I was designed to mimic my original human form as closely as possible."

Liam arched an eyebrow, and his gaze drifted south of Jules' navel.

"Not *that* closely," he chided, then changed the topic as he gestured to their room. "What do you think? Please, have a look around and get acquainted. This will be your home away from home for the next four and a half weeks as we travel through the colonies."

Liam looked around the living room. A four-seater dining table and a basic kitchen backed onto it. All of the finishings and appliances looked like they were top-of-the-line. The space was bright and inviting with smooth lines, light-colored furniture, and more of those glowing gold panels. Liam moved on from the picture windows to the first of the suite's two bedrooms. It was the master. A king-sized bed sat beneath an old-fashioned crystal chandelier. Rose petals in the shape of a heart decorated a cozy-looking white quilt. A row of golden throw pillows lined the headboard.

Liam took a deep breath, and his nostrils flared with the smell of fresh-cut roses. A crystal vase full of roses sat on the corner of a wardrobe beneath a large holoscreen at the foot of the bed. Tendrils of mist slowly wafted from that vase, making him suspect that it was the source of the fragrance.

Another picture window took up the far wall with a reclining chair in one corner and a jetted hot tub bubbling in the other. A transparent lid covered the tub, probably designed to prevent heat and steam from saturating the room rather than to keep the water from sloshing out. The *Starlit Dream* would have inertial dampeners to keep everything in place during maneuvers.

Aria's voice drifted to Liam's ears from the living room as she approached: "Have you seen the kids' room? It has all of the latest game consoles and two separate VR pods! They're already playing their favorite..." Aria trailed off as she walked into the master bedroom. She stood gaping in the entrance. Liam flashed a knowing grin.

"Have you seen *our* room?" he rejoined.

Aria glanced about quickly, then went to check a pair of closets on the other side of the bed. Two matching closets with a rack for shoes at the bottom, drawers on top, and hanging space above.

Liam smiled. "His and hers. Just like home."

"Hers and hers," Aria amended, smiling crookedly back. "You can have the wardrobe below the holoscreen."

Liam snorted and shook his head. "Just like home."

Aria went into the en suite bathroom next. She gasped, and Liam followed her there. It was a full five-piece bathroom, glittering with mirrors and lights.

"This is bigger than our bathroom back home!" Aria exclaimed.

Two sinks, another jetted tub, and a shower big enough for six people—with two separate shower heads and two sets of body jets. "You're right, it is," Liam replied.

Aria rounded on him with her arms crossed. "Spill it. How much did you spend on this trip?"

He hesitated. "Guess."

Aria made a show of looking around again and then threw up her hands in exasperation. "It must have been at *least* a hundred thousand."

Liam took a quick step back. "Are you crazy? I'd never spend that much."

"Then how much did you spend?"

"I told you, I got a deal. It was just over twenty thousand."

"That's *it?*"

He nodded.

Someone cleared their throat, and Liam turned to see Jules standing in the open doorway of the master bedroom. "Please pardon my intrusion. I couldn't help but overhear your conversation. Did you say you only spent twenty thousand for this room?" Jules asked.

Liam nodded to the bot. "That's correct, why?"

"Because Aria is correct. This suite has a base cost of sixty-nine thousand credits, with an additional ten thousand per meal plan."

Liam's brow furrowed, and he slowly shook his head. "Then how did I get it so cheap?"

"Perhaps you should verify your account statements, just to be sure that you have not accidentally spent more than you anticipated."

Just then, an announcement rippled through overhead speakers: "Ladies and Gentleman, this is Captain Harmond speaking. Welcome aboard the *Starlit Dream*. We are now just minutes away from launch. The inertial dampeners should buffer any turbulence, so there is no need to sit down or buckle in at an emergency station, but please do watch the security briefing on the nearest viewscreen and take a moment to familiarize yourselves with the safety features of this ship. The short version is that all of the suites along the ring decks function as independent lifeboats, and in the event of an emergency evacuation you must follow the red emergency light strips to the nearest ring deck.

"Rest assured, however, no stellar cruise in the history of the Union has ever needed to evacuate its passengers.

"While you're watching the security briefing at the viewports, do take a minute to enjoy the view as we make orbit and jump to our first stop: Kepler-22b, otherwise known as Aquaria. Our estimated flight time is six hours and ten minutes. Until then, feel free to wander around and explore the ship's many amenities.

"On behalf of myself and the crew, we hope you have a very pleasant afternoon, and an even better stay aboard the *Starlit Dream*."

As soon as the announcement ended, Liam went straight to the holoscreen at the foot of the bed and used a combination of mental commands and gestures to log into his bank account. He *really* hoped Jules wasn't right about additional charges to his account.

CHAPTER 4

Aria watched Liam log in to their account and check their credit statement. The deck rumbled and gently shook beneath their feet as the *Starlit Dream* took off. The crystal vase on the wardrobe shivered. All the while Aria's heart thundered in her chest. If Liam really had spent a hundred thousand credits on this vacation, then they were in big trouble.

Her husband's recent career change from highly paid defense attorney to the sole owner of a small family law practice had left them in a precarious position as it was.

"Look, there it is!" Liam said, pointing to the screen. "Twenty-one thousand, three hundred and five."

"Who discounts a trip by *that* much?" Aria asked, even as relief rippled through her.

"Maybe they needed to fill in for a last-minute cancellation?" Liam suggested. "I booked at the last minute. That's how you get a good deal. At least, that's what the booking agent said."

Aria looked to Jules for confirmation.

He wore a dubious frown. "I do not have access to the company's ticket booking records, but I suppose that it *is* possible. There would have to be multiple cancellations to account for such a dramatic discount, and it would certainly be the cheapest rate that *I* have ever heard of."

Feeling nervous again, another possibility occurred to Aria. Her eyes narrowed and found Liam once more. "Are you *sure* you read the fine print? What if you're on a payment plan and that was just the first installment?"

Liam shook his head. "I triple checked. It was all above board. You want me to call them and ask?"

"Yes!" Aria blurted.

"Fine."

She watched light from Liam's ARLs flicker across his eyes as he paced up to the picture windows next to the hot tub. Aria went to sit on the edge of the bed and watch the view. Her knees bounced nervously as she waited. Clouds scrolled down past the windows at an ever-increasing rate. A few seconds later, they fell away like cobwebs, and a vast blue sky domed the world. After about a minute, stars began pricking through, and the sky gradually darkened to black.

Liam was still standing there, quietly waiting to speak with someone.

"What's wrong?" Aria prompted.

Liam half-turned to her. "They're not answering."

Jules stepped into view. "Whatever the case may be, it is too late to do anything about it now."

Liam's frown deepened as he regarded the bot. "That's not reassuring."

"Perhaps not, but it is the truth. How about this: I will see what I can learn about your booking. In the meantime, please don't trouble yourselves. I can see that my well-meaning comments have caused you undue distress, and I sincerely apologize for that. Please relax, and leave everything to me."

Liam gave in with a grudging nod, and Aria let out a shaky breath.

"May I suggest a relaxing soak in the hot tub while we transition to orbit and jump through the gate to Aquaria? You will find that all of the viewports in your suite are configurable to provide real-time views from any of the ship's external cameras."

"That does sound nice," Aria said, eyeing the bubbling hot tub. "But I'm also hungry. Do you think any of the restaurants are serving yet?"

"Oh, yes, but if you prefer, I would be happy to bring whatever you like directly to your room."

Aria's mouth began to water. "Such as?"

"There are over one hundred restaurants on board, representing all of the most popular types of cuisine in the Union. No matter how refined your palate or eclectic your craving might be, you will find that the *Starlit Dream* has exactly what you're looking for."

"In that case, how about a mixed plate of sushi rolls, and whatever cocktail you'd recommend to go with it?"

"Of course."

"Oh, and please ask the kids what they would like. I know Nikolai was hungry. Payton probably is, too."

Jules inclined his head to that. "Gladly, Aria. And for you, Mr. Price?"

"A beer—actually, make that two. And a cheeseburger with fries. Nothing too fancy."

"Of course, sir." Jules smoothly turned to the wardrobe beside him and opened one of the drawers to reveal that it was a bar-fridge stocked with beverages. He withdrew a frosty-looking beer and removed the cap with a quick twist before walking over to hand it to Liam.

Accepting the reusable polycarbonate bottle, Liam took a big gulp while Aria watched him enviously.

"What else have you got in there?" she asked.

"Wine, spirits, and a variety of juices and carbonated beverages."

"Wine, please. White."

"Coming right up."

CHAPTER 5

Liam sat on the edge of the hot tub beside his wife, leaning against the wall with his feet dangling in the churning, steaming water. He took another bite of his burger, being careful not to spill sauce in the tub.

Aria sat beside him in a red bikini, deftly plucking sushi rolls from her plate with chopsticks and sipping a ginger-lemon cocktail.

They'd set the curving picture window beside them to show alternating scenic views from the aft, fore, and starboard cameras. Right now it showed Earth disappearing behind them, half of it cloaked in darkness with city lights blooming like orange flowers while the blue and green ribbons of an aurora borealis undulated above the North Pole. Spaceships came and went: fiery streaks falling through the atmosphere and glowing blue thruster-trails rocketing for orbit.

Then the scene switched back to a forward view and Liam saw the space gate to Kepler-22: a giant silver ring encircling a warped sphere of space-time, a wormhole.

The star field inside the sphere was actually over six hundred light years away. Dead center of the wormhole was a yellow star the size of the tip of Liam's thumb: Kepler-22, or Aquaria's Star. Aquaria was a water world, famous for its beaches, shallow lagoons, and crystal clear green oceans. Their striking emerald color was a combined product of atmospheric elements in the lavender sky and minerals in the water. Diving and snorkeling among the colorful alien reefs was one of the primary tourist attractions, but there was also plenty to see by touring the islands themselves.

A musical chime interrupted their silent contemplation.

"What was that?" Aria asked.

"It sounded like a doorbell." Liam activated his ARLs, and a flashing bar of text appeared at the bottom of his field of view:

Someone is at the door.

Liam mentally queried for a video feed and saw Markus and Elisa standing in the corridor. Once again Liam was struck by how familiar Markus looked. He frowned. "How did they find us?"

"Who?" Aria asked.

"That couple we ran into at the spaceport."

Aria's green eyes lit up. "Ask Jules to let them in. They've probably come to ask if we'd like to join them for dinner."

"We're already eating." Liam plucked a fry off his plate and held it up for emphasis.

"Don't be so grumpy. Isn't socializing one of the reasons people go on a cruise? Besides, Elisa seems nice."

Liam relented with a shrug just as the door chimed again. Liam was just about to contact Jules when the butler bot contacted him through the room's overhead speakers. "Would you like me to get the door for you?"

"Yes, thank you, Jules," Liam said. "You can bring them to our room."

"At once, sir."

A moment later, Markus and Elisa strolled in with Jules leading the way. Markus was wearing white shorts and a T-shirt and open-toed sandals, while Elisa wore a floral-patterned skirt and sleeveless top. They looked like they were already dressed for Aquaria.

"Hey there, Lee!" Markus said brightly. "I see you've found the hot tub."

"It's Liam, not Lee."

"But Lee is short for Liam, right?"

Liam smiled thinly and shook his head. "Liam's already pretty short."

"True!" Markus replied, nodding quickly.

Elisa stopped beside Aria and nodded to her plate of sushi. "That looks good. Where did you order it from?"

Aria shook her head as she sipped her cocktail. "I have no idea. Jules?"

"It's from *Tsugoi* on level fifty-six."

"We'll have to try that," Elisa replied.

"They're open until midnight," Jules added.

"Maybe tomorrow. We already ate at the spaceport," Markus said. "But we were hoping you two might join us for cocktails on Tahili Beach."

"Tahili..." Liam trailed off. "We're still hours away from Aquaria, aren't we?"

Markus snorted. "Not Aquaria. Deck seventy-one. It's a simulated beach."

"That sounds nice," Aria replied.

"It is!" Elisa added.

Markus nodded along with that.

"We could join you for a while," Aria said. "What do you think, Liam?"

He shrugged and emptied his beer. "Sure. Why not."

"Where's your bot?" Aria asked.

"We don't have one, just a virtual assistant," Elisa replied. "You don't really need one unless you have kids, so we decided to save the extra ten thousand for shopping."

Aria gaped at Elisa and rounded on Liam. "Ten *thousand?*"

He began shaking his head. The booking site hadn't cited any extra costs for Jules.

"Expensive, huh?" Markus replied, grinning like an idiot and nodding. "What did you pay for this trip? A hundred and fifty G's?"

Liam balked at that estimate and cleared his throat. "No," he said, thinking fast. "Captain Harmond is a personal friend of mine. He got us a good deal."

"Oh yeah? Lucky bastard. Wish I had friends like that!"

"So does Liam," Aria added, staring pointedly at him.

Markus missed the subtext. "Shall we head up to the beach?"

Liam swung his legs over the side of the hot tub and hopped down. It might be nice to have a distraction from Aria's repeated inquisitions. "Just let me change first."

"Change?" Markus asked. "Looks like you're already dressed for the beach to me."

"I'm not planning to swim," Liam said, shaking his head and heading for his suitcase lying open in the closet. He grabbed his shoes, a pair of fresh socks and pants and a short-sleeved button-up shirt. It might be odd to wear shoes and slacks to a beach, but after so many years of wearing suits for his job, he felt naked without at least part of that ensemble.

"I'll go ask if the kids want to join us," Aria said as she climbed out of the hot tub.

CHAPTER 6

"I heard the captain say that earlier, but what did he mean that our suites double as lifeboats?" Aria asked.

Markus turned to look at her from his lounger. He had to shade his eyes from the artificial sunset with one hand. "You guys didn't watch the security briefing?"

Aria shook her head. "We muted it and let it play in the background while we unpacked our clothes and changed into our swimsuits. We were planning to play it again later."

Payton squealed with delight, drawing Aria's gaze to where she and Nikolai were playing chicken with the waves crashing on the sandy shore. As she watched, Payton almost ran into a toddler. The kid fell over and began crying, but Jules quickly scooped him up and carried him over to his mother. "Watch where you're going, Paytie!" Aria called out.

"Sorry!" Payton called back.

There must have been a few hundred people on the semi-circular beach and in the water, but it didn't feel overcrowded because fully half of an entire deck had been devoted to this illusion, and the diameter of the ship's central column was over a hundred meters.

Not waiting for her attention to come back to him, Markus answered her earlier question: "Each suite is actually a detachable shuttle. They can even land on planets, but they're only activated in case of an emergency. The grav lifts are in the bottom of the rings, and the suites are in the rings, so each of them has its own set."

"Interesting." Aria looked away from Markus to squint at the simulated horizon over the sparkling water of what was essentially a giant wave pool. According to Jules, the water only went out twenty-five meters before it hit an invisible wall and merged with a hologram, but from this distance, it was impossible to tell where the real water ended and the illusion began. Holographic artistry at its best. On the other side of that wall was another VR deck—a winter wonderland with toboggan rides, ice-skating, hockey, and cross-country skiing.

"Well, I'm sure we won't need the lifeboats," Liam said between sips of his beer.

Jasper T. Scott

"Yeah, you're right," Markus agreed. "I mean, the *Starlit Dream* is over five hundred years old, and she's never had a problem."

That got Aria's attention. "Five hundred years? But it looks brand-new!"

Markus shook his head. "Not even close. She used to be a colony ship. She's been out here cruising the stars since before there were even any jump gates. The ship has been refitted multiple times since then, of course. At one point it was even drafted as a warship to fight in the first Gliesian War." Markus chuckled darkly. "I just hope there aren't any stress fractures left over from those days!"

Elisa sat up beside Markus, her lilac eyes squinting in the artificial sun. "Don't pay attention to him. He always does this—tries to scare everyone we meet. What he doesn't mention is that we've been on more than twenty cruises and we've never had any problems."

"*Twenty* cruises?" Aria asked. Markus and Elisa didn't look a day over thirty. There were ways to roll back the clock if you had enough money, but they were expensive and involved controversial abuses of alien rights. Aria's life's work at Vitatech revolved around finding a better, more humane way to extend human lifespans. She sincerely hoped Markus and his *consort* weren't *vitaholics*.

"You must have seen a lot of the galaxy," Liam put in before Aria could pry about their ages.

"As much as anyone can, I guess," Markus replied. "There are only so many places that have been connected with jump gates, and most of them really aren't worth visiting. On one planet we went to the gravity was so strong that we had to wear exosuits just to walk around. What was that one called, Elly?"

"Maragos."

"Yeah, that's right. They named it after the Hindu god of death because the colonists there all die of heart problems before they reach a hundred. If it weren't such a gold mine of rare elements, nobody would even live there. But I don't know why they don't just remote-operate it with bots. Who would willingly live on a planet that's going to cut your lifespan in half?"

"Well, not exactly half," Aria said. "No one has ever lived to be two hundred years old, but I'm working on it."

"Oh yeah?" Markus asked.

Liam sat up. "Aria works for a medical research company that's working on synthetic vitalics. They think they can extend people's lifespans by even more than the natural version once they get the formula right."

"No shit!" Markus said. "You must be some kind of genius. I thought synthetic vitalics were still a long way off?"

Aria hesitated. She didn't like to talk about her work. The research was too valuable and there was far too much at stake. Anyone could be a spy for the competition. As it was, they'd had three different break-ins at the lab. It had gotten to the point where they'd begun storing and encoding their research data in their own DNA in order to prevent it from being stolen, but no one knew about that besides Aria and a few other top researchers.

"We're still a long way off," Aria lied.

Markus's grin faded, and he sighed. He glanced at Elisa. "Looks like we'll have to keep using vitalics *au naturel*."

An angry heat rose in Aria's cheeks, and her breathing became suddenly shallow and fast. "You use vitalics?" she asked, her eyes like laser beams.

Liam placed a hand on her arm.

Markus's brow furrowed, obviously confused by her sudden change of demeanor. "How else do you think we stay looking so young at sixty?"

"Sixty! You'd have to be using vitalics twice a month for the last..."

"Thirty years?" Markus nodded. "I was an early adopter."

Aria couldn't even see straight. "That is unconscionable!"

"Why? It's not illegal. I don't know any of our friends who don't use them. I mean, if you can afford it, why not?"

"Because natural vitalics are harvested from live Vitari, and the harvesting process kills them."

Markus rolled his blue eyes and turned to his consort. "I think maybe we'd better go, Elly."

"I was just thinking the same thing," she replied.

Markus stood up and drained what was left of his frozen margarita. Elisa stood up beside him, her lilac eyes dipping to Aria. "They're not like us, you know. The Vitari."

Aria scowled. "You're right, they're better!"

"They're barely even intelligent."

"That doesn't give us the right to raise them in captivity and murder their children to extend our own lives."

"Better them than us," Markus replied. "You know, for most of human history, we raised animals for food. And yes, sometimes we killed and ate their babies—veal, for example."

"This is different. Vitari are *not* dumb brutes," Aria countered. "They're self-aware, they have a culture and even a language. They are the closest thing we've found to intelligent life so far!"

"If they're so intelligent, then why don't they fight back?" Markus challenged.

"Because they're non-violent! They're immortal herbivores. They had no concept of death until we came along. Thank God the explorers who found Vitaria couldn't remember how to get back there."

Markus snorted. "Couldn't remember, or purposefully forgot? At least they were smart enough to bring Vitari eggs back to Earth with them. Good luck with your synthetic vitalics. See you around, Liam."

Aria watched, speechless with rage as Markus and Elisa turned and began walking up the beach to a row of thatched-roof buildings that serviced the beach-goers. A holographic scene of tropical mountains soared above those roofs.

"*That's* where I know him from," Liam said suddenly.

"You *know* him?" Aria asked.

Liam nodded. "He's Markus *Leonidus*. His father is Varik Leonidus, the founder of Vital Corp."

Aria blinked in shock. "Are you sure? How come I've never seen Markus in the news? His father is..."

"Infamous?" Liam suggested.

Aria nodded. "Exactly."

"Varik's wife divorced him *in absentia* after his expedition went missing. Markus was still very young, and Varik didn't return until he was already fully-grown. He stayed out of the public eye because he was never in it to begin with. My understanding is that they reconciled sometime after Varik's return and Varik gave his son some of his shares in Vital Corp."

"Well, I guess that explains how Markus has been able to take twenty of these cruises."

"That's nothing to him. Markus is worth over a billion credits, and as the sole heir to Vital Corp he stands to inherit several thousand times that when his father finally dies."

"The rich get richer," Aria said.

"To hell with them," Liam replied.

"If only we had a hell to send them to..."

"Maragos sounds like a good candidate," Liam replied.

Aria smiled. "Yes, it does."

A rising commotion among the beach-goers interrupted their conversation, and Aria cast about for her kids. She found them racing up from the water with Jules hot on their heels. Everyone else was leaving the water, too.

Aria shot to her feet. "What's wrong?" she called.

Jules looked troubled. "We just exited the jump gate."

Liam chuckled nervously. "You say that like it's the end of the galaxy or something."

"Not the end of the galaxy, sir. The end of the line."

"What do you mean?" Liam asked.

Aria's heart began pounding in her chest. "Jules, you're starting to scare me. What's going on?"

The butler bot glanced at their kids. Payton's eyes were wide, and Nikolai's brow was furrowed with concern.

"Daddy, what's going on?" Payton asked.

"That's what I want to know," Liam said. "Jules? Spit it out."

The bot opened his mouth to speak, but before he could say a word, unseen speakers boomed to life, echoing through the virtual paradise. "Attention all passengers and crew, this is Captain Harmond speaking. We have experienced an unexpected departure from our intended flight plan. The jump gate appears to have suffered a malfunction which connected us to the wrong exit gate. Rest assured we have emerged safely from the wormhole, and there is no cause for alarm, but we will not be arriving at Aquaria as scheduled. I repeat, there is no cause for alarm, and we appreciate your patience while we work to resolve this matter. Thank you."

CHAPTER 7

Liam frowned at Jules. "The wrong exit gate? How does something like that even happen? We *saw* Kepler-22 while we were approaching the gate."

"Did you? Or did you see another star of the same spectral type? As to *how* it happened, I suspect it was a case of simple human error, but rest assured, it shouldn't be hard to correct our course. We will, however, be arriving at Aquaria several hours later than expected, so I suggest you all go get a good night's sleep. By morning the matter should be resolved, and the shuttles will be waiting to take you and your family down to a *real* beach."

Liam sighed and gave in with a nod. Someone tugged on his pants. It was Payton. She was squinting up at him with big green eyes. "Daddy, are we lost?"

He dropped to his haunches and regarded Payton with a warm smile. "No, sweetheart. We're just a little off course, that's all."

"Can you at least tell us where we are?" Aria asked Jules.

"Of course, one moment please."

Nikolai glanced about curiously. "Why is everyone so scared?"

Liam slowly rose to his feet. Niko was right. The people on the beach were gathering their things in a hurry, shouting at each other and at their assistants, virtual and real alike. The passengers looked to be on the verge of panicking.

"Hmmm," Jules said.

Liam rounded on the bot. "What's wrong?" His nerves were on a hair trigger at this point.

"I can't access our current location. The crew appears to have restricted access to that information."

"Why would they do that?" Aria asked.

"I'm afraid I do not know."

Liam could guess why. "Because they don't want us to panic when we find out where we are."

"Why would we..." Aria trailed off, her eyes widening in horror. "Do you think we're in Guild Space?"

"It's possible, but I wouldn't worry about that. Just because the Miners' Guild isn't part of the Union any more doesn't mean that they're out to get us."

"Maybe not, but Guild Space is poorly patrolled, and I've heard that pirates stalk the jump gates in their systems. What if a group of them somehow diverted us here?"

Liam thought about all of the ultra-rich people on board. How much could a group of pirates stand to gain by boarding them, or worse—by hijacking the entire cruise liner and holding the passengers for ransom? How much would Vital Corp's trillionaire founder pay to free his son, Markus? And he was just one of many wealthy passengers on board.

Liam remembered what Markus had said about the suites being lifeboats, and his gaze snapped to the nearest exit, behind a thatched-roof hut with stacks of colorful beach towels on the counter. "We should get back to our room."

Aria nodded quickly. She grabbed Payton's hand and began striding toward the exit. Liam looked to Nikolai. He was busy toweling off and raking hands through his wet hair, scratching the sand out of it.

"Come on! Let's go!" Liam urged.

Nikolai slipped on his sandals and wrapped the towel around his shoulders, and then they ran after Aria. Liam kicked up glittering waves of sand with his shoes as he went. Noticing that Jules wasn't with them anymore, he cast a quick look over his shoulder to see the bot collecting more towels and a few loose articles of clothing that the kids had left on the beach.

"Go on, sir, I'll catch up!" he said.

By the time Liam and Nikolai reached the exit, they were forced to press into a growing throng of grumbling masses. People were all-but trampling each other in their hurry to leave the virtual shores of Tahili Beach.

"Come on..." Liam ground out, standing on tiptoes as he struggled to catch a glimpse of Payton and Aria. But they were both too short to see over the heads of the crowd.

Nikolai huddled close, his shoulder brushing Liam's arm. "Where's Mom?" he asked.

"I don't know," Liam replied, shaking his head as they shuffled along with the crowd. Sweaty, sandy bodies pressed in on all sides. The elevators were right behind the exit, a bank of eight, each with a capacity of twenty or more, but there had to be almost a thousand people on the beach, and the sand traps were a major choke point. Even from a dozen feet back Liam could hear the jets of water hissing out to wash sandy feet and bodies, and hot air whistling from vents to subsequently dry them off. Liam took that as a good sign. The passengers couldn't be that scared if they were taking time to get clean before leaving the beach.

"Follow me, sir," Jules said as he strode up behind them. He went ahead, parting the crowds like a field of wheat.

Not asking questions, Liam grabbed the back of Jules' vest with one hand, and Nikolai's hand with the other. The three of them formed a train, chugging along and stepping on toes as they went. Jules made apologies for them which Liam repeated with a strained smile as angry faces turned their way.

But it worked. They reached the front of the churning masses just in time to see Payton and Aria disappear inside one of the elevators. Aria stood on tiptoes and waved to him as their eyes met.

"Come on!" Liam said, surging forward just as another elevator dinged and the doors parted. He accidentally elbowed a seven-foot man in the ribs, who rounded on Liam with a snarl. He recognized the tell-tale whir of motors and servos even before he noticed the exoskeleton lurking beneath the man's Hawaiian shirt and brown slacks. Probably a Martian or a Lunarian. A life lived in low gravity explained the willowy frame and the exoskeleton to support it. They were also notoriously ill-tempered.

Jules stepped between them and casually deflected a metal-wrapped fist with a hollow-sounding thunk. "Very sorry, sir. It is an emergency."

"You're not the only ones in a hurry," the man growled. "Mind your path."

"Yes, of course," Jules said.

Liam battled his way through to the open elevator with Nikolai and Jules just before it filled up. "You realize we're going *up*," Jules said quietly just as the elevator doors slid shut.

"What?" Liam glanced at the panel above the doors to see an up arrow. "Damn it!"

The elevator rose sharply under them, carrying them even farther from Aria and Payton. Liam sucked in a deep breath and let it out slowly. There could still be a benign explanation, a simple navigation error, for example. He tried to cling to that hope, but all of the other passengers in the elevator were speculating loudly about darker possibilities.

"Sir..." Jules whispered in Liam's ear.

He turned to the bot with eyebrows raised. Something in his tone set off alarm bells in Liam's head.

The bot's eyes darted around briefly as if worried about who might overhear him; then he leaned in and whispered again, "I think I know where we are."

CHAPTER 8

"**Y**ou *know* where we are?" Liam replied in a sharp whisper. Too loud. He drew curious glances from nearby passengers as the elevator made its first stop. Half of the passengers got off.

A chat prompt from Jules appeared on Liam's ARLs. He accepted it, and the bot's reply appeared at the bottom of his field of view.

I have been conducting a spectral analysis of the stars visible from the ship's external camera feeds.

Liam replied with a mental question via his Neuralink: *And?*

And, I cannot identify any known star systems.

Liam frowned. *So we're not in Guild Space?*

No, sir.

Then where the hell are we?

I believe we might be in another galaxy.

Liam's jaw dropped, but he quickly dismissed the possibility. *No one has ever jumped that far before.*

And yet, there is a jump gate behind us, which means the Union has *been here before.*

The elevator stopped again, letting off more people. *Maybe you don't recognize any stars because we're too far away from Earth?*

"Dad—" Nikolai interrupted, tapping him on the shoulder, "—what's that?"

Liam turned to his son with eyebrows raised just as the lights inside the elevator flickered, and the doors began sliding shut.

Nikolai was pointing to something on the other side of the closing doors—a shapeless shimmer, like a giant soap bubble, or the rainbow sparkle of mist in the sun. It flowed swiftly out of sight as the doors closed. A woman's muffled scream pierced the air, and then the elevator moved on, heading down.

Nikolai looked to Liam with wide eyes. Liam's heart jack-hammered in his chest as he tried to make sense of what he'd just witnessed. Rationalizations came and swept his fears aside, and he shook his head.

"Someone probably just stepped on that woman's toes." He squeezed his son's shoulder reassuringly.

"And that... sparkly thing?" Nikolai asked, his eyes narrowing beneath a knitted brow.

Liam shrugged. "Spray from a fountain, or mist from one of those essential oil diffusers. Right, Jules?"

The bot looked uncertain, but he nodded. "Quite likely."

The lights flickered again, this time plunging the elevator into darkness for several seconds. A ruddy glow of emergency lighting took over, and speakers crackled to life inside the elevator.

"Attention all crew and passengers, this is Captain Harmond speaking! We are under attack by unknown—" A muffled scream overlaid the transmission. Cracks of gunfire sounded, followed by more screams, and then the captain's voice returned, sounding out of breath. "All hands abandon ship! Repeat, all hands abandon—" The captain's voice cut off with a gurgle, followed by wet crunching sounds.

* * *

Aria tried not to think about what the captain was choking on. The lights flickered again just as she and Payton scrambled to board the tram with a throng of other passengers.

"Where's Daddy?" Payton moaned as she sat down beside a wide-eyed elderly man in the middle of their row.

"He's coming, don't worry," Aria replied as she took her own seat.

"He's not answering..." Payton sniffed.

Aria looked sharply at her daughter just as the tram jerked into motion. "What do you mean? You tried contacting him?"

Payton nodded quietly.

Fearing something might have happened to Liam or Nikolai, Aria tried to send her husband a message via her Neuralink. Neither of them had taken their comm pieces with them to Tahili Beach, but that didn't rule out text-based communications.

An error flashed at the bottom of Aria's ARL display: *No network.* Whatever was causing the ship's lights to flicker had already sent the ship's network into a tailspin. But how? Surely backup power would resolve any instability in the power grid. Aria grimaced and shook her head. At least the network failure explained why Liam was incommunicado. Darker possibilities flashed through her mind, but she shut them down.

"It's just the network, Paytie. I'm sure Daddy and Niko are fine." *Please be fine.* "They're with Jules," she added. "He'll keep them safe."

But Payton didn't look convinced. Neither was Aria. A horrible knot cinched off her throat, and her hands shook violently. What had happened to the captain?

The tram whispered down the tracks, picking up speed. The lights flickered again and then died. The corridor plunged into a silvery haze. Without any artificial light to compete, the stars beyond the transparent walls and ceiling of the spoke snapped into sharp relief, but there were vast patches of empty space between. A dark nebula curled over them to either side like breaking waves. It formed a bizarre tunnel around the ship. Stranger still, the nebula crackled and flashed with light from within. *Lightning?* Aria wondered. Was that even possible in space?

A sparkle of light caught Aria's eye, drawing her gaze to the front of the tram. A rainbow-colored shadow sat in the front of the tram, contoured like a soap bubble, and shaped like something with far too many arms and legs. It reminded Aria of a sea urchin—if sea urchins were made of liquid crystal. Aria shook her head and rubbed her eyes, expecting the aberration to disappear.

But the sparkling creature remained. A rising murmur spread through the tram as people began pointing to it. A squeal of brakes signaled the end of the tracks.

"Mommy what is—"

"Shhh." Aria grabbed Payton's hand hard and whispered, "Get ready to run."

Payton nodded quickly, her eyes never leaving the sparkling thing.

"What the hell *is* that?" the old man sitting beside Payton asked, pointing to it.

Aria caught his eye, but before she could reply, the thing began to move, drifting over the heads of the people in the first row of the tram. The passengers' murmuring turned to shouts and terrified whispers. Whatever that sparkling thing was, it was *alive*.

Glittering tentacles snapped straight and pierced straight through the back of five people's skulls at once. Blood and bone sprayed the people in the second row, and the tram erupted in chaos. People screamed and leapt over the sides as the monster descended on its victims, enveloping them. The bodies vanished under a writhing sea of sparkling limbs. Aria sat staring in shock at the spectacle.

"Run!" the man beside them snapped.

Payton was shaking Aria by her arm. "Mommy! Mommy!" she sobbed.

Aria snapped out of it and fled the tram, dragging Payton out after her. She darted into the milling crowd of debarking passengers, her heart pounding and palms sweating. They passed the front of the tram, swept up in the screaming crowd. The old man held Payton's other hand, letting her pull him along, his wrinkled face slack with shock as he stared at the ghostly monster devouring its prey. The front row of the tram and the glass railing were coated in blood, gleaming black in the darkened corridor. Wet crunching sounds trickled to their ears.

At the end of the spoke, a pair of big double doors barred the way to the ring deck and the suites beyond. Panicked voices rose in alarm, and people began clawing and climbing over each other, desperate to get away from the monster in the tram.

An elbow caught Aria in the ribs, and then a boot stepped on her shoulder, pushing her down. Payton cried out as people stepped on her, too. The old man with them was trying to shield her, but Aria could see a trickle of blood snaking down from his nose.

Biting back a scream, Aria curled her body around Payton and shielded her head with her arms, waiting for the stampede to pass. More boots came, stepping on Aria's legs, ribs, and shoulders. A mechanical grinding noise cut through all of the human noise, and then the crowd began to thin out. Aria risked looking up to see that the doors had cracked open.

Her body pulsing with the throbbing pain of countless bruises, Aria struggled to rise under a heavy weight. She twisted around just as that weight fell away. It was the old man who'd been trying to protect Payton. He slid off her back and fell on the deck in a shriveled heap. He'd been sheltering them both.

"Get up!" she screamed at him, torn between fleeing for safety with Payton, and repaying his selfless act. The man's green eyes were glazed with shock, blood trickling from his thinning hair, his hands bloodied and shaking.

"Go!" he croaked, trying but failing to rise.

Making a snap decision, Aria darted away from Payton and hauled him up by one arm. The bloody seats in the front of the tram were barely twenty feet away. The dead had been opened up like butterflied chickens, but the sparkling monster was thankfully nowhere to be seen.

"You can do it," Aria urged.

The man cried out and almost collapsed again. "My ankle," he breathed.

"Lean on me," Aria said. "Paytie?"

She stood shivering with spent adrenaline, her dark hair matted with blood and one eye half-swollen shut.

"Paytie!" Aria patted her daughter's hair looking for the source of the blood.

"It's not mine," Payton replied.

The old man leaning on Aria grunted and pointed to a trickling gash in the side of his head. "Guilty."

Relieved, Aria nodded and looked away. Everyone had already fled the spoke, leaving the three of them alone. She grabbed Payton's arm with her free hand. "Come on! We need to hurry."

They began taking lurching strides toward the half-open doors at the end of the corridor.

"It doesn't make sense," the man said as they slipped through the doors together. "The lights are out but there's still gravity and the tram worked."

"I wouldn't complain about that," Aria replied. "Can you imagine trying to run away from that creature without gravity?"

The man shifted his weight to lean more heavily on her. "No gravity sounds pretty good right about now," he said through clenched teeth.

Aria took a moment to get her bearings. Stars and flashes of lightning shone through the transparent ceiling. The doors to the suites were either glowing red or green, with crowds of people filing through the green ones into well-lit spaces. The suites must have had their own source of power. That made sense considering that they were lifeboats.

Lifeboats. That reminded Aria of her conversation with that *vitaholic,* Markus. Less than an hour ago he'd been talking about how everyone would have to flee to the suites in the event of an evacuation, and here everyone was doing exactly that. It was as if he'd *known* something was about to happen to the ship.

"Where do we go?" the man leaning on her prompted.

Before she could reply someone called out, "Aria! Over here!"

Speak of the devil! It was Markus, waving to her from the farthest door in view. A small group of people was busy filing into his suite. The door lay open, bright golden light spilling out like a beacon, drawing them in.

Putting her personal reservations aside, Aria pointed to the door. "That way!" They ran to reach the door.

Payton streaked ahead, then stopped and glanced back uncertainly.

"It's okay!" Aria urged. "We'll catch up!"

Payton nodded and sprinted ahead. Markus waved her on, urging her to hurry. "Come on, Payton!"

She dashed into his suite. Aria and her one-legged companion ran through next and collapsed, gasping inside the airlock. Markus shut the door behind them.

"That was close," he breathed.

The man beside Aria rolled over with a hand over his chest. "Too close," he whispered.

A loud *clunk* sounded from the door, followed by a *hiss*, and then a sudden jolt of movement. Payton darted out of Markus's living room and landed beside Aria, hugging her arm.

"What was *that?*"

Markus smirked. "Relax kiddo, just the mag locks releasing us. We're floating free now. Speaking of which, we'd better get out of the airlock."

"We've left the ship?" Aria's eyes darted to the outer airlock door. Liam and Nikolai were still on board! She jumped to her feet, dragging Payton up with her. "You knew this was going to happen!" She stabbed Markus in the chest with one finger.

He took a quick step back and regarded her with one eyebrow raised. "What are you talking about, woman?"

CHAPTER 9

"It's a hell of a coincidence, you talking about evacuation procedures right before an actual evacuation," Aria said.

"Are you suggesting I had something to do with it?"

"Maybe."

"You're crazy." Markus snorted and stormed out of the airlock.

Aria bent down to help the old man with the injured ankle. "What's your name?"

"Samos."

"I'm Aria, and that's my daughter, Payton."

Samos nodded as she helped him hobble into the suite. As soon as they cleared the inner door, it swished shut behind them. The rest of the evacuees stood by the picture windows on the far side of the living room. Aria helped Samos into an armchair and then went with Payton to stand with the others. It was the same stunning view as before: dark clouds curling over them, actinic flashes illuminating the clouds from within... but she saw something more this time: an open tunnel of space leading to a dark, bruise-colored planet. Behind it sat a much larger world, a super-earth painted in yellows, whites, and blues. Aria connected her ARLs to the suite's network so that she could check the view from another external feed without changing the view for everyone else in the process. The rear cameras showed the *Starlit Dream* falling away behind them, shrinking fast. A stream of rectangular lifeboats was streaking out of its three ring decks. Aria hoped to God that Liam and Nikolai were on one of them.

A dormant jump gate lay behind the ship. Here and there, bright specks of light drifted around the cruise ship. Smaller ships? Repair drones? Then one of the urchin creatures darted into view, its translucent tentacles writhing. Somehow, those things were floating around in vacuum as if it was their native environment. Aria tracked the creature, hoping it wouldn't take notice of them.

It didn't. Instead, it vanished with a forking blue flash of light. People began muttering and cursing in hushed tones. Blinking from the fading glare, Aria disabled her ARL overlay and stared out the picture windows once more.

She was just in time to see another urchin floating by, followed by a second forking flash of light. This time one of them materialized out of nowhere. Screams and startled shouts accompanied that feat of teleportation.

"I guess now we know how the Sparklers got on board," a woman standing beside Aria muttered. She had long, wavy red hair and bright magenta eyes set in a hard, angular face. She looked young, but with vitalics it was impossible to know her age just by looking at her.

Payton squeezed Aria's hand hard, tiny nails digging in. "What are they? What do they want?"

Aria glanced at her daughter. Payton was still wearing her one-piece blue swimsuit from their trip to the Starlit Dream's VR beach.

"It looked to me like they want to eat us," the red-haired woman said.

Payton whimpered and buried her face against Aria's leg.

Aria glared at the woman. "Do you mind? She's only seven."

"Sorry." The woman's lips quirked sideways as if chewing on the inside of her cheek. She sank to her haunches in front of Payton. "What's your name?"

"Paytie," she sniffled, peering around Aria's leg with one eye.

"Well, Paytie, you see this?" The woman opened her brown faux-leather jacket to reveal a big silver sidearm sticking out of a holster on her hip.

"Where did you get a gun?" Aria asked, withdrawing sharply and pulling Payton back.

The woman ignored her and patted the gun. "One of those things teleports in here, and I'll burn a hole in it faster than you can blink."

"Where did you get that?" Aria asked again.

The woman straightened and gave a crooked salute. "First Lieutenant Marshall, USMC. And yes, I know that's an ironic name for a space marshal to have."

Confused, Aria frowned and shook her head.

Marshall hesitated. "As in United Space Marine Corps..."

Aria shook her head. "I know what it means. You expect me to believe there's an armed Marine on a civilian cruise liner? You're not even in uniform!"

The lieutenant arched an eyebrow at her. "You've obviously never been on an interstellar cruise before. It's standard practice to have Marines scattered through the ship, undercover as passengers. It's a deterrent against pirates and hijackers."

"Why not police?"

Marshall snorted. "Yeah, I'd *love* to see the boys in blue trying to *run* after the bad guys after they've cut the gravity. Legs churnin' and arms flappin'..." She broke off chuckling. "Not to mention Zero-G will make most grounders throw up the first time it hits them."

Some of the tension left Aria's body, and she relaxed her hold on Payton. "How many of you were on board?"

"I had two squads under my command. Thirteen sets of boots in each, counting myself."

"Boots?"

"Less sexist than saying *men*."

Aria wasn't ready to believe this woman yet. "What about the hair? I've never seen a soldier with *long* hair before."

"Marine, not soldier," Marshall said, and then she smiled slyly and reached up. In one quick motion, she ripped her mane of red hair off and tossed it aside, revealing short, spiky blond hair underneath. "I guess I don't need to be undercover anymore. That's a weight off."

"Where are the rest of your men?" Aria asked.

Marshall gestured around. A few heads turned and nodded to Aria. "There are four here with me. The bridge security team. And I was in contact with some of the others before we left the ship. We lost Baller and Hatchet. Last I checked everyone else was still active on my grid. But now that my comms are out of range, who knows?" She touched a hand to her ear, drawing Aria's attention to a slimmer version of the scythe-shaped comm pieces that Aria and Liam had been wearing before they'd gone to the virtual beach.

Their comms were still in their suite, along with all of her clothes and other personal items. Hopefully Liam was there with Nikolai and safely away from the cruise ship by now. Aria looked back out the windows. Again she noted the curling walls of dark, flashing nebula to either side and the mottled blue and purple planet ahead. It was as if some alien god had parted the nebula for them. More likely, the tunnel had been blasted clear by a bow-wave of x-rays and gamma rays that had preceded them out of the jump gate. Maybe that was what had stirred up the Urchins.

Aria looked back to Marshall. "What now?"

"We wait to make landfall and just hope that none of those Sparklers teleport themselves aboard our lifeboat in the meantime."

"Sparklers?"

"Good a name as any."

Aria looked back out the windows, tracking a group of four spiky *Sparklers* as they drifted into a wall of dark clouds and disappeared. *What kind of creature can exist in a vacuum?* "Why *aren't* they coming aboard?" Aria wondered aloud. It was like their entire goal had been to get everyone to abandon ship, and now that they had, they were done scaring and gutting tourists.

Marshall shrugged. "Maybe they didn't like the way we taste?"

Payton clutched her leg and whimpered.

Aria decided to change the topic. "Where are we headed?"

"The autopilot will land us on the nearest habitable planet."

"And what if there aren't any habitable planets in this system?"

"Then it will choose the best one." Marshall glanced around the living room. "I count ten of us, including myself."

Aria counted, too. Marshall and her four undercover Marines made five. Three more between Payton, Samos, and Aria herself. And another two who kept to themselves—a big man with a black beard and a blond woman with a dollish figure sitting beside him. Ten people was right, but Markus and Elisa were nowhere in sight, and the door to their bedroom was shut. "Twelve," Aria decided. "There's two more in there." She pointed to the bedroom.

Marshall grimaced. "So we have twelve mouths to feed. We'd better hope the autopilot finds something habitable in range."

"But what if it doesn't? What about water? Air? We don't just have to worry about food."

"We can recycle most of what we have with the equipment on board the lifeboat," Marshall replied. "Should keep us going for a while. But there's no way to recycle food, so when our supplies run out, we're going to be drawing straws—if you get my drift."

Aria shivered and glanced down at Payton, but her face was blank, no sign of comprehension in her big green eyes. "What about a rescue? We came from *Earth,* not some backwater in Guild Space. By now someone must have figured out where we went."

"Then where's the cavalry?" Marshall countered. "It's been at least an hour since the captain announced we came out the wrong gate— probably more. And Aquaria was expecting us. By now everyone knows we didn't make it, and tracking us down should be as easy as one two three. So why hasn't anyone come looking for us?"

Aria felt her heart rate notching up. "Well... there has to be a record of our jump coordinates in the gate."

"And yet..." Marshall held up her hands in a shrug and looked around pointedly. "Still no cavalry."

"It takes time to organize a rescue. Or maybe they're hoping we'll come back on our own."

"The very first thing the gate controllers would do is open a wormhole to our coordinates and then make comms contact to check on our status, but the gate behind us has been offline since we arrived. The captain was trying hard to activate it and make contact with Earth before those Sparklers came aboard."

"How do you know that?" Aria demanded.

"Because I was on the bridge with my team right up until the captain gave the order to abandon ship."

"You *saw* what happened to him?"

"I shot the Sparkler that killed him. I think I got it, but I didn't stick around to find out if it bled red, blue, or green."

Aria peripherally noted that the other evacuees and Marines had gathered around. They were all listening intently to what Marshall had to say.

Aria's heart thundered in her chest, beating so hard that it hurt. "What are you saying?" She shouldn't have had to ask, but apprehension had muddled her brain.

Marshall glanced about, taking in everyone in the group. "I'm saying that I don't think we came here by accident, and whoever sent us here, they didn't just mess with our jump coordinates—they also erased them from the gate's transit log. No one's coming to rescue us, because they don't know where the hell we went."

* * *

All of the doors glowed red. Liam pounded on the one with their room number—258. "Aria! It's me! Open the door!"

But no one answered, and the door didn't slide open. Liam turned to Nikolai. His son's blue eyes were wide and glazed with shock. Liam could guess that his probably looked the same. *Now what?* He would have to find Aria and Payton on the surface of whatever planet they were evacuating to.

"The red doors indicate suites that are either already at maximum capacity or which have already departed the *Starlit Dream*," Jules explained. "We need to find a *green* door."

Liam glanced around quickly, noting that all of the doors in sight were glowing red. He nodded to his son. "Follow me." And then he took off at a run. Nikolai and Jules kept pace beside him. They flashed down the curving corridor, passing scattered groups of people who were running the other way—not a good sign.

"It would appear that all of these lifeboats have already left. We should try another ring deck," Jules suggested.

"How is that possible?" Liam demanded between gasps for air. No one would design a ship like this one without building in extra capacity for evacuees in case of an emergency. Had everyone somehow come to this ring deck to evacuate instead of going to one of the other two?

Or maybe the captain had authorized the lifeboats to leave before they were full. Was the situation that dire? And what was the glowing thing they'd seen when the elevator stopped to let people off?

Soon Liam's lungs and legs were burning, and he had to stop and lean against the wall to catch his breath. Up ahead people were pounding on doors and screaming for help. Liam noticed the number 243 glowing crimson on the door beside him. They'd run almost all the way around the ring, and none of the doors were green.

"Dad, what are we going to do?" Nikolai asked.

"I would advise that we head for ring deck two," Jules said again.

Not wasting his breath on a reply, Liam watched the scattered people up ahead grouping together like a pack of wild dogs. They came toward Liam and Nikolai in a noisy rush with, a clear alpha leading the pack. *One of the crew?*

"Maybe he knows why the doors won't open." Liam stepped away from the wall to put himself in front of the advancing pack. Jules and Nikolai joined him. The man in front slowed and then stopped with his legs planted in a wide stance. "Fall in," he said, his voice deep and commanding.

The man was tall with broad shoulders, dark skin, a square jaw, and striking yellow eyes that gleamed like citrine in the ruddy gloom of a nearby door. Starlight shone through the transparent ceiling, flashing periodically with those strange bursts of light they'd seen coming from within the nebula. Liam was about to do as the man said when he caught a flash of light reflected off a weapon on his hip. It was lurking behind a faux-leather black coat that reached down just past his waist.

"You have a gun," Liam said.

"That's right," he replied. "I'm with the *Dream's* security forces. Lieutenant Marshall."

CHAPTER 10

"You're a soldier?" Liam asked.

"A Marine. Under cover along with the rest of my unit as security for the *Dream*. You can call me Buck. Now fall in, we need to keep moving." Buck started forward, brushing by them. The murmuring group behind him surged in his wake, bumping shoulders with them as they swept past. Not satisfied to be one of the trailing masses, Liam ran to catch up with Buck.

"I'm Liam," he said.

Buck didn't respond, didn't even spare a glance. His eyes were everywhere, scanning the corridor top to bottom and left to right.

"What happened to the ship?" Liam asked, louder this time. "And where are you taking us?"

Buck stifled a sigh. "Those Urchin things came aboard. Attacked the passengers and crew. Killed at least a hundred people before the power went out—or at least the lights. Whatever they are, they seem to have moved on now."

"Aliens?" Nikolai asked, running up beside them with Jules.

Buck glared at him for a split second and then shook his head. "You three need to stay back."

"Of course," Jules replied, and pulled Nikolai back by his shoulders despite the boy's protests.

Liam stayed where he was, walking beside the Marine. "I need to find my wife and daughter. They would have come here, back to our suite."

Buck shook his head. "Then let's hope they made it."

"What if they didn't? I can't just assume—"

"You want to go look for them, be my guest, but you're going to make a lonely target for Urchins if you strike out on your own."

Liam glanced around, checking the curving stretch of corridor behind them. "What do they look like?"

"Like a cross between a sea urchin and a jellyfish, hence the name." Buck suddenly thrust up a hand and held it out like a stop sign. The whole group shuffled to a halt. Up ahead, a pair of wide doors were cranked half-open.

Buck drew his sidearm and stalked up to the opening. Planting his shoulder against one door, he peered around the edge with his gun. Something shifted in his stance, and his whole body went rigid.

Liam fought the urge to call out and ask him what was wrong. Seconds dragged, and Buck remained in that posture, peering around the door with his gun. At last, he peeled away and hurried back to them. He was breathing fast, his yellow eyes wide. "There are five dead in a tram, peeled open like fruit, but no sign of the Urchins."

The people behind them began murmuring anxiously and cursing with that news.

"Maybe we should try another spoke?" Liam asked.

Buck shook his head. "We press on. Next spoke is a hundred meters from here, and at least we know this one's clear. For now." Buck's eyes slid away from Liam to address the rest of the group. "Follow me."

Liam stayed where he was, but everyone else began hurrying through the doors after Buck.

"What about Mom?" Nikolai asked. "And Payton?"

That was what had Liam's feet rooted to the deck. He couldn't just *assume* that they were safe. Hopefully they'd already made it out, but even if they hadn't, Buck was right: he couldn't search the whole ship for them in the dark. "They left the VR deck ahead of us," Liam said. "They must have made it back to our suite in time to get away."

Nikolai frowned, looking like he wanted to argue.

"Your father is right, Master Nikolai," Jules said.

The last stragglers brushed by them, leaving them alone on the ring deck. "We'd better get going," Liam whispered and pushed his son ahead of him to the doors. An old adage came to mind: *You don't have to outrun the bear—you just have to outrun the guy next to you.* Except the guy next to him was his son, so that logic went in reverse.

They squeezed through the doors together and ran to catch up with Buck. The Marine was walking fast, sweeping his gun back and forth in a two-handed grip.

They passed the tram Buck had mentioned. At first Liam didn't even recognize the bloody pile of raw meat in the front row as human remains, but then he began to pick out strips of clothing, jutting white rib bones, and other familiar parts. Those people didn't look half-eaten, they looked like they'd been gutted and then left there as a warning. Liam's stomach flipped, and he looked away.

"Don't look," he said to Nikolai. Too late.

Nikolai was already staring fixedly at the corpses, his eyes wide with horror.

Liam caught a glimpse of something over his son's shoulder, through the transparent wall of the corridor. Something spiky, translucent and faintly sparkling was floating out there in space, pacing the group.

Someone else spotted it and cried out in alarm, pointing repeatedly. Voices rose sharply, and the crowd flowed away from the windows. Buck stopped, his gun sweeping toward the threat. Then the creature vanished with a forking flash of light.

"What the..." Liam stumbled into the person in front of him. Blinking fast to clear his eyes, he cast about, hands feeling for purchase in a hazy world of snaking green after-images.

The Urchin re-appeared, now standing *inside* the ship on the other side of the glass wall. Half a dozen spiky tentacle-limbs were planted under it like legs.

"Everyone, get down!" Buck yelled. He had his gun trained on the creature, but people were screaming and running in front of him in their hurry to get away, making it impossible for him to shoot without accidentally hitting one of them.

Liam stood beside Nikolai with his heart pounding and his mind screaming for him to run and freeze at the same time. A moment ago that creature had been floating impossibly *outside* the ship in a pure vacuum, and now, somehow it was on their side of the glass.

The Urchin shifted, rotating a few degrees on the spot. Then it began *rolling* forward, spiky tentacles flailing as they pushed off the deck, driving it faster. It was chasing after a screaming woman in a long, glittering indigo evening gown. She was trying unsuccessfully to run in high-heels. The fleeing woman glanced over her shoulder and screamed anew when she saw how close the Urchin was. Then she tripped and fell.

Buck tracked the creature with his gun, taking careful aim.

"Shoot it!" Liam yelled just before a loud *crack* split the air. A blinding white bolt of superheated plasma streaked out and hit the Urchin. An explosion of heat and light consumed the translucent monster. Liam could have sworn he heard it scream. It stopped chasing the woman and whirled around, now aiming for Buck.

"Shit!" he said and pulled the trigger twice more. Blinding white plasma flashed through the air. Two more screams tore from the Urchin before it surged toward Buck, leaving a glistening trail of clear fluid in its wake.

The Marine fired three more shots, backpedaling fast. Passengers ran screaming for the exits at both ends of the spoke.

The Urchin slowed but didn't stop. Buck fetched up against the glass wall of the spoke, firing constantly. The barrel of his gun glowed white-hot.

"Fucking die already!" Buck screamed. His weapon beeped with a familiar error sound that Liam recognized from holo-movies. His gun had just overheated.

The Urchin reached him, stopped, and brushed his cheek with one tentacle in a way that looked almost tender.

It wasn't.

Buck screamed as a bloody gash appeared where the Urchin had touched him. The creature rolled back as if to leave—or maybe to lunge.

Liam cast about for something he could use to distract it. But Nikolai had already beat him to it. Completely unarmed, Liam's thirteen-year-old son ran up behind the tentacled monster screaming like a Viking Berserker. Jules was hot on his heels.

"Master Nikolai!" Jules darted in front of Liam's son and caught him by his shoulders.

"Niko!" Liam sprinted after his son.

The creature tensed and three tentacle-arms snapped out of a seething mass of hundreds, piercing straight through both Jules and Nikolai in three different places. Sparkling, translucent spikes appeared sticking out of Nikolai's side, thigh, and shoulder. He cried out belatedly and collapsed to the deck.

Liam reached his son's side just in time to catch him as he fell. Blood bubbled steadily from his wounds. Liam planted his palms on the blossoming crimson stains in Nikolai's thigh and side to put pressure on the puncture wounds.

"Desist your assault immediately!" Jules ordered as he fended off repeated attacks, catching tentacles on his arms.

"Hang on, Niko!" Liam said. His son's eyes were rolling around like two marbles in his head. "Hey!" Liam released Nikolai's thigh and slapped his cheek repeatedly to wake him up. "Stay with me, buddy! Come on, stay with me..."

Liam dimly registered the sound of Buck's screams and more deafening cracks as he fired his gun over and over again. Something fell beside Liam with a thunderous crash, but he was too busy putting pressure on Nikolai's wounds to look. He hoped that hadn't been the sound of Jules' lifeless body hitting the deck.

"How is he?" Buck asked in a breathless whisper. "Shit, he's already unconscious."

Liam blinked through tears to see Buck on his haunches beside them, one half of his face bloody from the gash, one arm slick with blood and hanging limply at his side. The sleeve of his jacket had been flayed into bloody strips.

"We have to get him to med bay," Buck said.

"He's not going to last that long," Liam said. "He's losing too much blood!"

Buck pursed his lips. "We have to try."

Clanking footsteps approached. "Mr. Price is correct. We must stabilize Master Nikolai first." Jules appeared beside them, his clothes shredded, and the artificial skin covering his arms hanging in strips from the metal skeleton underneath. There were also three gaping holes in his body that corresponded to Nikolai's injuries. Ripping his shirt open at the belly-button, Jules opened a dented compartment in his abdomen. Artificial skin hung from the compartment like a tattered flag. Inside were three syringes with hypodermic needles already attached, and a small silver canister.

"What are those?" Liam asked as Jules withdrew all three syringes and the canister.

"Vitalics." Jules pulled the cap off one needle with his teeth and spat it on the deck. "Remove your hands."

Liam did, and blood began bubbling from his son's wounded side and leg once more. Jules squirted the contents of the syringe directly onto the wound in Nikolai's side. It began foaming and bubbling with pink froth. Jules removed the cap from another needle and then sprayed Nikolai's thigh with it. "Flip him over," the bot said as he uncapped the third needle.

Liam carefully turned Nikolai over, and Jules used the third syringe to spray the exit wounds in Nikolai's side and leg. They foamed as well. Moments later, the foam disappeared, leaving crusty red gore in its wake, but both wounds had stopped bleeding. Finally, Jules grabbed the canister and sprayed it on both sides of Nikolai's wounds, including his still-bleeding shoulder. A thin, gelatinous skin formed over all three injuries.

"There," Jules said, stepping back and returning the empty syringes and half-empty canister to the dented compartment where his navel should have been. He shut the hinged compartment and re-buttoned his shirt.

Nikolai stirred and woke up. "Ow..." he moaned as he twisted around.

"Careful," Buck said as Liam helped him to sit up. "Your wounds are still fresh."

Nikolai smacked his lips and worked his tongue around inside his mouth. "Can I get something to drink?" he croaked. "My tongue feels like it's made of sand."

Liam grinned like a fool and wiped fresh tears from his eyes.

"You're dehydrated," Jules explained. "There is only so much that vitalics can do."

"Probably sucked him dry to boost his blood volume back up," Buck added. Turning to Liam, he said, "We'd better get him to med bay anyway. He needs saline, and I could use a dose of vitalics myself."

Liam glanced at Buck's bloodied arm and nodded. He helped his son to his feet. Buck stood up with them and pointed with his gun to the half-open doors at the near end of the spoke. "That way."

As Liam followed that gesture, he noticed what had happened to the Urchin-creature. It was lying to one side in a tangled heap of now opaque, silver metal tentacles.

"They're machines?" Liam asked, his eyes flying wide as he stared at the 'dead' monster. Its previously sparkling, translucent body was pocked full of charred black holes where Buck had shot it with his plasma pistol.

"Apparently," Buck confirmed while checking the charge on his pistol. "Let's get out of here before another one shows up."

"What about everyone else?" Liam glanced around, noting that they were all alone now.

Buck shrugged. "They'll find us. Or if they're smart, they'll find the next available lifeboat and get the hell out of here."

Liam's eyes fell on the silvery metal Urchin once more. "I'm not sure they'll be any safer on the lifeboats. That thing teleported itself across at least twenty feet of vacuum to get on board."

"Yeah, that's a good point..." Buck trailed off, staring out into space with a furrowed brow.

"That is impossible," Jules said. The bot's face was drawn, his brown eyes narrowed. "Teleportation technology is still in the experimental stages throughout the Union."

Buck lifted one foot as if to kick the Urchin, then stopped short as he apparently thought better of it. The edges of those tentacles were sharp as razors. "All that means is that the Union didn't build them."

"So this is..." Liam broke off, shaking his head as he stared at the Urchin. "First contact?"

"Second contact," Buck replied. "That jump gate had to get here somehow. In fact, our teleportation tech probably comes from reverse-engineering one of these things. I bet there's a whole bunch of them sitting in an underground lab at a black site on Titan or Mars. That's why the jump gate out here is disabled, and why the Union has been lying and telling people that it's impossible to jump between galaxies. It's all part of some big cover-up."

"Why?" Nikolai asked, shifting his weight and removing his arm from Liam's shoulders so that he could stand on his own. He must have been feeling better.

Buck snorted. "You have any idea what teleportation tech would do? It's a game changer. The Guild and the Union have been jockeying for decades, pumping up their navies and recruiting bigger armies to defend their sovereignty. If one of them could figure out how to teleport Marines—or worse, bombs—directly onto rival ships and stations, that would be the end of it. The other side would just roll over and play dead. Game over.

"In fact, that's probably how we ended up here. The Guild found out about this place and used the *Dream* as cover to send a covert ops team to investigate."

"If that's true, then whoever sent us here is going to bring us back," Liam said.

"Or at least send someone to extract their team," Buck agreed.

"What about everyone else?" Jules asked.

Buck shrugged. "If we survive long enough, we might be able to hitch a ride with the extraction team or follow them back through the gate."

"I do not like your theory, Lieutenant Marshall," Jules replied.

Buck barked a laugh and smile ruefully. "You and me both, Bolts."

"My name is Jules, not Bolts."

"Every Marine needs a good call sign."

"I am not a Marine. I am a—"

"Honorary Marine. You and the kid saved my life. Thanks for that." Buck's gaze flicked to Nikolai. "How are you feeling?"

"Okay, I guess."

"Good. Maybe we can skip med bay and just get you some water. Faster we can get to the armory the better our chances will be against these things."

"What about your arm?" Liam asked.

He shrugged and flexed it a few times. "Just a scratch. Let's go."

CHAPTER 11

Aria stood in front of the picture windows, watching lifeboats rain down like meteors over the bruise-colored planet below. The suite shivered and shook around her; plates rattled on their racks in the kitchen, and glasses jingled like crystal bells. The planet grew larger and closer by the second. White clouds cast amorphous shadows on the blue and purple landscape. Bright crimson threads that might have been rivers snaked through alien jungles.

"You should sit down," Lieutenant Marshall said. She was sitting on the living room couch, checking the charge on her pistol and doing an inventory of her spare charge packs.

Aria glanced at the seat she'd got up from a moment ago, folded down from the far wall next to Payton and Samos. Everyone was seated in the emergency stations along the walls—everyone except for Markus and Elisa, who were still locked away inside their room.

Aria had stood up a minute ago, thinking that if the grav lifts and inertial dampeners could handle the descent without so much as breaking a glass in the cupboards, then she didn't have to worry about cracking her head open on the ceiling.

But just then the deck kicked up under her feet, almost knocking her over. She planted a hand on a nearby armchair to stop from falling over.

Lieutenant Marshall caught two charge packs in one hand as they leapt off the coffee table and grabbed her pistol just before it could slide off, too. "See?" She holstered the weapon and clipped the charge packs to her belt.

Aria climbed up a slanting deck to sit beside Payton. She buckled in and watched the remainder of their descent from the safety of her harness. Soon the black of space faded to a pale turquoise sky that gradually deepened in color. Clouds drifted by in hazy white threads, and then turbulence hit them in earnest. The ship bucked and skipped, and Aria felt her spine curling as power to the grav lifts suddenly increased, threatening to squash her flat.

"What's wrong with the dampeners?" Aria managed between gasps for air. She felt light-headed with all of the blood pooling in her feet.

Marshall had to yell to be heard over the roar of atmospheric entry: "Autopilot must have turned them off to supply more power to the grav lifts!"

The crushing sensation gradually eased as they dropped below the clouds, and Aria's weight went back to more or less normal as the grav lifts stopped braking their fall.

The lifeboat glided down over alien jungles. Sapphire and emerald-colored crystals jutted high, poking above the treetops like so many stalagmites on the floor of a cave. Alien trees sparkled in the sun with purple leaves and black trunks. Here and there a shining crimson river emerged, peeking between overhanging branches. The water seemed to glow from within, illuminated by phosphorescent bacteria or creatures of some kind.

"It's beautiful!" Payton cried.

Aria nodded in quiet awe.

A moment later, Payton began tapping on her arm. "I need to go to the bathroom," she said, wincing and squirming with obvious discomfort.

"You're going to have to wait a minute, sweetheart."

"Listen up everyone!" Marshall said, her magenta eyes glazed with a blue glow from an ARL overlay. "According to the lifeboat's sensors, this world is temperate, and the air *is* breathable, but only with a filter mask for toxins and to produce the right mix of air, so do *not* go outside without a mask. You will pass out, and you will die. In addition to that, bio-scanners are picking up a *lot* of lifeforms in those jungles, some of them as big as any dinosaur from Earth. We don't know if they are happy herbivores or if they'd rather take a bite out of you, so for now, everyone stays put while my team goes out to conduct recon and secure a perimeter. Are we clear?"

The man and woman Aria hadn't met yet nodded agreeably.

"I can't go anywhere, anyway," Samos added. His face was waxy and pale. He was struggling visibly with the pain of his twisted ankle.

Aria flashed a sympathetic smile. "There should be a medkit with painkillers around here somewhere. We'll fix you up once we've landed."

"No rush," Samos said with a grimace. "I'm okay."

Purple trees raced up fast, blurring by at several hundred kilometers per hour. Jutting crystals glinted in the sun, all different shades of blue and green. Aria estimated that they had to be hundreds of meters tall.

The treetops and soaring crystals fell away, and a clearing of purple grass emerged with a shining ruby lake in the center. The water was clear as glass all the way down.

The ship banked and circled around, dropping toward the grassy field around the lake. A sapphire crystal soared beside them. The ship set down with a muffled *thump*. Purple grass rippled out to the shining crimson lake, waving in a stiff breeze.

"Alpha Team, on me," Marshall said as she stood up from the couch.

"Copy," one man said as he stood up with three others in civilian clothes. They all wore jackets of various types, no doubt to conceal their weapons. Air filter masks dangled from the straps around their necks. They began lining up at the inner doors of the airlock. All around the suite other evacuees began unbuckling and standing up to stretch their legs.

Payton tapped on Aria's arm again, more insistently now. "Mom, the bathroom..."

Aria smiled tightly. "Right. Let's go find it." Truth be told, she needed to go, too. Unlike the suite she and her family had shared aboard the *Starlit Dream,* this one only had one bedroom and one bathroom. It was designed for a couple, not a family. Grabbing Payton's hand, Aria started toward the shut door to the bedroom.

She knocked on the door and listened for footsteps. When none came, she knocked again, louder. She cleared her throat and said, "My daughter needs to use your bathroom."

The door swished open to reveal that the bedroom was dark. *Had they been sleeping?* Aria wondered. Markus stood barring the doorway with his hands planted to either side of the frame. "Yes?"

"My daughter needs to pee."

He shook his head. "Not in our bathroom." Elisa appeared behind him, peering over his shoulder. "This is our private space," Markus went on. "We paid for it. The rest of you can have the living room."

Aria glanced behind her. "There's no bathroom in the living room."

"So?" Markus gestured to the rolling purple fields beyond the picture windows. "See that? It's all one big bathroom out there."

Aria frowned. "You can't be serious. What if it's dangerous? The lieutenant told us to stay here."

Markus's eyebrows drifted up, and he crossed his arms over his chest. "There are air filter masks under every chair. Environment suits and comm units, too."

Aria stood her ground. "We're all sharing this space equally. And I paid for a suite, too."

"Yeah, so why are you taking up space in mine?"

Aria narrowed her eyes at him. "Next you'll be telling us all of the food rations are yours and Elisa's as well."

Markus smirked. "If only. But no, I'm a reasonable man. The food will be shared equally. Our bedroom will not."

"Get out of the way," Aria insisted. She tried to shove him aside, but he was as heavy and solid as a statue.

Markus laughed. "What are you doing?"

Someone pulled her back by her arm. She rounded on the person and came eye-to-eye with Lieutenant Marshall.

"Leave it," she said, shaking her head. "Let him have his toilet. Every king should have a throne, even if it's a shitty one."

Markus's eyes flashed, but he said nothing at that.

"Come on. I'll watch your backs out there." Marshall went on, dragging Aria toward the lifeboat's airlock.

* * *

Terror crowded Liam's thoughts as they left the spoke and entered a short hallway lined with elevators: he was cut off from his wife and daughter with no way of knowing if they were okay or even alive. What if their lifeboat had crashed? What if they'd been attacked by one of those Urchin creatures? What if...

Liam forced his thoughts in a new direction, refusing to give in to his fears. Buck led the way past the elevators to a sweeping, three-level concourse lined with shops. A decorative fountain lay dormant in the center of the floor, water gleaming like glass beneath a giant crystal chandelier. Starlight poured in from a wall of windows framed by a pair of curving staircases at the far end of the chamber. Glimmers of light shifted on higher levels, catching Liam's eyes.

Buck dropped his good arm in front of Liam like a boom gate, stopping him and Nikolai from going any further. Jules fetched up behind them, and Buck jerked his chin to the upper two levels of the concourse.

Liam recognized the shifting glimmers of light for what they really were: two sparkling Urchins rolling aimlessly along the second level, prowling for their next victim.

"We need to get out of here," Nikolai whispered sharply.

"*Quiet,*" Buck growled.

Too late. The Urchins stopped rolling and began racing the other way, heading for the stairs. A metallic thunder like hundreds of knives scraping together accompanied them.

"Run!" Buck snapped. "I'll cover you!"

The first of the two Urchins hit the top of the stairs and began rolling down. Liam turned and saw that Nikolai and Jules had already fled to the elevators behind them. The up arrow was lit on the nearest control panel, and Nikolai was bouncing from one foot to the other, impatiently scanning the displays above each elevator to see which one would open first. Liam ran over to join them just as Buck fired off the first cracking shot from his pistol. The lights were out throughout the ship, but at least the elevators still worked.

"Hurry up, damn it!" Liam's gaze anxiously flicked between elevators, then back to Buck. Two Urchins were streaking around the fountain on the ground floor. Buck fired repeatedly on the nearest one, but it rolled furiously toward him, tentacles churning against the deck like so many legs. The sound of knives scraping grew louder and closer.

Ding.

One of the elevators opened. "Get in!" Jules urged, dragging Liam inside by his shirt just as the first Urchin reached the Marine.

"Buck!" Liam screamed. The doors began sliding shut, muffling Buck's shouts. The sound of metal shrieking on metal stopped, and a faintly sparkling shadow appeared through the narrowing gap between the elevator doors.

Time seemed to freeze: the doors closed, hairs rose on the back of Liam's neck, the elevator jerked upward, and a muffled metallic shriek sounded outside. Liam pulled Nikolai back against the side of the elevator just as the doors peeled open and sparkling tentacles came through like sharpened spears. Those mechanical limbs writhed around, blindly questing for them. More cracking reports sounded from Buck's pistol, and the tentacles withdrew with a loud, grating screech. The elevator continued upward, but got stuck and seized up with a groaning sigh.

"Stay back!" Liam said. He held Nikolai against the wall and strained to peer through one of the holes in the doors. Another metallic shriek sounded amidst the cracking reports of Buck's pistol, and then dozens more tentacles pierced the doors, turning them to Swiss cheese. The mechanical arms writhed around, searching for them again. Liam shuffled Nikolai into the far corner and put himself in front of his son as a shield. Jules stood in the opposite corner, cut off. But the Urchins weren't trying to reach him. Three shimmering tentacles snaked *around* Liam, reaching for Nikolai.

Another cracking report sounded, followed by two more, and this time something happened: half of the shimmering metal limbs grew opaque and silver. They clattered to the floor in a tangled mess. A final crack sounded, and the remaining half collapsed atop the first.

Liam blinked steadily at the dormant machines, trying to decide if it was safe for him to move now.

Yellow eyes appeared, peering through a hole near the bottom of the doors. The elevator was frozen half-way up from the level they'd been on a minute ago. "Is everyone all right?" Buck asked.

Liam stepped away from his son to check. There weren't any fresh blots of blood on Nikolai's clothes. Liam patted himself down—no sharp pains, no sticky-wet patches of blood. He glanced back to the doors and Buck's citrine eyes. "I think so."

"How are we going to get out of here?" Nikolai asked in a trembling voice.

Jules stepped over razor-sharp tentacles to reach the doors. He tried forcing them open. The doors shuddered open an inch before catching in the frame. Jules dropped to his haunches to speak to Buck. "We'll have to climb out the hatch and meet you on the next level."

"Don't bother," Buck replied. "Go straight to level sixty. Meet me at the armory."

"That's thirty floors up," Jules objected. "We will have to climb out on the next level and take another elevator anyway. It would be better if you were waiting there for us. You are the only one with a weapon."

"Not anymore. The charge is depleted," Buck explained. "We're defenseless until we get to the armory."

"I see." Jules stepped away from the doors and reached up to open a hatch in the elevator ceiling.

"I'll meet you there," Buck said.

"Wait!" Liam called through the doors.

"Yes?" Buck replied.

"How are you still alive?"

"I don't know... they completely ignored me this time even though I was shooting at them constantly. The only thing they wanted was to get at the three of you inside that elevator."

"So it would seem," Jules agreed.

"See you at the armory," Buck added.

Liam's mind flashed back to a moment ago: Jules standing in one corner, the Urchins ignoring him, Liam in the other corner shielding his son. He recalled tentacle-arms snaking *around* him to get at Nikolai. He turned to regard his son. Somehow, *he* was the one they were after.

But the first time they'd met one of the Urchins it had gone racing after a woman in high heels. It *had* attacked Nikolai, but only because he'd run out to confront it.

Something had driven these two to a single-minded frenzy, but whatever it was, it wasn't present during their initial encounter. Maybe the one that injured Nikolai had marked him somehow?

"Let's go," Jules said. He waved through the hatch from the roof of the elevator.

"After you, Niko," Liam said. He cupped his hands and boosted Nikolai up to Jules. Theories spun wildly through his head. What were the Urchins targeting? Was it genetic? Could Aria or Payton be a target, too? He hoped they were safe, but there was no way to know. Whatever had knocked out the lights had taken down the ship's network, too. Liam couldn't simply query the ship to find out where they were. No lights, no network, and some of the doors had to be manually cranked open, but the elevators were still working, and so was the ship's gravity. What kind of power failure was that selective?

"Your turn, Mr. Price," Jules said.

Liam shook his head to clear it. "Just call me Liam," he said as Jules reached under his arms and hauled him up through the hatch.

"Of course."

Liam stood up on the roof of the elevator. The shaft was pitch black except for the square of golden light radiating from the hatch. "I can't see a thing. Is there a ladder somewhere?"

Jules' eyes became blinding beams of light that swept around and landed on the rungs of a nearby ladder. "Over there." Metal-soled footwear clanged on the roof as he crossed to the elevator.

His curiosity peaked, Liam asked about it. "Jules, are you wearing mag boots?"

"Of course. They are mandatory for all of the ship's crew, in case of an artificial gravity failure."

"That makes sense." Liam thought back to Buck's silently padding footsteps. Wasn't he a part of the crew? Shouldn't he be wearing mag boots, too?

Unless he wasn't actually a Marine. He had a gun, but that didn't mean anything. Liam thought about that as his hands closed around cold metal rungs and he climbed the ladder behind Nikolai and Jules. Someone had deliberately brought the *Starlit Dream* here, and they only had Buck's word for it that he wasn't somehow a part of that plot.

Jules came to a halt above them, and Liam heard doors grinding open. A silvery slice of starlight poured into the elevator shaft from the level just above them.

"The way seems clear," Jules whispered down to them. He climbed out through the open doors, and Nikolai started up the ladder again.

Maybe I'm being paranoid, Liam decided as he followed them out onto the second level of the shopping mall. Stars shone brightly through a wall of windows looking out over the spoke where they'd first run into the Urchins. At the end of that spoke, the ring deck curved around with big gaping holes where the suites used to be docked.

Liam looked away. Jules had already hit the call button for the elevators. The up arrow was glowing orange. Nikolai stood beside the bot, eyes tracking the mezzanine floor beyond the elevators with its curving glass railings and darkened shops. More killer machines could be lurking inside any one of those stores.

An elevator sprang open, and they hurried inside. The doors slid shut, and it raced upward. The number *60* shone on the digital panel and display inside the elevator. They were on their way to the rendezvous with Buck at the ship's armory. One thing was for sure: whether or not Buck was hiding anything, *someone* definitely was.

CHAPTER 12

"Grab a mask from under your chairs," Marshall said. "And while you're at it, get yourselves a pair of environment suits. It's not exactly summer out there."

Aria glanced down at herself. She was wearing a loose-fitting knitted top and jean shorts over a bikini, while Payton was still wearing her blue one-piece swimsuit. Both of them were barefoot and wearing sandals. "What about our feet?" she asked as she went to grab air filter masks and environment suits from under her and Payton's chairs.

"I'll cook up some boots with the 3D printer," Marshall said. "It'll just take a minute."

"But I need to go *now!*" Payton complained.

"*One* minute," Marshall insisted, already striding toward a recessed panel beside the holoscreen in the living room. As Marshall touched the panel, it slid open, and a 3D printer slid out. "Shoe sizes?"

"Seven for me, three and a half for Payton," Aria replied. She withdrew an environment suit from under her chair. They were shrunken looking garments of a highly stretchable material, canary yellow, with reflective red piping. *One-size-fits-all*, Aria guessed. Not a fashion statement, but the material would be hard to miss, even on a dark night. A definite plus. It was bad enough being lost in some unknown sector of space, but getting lost on an unknown alien planet would be far worse.

The 3D printer began buzzing with activity, dozens of red lasers illuminating the interior as it printed their boots one layer at a time.

Aria handed a second jumpsuit to her daughter. "Put this on."

"Where do I change?"

Aria frowned, her eyes scanning the open living space for a place where prying eyes couldn't reach. But Markus and Elisa's bedroom was the only private part of the entire suite. Aria was just about to point that out and demand that Marshall enforce equal access to the bedroom when the lieutenant came striding over with a pair of boots.

"You can change inside the airlock," she said.

Aria regarded the other woman dubiously. "With your men looking on?" A few of them were already looking at her. "We should just insist that

Markus and Elisa give everyone access to their bathroom. This is ridiculous."

Marshall hesitated. Aria noticed the unidentified couple bobbing their heads in agreement.

"We'll deal with them later," Marshall decided. She led the way to the airlock and keyed the control panel to open the inner doors. "Look on the bright side, you and your daughter might be the first humans to ever set foot on this world."

Aria grudgingly followed Marshall into the airlock. The lieutenant shut the doors behind them, and then both Aria and Payton hurriedly stripped out of their clothes and into the environment suits and boots. The one-piece suits were built with convenient zippered openings in the rear and crotch. Fortunately, the planet had a thick enough atmosphere that they didn't need helmets and pressure suits just to go outside. Aria helped Payton with her air filter mask and then strapped her own mask on. When she was done, she activated the vacuum seals on both.

"Ready?" Marshall asked, her voice both amplified and distorted by the speakers inside her filter mask.

Aria double-checked the glowing rim of lights around her daughter's mask. Bright green. Good. Seeing the same emerald glow around the edges of her field of view, she nodded and gave a thumbs up. "Ready."

Marshall drew her sidearm and held it in a two-handed grip, aiming it at the outer doors.

Aria's eyes widened. "What's that for?"

"Just a precaution," Marshall assured her.

The outer doors swept open. A rippling, sunlit field of lavender-colored grass appeared. A gleaming blue crystal as tall and big around as most skyscrapers soared to one side. Beyond that, massive trees with black trunks soared. Broad, dark purple leaves formed an impenetrable canopy a hundred meters above the forest floor.

"Stay close," Marshall ordered. She walked to the edge of the airlock and then down a long gray ramp to the rippling lavender field. The lieutenant's aim tracked back and forth as she went, putting an exclamation point on the fact that this was an unknown world with unknown threats.

Aria waited to make sure nothing leapt out of the grass to eat Marshall before reaching for Payton's hand and following the lieutenant down the ramp. Their breath reverberated through their masks in quick, shallow breaths.

Thump!

Aria flinched at the sound and spun around to see that the outer airlock doors had shut behind them. Probably cycling so that Marshall's men could follow her out.

They continued on. Aria looked up as they reached the bottom of the ramp. The sky was greener than it was blue. Aquamarine in fact. The grass was knee high and sparkled faintly in the sun as if it were dusted with diamonds. A lonely wind howled, cold against their environment suits and exposed skin, but it brought with it a heavenly smell. Aria took a deep breath. Vanilla and fresh lemons. That fragrance immediately brightened her mood and cleared her head. She slowed down, some of the tension bleeding out of her. Glancing around, Aria couldn't help but smile.

"Mom..." Payton tugged on her arm.

"Right. Sorry."

Marshall waved them over from the base of the Sapphire-blue crystal. They hurried over to her, the long grass rasping against their legs.

"Behind the crystal," Marshall said. "That's our bathroom. Make sense?"

Aria nodded absently, unable to tear her eyes away from the deep, crystalline depths of the massive obelisk. It had to be at least thirty stories tall. It had a presence and a sense of ancient mystery to it that made the air seem to hum and shiver. Lieutenant Marshall led them around the base of the crystal until the lifeboat passed out of sight.

"Here we are," Marshall declared.

Aria dragged her eyes away from the azure pillar and helped Payton to unzip her jumpsuit. She crouched down and a steaming golden stream hit the ground. The grass immediately shriveled, turning black as if burnt.

"Guess this place doesn't see a lot of acid rain," Marshall commented.

Aria nodded absently, her gaze drifting back to the crystal. How could such massive crystalline structures occur naturally on the surface of a planet? Shouldn't crystals form in caves or inside of rocks? She recalled seeing plenty of others like this one cresting above the treetops as they'd flown in for a landing.

"Done," Payton said, standing up and zipping up her jumpsuit in a hurry. "Can we go back inside now?"

"Sure," Aria said, even though she was burning with curiosity to explore further. An alien world with so many unknowns had to be frightening for a child. It was scary enough for an adult. But it was also full of wonderment and bursting with possibilities.

"All right, about-face young lady," Marshall added. She began leading the way back to the lifeboat. Payton stayed close on her heels, but Aria lingered, her eyes scanning the labyrinthine depths of the forest around the clearing. What looked like a thick mist snaked around the bottoms of the trees. For some reason it dissipated just before reaching the clearing, as if it were a living thing, skulking in the shadows to avoid the sun. Aria stared into the shadowy gray depths of it. Shifting contours appeared, movement that her brain interpreted as *alive*. Aria squinted for a better look. *What was that?* she wondered.

"Aria?" Marshall called out.

Just air currents stirring the mist, she decided. "Coming!" she replied and ran to catch up.

They passed Marshall's men on their way back to the lifeboat, and she stopped briefly to give them orders.

"Set up a perimeter, no closer than fifty meters from the trees, and no one enters the forest. Yet." She produced a handheld scanner from one pocket of her jacket and turned the holographic display for them to see. Aria peered over Marshall's shoulder for a glimpse. The display showed a simplistic 2D representation of the clearing and the forest around them. A red blob for the lake. A blue hexagon for the crystal, lavender for grass, mottled black and purple for the trees. Red dots wove through the forest.

"There are lifeforms in there watching us," Marshall explained.

Aria's heart began thumping in her chest. "There are?" So it wasn't just air currents stirring the mist after all.

Marshall nodded to the Marine in front of her. "Is that understood, Corporal?"

He belatedly tore his eyes away from the scanner and nodded. "Yes, ma'am."

"Good. I'll be back out soon. Stay frosty."

"Oorah," the man replied and then jogged off with his rifle at the ready.

A rifle? Aria wondered. "I thought you were undercover? Where did your men get heavy weapons?"

"The armory," Marshall explained as she led the way back up the landing ramp. "Soon as we came under attack my men went there to upgrade their kit." The outer doors of the airlock swished open, and the three of them stepped inside.

"Did they manage to kill any of the Sparklers?" Aria asked.

"No, ma'am. The heavy weapons seemed to scare them off, though. A good deterrent if nothing else."

"Hopefully they don't find us down here."

"Copy that," Marshall said as the lights inside the airlock dimmed to a ruddy hue.

A warning beep issued from the airlock, followed by, "Decontamination commencing."

Acrid-smelling mist blasted them from jets on all sides for several seconds, followed by a blast of heat to dry them. Then the lights returned to normal, and a pleasant chime sounded, followed by, "All contaminants neutralized."

The inner doors sprang open, and a wave of warm, rose-scented air greeted them from the suite's essential oil diffusers.

Back inside the lifeboat, fatigue hit Aria like a wave. She stumbled aimlessly toward the living room couches, her feet shuffling as she fumbled to release the seals on her mask. She tore it off and let it dangle from one wrist as she helped Payton to remove hers. Once they were done, Aria cast about for something to do. "What now?" she asked, seeing that Marshall had opened another recessed panel in the living room. There was some kind of computer console behind it.

"Now, we see if we can make contact with any of the other lifeboats, and while we're at it, try to contact the *Dream*."

Aria's thoughts returned to Liam and Nikolai, and her heart began to pound once more. "Do you think anyone's still up there?"

"I don't know, but hopefully some of the crew stayed on board and managed to fend off the Sparklers."

"What about the other lifeboats? My husband and son might be on one of them."

"Might be," Marshall agreed.

"Can you ask?"

The woman laughed lightly. "There were three hundred and sixty lifeboats on the ring decks alone. They're programmed to spread out all across the most habitable zones of the planet, so we won't be able to contact more than a few of them."

Aria stared incredulously at the back of Marshall's head. "Why the hell would they spread out?"

Marshall half-turned from the console. "Because it increases our odds of survival. Studies show that stranding a lot of people in a hostile environment with limited resources leads to in-fighting. Gangs form. The strong prey on the weak. Tribal shit."

"But... what if there's some kind of external threat? There'd be strength in numbers."

"Sometimes. But imagine what would happen if the autopilots set us all down next to a volcano that's just about to erupt." Marshall framed an imaginary explosion with her hands. "Boom. No survivors."

Aria's mind raced. She felt dizzy with terror for her husband and son. What if she couldn't find them? She had armed Marines to keep her and Payton safe. But what did they have? "Do any of the other lifeboats have weapons?"

"No."

"Not even to hunt?"

Marshall glanced back at her. "You think it would be a good idea to give all the passengers on a cruise ship access to lethal weapons?"

"Then how do you expect them to survive?"

"There's a four-man rover mounted between the grav lifts on the underside of the hull and six armored exosuits hidden behind panels in the airlocks. The suits should keep even the most intrepid explorers from getting their limbs chomped off. But if they need weapons, they'll have to make do with the tools in the rover. Cutting torches, laser welders, knives." Marshall looked back to the console with a shrug. "Better than nothing."

"Can you at least ask the other lifeboats about my husband and son?" Aria asked. "If we can reach the nearest ones with our comms, maybe they can reach another few that are farther away, and then those ones can do the same thing. We can pass on a message like that, bouncing it from one transmitter to another."

"What are their names?"

"Liam and Nikolai."

"I'll try, but no promises. I'm still waiting for a reply."

"Thank you." Aria looked away, her eyes scanning the living room. Payton had curled up in an armchair. The two evacuees she hadn't met were still sitting at their folding emergency stations, talking in low voices. Aria angled for Payton, but stopped halfway there. The old man, Samos, was lying on the couch beside her chair, his twisted ankle raised on a pillow and visibly swollen.

She regarded him with a sympathetic frown. "Have you taken anything for the pain?"

"One of the Marines gave me something," he said.

"What about vitalics?" Aria asked, much as she hated to suggest it. "One injection and—"

The old man waved away that suggestion. "I'd rather limp than be the cause of an innocent creature's death."

Aria flashed a smile. A man after her own heart. No wonder Samos looked so old. He refused to be a part of the ubiquitous alien slaughter that stayed the hands of time and enriched the likes of Markus Leonidus. Aria glared at the bedroom door. For all anyone knew, he and Elisa were sipping wine in their hot tub right now—rich and entitled to the end.

She looked back to Samos. He was watching her through slitted eyes. "I'm sure your family is fine," he said.

Aria nodded. "Thank you. What about you, were you traveling with anyone?"

He shook his head. "Just me and my demons."

She cocked her head and looked at him with new eyes. *Why would he go on an expensive interstellar cruise by himself?* she wondered. "You do that often? Go on vacation by yourself?"

"I needed a break from work. Just because I don't have anyone doesn't mean I don't get tired of the same old routine."

"Sorry. What do you do?"

"I'm an engineer. Experimental technologies, mostly."

Marshall glanced their way, looking like she wanted to say something.

"What about you?" Samos asked before she could.

"I'm a biomedical researcher."

Samos winced as he shifted his position on the couch.

"I should probably let you rest..." Aria said, her eyes on his ankle.

"Yeah," Samos agreed. "Sorry. Rain check?"

"Of course." She found his hand and squeezed it briefly before leaving his side to go check on Payton. Still curled up in the armchair, Payton's eyes were shut as if she were asleep, but her brow was furrowed with anxious squiggles.

"Are you okay?" Aria asked, dropping to her haunches in front of the chair. She reached out to stroke Payton's hair, frizzy and tangled from a swim at the *Dream's* artificial beach.

Payton's eyes cracked to teary emerald slits. "No."

"What's wrong?" *Stupid question,* Aria thought.

"I was thinking about Dad and Niko. What if the Sparkles got them?"

Aria smiled and swept a frizzy lock of hair out of Payton's eyes. She cupped her daughter's cheek. "You mean Sparklers. Sparkles works, too, I guess." Her smile faded in a hurry as Payton's words hit home. Fear surged anew, and she withdrew her hand as it began to tremble. Desperately shoveling negative thoughts under mental carpets, she shook her head. "We're not going to think that way. Your father and brother are probably in our suite right now. They are probably just on the other side of this forest, with all of our stuff, wondering where *we* are and if *we* made it here safe."

"You think so?"

Aria sucked in a deep breath and summoned a smile despite the lump in her throat and the ache in her chest. "I *know* so."

"There is one lifeboat in range, but they're not replying," Marshall announced from the comms station.

Aria looked away from Payton. "Maybe they haven't heard you yet."

"Emergency messages are set to play over the PA system by default. They *had to* have heard me."

"Then maybe they don't know how to reply?"

"It's all automated and idiot-proof. All they have to do is talk back. I'm tapped into their internal audio-pickups, listening to everything they're saying."

"And?"

"Listen for yourself." A crackle of static hissed through hidden speakers in the living room. After a few seconds, Aria recognized a howling sound. The wind.

"Is that the wind?"

Marshall nodded. "The lifeboat must have cracked open on landing."

A skittering sound came over the speakers.

"What was that?" Aria asked.

Marshall's brow furrowed. "I don't know." She turned back to the control console. "Hello? Is anyone listening? This is Lieutenant Marshall, head of the *Starlit Dream's* security forces."

More skittering, but the sound was retreating now.

"Wildlife, maybe," Marshall suggested.

"Sounded like giant insects to me," the unidentified man said from where he sat with his wife.

Payton clutched Aria's arm suddenly, her fingers like talons. "Can they get in here?"

"No, sweetheart. We're safe."

"How do you know?"

Aria started to say something, then stopped. Empty reassurances got stuck in her throat. How *did* she know? The truth was she didn't know anything about this place, much less whether or not they were safe.

"I know because I'm your mother, and I'm going to keep you safe. No matter what. Alien bugs be damned."

CHAPTER 13

"Run!" Liam screamed. The armory was dead ahead at the end of the corridor. Seconds away, Buck was waiting there with the door already open. Metallic thunder chased them down the corridor from the elevators, growing louder and closer by the second.

Nikolai struggled to keep up, still weak from dehydration, his injuries only half-healed by the use of vitalics. Jules brought up the rear, shielding them with his body from a possible attack.

"Come on!" Buck urged, his yellow eyes flashing in the beams of Jules' bobbing optical lamps.

Liam grabbed Nikolai's arm and dragged him the rest of the way with a final burst of speed. They flew through the open door. Jules piled in after them, and Buck shut the door with just seconds to spare before the alien machines slammed into it. The door shook with the impact. Shrieking sounds followed as they began striking the door with their tentacles. Everyone stared at the door, watching as it shivered with repeated impacts. The assault grew louder and more frenzied with every passing second.

"Can they get in here?" Liam asked.

"No." Buck shook his head, then hesitated. "At least, I don't think so."

The assault waned and became more sporadic. The Urchins kept it up every couple of seconds, striking the door with a ringing *bang* to let them know that they were still there.

"Why don't they just teleport in?" Nikolai asked. He sat down beside a set of open metal shelves and leaned back against a supply crate. His face was pale and gray, a sheen of sweat had formed on his forehead and cheeks, and his blue eyes were worryingly dim.

"One of them wouldn't fit in here," Buck suggested.

Liam dropped to his haunches in front of Niko. "How are you feeling?"

"Sleepy," he said, his head lolling like he was just about to faint.

Bang. The Urchins struck the door again.

Liam glanced back at Jules. "He needs water. Or something to rehydrate."

Jules shook his head, a grave expression on his wrinkled face. His gray hair stuck up at odd angles, making him look like he'd just got out of bed.

"This is the armory," Buck said. "Plenty of guns but no food or water."

"Not even MREs?" Liam asked.

"Emergency rations are down the hall."

Liam glanced at the door just as it banged with another impact. "Great." He looked around. They were in a narrow aisle barely wide enough for two people to stand next to each other. It was fairly long, however, with shelves and racks of weapons lining both sides. "We could take them out," Liam suggested. "You and me and Jules. There's enough guns in here to start a war."

"I am not authorized to fire a weapon," Jules said.

"Not even in self-defense, or defense of another?"

Jules shook his head. "Not even then."

"Well, you and me then," Liam said, nodding to Buck. "There's just two of them. We back up to the far end of this locker, aim at the doors, and then you open them remotely. You said it yourself, the armory is too small for them to get in, so we should be safe as long as we stay out of their reach."

"Like shooting fish in a barrel. Sounds like a plan." Buck led the way to one of the gun racks.

Jules kept pace with them, using his optical lamps to light the way. The gun rack was replete with plasma and laser rifles, coil guns, and even old-fashioned slug throwers.

"Pick your poison," Buck said as he snatched a three-foot-long coil gun off the rack.

Liam opted for a laser rifle. It was a zero-recoil weapon which made it easier to aim. Buck handed him a pair of spare charge packs. "Put them in your pockets."

Liam checked the safety on his rifle as he did so and hauled back on the charging handle. The capacitors hummed to life, and the weapon began shivering ever-so-slightly in his hands to indicate that it was armed and ready to fire.

"Bring the kid over," Buck said to Jules. The bot went to where Nikolai was sitting and then scooped him off the floor. He carried Nikolai behind Liam and Buck and set him down once more.

"Down on one knee," Buck instructed. "Like this."

Liam crouched down to mimic the Marine's posture, being careful to keep the barrel of his rifle aimed at the floor. He braced his forearm on one knee to steady his aim.

"Ready?" Buck asked.

Liam aimed down the illuminated holographic sights on top of his rifle. "Ready."

The door thumped with another impact—

And then Buck opened it.

A sparkling Urchin surged into the gap, tentacles reaching blindly down the aisle. The screeching report of Liam's laser rifle sounded in tandem with the explosive *boom* of the coil gun. Lasers flickered through the armory in a pulsing wash of emerald fire, but Buck's supersonic rifle had already done the job. A hole the size of Liam's head had been punched straight through the Urchin. It was no longer sparkling and translucent, but silvery and opaque. Dead. The machine collapsed in a thunderous clatter of lifeless metal, blocking the entrance.

"Damn it," Buck said. He peered around his sights at the obstacle. "We'll have to blast it out of the way just to get out of here."

"Where's the other one?" Liam asked.

"My sensors indicate an energy signature just outside the doors," Jules put in.

"Sneaky bastard..." Buck's brow furrowed. "It's camping there, just waiting for us to come out."

"So what do we do?" Liam asked.

"I don't know."

"What about a grenade? We could toss one out and clear the way."

Buck chuckled darkly.

"What?"

"What do you think this is, a warship?"

"You've got an armory with coil guns in it," Liam pointed out.

"Yeah, but that's as heavy as the weapons get. Civilian ships aren't allowed to stock explosives of any kind."

"So, what do we do?"

"Get back."

"What?"

"You heard me—all the way to the end."

Liam did as he was told, and Jules carried Nikolai to the end of the armory.

"Take cover," Buck said.

Jules set Nikolai down and went to stand between them and Buck as a shield.

Liam frowned. "What are you—"

An explosive *bang* cut him off, followed by another, and another. Shrapnel pinged around the armory and clattered to the deck. When no more explosions sounded, Liam peered around Jules to see that the Urchin blocking the door had been reduced to a ragged pile of molten orange metal.

"How about now, Bolts?" Buck asked. "Still reading an energy signature out there?"

"Yes, but it is farther away now."

Buck grunted. "They don't scare easy." The door to the armory slid shut, pushing the molten remains of the Urchin aside. He stood up, holding the coil gun one-handed, the white-hot barrel nearly scraping the ceiling.

"We can't just stay in here until it gives up and goes away," Liam said.

"I agree." Buck nodded at the ceiling, to the grille of an overhead duct. "How are you at army crawling?"

CHAPTER 14

"Still nothing," Marshall said over the persistent crackle of static.

Aria swallowed hard past the lump in her throat. "What about the *Starlit Dream?*"

"No reply from them, either. Not even a ping reply. Their comms must still be down. We're on our own."

"What could have happened to that lifeboat?" Aria asked.

"I'll tell you what happened," one of the two evacuees that Aria hadn't met yet said. He was a big man wearing a form-fitting blue suit and a white shirt with no tie. His immaculately trimmed black beard and stylish haircut made Aria think he spent far too much time worrying about appearances. A stunning woman with long, straight blond hair sat beside him. Smoky eye make-up framed brilliant purple eyes, and she had an exaggerated hourglass figure that was almost painful to look at.

"They're all dead," the man said.

"We don't know that," Marshall replied.

"You said it yourself, they should have replied by now. At the very least we'd be able to overhear them talking. And what about that skittering sound we heard?" He shook his head.

"We won't know for sure what happened until we get over there," Marshall insisted.

Aria looked away from the big man and his wife, back to Marshall. "You think you'll be able to find them?"

She nodded. "We can track their emergency beacon."

"How far away are they?"

"Five point nine kilometers."

"Even if they are all... *dead*—" Aria's voice shrank around the word. "—maybe we can use their comms to reach the next closest lifeboat."

"My thoughts exactly," Marshall replied.

"You said the autopilot separated us for a reason," the bearded man interrupted. "So why are you trying to make contact with the other lifeboats?"

"Because my family is missing!" Aria snapped.

Black Beard flinched at the force of her outburst.

Marshall added, "We also need intel. We need to learn from each other's mistakes and triumphs if we're going to survive down here until a rescue comes."

"You mean *if* a rescue comes," Black Beard said.

Marshall's magenta eyes narrowed. "What's your name?"

"Mattias Corvus." He turned and nodded to the blond woman sitting quietly behind him. "And my wife, Asha Corvus." At the mention of her name, she looked up.

"Nice to meet you both. You know what the difference between a survivor and a corpse is, Mr. Corvus?" Marshall asked.

"The smell?" Mattias suggested.

Marshall's mouth twitched up in one corner. "No, the difference is the survivor held on, and the corpse gave up. You tell yourself that no one is coming to save us, and you might just end up flying home in a body bag when the rescue ships finally do get here."

"Yeah, whatever," Mattias waved his hand at her and went back to sit beside his wife.

"How do we reach the other lifeboat?" Aria asked.

"We have to scout the forest, see if we can drive the rover through it. If not, we'll have to hike over."

"Can I go?" Aria asked.

Marshall's gaze landed on Payton. "What about your daughter?"

"Samos can watch her."

"The guy with the twisted ankle?" Marshall shook her head. "If something happens to you, your girl is going to be all alone. You can't risk that."

"She's not the only one who needs me. I have to get on the comms in the other lifeboat. I have to convince the other passengers to spread the word and find out where my husband and son are."

"I can pass on the message for you."

"I'll be more convincing," Aria replied.

Marshall's lower jaw zig-zagged briefly. "Tell you what. If we find out that the rover can make it through the trees, you and your daughter can both come. We should be safe enough inside."

"Thank you."

Marshall smiled tightly. "No problem. I'm a wife and a mother, too. I know how it is."

Aria's eyes widened and flicked up and down the lieutenant, studying her short, spiked blond hair, dark pink eyes, and sharply angled features.

"What's the matter?" Marshall asked through a smirk. "I don't look like the family type to you?"

"No, no, it's not that, it's—"

Marshall rolled up her right sleeve to reveal a wiry forearm with veins popping out. A stylized name appeared glowing red and blue in a barbed-wire font: *Maddy*.

"The other arm has my husband's name on it," she said.

Aria smiled wanly. "How old is Maddy?"

"Three," Marshall said as she rolled her sleeve back down.

"That's a cute age."

"Yeah."

"Sorry for my reaction. It's just that you look—" Aria shook her head.

"Like a hard ass?"

Aria laughed. "Exactly."

"Can we all focus on the situation at hand?" Mattias interrupted. "You said you need to scout the forest. And we also need to eat. Where's the food around here?"

A dark cloud passed over Marshall's face. "The synthesizer in the kitchen is fully stocked."

"I've never used a synthesizer in my life," Mattias said, his upper lip curling at the thought.

Marshall's eyes rolled. "You were expecting one of us to cook your meals for you?"

Mattias's cheeks turned red. "No, I meant I don't know how it works."

Marshall blew out a breath. "Unbelievable," she muttered. "I bet he doesn't know how to wipe his own ass either."

"Hey!"

"I'll take care of it," Aria interrupted.

"The food, or his ass?"

"Have some respect," Mattias growled.

"Thank you," Marshall replied, ignoring him. She strode toward the airlock. "I'll be back as soon as I can."

"Be careful," Aria called after her.

"Don't worry. I didn't live through the second Gliesian War just to get eaten by some fucking alien." The inner airlock doors swished open, and Marshall walked in. The doors slammed shut before Aria could reply.

The second Gliesian War ended in 2542 AD— 55 years ago. If Marshall had fought in that war, she had to be at least seventy-five years old, and somehow she had a three-year-old daughter. Another living example of the power of vitalics, but that wasn't the problem: Vitalic serum cost around five-thousand credits per dose. She needed two doses a month to stay so young and vital at seventy-plus years old, and there was no way that a Marine lieutenant was making over ten thousand credits a month. Something definitely wasn't adding up. Aria glanced around, searching for signs of recognition on Mattias's and Asha's faces, but they were whispering among themselves once more, seemingly oblivious to the incongruity between Marshall's apparent age and economic status.

What if Marshall wasn't actually a Marine? What if she was part of whatever plot had brought them all to this place?

The answer came unbidden to Aria's mind: if Marshall wasn't actually who she said she was, then she could be dangerous. No one who went to this much trouble to divert a cruise ship would want their plans exposed.

On the bright side, it meant that they weren't actually lost. Marshall likely knew where they were and how to get them home.

So what is she waiting for? Aria wondered.

"Hey, hello... lady, are you there?" Mattias was waving his hands to get her attention. "You said you were going to whip something up in the synthesizer..."

"It's Aria, not *lady*, and I'll whip you up a well-seasoned shoe if you don't learn some manners."

A dark look flickered across the man's face, but his wife patted his knee. "She's right, Matt. You could be a little nicer."

He glanced at her, then back to Aria. "I apologize. This situation is bringing the worst out in me. Perhaps you could show me how to work the device, and then I can prepare my own food?"

"Fair enough. Come on," Aria said, already headed for the kitchen.

CHAPTER 15

Liam army-crawled through the duct behind Buck. Both of them wore optical enhancers, one camera stuck beside each eye with nano-adhesive pads. The enhancers provided perfect night vision via an overlay on their augmented reality lenses. Buck had dug them out of a cabinet in the armory just before they'd left. It was military-grade tech that had no business being on a cruise ship, but then again, undercover Marines and coil guns had no business being there either.

Besides the optics, the only equipment they carried were a pair of short-barreled laser rifles and in-ear comms.

"How are you doing back there?" Buck whispered.

"Good," Liam panted. "What do you see up ahead?"

"Looks like a corner coming up."

"Great." Slithering along the duct was more exercise than he'd imagined. Liam stopped, gasping and sweating, feeling like he couldn't breathe.

"What's wrong?" Buck asked.

"Is it getting narrower or is it just me?"

"It's all in your head. Keep your shit together."

Liam grimaced and began slithering once more. He tried not to think about it, but if they got stuck, there was no way in hell he'd be able to crawl out backward.

They reached the corner, and Buck expertly wiggled his way around it. Liam tried to mimic that movement but ended up with his shoulders wedged. *Shit.* His heart thundered in his chest, and his head pulsed with a dizzying wave of terror. Liam tried to kick his way through, drawing thunderous reports from the sides of the duct.

"You okay?" Buck called back to him.

"I'm stuck," Liam said, fighting back a fresh surge of panic that left him cold and shaking. There was a maddening itch between his shoulder blades that he couldn't scratch. His nose and scalp itched, too. Liam squeezed his eyes shut and focused on his breathing to calm down.

"Try turning your shoulders, the duct is wider along the diagonal."

"Okay..." It worked. "Thanks," he breathed.

"Keep it moving. Looks like there's a vent up ahead. Maybe our exit."

Liam nodded and worked some moisture into his dry mouth. "Good."

"Keep the safety on until we're clear," Buck added.

"Don't worry. It's not my first time around a gun."

"All the same. If it were your ass in my sights..."

Liam smiled. "Yeah. I get it."

After a few seconds, Buck stopped crawling, and Liam heard metal striking metal as he knocked on the vent from the inside with the butt of his rifle.

A moment later, the grate popped free with a *ping* of snapping screws. It clattered on the deck below. Liam held his breath, waited to hear Urchins rumbling toward them.

"Clear," Buck whispered, and then crawled halfway out. He twisted around inside the duct, his torso leaning out, his rifle dangling from the strap; legs, abs, and hands supporting his weight as he pulled out one leg at a time and then dropped down with a soft *thump*. "Your turn," he whispered up to Liam.

Buck's maneuver looked like something only an acrobat or a stunt man could do—not a lawyer with a middle-aged spread. Liam imagined himself tumbling headfirst from the duct and smashing his face on the deck.

"Coming," Liam said.

The corridor beyond the duct was lined with a curving wall of windows. The dark, flashing nebula concealing the stars. A sudden flash of light blinded Liam's optics, and then a familiar shimmering form appeared right in front of them, close enough that Buck could have reached out and touched it. He stiffened, his aim shifting casually to the Urchin. Liam did the same, sliding the safety off and slipping his finger past the trigger guard.

The Urchin remained where it was, no discernible face or eyes staring at them, but its razor-sharp tentacles drifted around like snakes, as if it were restless with indecision, or maybe just savoring the kill. They could shoot it, but it could definitely kill them before they disabled it. The memory of those translucent tentacles piercing Nikolai in three different places flashed through Liam's mind's eye. Niko had been lucky. If it had stabbed him through an eye or his heart...

The Urchin made its move. Liam's finger tensed on the trigger.

But it was rolling *away* from them. Tentacles scraped the deck with a muted rumbling sound. The machine rolled around the curving corridor and out of sight.

"What the hell?" Buck breathed.

Liam let out a stale breath. "Why didn't it attack us?"

Buck turned to him. "They were desperate to get at you in the elevator. So desperate that they rolled right past me even while I was shooting them." Buck's eyes pinched into confused slits, and he shook his head.

"They're not killing indiscriminately," Liam decided. "The first one we met went chasing after a woman in heels. It only broke off and turned on you when you started shooting at it."

"But it didn't kill me when it could have. It just scratched my cheek and slashed my arm open," Buck said.

"Exactly. But when Nikolai tried to distract it—"

"It ran him through in three different places," Buck finished. "So they're after *him?*"

Liam struggled to get out of the duct. "A little help?"

Buck let his rifle dangle from its strap and helped him down.

"Thanks," Liam said as his feet touched the deck.

"If your son is their target, we might not be able to get him out of the armory," Buck said.

"It might not be *him.* Jules ran out to protect him. Maybe Niko only got stabbed because he was standing behind Jules."

"So you're saying they have a thing against their own kind? Machines killing machines?"

"No, because it went after the woman in heels first. And another one killed the people we saw in the front of the tram."

"Not to mention the captain," Buck added. "Seems like random killing to me. There's no pattern to it. Maybe the one we just saw didn't attack us because it realized we're armed with heavy weapons and we're not easy targets anymore."

"Yeah, maybe," Liam agreed. "We need to find some water and get back to Niko."

Buck nodded down the corridor. "We're still on level sixty. It's just a storage level. No water here. Sixty-one through sixty-three are filled with bars and clubs."

"Perfect. Lead the way," Liam said.

Buck started down the curving corridor in the direction that the Urchin had gone, then stopped and turned the other way. "Maybe we shouldn't tempt it," he said.

They hurried down the corridor, periodically throwing glances behind them to make sure no Urchins followed. Dark signs hung from the ceiling marking the way to various numbered storage rooms, elevators, and stairs. Following the signs, they soon came to a short hall lined with elevators on both sides. Liam activated the call button via his ARLs, and the up arrow glowed orange. The ship's network still wasn't working, but most of the wireless ARL interfaces still worked.

Liam glanced about as they waited. Beyond the banks of elevators was a familiar door-lined corridor. The door to the armory stood halfway down to the other end with a faintly shimmering Urchin lurking beside it. The machine made no move to approach them, apparently content to wait out its cornered prey. "Son of a bitch," Liam muttered. "Look—" He gestured with the barrel of his rifle, sighting down it to the Urchin. "We could shoot it from here. There's enough distance between us that we've got the upper hand."

Buck pushed his rifle aside. "But it's not the only one on board. Your son is safe in the armory, and right now, for whatever reason, the Urchins aren't hunting *us.* That means we have free reign to get to the bridge and figure some other shit out."

Liam glanced at him just as one of the elevators dinged open. "Such as?"

"Such as where the hell we are and how to get the jump gate in this system working so we can get home. Or at the very least, where the lifeboats went so that we can join them."

"We have to get water for Niko first."

"Agreed, but if those things really don't give a shit about us anymore, we may as well push a little farther and hit the med bay. Saline's better than water, and I could still use a shot of vitalics." Buck nodded sideways to indicate his bloody arm.

"Where's med bay?"

"Nearest one is on deck one hundred."

"Let's go." Liam led the way into the open elevator and mentally pre-selected *D100(MD)* from the digital directory. The elevator rose swiftly, covering forty floors in just a few seconds. When the doors dinged open, three shimmering Urchins were waiting for them.

Liam's and Buck's rifles snapped up in the same instant. Razor-sharp tentacles skittered on the deck as the Urchins shifted toward them. Bright red blood sparkled on their transparent limbs, and a ragged human corpse lay at their feet.

CHAPTER 16

"**W**hy aren't they attacking us?" Liam whispered. The Urchins waiting outside the elevator went back to whatever they were doing with the corpse—tentacles striking flesh with metallic scissoring sounds.

"Maybe it's a trap," Buck suggested. The elevator doors slid shut, and the elevator whisked up for half a second.

Liam glanced at the panel above the doors just as they dinged open once more. "Level 101?"

"Also the med bay," Buck replied. This time the way was clear. "Come on." He walked out with his rifle raised, scanning both ways for targets, but there were no alien machines on this level.

"What were they doing?" Liam asked, keeping his rifle aimed down and to one side to avoid pointing it at Buck.

"Don't know."

"Feeding?"

"With what mouths?" Buck strode quickly through a patient waiting area and around an abandoned reception desk with the words *Starlit Medical Services* above it. From there he led the way down a hall lined with doors to an open area with green curtains, beds, and medical equipment. He walked purposefully toward a refrigerated medicine cabinet with heavy metal doors, but halfway there, his steps faltered.

The doors were dented and punched full of holes, peeling open in several places to reveal broken glass vials. Shards of glass lay all over the floor in front of the cabinet, but no signs of whatever liquid they had contained.

"Whatever was in there, the Urchins wanted it bad," Liam said.

Buck turned to him. "They're after the vitalics. That's what they're targeting, and that's why they were after Bolts. He had three vials in a storage compartment in his stomach. Like you said, your son only got hit because he was standing behind the bot."

Liam's eyes widened. "But Jules used the vitalics on Niko!"

"Which is why they were so desperate to get at him in the elevator. Anyone who's dosed recently with the serum becomes a target for them."

"You mean everyone on board?" Liam asked. The ultra-rich were all habitual users. Who would die young or grow old if they could afford not to?

Buck shook his head. "You only have to dose twice a month. Some people will have dosed recently, but not everyone. The amount of time elapsed since a person's last dose probably determines the degree to which the Urchins focus on them."

"That explains why they never went after me," Liam said. "I'm not a user." A ripple of relief spread through him as he realized that meant his wife and daughter weren't targets either. They'd almost certainly made it to one of the lifeboats. But Niko wasn't so lucky. "My son received *three* doses."

"He'll have to stay in the armory until enough time passes for him to come out safely," Buck replied. "Or, until we find a way to clear the Urchins off the ship." He walked over to another cabinet and yanked it open. "Bingo." He began pulling out items: wads of gauze, a bottle of disinfectant, and a spray can of synthskin.

Setting the items on a steel cart beside him, Buck unslung his rifle and shrugged out of his jacket to reveal a pair of ragged, crusty red gashes running down his left arm. He sat on the edge of a nearby bed and began pouring the disinfectant over the wounds. Pink rivulets trickled down to his hand and dribbled to the floor. Buck gritted his teeth against the pain and began pouring more disinfectant on the gauze and using it to clean away crusted blood. When he was done, the wounds were bleeding again, but he quickly sprayed them with the can of synthskin. A translucent layer formed over the gashes and they stopped bleeding.

"Good enough," Buck grunted.

"How long before Niko can come out of the armory?" Liam asked.

Buck looked up. "My last dose was ten days ago, and the Urchins are ignoring me."

"Your last dose?" He trailed off, wondering about that. Buck was a user? "What about the gashes in your arm and cheek?"

Buck reached up to touch the crusted wound in his cheek as if only remembering it now. He poured more disinfectant on a clean wad of gauze and used it to rub away the dried blood. "Maybe that was self-defense. I was shooting the thing at the time. Anyway, I only used one vial of vitalics. Your son used three, and he's probably half my weight. I figure that means his blood concentration is six times as much as mine was when I took my dose ten days ago. The half-life is roughly two days, so to get to the same serum blood levels as me..."

Liam ran the calculations mentally with his Neuralink. "It would take between fourteen and sixteen days."

Buck nodded. "Then that's how long he has to stay in there."

"He'll die."

"We'll take him rations."

"There's no plumbing."

"Ever heard of a bucket?"

"Shit..."

"Yeah, there'll be lots of that," Buck said, chuckling darkly.

"It's not funny."

"It is a *little* funny." Buck hopped down from the bed and slung his rifle crosswise over his shoulders. "Look on the bright side. At least now we know how to avoid getting speared to death by the Urchins. We've just caught a hell of a break."

Liam frowned but said nothing.

"Let's get that saline for your son and go break the bad news."

Liam nodded absently. Something was niggling in the back of his mind, a puzzle piece that didn't quite fit. Buck found a bag of saline in another storage locker along with an IV line and some surgical tape. He went back for the bottle of disinfectant and the remainder of the gauze. "Here, take these."

Liam accepted the bundle of items and tucked them under his left arm as he followed the Marine back the way they'd come. Liam's thoughts cleared, and he realized what was bothering him. "Buck..."

"Yeah?"

"You mentioned your last dose was ten days ago."

"Uh-huh, and?"

"I was just wondering... how can you afford vitalics on a Marine's wages?" Liam stopped and brought his rifle up, awkwardly aiming it one-handed at Buck's back. The safety was on, but Buck didn't know that.

The Marine stopped and slowly turned around as if he could sense the crosshairs between his shoulder blades. He held his own rifle crosswise, the barrel pointing down.

"Well?" Liam demanded.

Buck's yellow eyes glittered darkly in the light of Liam's optical enhancers. "In the corps, they teach you never to point a firearm at someone unless you intend to shoot, and never to shoot unless you intend to kill," Buck said.

"Stop stalling and answer the damn question," Liam said, shaking his rifle at the self-proclaimed Marine. "Someone was responsible for bringing us here. And if you're lying about being a Marine, then what else are you lying about?"

Buck took a quick step toward him. Liam flinched, his forefinger reflexively squeezing the trigger, but of course, nothing happened. Buck grabbed the weapon barrel with his good arm, pushing it aside, and then sucker punched Liam in the gut with his injured arm. He yanked the rifle away. Liam dropped the bag of saline and other articles as he stumbled back, gasping soundlessly for air.

CHAPTER 17

Sparkling lavender-colored grass waved in the breeze. Marshall gripped her sidearm in a tight, two-handed grip as she approached the gleaming obsidian trunks of the towering alien trees. Two of her men flanked her to either side, their rifles up and tracking.

A gloomy silver mist concealed the forest floor. Intrepid tendrils snaked through the grassy field as far as the shadows around the trees, stopping before they reached sunlit ground. High above, dark purple leaves blocked out the sun. The leaves only started a few hundred feet up, and each of them was big enough to form the roof of a small house. The sun backlit some of them to a luminous, pinkish hue, revealing fat black lines snaking through that looked just like veins.

Bringing her gaze back down, Marshall paid special attention to the ARL overlay that showed what the scanner in the inside pocket of her jacket could detect. Flickering red outlines between the tree trunks denoted lifeforms. Numbers alongside those overlays gave her estimates of the creatures' distances and sizes. The nearest ones were as small as squirrels, a few others as big as dogs. Further in, some of the blips reached the size of elephants, and at a range of two kilometers, a single flickering red blip was estimated to be twenty feet tall and sixty feet long. The size of a large dinosaur.

Marshall stopped at the edge of the clearing, right where the mist went from wedding-veil thin to primordial soup thick. The sound of her breath rasping through the filter mask was loud in her ears.

A sudden *cracking* sound sent her heart-rate soaring, and she whirled toward it, her plasma pistol tracking up. The noise went on, crashing down through the trees...

A massive leaf appeared, fluttering down with a sound like a helicopter's blades turning in slow-motion. Twigs and bits of broken branches thumped down ahead of it. The massive leaf flipped and flopped as it fell, then vanished into the concealing mist with a quiet *thump*.

Just a leaf, Marshall said via silent comms—text only. Tiny red-shaded creatures had scattered away from the falling debris, leaving only half as many of them in the range of the scanner. The small, squirrel-sized blips were only detectable at a short range.

Big ass leaf, Thespian replied, his rifle tracking back and forth across the drifting wall of mist.

We should go in and take a look around, Hunter added.

Marshall hesitated, wondering if that was necessary. From here they could clearly see that the trees were far enough apart for the rover to weave a path around them. Hunter probably reasoned that with the mist concealing the ground there was no way to tell what kind of obstacles were lying in there. They might only get a few feet in with the rover before getting it stuck on a fallen branch or log.

That's a negative, Marshall decided. *Visibility is for shit. We could fall in a hole or get bitten by some alien snake. The rover's optics will help us image whatever is hiding in the mist. We'll drive it over here and take a look. If there's a path, the rover will find it.*

Copy that, Hunter replied.

Marshall was just about to start backpedaling when a red blip came creeping out of the mist on two legs. As it emerged, the shaded overlay disappeared, and the creature snapped into focus.

Marshall gasped and stumbled back a step.

"What the..." Thespian trailed off, too shocked to speak silently over the comms.

"Is that what I think it is?" Hunter asked.

Hunched like a tiny dinosaur, the creature fluttered translucent, rainbow-colored wings before folding them along its back. It cocked its head at them. Big green eyes wide and blinking. Its ears were long and pointed like a rabbit's. Fine blue and green fur sparkled with dew drops all over its body. Just then, spindly arms unfolded to a few feet in length, reaching out with dexterous hands as if to touch them. But anyone who knew their body language knew that this was a wave hello. The creature warbled something at them. A question.

Marshall's *Vitari* was rudimentary at best, but she understood it well enough. It roughly translated to: *do you kill for food?*

The answer—which of course would be a *no,* thanks to the prevalence of synthetically-grown meat products—would put the creature at ease. Little did the poor thing know just how many other reasons there were to kill—especially a Vitari whose blood was a fountain of youth for other lifeforms.

"We landed on Vitaria?" Thespian asked, his voice rising in disbelief.

* * *

"So just because I'm a Marine, I can't be rich?" Buck asked.

"Well, no but..."

Jasper T. Scott

"What if I told you it's family money. Would that make more sense?"

Liam nodded slowly. "I suppose it would."

Buck checked the safety on Liam's rifle, smirked when he saw it was still on, then passed it back with the barrel aiming at the ground. "Here."

Liam accepted the weapon, then bent to pick up the bag of saline and the other items he'd dropped.

"We're in this together," Buck said. "I don't know anything more than you do. And if someone *does* know what happened to send the *Dream* here, I'll be first in line to beat the answers out of them."

Liam nodded again.

"That's why we need to get to the bridge. I want to see what happened. We heard gunshots over the PA when the Captain ordered everyone to abandon ship. It's possible they were shooting more than just Urchins. They might have been dealing with hijackers."

"From the Guild," Liam suggested.

"That's one possibility."

"My butler bot said he analyzed the position of the stars around us."

"And?"

"He couldn't recognize anything. He thinks we might be in another galaxy."

Buck frowned. "Jumping to another galaxy is impossible."

"Then how do you explain what Jules found?"

"The bot's wrong. Simple as that," Buck replied. He jerked his head sideways to indicate the way they'd come. "Let's move."

* * *

Marshall turned to Thespian. His blue eyes were wide. This shouldn't have been possible. Supposedly no one knew where Vitaria was, not even Markus's father, and he was the only living person to ever have been there.

"Leonidus is behind this," Thespian said. "He brought us here on purpose."

"If that's true, then his family has been keeping a hell of a secret all these years," Marshall said. "But why trick us into coming along by hiring us for an entirely different mission?"

"Maybe so we wouldn't get spooked or ask for more money," Hunter suggested.

"Maybe also so we couldn't sell the family secret to the highest bidder," Marshall mused, her eyes on the Vitari standing in front of them. It raised its spindly arms once more in a reaching gesture. Another greeting. It warbled again. *Are you friend?*

"Whatever the reason, we need to get back and confront him with this." Hunter's rifle snapped up to his shoulder.

"Wait!" Marshall said.

A sharp *crack* split the air as a bright flash of light tore from the barrel. The Vitari fell over with a muffled thump, green eyes already glazed with death.

"What the hell, Hunter?" Marshall demanded.

"What?"

"You mean besides the fact that the sound of your rifle going off could attract the other creatures in the forest?"

He shrugged broad shoulders and rolled dark red eyes at her. "If anything does come sniffing around here, we've got the firepower to take it down."

Marshall let out an annoyed hiss. "Grab the carcass and let's go."

"Oorah."

"Cut that shit out. You're not even a Marine."

"Neither are you."

"At least *I* was," Marshall replied. "Once a Marine always a Marine."

"Once a bitch always a bitch."

Marshall mentally set her pistol to stun and dialed it all the way down. Then she shot Hunter in the head. He collapsed, his limbs jittering noisily in the grass.

"Woah," Thespian said, then burst into laughter. "Shit. He's gonna be pissed when he comes to."

"Good for him. Grab the carcass and let's go."

"You're just gonna leave him there?"

"For now. It was dialed down to the lowest setting. He'll only be out for five or ten minutes. After that, he can make his own way back."

"Copy."

Thespian grabbed the Vitari carcass and hoisted it up by its ears like a dead rabbit. Wings and arms unfolded limply and dragged through the grass as they went back to the lifeboat.

CHAPTER 18

Aria heard the airlock chime. She twisted around in the armchair she was sharing with Payton to watch as the doors parted. Marshall and one of her men stormed out. The man was carrying something...

A dead Vitari.

Aria's heart leapt into her throat, and her thoughts began to spin. Her connection to reality felt suddenly tenuous—a thin thread just about to snap. This had to be a dream. She must have fallen asleep in the chair with Payton. That was the only reasonable explanation.

Samos sat up with a groan. "Is that what I think it is?"

Neither of the two Marines replied nor showed signs of stopping.

Mattias shot to his feet, his dark blue eyes becoming flinty. "Where did you get a Vitari?"

Marshall strode straight by him and stopped at the door to Markus's and Elisa's bedroom. She pounded on it with one fist.

"Leonidus!" She roared. "It's Marshall. Open the door." She waited a beat. "If I have to ask again, I'm going to blast it open." Another beat.

The door slid open. Aria peered in, but the room was dark inside. *Why did they turn off the lights?* she wondered.

"Get in," a familiar voice said.

Aria opened her mouth to say something. Both Marshall and the other Marine crossed the threshold. Seeing her chance to get in there, Aria jumped up, almost knocking Payton to the floor as she did so.

"What's wrong?" Payton asked sleepily as Aria raced toward the bedroom.

The door slid shut with a muffled *thump* a split second before Aria reached it.

"What the hell was that about?" Mattias asked, looking to her as if she somehow knew more than he did.

Aria pounded on the door just as Marshall had done. "Lieutenant! Open the door! We deserve answers, too!" She waited, heard muffled voices arguing, but no footsteps approaching. She was about to knock again but decided to press her ear to the door instead.

"...Vitaria!" Marshall screamed.

A quiet male voice replied. The voice was too soft to make out, but she guessed from the context that it was probably Markus rather than the blue-eyed marine dragging the Vitari carcass.

"You're full of shit," Marshall said.

More muffled words.

"If this is a bluff, Thespo is going to burn a hole between your eyes," Marshall added.

Another indistinct reply. Then lots of silence. When Marshall's voice returned it was quieter, and it was no longer possible to make out the words.

"What are they saying?"

Aria jumped at the sound of Mattias's voice. She turned to glare at him and placed a finger to her lips.

He replied with an open-handed shrug.

Aria placed her ear to the door once more.

More muffled voices. A few more minutes passed. Aria's ear began to hurt from being pressed against unyielding metal for so long.

Footsteps sounded, approaching fast.

Aria flew back to the armchair and squeezed in beside Payton. The door slid open. Mattias remained where he was, arms crossed, staring at Marshall and the other Marine as they came out. He tried to peer around them, but the bedroom was still dark, and the door slid shut almost immediately. The Marine standing beside Marshall held the dead Vitari in one hand, his rifle in the other. Aria got the impression that Markus's reasons for keeping the bedroom private had nothing to do with his sense of entitlement or presumed ownership of the space. He was hiding something in there.

"Well?" Mattias demanded. "Are you going to tell us where you found a Vitari?"

Marshall nodded once. "Outside. It came out of the forest to say hello. Thespo overreacted and shot it."

The one called *Thespo* regarded his kill with a convincingly remorseful look. "Sorry, little buddy."

Aria gaped at him. "You *killed* it?"

"By accident."

Realization dawned belatedly. "Wait—we're on *Vitaria?* The planet has been lost for decades!"

"Not anymore," Marshall said.

"But how... how did we get here?"

"That's why I went to speak with Markus. His father is the only one who has been to Vitaria and returned to tell about it, so I assumed that Markus might have had something to do with bringing us here."

"And?" Aria pressed. "What did he say?"

"He said that he has no idea how we ended up here, but he recognized the Sparklers from the stories his father used to tell. He was hoping he was mistaken."

"And you believe him?" Aria asked.

"He opened his Neuralink so that I could get a look inside his head. Unfortunately, he's telling the truth."

But are you? Aria wondered.

"*Unfortunately,* he's telling the truth?" Mattias echoed. "How would it be better if he had plotted to bring us here?"

Marshall arched an eyebrow at him. "Because it would mean he knows how to get us home. Regardless of *how* we got here, knowing where we are is both good and bad news. The good news is Markus knows a few things about Vitaria from his father's stories. Leonidus senior had retrograde amnesia when he returned, so he didn't remember much, but what he did remember, he shared with his son. The Sparklers aren't what we should be afraid of."

"No?" Mattias asked. "They seemed pretty damn scary to me."

His wife, Asha, quiet until now, looked up and spoke in a melodious voice: "They tore our butler bot open like he was made of paper."

"To get this." Marshall held up an empty glass vial. "Vitalics. There's a reason none of them boarded us as we left the *Starlit Dream*. Markus suspected what the Sparklers were after, and he flushed all of their vitalics down the drain.

Unfortunately he was the only one who knew to do that. All of the *Dream's* crew, including its robotic assistants, carry vitalics on them in case of an emergency."

Aria's eyes widened. Vitalics withdrawals were no joke. Go too long between doses and the symptoms could actually kill you. Therefore, the term *vitaholic*.

Mattias slowly shook his head. "You're saying they only killed the people who were carrying vitalics around with them?"

"No. Anyone who dosed recently is also a target."

"Great," Mattias muttered. "We're due for our next dose in just a few days. I was about to ask if anyone had any vitalics on them."

"Even if Markus hadn't dumped their supply, it wouldn't be a good idea," Marshall replied.

Aria felt a wave of relief spreading through her. If the Sparklers were only after vitalics and users, then Liam and Nikolai would be safe. Except that if Marshall was right, then Jules would have vials of vitalics on him, and he would draw the Sparklers straight to them.

Aria prayed that Liam and Niko were smart enough to stay out of the way.

"There's something else," Marshall said. "Apparently the Sparklers are machines. They can detect the quantum signature of vitalics from a long way off, even across a vacuum. That's why they boarded the cruise ship in the first place."

"Machines?" Aria echoed.

Marshall nodded. "Harvesters. And the Vitari are their crop."

CHAPTER 19

"If they're machines, then who built them?" Aria asked.

"Markus doesn't know. Apparently his father never found out or couldn't remember, but if you ask me, the aliens that built them are the real threat. They built machines that can *teleport,* so they're way beyond the Union's level of technology."

The Marine called Thespo nodded gravely. "We need to keep a low profile," he said.

Aria's attention shifted to the bedroom door. "Why isn't Markus out here telling us all of this himself?"

"He's... dealing with Elisa. She's not taking the news very well."

Aria's eyes tightened. "So he's not hiding something in there?"

Marshall's eyebrows inched up. "Like what?"

"You tell me."

"Nothing besides a broken woman weeping in a corner."

"And we just have to take your word for that?" Mattias asked.

Marshall shrugged. "Go pound on his door if you want. Maybe he'll let you in. But I've got better things to do than fight a war over personal space. Now more than ever we need to get to that other lifeboat and make contact with the others."

"Why?" Mattias replied. "If what you're saying is true, then won't we alert whatever aliens we're hiding from by using our comms?"

"It's too late for that," Marshall said. "We already used them."

"That doesn't mean we should keep doing it!"

Marshall smiled thinly at him. "Here's the problem: right now we're the only ones who know all of this. There are probably people out there dosing with vitalics as we speak, oblivious to the fact that they could be about to get their guts ripped out because of it. We need to spread the word and warn them before it's too late."

"They'll just die of withdrawal," Aria said.

"Maybe. Or maybe we can get away with minimal doses. Enough to stave off withdrawals, but not enough to draw the Sparklers to us. At the very least, people deserve to know so that they can prepare for an attack."

Aria stared at the dead Vitari in Thespo's hand. "What about your kill? Its blood is the *source* of vitalics."

Marshall stiffened and rounded on Thespo. "She's right. Get it out of here."

"Copy that." Thespo was already on his way to the airlock.

Marshall followed him there.

"Where are you going?" Aria asked.

"We still have to finish scouting the forest to see if the rover can make it through."

"Wait! What about us? You promised we could go with you."

Marshall glanced over her shoulder. "If it looks like the rover can make it, we'll come back for you."

The inner airlock doors swished open, and Aria watched as both Marines began to leave. Then she realized something: one of them was missing.

"Hey, where's your other man?" she asked, just as Marshall entered the airlock.

"Guarding the perimeter."

The doors slid shut, leaving Aria alone with her spinning thoughts. Her instincts were screaming for her not to trust Marshall. She didn't buy that Elisa's breakdown was the reason for Markus's solitary behavior. Aria stared at Markus's bedroom door. *He's hiding something, and Marshall knows what it is. That must be why she took Payton outside to pee instead of forcing Markus to open his door. But what is he hiding, and how can I find out?*

An idea sprang to mind, and a slow smile curved her lips. She cast about the living room, looking for something they could use. Her eyes landed on the electric stove in the kitchen. Perfect. Now she just needed something flammable that she could burn. A high-fat meal from the synthesizer would do it.

"Does everyone have a filter mask?"

"I have mine," Payton said, wriggling in Aria's lap to pluck her mask off the floor.

"What for?" Mattias asked.

Aria ignored the question and looked to Samos. He shook his head.

"I'll get you one." She stood up from the armchair and headed for a pair of empty emergency seats beside Mattias and his wife, Asha.

"Are you going to explain what you're doing?" Mattias asked.

"Keep your voice down," Aria whispered. "We're going to see what Markus is hiding in his room."

"What do filter masks have to do with that?"

"We're going to smoke them out."

* * *

Liam was not happy about army-crawling back through the ducts, but neither he nor Buck wanted to push their luck by opening the armory door with an Urchin camping right beside the entrance. This time Buck made Liam go first. He didn't trust Liam after their brief confrontation about his use of vitalics.

Liam saw the glow radiating from Jules' eyes even before he reached the hole in the bottom of the duct. He had to tone down the light amplification settings on his optical enhancers so that he could see despite the sudden increase in visible light.

When he reached the opening of the duct, Liam realized that he was in a familiar position—he couldn't crawl out without doing a face plant on the deck.

Jules looked up. The bot's glowing eyes blinded Liam, and he threw up his forearm to block the glare.

"Master Nikolai, your father has returned."

"Dad?" Nikolai croaked.

He didn't sound good. "Are you okay, Niko?" Liam asked.

"No. My head hurts a *lot*."

"Master Nikolai has all the symptoms of severe dehydration," Jules said. "Did you manage to find water for him?"

"Even better. We found a bag of saline and an IV. Could you help me down?"

"Of course."

Jules reached up and pulled Liam out. His armpits ached sharply from bearing his entire weight, but he ignored the pain. Turning to look at Nikolai, he ran a quick appraisal of his son's condition. Not good. His lips were cracked and bleeding. Eyes half-lidded.

Boots struck the deck beside Liam as Buck jumped down. Liam had already unfurled the IV line and was connecting it to the saline bag. He positioned the bag on one of the room's open shelves and then began checking Nikolai's wrist for a place to insert the needle.

"Allow me," Jules said, and formed a tourniquet around Nikolai's arm with his hands.

The needle went in easily, and Buck taped it into place. "If you start feeling cold you can ask Jules to turn down the flow, but try to leave it the way it is for a while. You need the fluids."

Nikolai nodded.

"If you need to pee..." Buck searched around for something. He spied an open metal crate on one of the shelves, dragged it out, and began emptying the contents.

Liam sat beside his son and wrapped an arm around his shoulders. "You're going to be fine."

Nikolai's head bobbed quietly.

Buck dragged the empty crate over. "You can use this for a toilet."

"We're stuck in here?" Nikolai asked, his brow furrowing. He brushed thick dark hair out of his eyes.

"*You* are," Buck replied.

"Just me?" Nikolai looked to his father. "What happened to getting to a lifeboat and finding Mom and Payton?"

"We'll still do that, but you need to stay here. We figured out what the Urchins want. It's not safe for you to leave here. Not yet."

"Indeed?" Jules straightened with sudden interest and moved closer to them.

"What are you talking about?" Nikolai asked, his eyes flicking between Liam and Buck.

"They're after vitalics and anyone who dosed recently with them," Buck explained. "We ran into multiple Urchins, but none of them tried to attack us. Then we found a vitalics storage cabinet that they'd torn open."

Jules touched the ruined compartment in his stomach and peered down at it with sudden interest. "That is why they attacked me..."

"They attacked me, too," Nikolai said. "And that was before you used vitalics on me."

"They only attacked you because you were standing behind Jules," Liam explained.

"Well, what about him?" Nikolai nodded to Buck.

"He's a user," Liam explained.

"It grazed my cheek first," Buck said. "Probably checking the concentration in my blood. Lucky for me it's been a while since my last dose. You, on the other hand, just received a triple, and that was only a few hours ago. That means you're going to be stuck in here for a while."

"How long?" Nikolai asked.

"At least two weeks."

"Two weeks!" Nikolai's voice cracked into a hoarse whisper. "No..."

"We'll bring you food and water," Liam said while rubbing his son's shoulders. "It'll be okay."

Nikolai groaned and subsided in Liam's arms, too tired to argue further.

Jules broke the momentary silence. "I wonder how they know what vitalics are?"

"I wanted to ask you about that," Buck said. "What did you find when you tried to identify our position?"

"None of the stars around us match any known stars within the Milky Way," Jules said.

"Are you sure?" Buck asked.

"Positive."

"Then what galaxy do you think we are in?"

"That is impossible to say without additional data."

"So we could still be in the Milky Way," Buck concluded.

Jules hesitated. "Perhaps, but only if we are on the opposite side of the galactic bulge."

"The bulge?" Nikolai whispered sleepily. He nestled against Liam, head tucked into Liam's shoulder in a way that he hadn't done for a long time. A memory flickered through Liam's mind's eye of cold winter nights by the fireplace in their home outside Philadelphia—baby Payton resting in Aria's arms, contentedly sucking her thumb while Nikolai snuggled up on Liam's other side. All four of them sitting under a loosely-woven blanket as they watched holo-vids on the screen above the fire.

"The bulge is the center of the galaxy," Jules explained. "It is the whitish smear of light that appears in the sky on a clear dark night. The density of stars and dust around the galactic center make it hard to see the other side. If we are on the opposite side from Earth, that might explain why I couldn't recognize the stars around us."

"We'll know more when we get to the bridge," Buck said. Looking to Liam, he asked, "Are you coming with or staying here?"

"I'll go," Liam replied. "Just give me a minute."

"I would also like to join you," Jules added. "It would be useful to see what else I can learn about our surroundings from the ship's sensors."

Liam frowned. "We can't leave Nikolai alone."

"Then maybe *you* should stay," Buck put in.

Liam hesitated. "I need to find out where my wife and daughter are. I was hoping to use the ship's comms to contact the lifeboats."

"It's more important for Jules to help us figure out where we are," Buck argued.

"Excuse me," Jules said. "Perhaps I can solve this dilemma."

"How's that?" Buck asked.

"All you need to do is bring the ship's network back online. Once you do that, I'll have remote access to all of the data I need. I will even be able to accompany you virtually on the bridge via your augmented reality lenses."

"Problem solved," Liam said. Nikolai stirred and sighed. Liam glanced down at him and saw that he'd fallen asleep. Or passed out. Suddenly worried about that, he placed a hand on his son's chest to check his heart rate and breathing.

"Don't worry," Jules said. "His vitals are all within normal ranges."

Liam nodded. "Would you mind taking my place over here?" He was losing the feeling in his legs from sitting on the hard deck.

"Of course."

He and Jules traded places so that Nikolai lay against the robot's chest instead of his.

Liam stood up and shook out his legs to clear away the pins and needles.

"Ready?" Buck asked, jerking his chin to indicate the duct.

"For more army-crawling down a coffin-sized tunnel?" Liam nodded, and Buck smiled. "Ready as I'll ever be."

CHAPTER 20

The smoke was so thick that Aria could hardly see through it. Thanks to her air filter mask at least she could breathe. The smoke detector screamed incessantly, but still, the bedroom door didn't open. Maybe the room was soundproof?

Then the overhead sprinklers came on, dousing everything in water. Mattias and Asha began cursing and muttering about Aria's *stupid plan*.

"This had better work!" Mattias said.

Aria's and Payton's environment suits were waterproof, so only their hair got wet. Aria chewed her lower lip inside her mask, her gaze locked on the door. She stood right beside it, plastered to the wall. Any minute now. Her muscles tensed.

The door slid open, and Markus stormed out. "What the hell is—"

Aria burst out of hiding and slipped through the open door before he could react.

"Hey! You can't go in there!"

Markus's hands snagged the slick material of her environment suit and slid off.

Aria stumbled through the dark, smoky bedroom. "Lights!" she said, and they snapped on. Footsteps pounded after her, and the door slid shut, locking out the source of the smoke. Aria turned in a quick circle, taking in the entire room and looking for whatever Markus and Elisa could be hiding. Markus was standing behind her, the one who'd shut the door. His eyes blazed at her in the smoky gloom.

"What do you think you're—" He broke off, coughing into his arm.

Aria felt hands on her shoulders and heard more coughing. "Get out," Elisa said.

Flinching away, Aria backpedaled quickly, shaking her head. "Not until you tell me what's going on here. What are you hiding?"

"Nothing! Look for yourself!" Markus snapped, spreading his arms to indicate their suite.

Aria fetched up against the bathroom door. Her eyes darted around the room, seeing nothing unusual other than the fact that there were two queen beds instead of one king. Both were unmade and Elisa stood beside the nearest one. Maybe *consorts* didn't sleep together.

The hot tub lay uncovered and steaming in the corner by the picture windows. Blinds were drawn across those windows with suitcases piled on the floor in front of them.

Aria shook her head, refusing to believe that they had nothing to hide. She turned and yanked open the bathroom door—

But it was empty. The only thing out of place was the pile of used washcloths and towels and the fine coating of sand on the floor. Wet swimsuits were drying on towel racks.

"Looking for something?" Markus asked from the open doorway.

Aria rounded on him. "What are you hiding?"

Markus snorted. "Hiding? I don't have anything to hide. Now get out of our room, and go put out that grease fire you started."

Aria nodded agreeably. "Fine."

She pushed past Markus in the entrance of the bathroom. His hands landed on her shoulders and dug in like talons, guiding her out. But as soon as she cleared the bathroom door, she ducked out of his grasp and darted to the closet.

Markus lunged after her. "Get her!" he screamed.

Elisa sprang after her.

Aria wrenched the closet doors open—

Markus pulled her away so violently that he knocked her over. She landed on her rear with a sharp spike of pain and sat staring up at the reason Markus didn't want anyone in his room.

"You're too late," the man in the closet said.

"Am I?" Markus loomed over Aria with both fists clenched by his sides.

The man hiding in the closet stepped out with a sigh and placed a hand on Markus's shoulder. "Settle down, son. There's no point in trying to hide me any longer." He reached down to help Aria up. She hesitated before taking his hand. He pulled her off the floor with surprising strength considering how old he was.

"*You,*" Aria said. Anyone in the Union would have recognized him as Markus's father, the founder of Vital Corp. He and Markus shared a few obvious features—their blue eyes and long straight nose, their height and rakish good looks.

The man inclined his head to her. "You likely know me from the news, but I don't believe we've formally met." He thrust out his hand again. This time Aria didn't accept it.

"Varik Leonidus," he said, smiling tightly as he returned his hand to his side. "You must be Aria Price. It is a privilege to finally meet you. I am a big fan of your research."

"I'm surprised you know my name."

"You could say it's my business to know the competition, even when said competition has yet to reach the market."

Aria crossed her arms over her chest and asked the obvious question: "Why are you hiding in here?"

CHAPTER 21

Varik Leonidus smiled and spread his hands. "By now you've heard from Lieutenant Marshall that this is the lost world of the Vitari. And you likely also know that I am the only survivor from the original expedition to Vitaria."

Aria nodded. "Which makes your being here either an astronomical coincidence or a plot."

"You see? You already suspect me. *That* is why I hid. If people learned that I am here, they would blame me for our current predicament. They would also assume that I know how to get them home."

"Those seem like fair assumptions to me," Aria said. "You found your way home once before."

"But I don't remember how. When I returned, there were big gaps in my memory—whole decades of my life that I could not account for. I came back *twenty-nine years* after I left, but with almost no memories from that time. Furthermore, I returned with nearly the same apparent age as I had left. My son, Markus, was only one year old when I left, but when I came back, he was thirty. People would say we are brothers if they didn't know any better."

"I remember," Aria replied. "You were on the news every day for weeks." Aria had been Payton's age when Varik had returned from Vitaria. Over thirty years had passed since then, and in that time he had built the biggest empire in history thanks to the Vitari eggs he'd brought back with him. "I've already heard your excuses through the media," Aria said. "But obviously Vitaria has been lost all these years because it's convenient to you and Vital Corp to have a monopoly on Vitalics. If other people could have simply flown to Vitaria and collected their own Vitari eggs, you would have had a thousand competitors overnight."

Leonidus smiled. "That seems like a reasonable explanation, doesn't it? But you're forgetting that there was a criminal investigation. People assumed that because I was the only survivor, and because I returned with such a valuable commodity, that I must have either killed or left the rest of the crew behind. Police obtained the necessary warrants to connect with my Neuralink. They searched my memories with a fine-toothed comb, but they never found anything that they could use to convict me. Not a thread of evidence to support the theory that

I was some evil mastermind trying to monopolize the greatest discovery in human history."

"And yet that's exactly what you did," Aria replied. "You built an empire around raising intelligent aliens for the slaughter. Before you came along, raising anything for the slaughter was a barbaric practice from a bygone era."

"Which is where you come in," Varik said. "Just as the creation of synthetic meat put a stop to killing animals for food, so too will synthetic vitalics." Varik smiled again. "I'm just the fat cat rancher who profits from the natural version in the intervening years."

"Screw you." Aria spat at him. She was aiming for his face, but the spittle landed on his shoes instead.

Varik's gaze dipped down and then back up. His blue eyes glittered darkly at her. "You might be surprised, but I'm waiting anxiously for you to succeed and put an end to the slaughter."

Aria snorted. "Sure you are." Varik would never want her to succeed. Synthetic vitalics would wipe out his business overnight.

"Of course you have every right to be skeptical, but my interest runs deeper than you know. My sources tell me that you are very close to a breakthrough."

Aria said nothing to that, but a wild theory began to coalesce in her mind. *What if Varik detoured an entire cruise ship to a world where no one would ever find them just so that he could quash my research? Is he capable of such a heinous act?*

But there were holes in her theory. Aria wasn't the only researcher in the company. Varik wouldn't be able to take down Vitatech just by removing her from the picture.

Something was definitely up, but Aria decided to play it safe and tone down her confrontational approach. She uncrossed her arms and wiped the scowl off her face. "All right, I'll give you the benefit of the doubt: what do you stand to gain from synthetic vitalics?"

"They're supposed to be more effective than the natural ones, right? I'm already ninety-four, and I won't live forever."

"That's a weak excuse. The natural serum will give you at least another sixty years."

"But with your product, I could have a hundred or more."

"And lose all of your money in the process."

Varik shrugged. "Some, not all. Besides, you can always make more money, but you can't make more time to enjoy it."

"Said the ninety-four-year-old trillionaire who looks like he's thirty," Aria quipped.

"Yes, well, speaking of money, where did your start-up capital come from?"

Aria's brow tensed, and she shook her head. "What does that have to do with—"

"Ten million and change came from a venture capitalist by the name of Kravi Dunelios. And he's reinvested several times since then, hasn't he?"

Shock flooded through Aria's thoughts.

Varik favored her with an icy smile that never reached his eyes. "Kravi Dunelios is an actor, and his name is an anagram for my own. Your company, Vitatech, is financed by me, and *I* own the vast majority of the shares."

Aria's shock blossomed to cataclysmic proportions, and she swayed on her feet. "I need to sit down." She stumbled over to the bed. Her theory that Varik Leonidus might have abducted her to do away with his competition evaporated, burned away in the light of the truth: there was no competition. Varik Leonidus had a monopoly on synthetic vitalics, too. And the worst part was that Aria's life's work, her noble quest to end Vitari suffering, had been financed with their blood.

CHAPTER 22

On their way to the nearest bank of elevators, Liam and Buck encountered several more Urchins, but yet again, none of them attacked. Still more proof that their theory was correct.

The nearest elevator dinged open, and Buck stepped inside. Liam followed him and saw that the control panel was already illuminated with B203.

"That must be near the top," Liam commented as the doors slid shut. A brief sensation of acceleration pressed them into the floor as the elevator rocketed up from level 60.

"Top, nose—whatever you want to call it," Buck replied. "The bridge encompasses the uppermost and foremost three decks of the *Dream.*"

Just under a minute later the elevator dinged once more, and the doors slid open. They emerged in a short corridor lined with exposed and sparking conduits. With each flicker of light from the damaged conduits, a collection of dismembered bodies snapped into sharp relief. The walls and floors were slick and gleaming with blood.

Liam sucked in a breath.

Held it.

At the end of the corridor, a pair of blast doors repeatedly opened and shut, coming up against a tangled knot of crewmen who'd died on top of each other in the doorway.

"What the hell happened here?" Liam whispered.

"All of the crew had vitalics on them, remember?" Buck said. "That made them targets for the Urchins."

Liam slowly shook his head as they picked their way down the corridor, dodging sticky puddles of blood and grisly bits that Liam couldn't even identify. A snaking tangle of intestines protruded from one man's abdomen. Liam's stomach lurched, and he looked up sharply. *Eyes up,* he chided himself.

"Keep your weapon ready," Buck whispered as they reached the restlessly slamming doors.

Liam nodded. The Urchins might not be interested in them for the moment, but the carnage here was a vivid reminder of what those machines were capable of if they changed their minds.

There was no way through the doors without stepping on the dead bodies blocking them. Buck went first. The Marine's boots made squelching sounds as he tromped over and through. Liam's guts clenched.

Buck spent a moment scanning the bridge on the other side with his laser rifle; then he half-turned and waved.

More squelching as Liam went through. He refused to look and tripped over an outstretched leg.

Buck caught him as he fell. "Careful."

Liam nodded as he looked around the bridge. It was a vast chamber at least three floors high. A transparent, dome-shaped ceiling came all the way down to the deck and gave them an impressive view of space. Dark nebular clouds curled around them on all sides, but they were no longer flashing with the lightning of Urchins teleporting to and fro. Directly above them—dead ahead with respect to the ship's momentum—was a mottled blue and purple planet in front of a much larger yellow, white, and blue monstrosity.

"Let's see if we can do something about the lights," Buck said. He began hunting around the bridge, checking control stations as he went.

There were dozens of stations, most with dead officers slumped over the controls or lying beside their chairs. The majority of the crew had been killed quickly, before they'd even had a chance to flee.

Buck reached one of the stations and abruptly stopped. He let out a string of curses.

Liam hurried over. "What's wrong?" He glanced at the control station in front of them. A man was strewn over the controls. Congealed blood had spattered everywhere in thick, sticky puddles.

"This is the operations console," Buck explained. "It controls the lights, the ship's internal network, comms, and a bunch of other systems. The blood leaking into the console must have shorted out at least half of them. That's why all of the lights are out. Probably explains the network and comms outages, too."

Liam scanned the bloody mess with a wrinkled nose. "Can you fix it?"

"Short of disassembling and cleaning everything?" Buck shook his head. "We'll have to manually cut the power to any damaged consoles up here. After that we can head down to engineering and use one of the auxiliary control stations to bring everything back online. Then all we'll need is the right access codes and we'll be able to control everything remotely through our ARLs."

"Do you have the access codes for that?" Liam asked.

Buck shook his head. "No, but I'm guessing Bolts will."

"You're guessing?"

Buck waved a hand. "Figure of speech. He *has to* have the codes. Ships like this one have an elaborate chain of command. Since all of the crew are either dead or evacuated, technically *he's* next in line for captain."

"What about you?" Liam asked. "Aren't undercover Marines a part of the crew?"

"Not in that sense. We're not trained to fly spaceships."

"And a butler bot is?"

"Just because his primary job is to babysit kids and wait on passengers doesn't mean that's all he can do."

"I guess." The Union's labor laws favored humans and heavily taxed robotic workers in skilled-labor positions, but bots were still allowed to have auxiliary programming that enabled them to fill in during emergencies. "Sounds like a plan. Let's get down to engineering," Liam said.

Buck nodded and led the way back to the endlessly-slamming doors. The sooner they rebooted the ship's systems, the sooner Liam could get on the comms and find out where Aria and Payton were.

CHAPTER 23

Aria sat on the edge of one of the room's two beds, eyes wide and blinking. "Now what?"

"I have an idea about that," Varik said.

"We need to make contact with the aliens who built the harvesters," Markus added.

Elisa nodded. "They might be able to help us get home."

"Lieutenant Marshall said they could be dangerous," Aria replied.

Varik arched an eyebrow. "Why? Just because they're more advanced than we are?" He shook his head. "I'm surprised that an alien rights activist like yourself would be so quick to ascribe bad intentions to another species."

Aria snorted. "Maybe that's because I've spent too much time with my own species."

A knock sounded on the door. "Leonidus?" It was Marshall. "We need to talk."

"*Again?*" Markus asked. He looked to his father, and Varik nodded. "Come in," Markus said as he waved the door open.

Marshall stepped into the room, looking tense and worried. She didn't even bat an eye to see Varik standing there with his son.

Payton called out, "Mom?"

"I'll be out soon, Paytie!"

Markus waved the door shut. "Well?" he prompted.

Marshall's eyes flicked briefly to Aria, then back to Markus and his father. "I guess we're not keeping secrets anymore."

"She snuck in and found me hiding in the closet," Varik explained. "What do you need, Lieutenant?"

Aria frowned. The dynamic between them was off. If anything, Marshall should have been the one in charge, but here she was reporting to them as if they were her superior officers.

"You're not really a Marine, are you?" Aria asked before Marshall could say anything.

The other woman bristled. "I am."

"She *was*," Markus clarified.

"Once a Marine, always a—"

"Yeah, yeah." Markus waved dismissively at her, and Marshall's eyes flashed. "She's a mercenary," he explained. "They all are."

Aria shook her head incredulously. "And you expect me to believe that you had nothing to do with the *Starlit Dream* getting lost out here? Why would you hire mercenaries to join you on a cruise ship unless you were expecting trouble?"

Varik answered, "We *were* expecting trouble. There have been six attempts to abduct members of my family over the last year alone. Everyone wants to know where Vitaria is. Ironically, after this, we might actually be able to tell them."

Markus nodded. "We don't go anywhere without our bodyguards."

"And the cruise line allows that?"

"Marshall and her men are duly-licensed to carry weapons if that's what you mean," Varik said.

Marshall spoke up, "Speaking of your bodyguards. You might have one less now."

Varik's expression darkened. "What do you mean?"

"Hunter is missing. We left him outside. He was getting lippy, so I stunned him to shut him up. When we went back for him a few minutes later, he was gone, and there was a trail of blood leading into the forest. We followed it for a few hundred feet before we lost it."

"Shit," Markus muttered. "You idiots are supposed to be protecting us, not shooting each other!"

Marshall nodded stiffly. "I take full responsibility, sir. We *will* find him."

"No," Varik said. "It's too dangerous, and we have other priorities."

"With all due respect, sir, I'm not taking no for an answer."

Marshall and Varik glared at one another. "You work for *me,* Lieutenant, and as you so eloquently stated, this is your fault."

"Then maybe it's time that we changed the status quo," Marshall replied. "Your money's no good to us out here. We don't even know when or *if* we'll get home to spend it."

"We all want to get home, Lieutenant Marshall. That is the priority I'm referring—"

The overhead speakers crackled. "Hello? This is Lieutenant Marshall aboard the *Starlit Dream,* calling to all lifeboats."

There came a brief pause and then the speaker went on, "What is your status? Reply 10-4 if all is well, or else let us know if you need assistance. We will follow up on all replies as fast as we can. Until then, be advised, the alien entities that we encountered are after vitalics. If you have any serum on board, get rid of it and do not dose yourselves. They can detect it in your blood, and they will carve you open to get it. If you are already due for your next dose or have dosed recently, please let us know immediately. Marshall out."

Aria stared suspiciously at the former Marine with magenta eyes and spiked blond hair. "I thought *you* were Lieutenant Marshall?"

CHAPTER 24

"I *am* Lieutenant Marshall, but so is he. I was a first lieutenant, he was a second. My name is Jacey. Ace for short. He's Buck."

Aria took a moment to process that. "So he's your..."

"Husband."

Aria looked to Varik and Markus for confirmation.

"He's also working for us," Varik said. "There were six of them. Until now we were worried that Buck might not have made it."

Marshall looked to him. "We should reply before their comms log fills up with messages from the other lifeboats."

"Agreed." Varik raised his eyes to the ceiling and said, "Activate comms, reply to last message." A moment later, he added, "Buck, this is Varik Leonidus. We made it down safe."

"Except for Hunter. He was dragged off by something," Marshall added with a scowl.

Varik's eyes swept to Marshall. "Yes... anyway, it would appear that we're not lost after all. We have been brought to Vitaria, of all places. I know how that looks, believe me, but I am not behind all of this—end message."

Varik looked to Marshall. "We should make contact with the aliens running the harvesting operation."

"Why the hell would we want to do that?" Marshall asked. Her magenta eyes turned flinty. "What haven't you told us?"

"I believe that they can help us get home."

"Based on what?"

Aria nodded her agreement. "I thought you couldn't remember anything from Vitaria."

"That's not what I said. I said there were gaps in my memories, and I couldn't remember exactly how I got home, but I still remember plenty about my time here. The last thing that I remember was breaking into an alien depot where the harvesters store raw vitalics. The next thing I knew, I woke up in my bed next to my wife, and twenty-nine years had passed. You can imagine her shock and mine—a sixty-four-year-old woman waking up beside her long lost husband, who was somehow still the same age as when he left."

"You probably stayed young because you were exposed to vitalics while you were here," Aria said.

"Most likely."

Marshall looked unimpressed. "Okay, so you went to the nearest depot, broke in, and somehow woke up back home twenty-nine years later."

"Yes."

"It sounds like they used their teleportation tech on you," Marshall said.

"I agree."

"But why? Why help you get home? And why just you? What happened to the others in your expedition?"

"The others were scared of the depots. After seeing the harvesters in action, they didn't want to meet the aliens who had built them. I was more optimistic about first contact. It seems my approach was best."

"I don't remember you mentioning any of this on the news," Aria said slowly.

"The Union classified the details of first contact and confiscated the vehicle that sent me home. Where do you think the Union's own teleportation technology comes from?"

"They're still far from making it work," Aria said.

"But they have a working alien prototype. Or at least they did before they tore it apart to reverse engineer it."

Marshall spoke up, "Okay, so we get to the nearest depot, meet the aliens, and ask them to help us get home. That's the plan?"

"Unless you have a better one," Varik replied.

"What about the jump gate?" Aria asked. "There's one in this system. What if we could get it working?"

Varik shook his head. "It won't work. The gate's power supply is missing."

"How do you know?"

"Because my expedition took it out as a precaution when they realized there might be an advanced alien civilization on this end. They never had a chance to put it back and escape."

"Well, maybe we can supply power to the gate from the cruise ship," Aria suggested.

"If starships could generate that much power on their own, we wouldn't need space gates."

Aria shook her head. "So you're saying the only way we're getting home is to go to one of the depots and meet the aliens that sent you home the first time."

Markus snorted. "You catch on fast."

"Maybe I should stay here. I'll see if Buck can help me find my husband and son with the *Starlit Dream's* comms."

Varik shook his head. "I wouldn't recommend that. This planet is dangerous."

"We'll stay inside the lifeboat. Now that we don't have to go outside to go to the bathroom that should be easy."

Varik's eyebrows lifted. "You would think you'd be safe in the lifeboat, but my original ground team landed in an armored shuttle. That night a monstrous creature ripped it open while we slept, and more than half of us were killed. The rest fled. We found one of the depots, and I went inside. The others decided to wait for the next shuttle to come down and pick them up."

"Wait, I thought you were gone for twenty-nine years?" Aria said. "You're implying that you were only down here for a day."

Varik nodded gravely. "That's how I remember it. I don't know what happened after I went inside the depot. Maybe the aliens kept me on ice for twenty-nine years before they finally decided to send me home."

Aria blew out a breath. "And you want us to meet them?"

"I'm the only one who made it home, remember? You wanted to know how I did it. That's how. You're welcome to stay behind, but I can't say I recommend it. So what's it going to be, Aria? Are you staying here or are you coming with us?"

Aria struggled to absorb everything that Varik had just dumped on her — on *them.*

Marshall didn't look happy about it either.

Aria didn't trust Varik. The fact that they'd somehow found a lost planet that only he had ever been to was too strange to be a coincidence.

Before she could say anything, a chime sounded, and Varik suddenly straightened.

"What was that?" Aria asked.

His ARLs flickered with imagery. "It's a message from the *Starlit Dream.*" He smiled. "Perhaps this will help you make up your mind. It's from your husband, asking for information about you and your daughter. Apparently he's safe. Would you like to send a reply?"

"Yes!"

Varik nodded and spoke to the ceiling once more. "Activate comms, reply to Liam Price." He nodded to her.

Aria began, "Liam? Is it really you? It's Aria. Payton is here with me. We're in Markus's lifeboat. His father, Varik, is here too. I was so worried about you! Are you and Nikolai okay? Please reply as soon as you can."

"End message," Varik said for her. "We should get going."

Aria shook her head. "Maybe just a few of us should go..." She looked to Marshall. "You and a

— 209 —

few of your men could scout ahead and then report back. That would be safer, wouldn't it?"

"I have an even better idea," Marshall said. She promptly drew her pistol and aimed it at Varik's chest. "It's time for you to tell us what's really going on."

CHAPTER 25

"They're all replying at once!" Buck said, shaking his head. They'd gotten the ship's systems working again after cutting power to the bridge and resetting everything from engineering. Now they were back in the armory. "Apparently everyone thinks they need assistance," Buck went on. "There's not a single 10-4. It's going to take hours to reply to all of these!"

Liam sat beside Nikolai, using his ARLs to watch the scrolling list of replies coming in through the ship's comms. Just as Buck had predicted, Jules had the access codes they needed to remotely access the ship's systems.

"I need to ask if anyone's seen my wife and daughter," Liam said.

Buck's eyes flicked to him, bright with imagery from his ARLs. "Yeah, sure, go ahead."

"Thank you."

Liam took a moment to gather his thoughts, then set the comms to broadcast a message on an open channel to all of the lifeboats. "This is Liam

Price, a survivor aboard the *Starlit Dream.* I am with Lieutenant Buck Marshall and my son, Nikolai, and I am looking for my wife and daughter—Aria and Payton Price. Aria is Caucasian with long dark hair and green eyes. My daughter Payton looks just like her and is seven years old. If anyone has information as to their whereabouts, please reply immediately. Thank you in advance for your help." Liam sent the message and let out a shaky sigh.

Jules favored him with a sympathetic smile. "I am sure you will hear from them soon."

"I hope so..." Liam turned to look at Buck. He was still using his ARLs to skim through the list of incoming messages. "What are you looking for?"

"A reply from *my* wife," he said.

Liam's eyebrows shot up. "Your... wife? She was on board?"

Buck nodded. "She's an undercover Marine like me."

"Oh."

"This one looks interesting," Buck said. "Message begins: *Buck, this is Varik Leonidus...* and... well, that's even more interesting."

"What is? Wait, Varik Leonidus?" Liam echoed. "Varik is here? I thought only his son was on the cruise?"

But Buck gave no reply. He was too busy reading the message.

Liam scanned the list of incoming comms for himself, searching for the one Buck was talking about. But a different message caught his eye: *Liam? Is it really you? It's Aria(...)* Liam expanded the message by focusing on the ellipsis after the first few words.

—Payton is here with me. We're in Markus's lifeboat. His father, Varik, is here too. I was so worried about you! Are you and Nikolai okay? Please reply as soon as you can.

"I found my family!" Liam crowed.

"Good for you."

"They're with Varik."

"They are?"

Liam was tempted to play the audio version of Aria's message just so that he could hear her voice, but he didn't want to waste any time. Not waiting for permission, he activated the comms once more: "Aria! I was so worried about you! We're both fine. Nikolai had a run-in with the alien machines that boarded us, but we used vitalics to treat his injuries. Unfortunately, that makes him a target, so we're stuck hiding in the armory with him. Oh, and Jules is here. The bridge is a nightmare... everyone was slaughtered. I don't think a single crewman survived anywhere on the ship. What is the planet you landed on like? Is it safe? Is the air breathable? We'll probably be joining you soon. Please reply as soon as you can—ah... over."

"Are you done?" Buck demanded.

"Yes. Sorry."

"I get it. I found my wife, too. I heard her in the background of Varik's message."

"That's great!"

Buck nodded. "There's more. We're not as lost as we thought. We're on Vitaria."

Liam did a double take. "Vitaria? How is that possible? Are they sure?" Right on the heels of that shock came a fiery burst of outrage. "Wait—we've found Vitaria, and Varik, the only one who's ever been there is mysteriously here with us? That can't be a coincidence."

"Varik claims he doesn't know how we ended up here."

"Of course he doesn't," Liam said.

"I don't know. I think he might be telling the truth."

Liam shook his head. "What? Why?"

"Because I've worked for him for a long time."

"You're working for Varik?"

"It's probably time that I leveled with you."

"I agree," Liam said, his heart suddenly pounding.

"I'm a mercenary."

Liam could feel his eyes popping. "A mercenary."

Buck must have seen the look on his face, because he hurried to add—"Nothing illegal, but yeah. I'm a merc."

"I thought you said you were a Marine?" Liam said slowly.

"I was. The rest of my team, too. We're all former operators—except for Hunter, who washed out of boot camp. We've been working for Varik on and off over the last five years. By this point, I feel like I know him pretty well, which is why I say that maybe we should trust him. Varik brought us along for protection. We were staying in the suite next to his."

"Protection from what?"

"There have been repeated attempts to abduct him and the other members of his family over the years."

"I don't like it," Liam decided. "This is too much of a coincidence. I'm going to warn my wife to stay away from Varik until we know more."

Buck inclined his head at that. "Make sure you use a private channel this time."

"Right." Liam had forgotten with his last message that he could contact Aria directly via her ARLs. He hurriedly configured the comms to do just that—text only.

Into the Unknown

Aria, don't trust Varik. Keep your distance from him and Markus. And keep Payton safe. I love you.

CHAPTER 26

Aria fled the bedroom, not even bothering to shut the door behind her. She scooped Payton out of the armchair in the living room and ran with her behind the couch. Liam's message reached her a second later. *Aria, don't trust Varik. Keep your distance from him and Markus. And keep Payton safe. I love you.*

She replied silently via her ARLs. *I'm already ahead of you.*

Varik's voice drifted out the open bedroom door: "You're making a big mistake."

"We'll see about that," Marshall replied.

Aria could see that she had her pistol trained on all three of them: Markus, Elisa, and Varik.

Meanwhile, the one called Thespian stormed back in from the airlock carrying several loops of rope that Marshall had sent him to get from the survival kit in the rover.

"Ow! Careful!" Markus hissed as Thespian tied his hands behind his back.

"Shut it," Thespian growled back.

"Serves the bastard right," Mattias said, rolling his big shoulders and flexing his fists. He was watching the confrontation from what he judged to be a safe distance.

After a few minutes Aria could see that Marshall had all three of them on their knees. "Start talking," she said.

"We've already told you everything," Markus replied. "I gave you access to my Neuralink, remember?"

Marshall snorted. "Yeah, what about his?" she jerked her chin to Varik.

"The information in my head is too valuable. How do I know you won't sell it?" Varik replied.

"To who?" Marshall scoffed.

"After we get home you could sell whatever you learn. Besides, how do *I* know that you weren't responsible for us coming here? Maybe my abductors paid you off and this is where they had you take me?"

"I'm not even going to dignify that with a response. Thespo—"

"Ma'am?"

"Shut the door. It's time to go to work. We'll get the truth out of them the old fashioned way."

"Now hang on just a—" Whatever Markus had been about to say it was cut off as the bedroom door slammed shut.

The first muffled *smack* reached Aria's ears, followed by a woman's scream. They were working on Elisa first. Aria winced and clapped her hands over Payton's ears.

Her daughter's eyes were huge, "Are they going to kill them?"

"No, honey." But she wasn't sure that was true.

Samos sat up in front of them. He was still lying on the couch. "If they do kill them, we might never get home. Varik is the only one who knows the way."

Another scream interrupted them, followed by both Markus and Varik shouting for them to stop. Aria's perception of who the good guys and bad guys were shifted, and suddenly she was no longer sure who to trust.

Elisa's screams went on and on, then stopped. And then the men's cries began. Aria kept her hands over Payton's ears, but there was no one around to do that favor for her. She became increasingly sick to her stomach, and even Mattias began to look troubled. His wife, Asha, looked like she was on the verge of a panic attack.

"We have to stop them," she whimpered.

"Yeah, maybe we should..." Mattias tried the door controls and shook his head. "It's locked." He cast about, as if looking for something they could use to bash open the door.

Another cry. Female, but this time it wasn't a cry of pain, and it wasn't Elisa's high voice. It was Marshall's.

A man shouted in alarm, and a gun went off with two loud *cracks* in quick succession. The muffled *thumps* of two bodies hitting the floor came next.

"What the hell is going on in there?" Mattias wondered.

A few minutes later the door swished open and a battered-looking Varik stepped out, holding a small pistol. One of his eyes was half swollen shut, the other bloodshot and blazing with fury.

The bloodshot eye settled on Mattias and promptly narrowed. "You. Take out the trash." He gestured with his gun to two bodies lying on the floor in the bedroom. From where Aria was hiding behind the couch, it was hard to tell who they were, but then Markus and Elisa walked out behind Varik, bruised and beaten within an inch of their lives, and holding the mercenaries' weapons.

That confirmed the identities of the fallen.

But it raised a new question: how had Varik broken his bonds and gotten the upper hand on two former Marines?

CHAPTER 27

"Are th-they dead?" Mattias stammered.

"Stunned. Unconscious, but they're damn lucky I don't make it permanent," Varik replied.

Aria blew out a breath. Her whole body was shaking from the adrenaline. Tired of sitting on the sidelines, she jumped to her feet. "You're just going to throw them out the airlock?"

"That's right. What's it to you?" Varik snapped.

"Well, for one thing, there's another two of them outside. If they find out what you did, they could come storming in here, guns blazing. Besides, if you only stunned them, then they'll wake up sooner or later. You should be worried about reprisals."

Varik shook his head. "We won't be here. We're taking off and flying to the nearest depot."

"But..."

"But nothing. It's our best chance of survival and of getting home. You're just going to have to trust me on that."

"Will we be able to take off again after that? In case we need to get back up to orbit?"

"Yes, but we won't need to. We just need to make contact. The aliens will do the rest."

"You seem pretty sure about that for someone who can't remember anything about the beings we're going to meet."

"This is not a democracy. If you don't like it, there's the airlock." Varik pointed to it with his gun.

Aria looked to Markus and Elisa. Their faces were swollen and smeared with blood from broken noses and split lips, but they seemed determined to follow Varik's plan.

"You," Varik said, gesturing to Mattias with his gun. "I told you to get them off my ship."

Mattias frowned uncertainly, but said nothing and made no move to obey. Payton was peeking over the top of the couch, eyes wide with horror.

"What about my husband and son?" Aria said. "Even if you're right and the aliens will send us home, I can't go home without them. Not to mention there's a cruise ship full of people still stranded on this planet."

"I'll tell them to meet you at the depot. And we'll discuss the others once we're there."

Aria nodded uncertainly, her mind spinning.

Varik nodded to Mattias. "Well?"

This time he did as he was told, dragging first Marshall, and then the other mercenary into the airlock.

"There!" Mattias declared.

"You're not done. Put their masks on and dump them outside."

Mattias went down on his haunches to put Marshall's mask on. It was dangling from her neck by the straps. He went to do the same for the other Marine. That done, Mattias straightened and slipped on his own mask, also dangling from his neck. The swished shut a moment later.

Aria's thoughts returned to the mystery at hand while Mattias took the unconscious mercenaries out. How had Varik gotten the upper hand on two former Marines? Even if he'd had a concealed weapon that they didn't know about, how had he managed to use it with his hands tied? Aria thought about asking Varik, but she doubted she'd get an honest answer out of him.

"Do you have something on your mind, Mrs. Price?" Varik asked.

She shook her head. "No."

* * *

"Ace isn't answering me anymore," Buck said.

"Maybe she's busy?" Liam suggested.

"Yeah, maybe..."

The envelope icon at the top of Liam's ARLs began flashing, and the number 1 appeared in the corner beside it. He'd just received a new message. He focused on the icon to read it.

Liam. It's Aria. There's trouble down here. Somehow Varik got the upper hand. The mercenaries are stunned and Varik is throwing them off the ship. We're going to fly to some kind of alien depot where raw vitalics are collected. Varik says you and Niko need to meet us there. He says the aliens will help us get home. He'll provide coordinates and instructions to use them with another lifeboat's autopilot. But I don't know who we should trust... Varik wants to go meet the aliens, but Marshall thought he was hiding something. She and one of her men beat him, Markus, and Elisa within an inch of their lives before Varik somehow turned the tables. Liam, I'm scared! You need to come for us. Please hurry.

"Everything okay?" Buck asked. He must have noted how quiet Liam suddenly was. Probably saw the glowing overlay on Liam's ARLs, too.

"Aria just sent me a message."

"Oh yeah? And?"

Liam hesitated, wondering how much he should say. How much he should trust this mercenary. But Buck had come clean about that, and at this point that was one better than Varik and Markus had done. "You're not going to like it," Liam said, and then he read the message aloud.

When he was done, Buck said nothing for a long time, but his eyes were flickering and flashing with ARL overlays.

"We have to get to Mom," Nikolai said.

Liam glanced at him. He looked wide awake and strong enough to travel now, but he was still a target for the harvesters.

"You're not going anywhere," Liam said.

"But—"

"Your dad's right. You three should stay here, but I need to get down to the surface." Buck stood up, hands flexing on his laser rifle as he scanned the racks of weaponry in the armory. He went over to a wall full of handguns and picked two off the rack. Next he went to a shelf and dug around inside a crate before pulling out a pair of suspender-style body holsters.

Liam warred briefly with himself as Buck shrugged out of his jacket and strapped the holsters on. Aria had begged him to go get her and Payton. He couldn't ignore that.

"Niko, you're going to have to stay here with Jules. I have to go, too."

"What? No. I'm coming with you."

"You can't. It's not safe for you."

"Well, I can't just stay here! I could starve or die of thirst. Or—"

"I will take care of your needs, Master Nikolai," Jules replied.

"How?" he demanded, rounding on the bot.

"By crawling out through the ducts, just as your father and Lieutenant Marshall have done."

"But—"

"It's the only way, Niko," Liam insisted. "Your mother and Payton need me. Varik is up to something, and we don't know if the aliens that they're going to meet are friendly."

"Doubt it." Buck looked up from clipping charge packs to his belt. He had three pistols now, two in the body holsters and one in his own hip-slung holster. "If you're coming with me, then you'd better kit up."

"Kit..."

"Gear. In this case, weapons and ammo. As much as you can carry and still crawl through the ducts."

"Right." Liam climbed to his feet and walked over on shaking legs.

Buck grabbed their laser rifles from before and thrust one of them at Liam. He slung the other across his shoulders and double-checked the safety before he let it dangle. "This is your primary weapon." Buck grabbed a pair of matte black plasma pistols off the rack and held them up, muzzles down. "These are your secondary weapons. What kind of holsters do you prefer?"

"Um..."

"Hip holsters it is." Buck grabbed two, then helped Liam strap them on.

He holstered the weapons and let his hands dangle awkwardly beside them. He felt like a pirate from Guild Space.

Buck passed over spare charge packs from the table below the gun rack, and Liam clipped them to his holster belts. He was glad he'd changed into slacks before going to the ship's VR beach with Markus. He would have looked absurd with a pair of sidearms strapped to his swimming trunks and dangling just above his hairy legs. "Are we good to go?" Liam asked.

Buck gave him an appraising look, as if silently asking himself the same question. Liam took a mental inventory. He already had optical enhancers for night vision. A comms piece for short-ranged communications. Weapons and charge packs a-plenty. What else did he need? Rations? There weren't any in the armory.

Buck looked away, scanned the ammo table, and grabbed another piece of equipment. It was a thin rectangular device with a holo projector at one end. "A handheld scanner," Buck explained. "It links up to your ARLs if you prefer to keep your hands free. Put it in your pocket."

Liam did so, and Buck grabbed a second scanner for himself. "Now we're ready."

"What about food and water?"

"We'll hit one of the other storage rooms before we go," Buck said.

"I'm hungry, too," Nikolai put in.

Jules perked up. "If you like, Master Nikolai, I can go with them and get rations for you as well."

Nikolai shook his head. "No. Never mind. I can wait."

Liam frowned. "But not forever. You need to eat."

"Not yet," Nikolai insisted.

Liam walked over to his son. Dropping to his haunches, he grabbed both of Nikolai's shoulders. "I'll be back."

Nikolai looked uncertain. His eyes slid away.

"Hey." Liam shook his son gently. "I mean it. I'm not going to leave you alone up here. I promise."

Nikolai's head bobbed quietly, but he said nothing.

"I love you, son."

"Love you, too..."

"You'll be safe here," he added. "Jules will make sure nothing happens to you."

"Yeah."

"We need to go," Buck said. "Every second we waste is another second that Varik has to accomplish whatever he came here to do."

Liam stood up. "I'm ready."

Buck cupped his hands and jerked his chin to indicate the overhead ducts. "After you."

CHAPTER 28

Marshall awoke in a bed of soft, lavender-colored grass with Crash and Mime standing over her. Mime's blue eyes widened with relief, but he said nothing. Silence was his default setting, hence his call sign.

Crash blew out a breath. "Finally!" He glanced behind him, looking nervous, hands flexing on his rifle.

The sun was gone, having sunk below the trees, and the entire clearing now lay in a deep pool of shadows. Thin tendrils of mist drifted through the air, encroaching from the trees like a living thing.

Marshall took stock of her situation, trying to remember how Varik had turned the tables on her and Thespian.

"What happened, Ace?" Crash asked, looking back to her.

Memories drifted back, and she sat up suddenly, twisting around to look for the lifeboat—

Jasper T. Scott

And saw nothing but a patch of flattened grass where it had been.

"Son of a bitch!" Marshall pounded the grass with a fist. It flattened and curled, shrinking away from the impact. Marshall frowned, wondering if the vegetation on this planet was more *alive* than usual.

"Boss?" Crash prompted.

"Varik. That's what happened."

A groan drew her attention to Thespian as he sat up beside her. He glanced her way, blue eyes wide and forehead wrinkled up to his shaved scalp. He gave his head a slight shake.

"We tied them up, but somehow Varik got free," Marshall began, looking back to Crash.

"You tied them up? Why?" A puzzled frown marred Crash's Latino features.

"Varik wanted to drag us all off to meet the aliens who built the Sparklers. He claims they're the ones who helped him get home the last time he was here."

"The *last* time? Varik has been here before? When?" Crash looked around. "And where's Hunter?"

Marshall hesitated, realizing that Crash and Mime hadn't been there when the Vitari had come out of the forest and Hunter had shot it. They hadn't been there for the confrontation with Markus and his father either.

"You have a lot of catching up to do," Marshall said, wincing as a residual wave of pins and needles went sparking through her entire body.

She gave them the highlights.

Mime's jaw dropped, and he scratched a hand through his short red hair. "This is Vitaria?"

"Yeah."

"No wonder you tied them up," Crash said.

Marshall nodded. But that hadn't been the catalyst. The tipping point had come when Varik insisted that they all go have tea with the aliens who'd built the Sparklers. No way did that make sense. Unless Varik knew more than he claimed. Unless he had an agenda and he really was responsible for bringing them all here. And that would mean that he was responsible for getting hundreds of people killed. He'd deserved every ounce of the beating he'd taken. But what had happened next? And what did it mean? The details felt hazy, more dream-like than real. A side-effect of taking a high-powered stun blast to the chest.

Thespian walked over, long grass rasping against his cargo pants. "Marshall," he prompted. "We need to talk about what happened."

"What *did* happen?" she asked, slowly shaking her head. Her eyes drifted out of focus as memories swirled back to her—

Varik, Markus, and Elisa were lying on the floor, their hands bound behind their backs, faces bloodied and bruised, only half-conscious.

Marshall remembered walking up to Varik, grabbing him and hauling him up by his blood-stained shirt. She'd cocked a fist back, promising to knock him into oblivion.

He'd smiled and spat blood in her face; then a flash of light had blinded her, and when the glare faded, Varik was gone.

A few seconds later another flash of light had torn through the room and Varik had appeared standing behind her. His hands were no longer bound, and he'd been holding a small stun pistol.

"Boss?" Crash prompted. "What is Thespo talking about? What happened?"

"Varik got free and stunned us both..." Marshall said in a faraway voice.

"He was tied up," Thespian objected. "They all were."

Marshall looked to him. "What do *you* remember?"

"Well..." Thespian's scalp wrinkled, and he heaved his broad shoulders. "What I remember doesn't make sense."

"Sure it does," Marshall said. "The Sparklers can teleport. There's experimental versions of that tech back home in the Union, so it doesn't take much of a leap to imagine what happened."

Thespian arched a dark eyebrow. "Varik teleported? Where? He was only gone for a few seconds. How did he get free that fast? And where did he get a gun? I patted him down myself."

"The better question is how does Varik have a working version of an alien technology that even the military hasn't cracked yet?"

"Maybe he..." Thespian trailed off.

Crash snorted. "That explains why none of the attempts to abduct him ever succeeded. So much for hiring us to keep him safe."

"So why *did* he hire us?" Marshall asked.

"Good question," Crash replied.

"He could be working with the aliens somehow," Thespian decided. "That would explain how he has their tech, and why he wants to go meet with them."

"That's a cozy thought," Marshall replied. "But what do the aliens get out of it? What has he done since they sent him back to Earth?"

"Made himself stinking rich by getting everyone hooked on vitalics," Crash replied.

"That's a connection right there," Marshall replied. "The aliens built the Sparklers to harvest vitalics from wild Vitari, but maybe the vitalics aren't for them. Maybe they're stockpiling for us. Think about it. If they get Varik to somehow suddenly cut off our supply, billions of people would die."

"Only the rich," Crash said. "And grubbing Vital Corp employees like us."

"So who would be at risk?" Marshall began counting off on one hand. "Politicians, high-ranking military officers, wealthy businessmen, and highly-skilled laborers—doctors, engineers, and so on. Humanity's best and brightest would all die ignominious deaths."

"Money and brains don't always go together," Thespian said.

"No, but money and power do. So let's say these aliens, whoever they are, want to invade us, but they don't want a war. How do they get us to surrender? They get us all hooked on vitalics and then take away our supply. They wait until all of our leaders are at death's door, and then they sweep in and promise to save their lives in exchange for the keys to the kingdom." Marshall snapped her fingers. "Just like that, humanity rolls over and gets enslaved."

"Shit," Crash said. "But that can't be right. When Varik came home, the authorities scanned his Neuralink to find out what happened to the other explorers. There's no way he could have hidden his involvement with a plot like that."

"Maybe he really did have amnesia," Marshall said. "And maybe his memory only came back later."

"We're going to have to catch up with him if we want to find out the truth," Crash said.

"I agree," Marshall replied. "For that we need to reach Buck and call for a pickup. We can regroup on the *Dream,* kit up, and then come back down and find that bastard."

"Sooner the better," Thespian said. "I'm already due for my next dose of vitalics."

Marshall nodded. "I'm due in a couple of days. The clock's ticking. If this planet doesn't kill us, the withdrawal symptoms will."

"There's a problem," Thespian said. "The lifeboat's gone, and we were using its comms to communicate with Buck."

Marshall ground her teeth. "We'll have to hike over to that other lifeboat—the one that wasn't responding to our hails. We can use their comms to reach the *Dream.*"

Crash glanced over his shoulder to the pitch black wall of trees that encircled the shadowy clearing, then looked up to the sky. It had deepened from dark turquoise to dark olive, and the mist in the clearing was growing thicker by the second. The air had a sharp bite to it now. Cold as ice. Marshall shivered.

"Maybe we should wait for morning," Thespian said, also scanning the trees and sky. "Varik said the nights are the most dangerous on Vitaria."

Marshall pushed off the ground just as Mime gave her a hand up. "I don't know how much of what he said we can actually believe."

A gust of frigid air whipped through the clearing, and suddenly Marshall realized that she couldn't feel her ears. Short hair might be practical in her line of work, but it did nothing to keep her warm. She found herself wishing she hadn't discarded her wig. "If we keep moving, we should stay warm," she said. She felt around absently for her sidearm, but it was missing from the holster. *Great.* "Anyone have a spare *leg-warmer?*"

"Here, boss, take mine," Crash said as he handed her his plasma pistol.

"They took mine, too," Thespian said.

Mime made a discontented noise and handed his sidearm over.

"Thank-ya kindly," Thespian said.

"GTG," Marshall added. "Fall in, ladies." She began marching toward the dark wall of trees, aiming for a green diamond she'd marked on her scanner the last time she went out with Thespian.

At least Varik hadn't taken the scanner. The mist quickly grew thicker as they approached the trees. Marshall held her plasma pistol out in a two-handed grip and activated the under-barrel flashlight. More lights flicked on around her as the others did the same. Shadows fled and the mist shone bright silver. Lavender grass rippled out under four marching cones of light.

They had just two plasma pistols and two laser rifles to face the night and an alien forest full of unknown terrors. Marshall could see them creeping through the trees—dozens of red-shaded blips highlighted on her ARLs by her scanner. Marshall studied the scale numbers and range for each blip, trying to decide which of them represented the biggest threats. That sixty-foot-long, twenty-foot-tall creature she'd seen earlier was still out there, but now it was just six hundred meters away, and it was more or less directly between them and the other lifeboat. Was it hunting them? Maybe it had been drawn in by the sound of the lifeboat taking off.

"That big sucker is still out there," Thespian said.

"I see it." Marshall picked up the pace and angled away from the blip. "Let's go around. Just in case."

CHAPTER 29

"**W**e should check if there's anyone else on board," Liam said as they ran around the ring deck to reach one of the *Starlit Dream's* few remaining lifeboats. Pistols and charge packs rattled on their belts and in their holsters as they ran. "You were with a group of people when I met you," Liam added.

"The ship's internal sensors show several scattered groups hiding in their rooms," Buck said.

"You've already checked?"

"Yes."

"Shouldn't we tell them to meet us here? Or go get them?" Liam asked.

Buck skidded to a stop in front of the only door in sight with green lights around the frame. The color indicated that the lifeboat behind the door was still available for launch.

Buck turned from the door to face Liam. "At this point, if they're not already dead it's because the harvesters aren't interested in them. That means they're safer up here than they are down on

Vitaria where the air is toxic, and food and water will be limited."

"We should at least warn them about the harvesters going after people who've used vitalics recently."

"Be my guest."

Liam got on the comms and did exactly that while Buck fiddled with the control panel beside the doors. An error beep issued from the panel, and Buck pounded on the door with his fist.

"What's wrong?" Liam asked.

"It won't open! The door must be jammed. We'll have to find another one." Not waiting for a reply, Buck sprinted down the corridor once more. Liam ran after him. After just a few seconds Buck stopped next to a glowing red door frame. It had the number 312 emblazoned on it, also glowing red.

Liam's brow furrowed. "Aren't we looking for a green door?"

"Look." Buck pointed to the bottom where a human hand was sticking out. The door was cracked open as a result. The marine stepped to the control panel and keyed the door open.

Liam gasped.

"Shit..." Buck muttered.

Adrenaline surged in Liam's veins, making his heart pound at a furious rate. A bloody pile-up of dead bodies had jammed the inside doors of the airlock open as if everyone had tried to flee at the same time.

One man had apparently died while dragging himself toward the outer doors. He was the one with his hand sticking out into the corridor.

"I guess we know why this lifeboat is still here," Buck said, kicking the man's hand out of the way. They walked into the airlock and Buck waved the outer doors shut. They climbed gingerly over the bodies piled across the threshold of the inner doors. From there, Buck led the way to the living room windows and stood looking out at a dense, starless black nebula. A lone harvester drifted lazily by, its armor translucent and vaguely shimmering with what Liam assumed to be some kind of energy shield. Yet another technology that the Union hadn't developed past the experimental stages.

His son called him on the comms. "Did you find a lifeboat?" Niko asked.

"Yeah. Number three twelve. We're about to launch."

"Okay," Niko replied.

"Stay safe. Don't leave the armory."

"I won't."

"Good. Talk to you later, Niko."

"Bye."

Buck was busy pacing the floor in front of the windows, studying the deck, obviously searching for something.

"What are you looking for?" Liam asked.

"This." Buck stopped, and a floor panel slid open in front of him. A mechanical groaning sound began, and then several other floor panels slid open. Liam jumped back, almost falling into the recessed compartment that those panels had revealed. Something began rising out of it in front of the windows.

A chair and a control console.

"The manual flight controls," Buck explained. He sat down, already stabbing physical buttons and swiping at holograms that only he could see.

"Now what?" Liam prompted. "Can you figure out where Aria and Varik went?"

"I'm tracking them," Buck replied. "But I don't think we should go after them yet."

"What? Why not?"

"Because they kicked my wife and the rest of our team off their boat. They could be in serious trouble down there. That's more imminent than whatever Varik has planned for the people riding with him. Not to mention we could probably use the backup."

Liam felt torn. Buck's arguments made sense, but his wife's pleas for a rescue weighed heavily on him, and he didn't want to delay any more than he had to. "How long will it take to pick up your team?"

"Not long. An hour at most."

"Okay," Liam decided. "We'll do it your way."

Buck snorted. "I wasn't asking for permission."

The lifeboat detached with a *thunk* and a fast-rising roar of thrusters firing. Dark tentacles of nebula swept by, and a bright blue and purple planet appeared—half-lit by the system's sun, half-shadowed by the massive yellow, white, and blue planet that it orbited.

"The smaller one is Vitaria," Buck said.

An insistent trilling sound began, and a blinking red light appeared on Buck's console.

Liam pointed to it. "What's that?"

"We're being hailed."

"By who?"

Rather than answer, Buck flicked a switch on the panel, and a bruised and bloodied face appeared in the top right corner of the picture window where Buck sat. That man managed to smile despite his split lip.

"Varik," Buck said. "You've looked better."

"Your wife has a mean right hook," Varik replied.

"What the hell is going on?" Buck asked. "You hire us for protection, and then you turn on us?"

"I'm afraid you have that story backward."

Liam noticed Markus and Elisa standing to either side of Varik, their backs to the camera, weapons trained casually on the others in the room. He caught a glimpse of Aria and Payton huddled together in an armchair. A warm swell of relief overcame him to see that they were alive and well. Right on the heels of that, outrage surged at the sight of weapons being aimed at them. Neither Aria nor Payton had reacted to seeing *him*. Their eyes were glazed and unseeing.

Thinking he must be out of the camera's field of view, Liam bent down in front of Buck's console. "Aria! Paytie!"

Payton was the first to react. She jumped out of her chair and pointed at the camera. "Daddy!"

Aria straightened, eyes blinking.

Varik's swollen eyes tightened, and he glanced behind him. "Keep them back," he said.

"I see you've learned well from your would-be abductors," Buck said.

Varik slowly shook his head. "I know what this looks like, but it's not like that. I'm just trying to get us all home. I didn't harm your wife, Buck. Or any of her men. Which is a lot more than I can say for her. She almost beat us to death. Even poor Elisa."

Buck jerked a thumb over his shoulder to the pile of dead bodies still lying half-in, half-out of the lifeboat's airlock. "I've got a couple hundred corpses that say you deserved every ounce of the beating Ace gave you."

Varik sighed. "That's the problem. You both think this is my fault."

"Isn't it?"

"No, and I can prove it. Meet me at the depot, and you'll learn the truth."

Buck's eyes pinched into slits. "You're making it sound like the aliens brought us here."

Varik's chin came up, his blue eyes bloodshot and glittering. "Now that's an intriguing possibility."

"And that doesn't frighten you?" Buck asked.

"No. It excites me. You're not the only one looking for answers. Now, you have a choice, you can come get those answers with me, or see how long you last waiting for a rescue. But if I can give you the benefit of my experience..." Varik trailed off, shaking his head. "No one is coming, and Vitaria is a dangerous place to wait—especially for vitaholics like yourselves."

"You bastard. You were the one handing vials of serum out like candy as bonuses for our last two contracts. If anything happens to any of my men—"

"They're heavily armed. Besides, it hasn't been long. I'm sure they're fine. Go pick them up and then come meet me at the depot. I'm sending you the coordinates now. Remember, you still have a job to do and more *bonuses* to collect. Hope to see you soon, Buck. Varik out."

The swollen face disappeared, and Buck screamed, "I'm going to kill him!"

CHAPTER 30

The mist was so thick that it made their flashlights all but useless. Marshall struggled to even see the ground she was walking on, and they had to go slowly to avoid tripping over unseen obstacles.

Red-shaded blips swarmed around them like curious monkeys, but Marshall never glimpsed more than a fleeting shadow. She kept hoping one of them would resolve into a human shape, which would indicate that Hunter was still alive and well. But there was no sign of him anywhere.

A massive black tree trunk came swirling out of the gloom, and Marshall almost smashed her face into it.

"Damn it..." she muttered. That was the third time in as many minutes. As she led the way around the mighty trunk of the tree, a group of three large, undulating shadows appeared, shaded bright red by her scanner. She stopped cold and tightened her grip on her plasma pistol, tracking the nearest lifeform.

Heads up. Alien lifeforms ahead, she thought over her Neuralink.

The comms piece in her ear conveyed a simulated version of Thespian's voice: *They look like big ass worms.*

We don't know if they're hostile, Marshall added. *Better let them pass.*

A loud *crack* sounded somewhere in the trees overhead. Followed by the *whoop, whoop, whoop,* of several giant leaves falling.

Marshall's head snapped up, tracking the noise. There were four-legged lifeforms in the trees. Forty meters up. She studied them a moment. Each was the size of a grown man. Alien monkeys? They weren't approaching. Not yet.

Whoop, whoop, whoop...

The falling leaves were close. How heavy were they? Marshall began backing up slowly.

Watch for falling—

One of them landed in front of her with a muffled *thump*, cutting off her thoughts in mid-stream. She flinched and leapt back instinctively. Another leaf landed a few feet to her left, and Crash cried out.

Status? Marshall asked.

Just a bump on the head, Crash replied. *GTG.*

Marshall swept her pistol around, the under-barrel flashlight bouncing off shifting curtains of silvery mist. Range to the nearest of the three undulating worm creatures was fifteen meters now, and they were no longer blocking the way to the objective. Turning in a quick circle, Marshall confirmed that the other lifeforms were still keeping their distance. All except for one. That giant sixty-foot creature was only four hundred and ten meters away now.

Four hundred and one.

Three ninety-two.

Three eighty-six.

Marshall spun the other way, checking the range to the green diamond on her ARLs. The lifeboat. *We're still five hundred meters from the objective.*

She glanced back at the approaching monster.

That big mofo is getting closer, Thespian said as he emerged wraith-like from the mist. His flashlight joined hers, creating a bright spot on the wall of condensation in front of them.

It's definitely tracking us, Crash added.

Range is now three hundred sixty meters, Marshall noted.

Three fifty-three, Thespian added a moment later.

It's charging, Mime said.

"Scanner clocks it at thirty klicks per hour," Crash put in. "How the hell is it moving that fast in this shit? It should be running into trees every five seconds!"

"Don't know, don't care. Double time it!" Marshall yelled. She whirled toward the green diamond and ran as fast as she dared through the murky forest. Branches cracked, and leaves crunched underfoot. Black tree trunks whipped by, swirling out of the gloom as she raced by.

An obsidian wall emerged dead ahead. Going too fast to stop, she pushed off the trunk with both hands to redirect her momentum. Her arms buckled and her shoulder glanced off the tree, landing her in a thicket of cone-shaped red plants that hissed and rattled like snakes. They oozed a foul-smelling black sap all over her.

"We can't out-run it!" Thespian said as he yanked her out of the thicket.

Marshall checked range to the monster chasing them. Three hundred and ten meters now. Thespian was right. "Let's find a defensible position and dig in!"

* * *

Aria watched the view from the armchair that she shared with Payton. The treetops flashed by, blue and purple leaves shining gold in the setting sun. Here and there blue and green crystals jutted up, rising to even more impressive heights than the trees. Up here, above the canopy, it was still day-time, and they were chasing the sun around the curve of the planet, causing it to rise higher in the sky instead of setting.

Varik sat behind the controls. Markus and Elisa stood to either side of him, facing the inside of the lifeboat, the weapons they'd stolen from Marshall and Thespo held casually at the ready.

"How much farther is it?" Aria asked.

"Not far," Varik replied.

"What happens when we get there?"

"You'll see."

Aria scowled, and Mattias muttered something colorful under his breath. Samos was still lying on the couch, obviously in too much pain from his broken ankle to react.

Up ahead the trees thinned out, and Varik slowed the lifeboat. Blue and green leaves gave way to naked black branches. Bulbous brown growths sprouted along them with a mesh of giant blue and purple leaves interlaced to form bridges and crossings from one branch to another. Familiar-looking winged creatures with colorful feathers perched on the branches and leaf bridges, walking from branch to branch or diving off to lower levels. Dozens of others took flight and darted around the lifeboat, making close flybys in an attempt to scare off the intruding metal bird.

Varik circled the area. "That's a Vitari village— or a farm, depending how you look at it."

They flew over the denuded trees to a broad clearing of lavender-colored grass. In the center was an emerald-colored dome with a honeycomb structure that shone bright green in the sun. It curved over a glittering crimson pond.

As they flew over, Aria spotted silver Vitari eggs at the bottom of the pond, and their cocoons dangling from the honeycomb framework above.

"And that's a Vitari nest," Varik explained.

Aria had seen pictures of their honeycomb nests before—built over artificial ponds inside of giant factories—but this one was unlike any she'd seen before.

"It's beautiful," Payton whispered.

"It is, isn't it?" Aria replied. It looked to be carved from solid emeralds. The stump of a crystal obelisk lay on the other side of the nest. Emerald-colored rubble traced the path where it had been felled like a giant tree and then whittled away to build the nest.

Varik circled back around, and Aria studied the cocoons and gleaming silver eggs once more. Vitari had two distinct life cycles. One as tadpoles that matured into amphibians with four legs and a tail—they were the ones who built the honeycomb nests and laid more eggs. And a second life cycle as the bird-like creatures that emerged from the cocoons. The avian Vitari were mysteriously sterile but theoretically immortal. They were the ones with compounds in their blood that could rejuvenate other forms of organic life.

The lifeboat circled back once more, but this time Varik accelerated and kept on going. The sun rose to about sixty degrees, somewhere in the middle of Vitaria's afternoon, and then Varik slowed the lifeboat once more. In the distance, a range of jagged, snow-capped mountains soared, and a snaking crimson lake came peeping through the trees, sparkling like rubies in the sun. As the trees fell away, Varik dived down, and in seconds the lifeboat was racing low over the rippled red water. Whole schools of giant green fish with fins the size of wings came leaping high out of the water as the lifeboat flew over.

"Mommy look!" Payton cried. "There's so many of them!"

"Amazing," Aria replied. She heard several of them thumping mindlessly into the underside of the lifeboat, having jumped just a little too high.

"The shadow we're casting makes them think we're a flock of Vitari," Varik explained. "Even the fish on this planet evolved to hunt them. Increasing one's procreative lifespan is quite the evolutionary advantage."

"Unless you decide not to have kids," Mattias put in.

"Humans are particularly good at thwarting evolutionary progress," Varik replied.

They reached the opposite shore of the lake, and Varik slowed the lifeboat to a crawl. He hovered down into a field of tall, lavender-colored grass that was freckled with bright green flowers. The snow-capped mountains soared above the treetops, looming over them. Varik rotated the Lifeboat on the spot to face a crimson river. It raced through the sunlit field and emerged in a broad delta in the sandy white shores around the lake.

Aria heard the sound of buckles on Varik's safety harness rattling. He rose and turned to face them. "Time to meet the masters of this beautiful world."

"Where's the depot?" Mattias's wife, Asha, asked.

"Yeah," Mattias began, his eyes narrowing to suspicious slits. "I didn't see any buildings when we flew in."

"Nor would you. The facility is below ground," Varik said.

"Bull. This close to the water it would be flooded if it were underground."

"Did I say it was here?" Varik replied. "We have to go through the trees to reach it. There's nowhere closer to land."

"It's an alien depot for resource collection, and there's nowhere to land?" Mattias asked. "That doesn't make any sense."

"It makes plenty of sense if you can teleport cargoes directly from point to point."

Mattias's gaze widened, then narrowed again. "I don't care. You're up to something, and I'm not going to let you lead us off like Vitari to the slaughter. We're staying here."

Aria nodded along with that. "So are we."

Varik regarded them with a subdued sneer. "Then you can forget about going home. Maybe you can become fishermen and build yourselves a nice cabin by the lake. Oh, but no, that won't work because the air on this planet is toxic. Better make it airtight and put in a good filtration system. I suppose you could use this lifeboat as your home... it has an airlock and an air filtration system. You should be fine for at least a couple of hours. Until night falls and the predators find you." Varik smirked. "Take it from me, there are monsters here that make T-rex look like a puppy. They'll peel this lifeboat open just to get at you."

"Then leave us one of the guns," Aria suggested.

Varik looked to Markus, then Elisa, then shook his head. "I'm afraid we're going to need them."

Aria frowned. "Well, we should at least wait until Buck and Liam get here."

"They'll go pick up Marshall and the rest of her and Buck's team first, and you can bet that when they get here, they'll be spoiling for a fight. No, I don't intend to be here when they arrive. I'll be in the depot. If they're smart, they'll come and join us." Varik's eyes bored into Aria's. "And if *you're* smart, so will you. Waiting here is not safe."

"And we're just supposed to take your word for that?" Mattias challenged.

"What about Samos?" Aria asked. "He's not going anywhere with a twisted ankle."

"Actually I think it might be broken," Samos lamented.

Varik's eyebrows shot up as he glanced between the two of them. "We're not going on foot. We're taking the rover."

"You have an answer for everything, don't you?" Mattias asked. "You're not going to change our minds."

Varik sighed, reached over, and grabbed the rifle Markus was holding.

Mattias jumped to his feet and sprinted across the room to reach Varik.

"Stop!" Elisa screamed. "I'll shoot!"

"Hold your fire!" Varik growled.

Aria cringed and curled her body around Payton, acutely aware that they were in the line of fire. Varik casually flicked a setting on the side of the rifle and raised it to his shoulder.

An arcing blue-white bolt of energy snapped out and struck Mattias in the chest. Electricity crackled and leapt off his body. He collapsed to the floor, already unconscious from the combination of tranquilizers and electric shocks delivered by the micro-darts packed into the stun shell. A growing pool of water appeared on the deck. He'd been stunned with a full bladder.

"Does anyone else need to be stunned in order for me to save their lives?" Varik asked.

A shocked silence answered him.

"I'll take that as a no. Good." He gestured to Markus. "Put his mask on and get him into the airlock."

Markus's upper lip curled and his nose wrinkled. "He's covered in piss."

"Do I need to stun you, too?"

Markus blinked, his eyes widening as he stared at his father in disbelief.

"Well?"

"No."

"Good. Then let's stop wasting time."

CHAPTER 31

"**S**hit. They're not here," Buck said.

Liam stood at the picture windows beside Buck's control station, peering down on a dark, misty clearing. "Are you sure? How can you tell? I can't see anything down there." The lifeboat's floodlights reflected back off the mist and dazzled his eyes as Buck slowly flew over the clearing.

"I can't reach them on the comms." Buck tapped the comm piece in his ear. "They can only transmit around ten or twelve klicks. Less with all of the interference from the moisture in the air."

"Klicks?" Liam asked.

"Kilometers."

"Well, where would they go?"

"That's a good question...." Buck spent a moment swiping at an interface that only he could see. Then a holographic map sprang from his control console. The terrain was shaded bright blue but stripped bare of the enshrouding mist and ground cover. Black trees soared around the clearing with a myriad of red blips milling around and in-between.

"Is there any way to tell if one of those life signs is human?" Liam asked.

"At this range?" Buck shook his head. "We'd have to be right on top of them to distinguish detailed shapes. Best we can do is rule out the ones that are either too big or too small." Buck scanned the map, scrolling around by swiping the air above it.

"What are you looking for?"

Another clearing and lifeboat swept into view. Buck stopped scrolling and centered on it. "That's where I'd go if it were me. Assuming they know it's there. They can use that boat's comms to make contact with us."

Liam frowned. "Another lifeboat? It looks like it's in bad shape..." And that was an understatement. The top of the ship had been peeled open like a piece of fruit, metal panels curling up to reveal the living room furniture. "Is that imagery accurate?"

"Very. I performed a deep scan of the surface on the way down, so everything you see is based on actual data."

"You think your wife would head there, even though the lifeboat is damaged?"

Buck shrugged. "Again, I would. I'm getting a ping from its comms system, so we know that it's still working. Besides, some shelter is better than no shelter at all."

"So what do we do?"

"Head there and wait for them," Buck replied. "And see if we can make contact along the way."

"How far is it?" Liam asked.

"Four klicks and change. They'll be on foot, but they have a good head start, so they might already be close to it." Buck dropped a green diamond on the map beside the damaged lifeboat and then made a pinching gesture, shrinking the map to a miniature version. Grabbing the flight yoke in both hands, he pulled up from the clearing and rocketed over the treetops. Liam struggled to remain standing as the deck tipped up under his feet. Fortunately the inertial dampeners took care of the sudden acceleration.

Buck banked sharply until the green diamond of his waypoint swept into view—along with a monstrous yellow, white, and brown planet cresting over the horizon. The forest canopy gleamed like a sea of gold in its glow.

"That's a hell of a moon," Liam said.

"Technically, *this* is the moon," Buck replied.

"True." Although Vitaria itself was almost the size of Earth, its parent planet dwarfed it. "The gravity on that other planet must be deadly."

"Two point seven five G's," Buck confirmed. "Living there would cut your lifespan in half. Or worse."

"But the vitalics on Vitaria could double it."

"Your point?"

"It's just ironic, that's all," Liam said.

"Irony's a shameless—hang on... I'm getting something on the comms." Buck spared a hand from the flight yoke and flicked a switch.

A deep female voice blared through hidden speakers: "Weapons free!" A flurry of weapons fire crackled over the comms, followed by the sound of something squealing and hissing.

"Contact right!" a man said.

"Shit!" another added.

More weapons fire.

"It sounds like they need help!" Liam said.

By way of reply, Buck pushed the throttle all the way up. The thrusters roared, and the entire lifeboat shuddered from the strain. Buck banked a few degrees right of his waypoint and angled down, skimming dangerously close to the treetops.

Branches shrieked and snapped against the underside of the hull. Overtaxed inertial dampeners began to fail, and Liam nearly fell over as a collision with a particularly thick branch knocked them sideways.

"Sit down and buckle up!" Buck said.

Liam whirled around, looking for a place to do just that. But all of the emergency stations were on the other side of the living room, by the airlock.

"Brace!"

Liam dropped down behind Buck's chair and wrapped his arms around the base of it. A sharp ferrous smell greeted his nostrils as he neared the deck, and he spied a sticky river of dried blood several inches from his nose. He'd almost forgotten how they'd found this lifeboat—with gutted corpses strewn across the floor.

Buck hit the air brakes and reversed thrust at the same time. Liam's body wrapped around Buck's chair like a ground car around a lamp post, and his head ached sharply as all of the blood pooled behind his eyes and forehead. Wind roared against the hull, and loud thumps sounded from the inner airlock doors as the bodies they'd dragged in there went airborne. There came a brief moment of silence, and then branches shrieked and snapped in a deafening roar as Buck deliberately crashed through the treetops.

"You're insane!" Liam gritted out.

"Nah, just a Marine!" Buck replied.

CHAPTER 32

Marshall's team found a particularly large tree with a cleft in the trunk that formed a shallow cave. There was a burrow inside big enough for one of the worms they'd seen earlier to wriggle down.

But they had bigger problems than whatever might be hiding in the burrow. Much bigger. Marshall tracked the red blip that chased them. It grew swiftly larger as it approached. One hundred and nine meters. One hundred and one. Ninety-four.

"Ten seconds!" Marshall estimated. "Ready up! Shortest to the front and take a knee!"

"Copy," Crash said.

Mime shuffled forward with him, and they both dropped to one knee. Marshall and Thespian took aim over their shoulders with their plasma pistols.

All four of their under-barrel flashlights pooled against the silvery wall of mist beyond the entrance of the arboreal cave, doing almost nothing to improve visibility.

"Lights off. Scanner overlays only," Marshall decided. "Maybe we'll get lucky and it won't see us."

"Rog," Crash said.

"Copy," Thespian replied.

Lights clicked off in quick succession—one, two, three—and plunged them into utter darkness. Marshall switched to an ARL overlay from her scanners. A shaded blue wireframe marked the tree around her and the trunks of other trees beyond. Shaded-green silhouettes marked her men. Mime beside her. Crash and Thespian kneeling in front. A growing red blob marked the incoming monster.

Fifty meters! Thespian said, switching to silent comms.

Someone shuffled their feet, and a twig snapped. Then all went still and silent, but for the sound of Marshall's heart thumping in her ears, and the team's breath rattling loudly and unevenly through their filter masks.

Then the ground began to shake: *Boom—thud-thud-thud-thud-thud—BOOM—thud-thud-thud-thud-thud... BOOM.*

Marshall stared at the approaching blob, trying to make sense of what she was hearing. It was beginning to take shape: six long legs, two arms folded and held up like the forelegs of a praying mantis; pincers protruding from a giant, triangular head, and a lumpy, bulbous body. It reminded Marshall of a spider, but much, much bigger and with longer legs. It was alternately running along the forest floor and springing from tree to tree, covering half a dozen meters with each leap.

Ten meters, Marshall said over silent comms.

Thud-thud-thud-thud... thud. It stopped right beside their tree and hoisted its giant high, snorting like a whole stable full of horses.

Marshall held her breath. From the sudden absence of their rasping breaths, the others must have been doing the same. She flexed cold, sweaty hands around the grip of her plasma pistol, trying to work some feeling into numb fingers. They'd kept themselves warm by running until just recently, but now the cold was making a comeback.

The snorting stopped, but a new sound split the air: muffled thumps sounding in quick succession. A pitter-patter of light footfalls. And then the giant red blip spawned dozens of smaller versions of itself, each as big as an adult human.

Oh shit, Thespian said.

Marshall watched as dozens of spiders came rushing around the tree. "Watch your left!" Marshall whispered over the comms.

The leader rounded the opening of the cave, followed by three more. They spread out, cocking their triangular heads back and forth, and snapping their pincers restlessly. Then one of them bent its legs, getting ready to spring.

"Weapons free!" Marshall said.

All four of them opened fire at once. Emerald laser beams and white-hot plasma converged, and the creature burst into flames. It ran around aimlessly, squealing and hissing. To the right, another spider crouched.

"Contact right!" Thespian said.

"Shit!" Crash added.

They opened fire again, cutting the second spider down in mid-air as it leapt toward them. It collapsed at their feet in a shriveled heap with flames leaping high off a glossy blue and purple body. A welcome heat washed into the hollow of the tree, along with a sickly-sweet, burnt-marshmallow smell. The other spiders flocked to the light and heat like moths, but this time none of them attacked.

"What are they waiting for?" Thespian mumbled. He got his answer a second later as a massive red blob appeared in the opening of the cave.

Mommy spider? Marshall wondered. Its jaws gaped wide in a serrated horror of teeth. Sticky globs of green saliva drooled from chitinous jaws and pincers. *Plop, plop... plop.* The creature's hot breath piled into the cave, sweet and rancid at the same time.

Nobody move, Marshall said, switching back to silent comms.

One of two arms folded out, tentatively reaching for them with a slender hand the size of her torso. It had three long fingers, each the length of her entire arm. Six-inch claws gleamed in the flickering orange light of the fire leaping from the dead, shriveled spiders in the entrance of the cave. The other babies chittered and clacked their pincers.

Marshall kept hoping the giant spider would hesitate, that it would think twice and withdraw, but that hand glided out steadily, determined to find out whatever was inside of the tree. Marshall wasn't going to give it the chance.

"Fire!" she screamed.

A staccato burst of plasma and laser fire erupted once more, dazzling Marshall's eyes. The giant spider screamed, and the hand shot out and wrapped around Crash, dragging him out into the swirling mist in the blink of an eye.

They all stopped firing for a split second to avoid hitting him.

Then came a muffled scream that cut off sharply with a sickening *crunch.*

"Kill it!" Marshall screamed.

Another hand darted in and wrapped around Thespian.

"Ahhhhh! Get it off me!" Another *crunch* and he sagged inside the monster's fist. The spider withdrew sharply, flinging his lifeless body away.

Marshall's eyes stung with tears. She screamed again and ran out of the hollow, firing steadily up at the massive creature. White-hot plasma bolts snapped out in quick succession, filling the air with the cloying smell of charred spider flesh.

A monstrous hand came snaking out of the mist. Impossibly long fingers wrapped around Marshall's body and squeezed, grinding her ribs together in a breathless, blinding agony. She ignored the pain, struggling to hold onto her pistol and pull the trigger as fast as possible, aiming for that massive, triangular head. Something in her chest cracked, and Marshall cried out with what little breath she had left.

Dark spots swam over the bright overlays on her ARLs, multiplying and clustering together.

Mime ran into view, shooting his rifle point-blank on full-auto into the spider creature's wrist. It released her suddenly and grabbed Mime instead. His eyes bulged as massive fingers curled around him in a giant fist. And then he was jerked suddenly away, flung into swirling clouds of moisture.

"Mime!" Marshall cried. She fired her pistol over and over until it clicked. Charge empty. She threw it aside and scanned the forest floor for another weapon.

Crash's rifle lay a dozen feet away. She ran for it, but an explosion of pain from her cracked ribs forced her to limp. She clutched her side and gritted her teeth. Scuttling feet hammered after her. An alien shrieked somewhere close behind her, and she felt something brush her back...

She dived for the weapon. Her hands closed around it, and she tucked and rolled with a nauseating wave of agony. She came up in a crouching stance and faced a scuttling horde of spiders, each the size of a grizzly bear. The nearest one stopped in front of her and reared up on hind legs, pincers snapping.

Marshall unleashed an emerald torrent of fire from the rifle. Green gore splattered her, and the sickly-sweet smell of burned chitin streamed through her air filter mask. The monster collapsed on top of her, and she cried out as her already wounded ribs took the brunt of its weight. She struggled to drag herself out even as the next spider leapt into the air, pincers gaping and aiming for her neck.

CHAPTER 33

As the thunder of cracking tree branches quieted, Liam risked looking up. An enormous black spider rose like a sea monster from the mist as they hovered down between the trees. The lifeboat's floodlights reflected purple off the creature's glossy black armor. It stood on six legs and used two arms to swipe blindly at a moving target on its back: a human woman, firing emerald laser beams into the joins between its plates of armor. Smaller spiders were leaping up to get at her, but she kicked them off and shot them as fast they could get up.

"That looks like Ace!" Buck said as the lifeboat touched down with a violent *thud* that clacked Liam's teeth together.

Liam peeled his cheek off the deck.

"I have to go help her, stay here!" Buck said.

It took Liam a moment to process that. Buck was crazy if he thought he could face that monster alone. Liam's mind flashed to the pair of plasma pistols holstered to his thighs, and to the laser rifle he'd tucked barrel-first between the couch cushions. Springing up from the floor, he whirled around just in time to see Buck swipe open the inner airlock doors. A bloody tangle of corpses appeared, piled against the doors like driftwood against a dam.

Liam sprinted to the couch, snatched his rifle from the cushions, and darted into the airlock beside Buck.

"What are you doing?" he demanded.

"Helping you."

Buck snorted and shook his head. "Your funeral." He opened a sliding compartment to reveal oxygen tanks and masks. Grabbing two masks, he handed one to Liam. They both put them on, and then Buck swiped the inner airlock doors shut. The doors jammed on a dead woman's stiff, outstretched arm. Buck jumped up onto the pile of bodies and yanked the arm out of the way with a grunt of effort. A bone snapped, and Liam's stomach spasmed. The doors banged shut, and warning lights flashed crimson in time to a klaxon. Buck strode up to the outer doors, checked his rifle, and flicked off the safety.

"Ready up." He snapped a grim look over his shoulder and tapped a pair of fingers to the camera beside his left eye. "Put your optical enhancers on."

Liam touched a hand to his own temples, found them naked, and then remembered he'd placed the devices in his pocket before leaving the *Starlit Dream*. He grabbed them and stuck them to his skin, one to either side of each eye. He mentally activated them via his Neuralink and flicked the safety off on his rifle.

Buck nodded and turned around.

The outer airlock doors sprang open, and mist swirled in along with the screeching reports of a laser rifle and the alien screams of the giant spider.

"On me!" Buck said as he raced out of the airlock and down the landing ramp.

Liam's heart pounded frantically at the thought of what awaited them, but it was too late for second thoughts now. He sucked in a quick breath and ran after the Marine.

* * *

Liam stuck to Buck's heels, afraid to lose him in the mist. The former Marine screamed like a madman and fired steadily at the six-legged monster standing beside their lifeboat. Liam aimed his rifle up and squeezed off a long burst of dazzling green laser bolts. The creature bucked and swayed under their combined salvos, but didn't seem to notice that two new adversaries had joined the one still clinging to its back.

The smaller spiders were another story. A group of four came springing toward them. Buck's line of fire tracked down, catching one of them and cutting it into smoking pieces just as it sprang off the ground to reach him.

Another one jumped in from his left. Buck spun around, bringing his rifle to bear, but he was too late.

Liam swung his weapon into line and squeezed off a trio of laser bolts. The first one struck the creature dead center of its body. The other two missed. The spider landed on Buck, legs scrabbling in the dirt. It was small, the size of a dog. He threw it off, and it landed a few feet away, still thrashing. He fired a second laser bolt straight into its triangular head, and green gore splashed him.

Liam hurried to Buck's side, and then they were both tracking new targets, standing back to back and firing steadily into the advancing hordes of spiders. All the while, the mother spider hammered the ground, and Buck's wife continued her assault.

A pair of baby spiders scuttled in, lunging in tandem at Liam. He shot the one on the right, but the one on the left knocked him over. He dropped his rifle and grabbed the pair of giant pincers protruding to either side of the creature's serrated jaws. The pincers were like knives, and they sliced his palms open. He cried out and gritted his teeth against the pain, trying to hold those scissoring blades away from his throat.

A screeching report from Buck's rifle ended the struggle, and Liam jumped back up.

"You okay?" he asked.

Liam nodded. His blood-slicked hands found his rifle dangling from the strap around his neck just in time to cut down three more spiders as they scuttled toward him. At least half a dozen more came scurrying out of the mist.

"There's too many of them!" Liam said.

An ear-rending scream stole Buck's reply, and Liam looked up in time to see the mother spider crumpling to its knees. A staccato burst of emerald fire illuminated the monster from within, and bright purple lines marked the joints between thick plates of armor. The spider collapsed with a thunderous *boom.* Liam stared at it in shock. The little spiders screamed in unison and scattered, scurrying away in all directions and vanishing into the mist.

Silence rang painfully in Liam's ears. He turned in a slow circle, taking stock of the carnage. The mist had retreated somewhat to reveal dozens of the small spiders lying dead and smoking on the forest floor—as well as three human men.

"Where is she?!" Buck cried.

"Who?" Liam asked, blinking in a daze.

"Ace!"

Then Liam remembered the woman on the mother spider's back... and the luminous flashes of lasers illuminating the creature from within. She'd been swallowed whole.

Buck was whirling around wildly. "Ace!" he screamed. "Ace!"

Liam pointed to the fallen monster. "She's inside it!"

Buck stared at him in horror. "Are you sure?"

He obviously hadn't seen the flicker of laser fire coming from within the beast.

"Yes!"

Buck ran for it, ducking under bent and curling legs the size of trees. He scanned the sides of the beast. "There!" He aimed his rifle at a point midway along the creature's torso that leaked green blood from multiple charred black holes. "One life sign. She's alive." Buck flicked a setting on the side of his rifle and took aim. A green laser beam shot out, drawing a fiery line between plates of armor. The spider's flesh crackled and smoked with the stink of burning sugar. Buck traced a line at least ten feet long. Green blood gushed out, along with gelatinous white mush, and a glossy, balloon-like organ with a dark shadow inside. A human shadow, curled into a fetal position. Buck stopped firing and drew a wicked-looking knife from his belt. He slashed the balloon open, and water gushed out followed by an unconscious woman, her skin pink and raw from whatever digestive juices churned in the spider's gut.

Buck slapped her face a few times. "Ace!" No response. He laid her out and set to work pumping her chest. "Come on, Ace!" More compressions. "You can do it..." A trickle of moisture slid down Buck's cheek. "Come on!"

CHAPTER 34

Liam looked on as Buck wept and cursed, alternately pumping his wife's chest and delivering mouth-to-mouth.

"Don't you leave me, you selfish bitch!"

Liam winced at Buck's language. Maybe he'd already reached the anger stage of grief. He took a hesitant step toward the former Marine. Reached out—

Buck rounded on him, yellow eyes blazing. "Don't you fucking touch me!"

More chest compressions. More mouth-to-mouth.

"Come on, Jacey!"

Liam could feel the anguish pouring off Buck in waves, his refusal to give up and accept the truth.

Long minutes passed, and the mist swirled back in, thickening and choking their line of sight. Red blips began pricking through, lifeforms identified by the scanner in Liam's pocket.

He looked back to Buck, risked interrupting the man's whispered pleas and muffled sobs. "We have to go. It's not safe here."

The other man ignored him.

"Buck..."

Still more chest compressions.

How long had it been? Ten minutes? She was gone. He had to know that.

Liam tried to imagine if it were Aria, but that thought triggered a mental knee-jerk, and he violently shook his head to clear away the image of *her* face blistered and torn, half-digested by alien stomach acid.

"Buck," Liam tried again.

The Marine stopped and leaned back on his haunches, breathing hard. "I'm going to fucking kill him," he croaked. "This is all Varik's fault."

Liam didn't know what to say to that. Buck was right. It was Varik's fault, but they couldn't make everything from this point on about revenge. They had higher priorities. Or at least Liam did. He needed to find his family and get them all home.

Buck looked to him with unseeing eyes, red from crying, tear-streaked cheeks agleam in the amplified light of Liam's optical enhancers.

"What am I going to tell Maddy?"

"Who?" Liam asked quietly.

"Our daughter!"

"I..." Liam's brow furrowed. "I'm sorry. I didn't know you had a daughter."

"She's three," Buck said. He wiped his nose and cheeks on one sleeve, and his mouth quirked up in one corner. "Spitting image of her mother." His eyes tightened, then relaxed and swam out of focus. "What do I tell her?" he asked again, this time in a faraway voice.

Liam swallowed thickly. "First you have to get home. Make sure she doesn't lose you, too. That's priority one."

Buck's lips curled. "I'm not going back empty-handed. I'm taking proof that the bastard who killed her is dead."

"You mean the... spider?" Liam glanced at the creature beside them.

"No, Varik. His head is riding home with me in a box. That's the only way to make this even half right."

Liam smiled tightly, not sure what he could say to that.

Buck reached under his wife's legs and back and lifted her off the ground. She looked like a child in his arms. He jerked his chin to the landing ramp. The number on the outer doors of their lifeboat glowed brightly through the mist, like the lantern at the top of a lighthouse—*312*.

"Let's move," Buck croaked and started trudging toward the light.

* * *

"What is it?" Nikolai asked sleepily. "Can I see?" The armory was dark again. Jules had turned off the lights so that Nikolai could rest.

Jules was silent for a long time.

"Hey, did you hear me?" Nikolai said, tapping the bot's shoulder repeatedly. A few hours ago, Jules had launched one of the *Starlit Dream's* probes into the nebula in the hopes of finding out more about where they were. Now the probe had found something interesting, but Jules was being annoyingly secretive about it.

The bot nodded slowly as if only now hearing him. "One moment."

A request to stream live video from the probe popped up on Nikolai's ARLs. He confirmed the request and a virtual screen appeared, front and center of his field of view. The probe was racing through dark nebular clouds. Here and there stars pricked through the dust.

"I don't see anything..."

"Be patient, Master Nikolai."

Multiple flashes of light illuminated the nebula from within, revealing dark, jagged shadows. One of the harvesters darted across the probe's path as if to scare it away.

"What are those shadows?"

"Spaceships, I believe."

"Alien spaceships?"

"I cannot say," Jules replied. "But I think we're about to find out."

The probe flew on, racing toward the shadows. Moments later, the nebula parted as though a veil had been lifted, and the probe emerged in a relatively open space.

Nikolai sucked in a breath. "There's dozens of them..."

"Twenty-three to be exact," Jules replied. "An entire fleet."

The live stream zoomed in on the side of a particular starship, and a familiar symbol snapped into focus: fifty-seven stars, one for each of the colonized star systems in the Union, arranged inside of a triangle and surrounded by a circle. The image zoomed out and then zoomed in on the side of another ship. The same symbol appeared once more.

"They're Union ships!" Nikolai said. "Can you contact them?"

"No. They're derelicts."

"Derelicts?"

"It means they're abandoned or offline. I cannot detect any signs of external damage, but there are no life signs on board."

"Maybe the harvesters attacked them, too. How long do you think they've been here?"

"I couldn't say, but one thing's for certain, this star system is not as lost as everyone seems to think."

"Then that means someone is going to come looking for us!" Nikolai said.

Jules just looked at him. "The Union lost an entire fleet here. Even if they knew where we went, I doubt they would risk following us."

Nikolai's heart sank. He went on staring at the video feed. After a few moments, he spotted something unusual in the imagery. Two rings of light interlocked at ninety-degree angles around an empty black circle. A delicate framework of silvery lines encompassed it like a ball of yarn, or a spider's web in spherical form.

"What's that?" Nikolai asked, pointing to it.

"What is what?" Jules replied.

Nikolai frowned. Of course the bot couldn't see what he was pointing to. "The rings of light with the lines around them."

The wrinkles in Jules' brow grew suddenly more pronounced. "Oh my..."

"What?"

"It's a black hole. With a Dyson sphere around it."

CHAPTER 35

"**A** Dyson what?" Nikolai asked.

Jules looked at him. The twin beams of light shining from the robot's eyes forced Nikolai to look away and shield his eyes with his arm.

"It is a megastructure of unimaginable size that encircles a sun or a black hole to draw power from it," Jules explained. "Whoever built it would have had to strip hundreds of star systems just to get enough materials."

"Hundreds of star systems?" Nikolai's voice shrank into a whisper as he contemplated that.

Jules nodded. "Easily more than a thousand planets, all stripped to the core."

"The harvesters did that?"

"No, they're not big enough to mine planets. But whoever built them must have other machines that could."

"Why? Why not just live on a planet, or many planets, like we do?"

"Who knows? There may be many reasons for that. The black hole is a good source of power.

There's also a strictly-defined locality to a Dyson sphere which an empire spanning multiple star systems wouldn't have. It would be easier to manage. Just one point to supply and defend, one infrastructure, one culture, and one government versus hundreds or thousands."

"What do you think it means for us?"

"It means that these aliens are far beyond our level of technology. But we already knew that from the harvesters," Jules added.

"So maybe that guy Varik was telling the truth, and the aliens really can help us get home," Nikolai said.

"Yes, I believe that's exactly what this means."

Nikolai watched the probe fly between a pair of derelict destroyers, each bristling with weapons that they'd never had a chance to use. The harvesters would have boarded them just like they'd boarded the *Starlit Dream*. They'd defeated those ships by slaughtering their crews directly.

But why? There was no way the crews of those ships had been using vitalics, too. Maybe the captains and their first officers, but no one else in the Navy would make even close to enough money to afford regular doses. "They attacked this fleet on purpose," Nikolai realized. "Not because of automated programming."

"What makes you say that?" Jules asked.

Nikolai explained his reasoning.

The bot blinked, long and slow, as if only now coming to the same conclusion. "Perhaps the Union fired the first shot?"

Nikolai shook his head quickly. "They wouldn't do that. Not with first contact."

"Then, why send a war fleet?" Jules asked.

"Because maybe they already knew how dangerous these aliens are. Or maybe they just wanted to be careful."

"Then they weren't careful enough," Jules replied.

"We have to contact my dad and Buck to warn them. They could be flying into a trap."

"Yes... you might be right," Jules said. "I'm going to call them right now."

"When you do, put me on to my dad. I want to talk to him, too."

"Of course."

Nikolai anxiously curled and uncurled his fists while he waited. "Well?"

Silence. Jules' brow furrowed, and he shook his head. "There is no reply."

"What? Why not? Let me try."

"Do you know how?" Jules asked.

"Maybe."

"Look." A screen-share prompt popped up on Nikolai's ARLs.

He accepted it, and a bar of text appeared at the bottom of his field of view:

Hailing Lifeboat 312...

The three dots trailing the number kept disappearing and reappearing. Nikolai waited for several minutes before letting out a frustrated sigh.

"Like I said, they're not answering. I'll leave them a message," Jules said. He wrapped an arm around Nikolai's shoulders. "Don't worry. Everything is going to be okay."

Nikolai nodded even though that reassurance sounded hollow to him. He wanted to believe it, but there were too many unknowns. Gruesome images of his parents' bodies torn open by harvesters flashed through his head. "What do you think they want from us?" he asked.

Jules regarded him with bushy gray eyebrows raised, his dazzlingly bright eyes the only light inside the armory. "What makes you think they want something?"

Nikolai looked at the deck to avoid the brightness of Jules' gaze. "If Varik is up to something, and he wants us to meet the aliens, then he's probably working with them or for them. I think they sent him home for a reason."

"That does seem logical. You are a very intelligent boy, Master Nikolai."

"Thanks, I think... So, the question is, what does a highly advanced alien race want with us? They don't just want to kill us. Not all of us, anyway, because they let us evacuate the ship."

"I wish I had answers for you. Whatever it is that they want, I believe your mother is about to find out."

"Yeah, that's what I'm afraid of," Nikolai said.

CHAPTER 36

Aria alternately peered out the front and side windows of the rover, watching as thick black trunks of ancient alien trees faded in and out of the mist. It had been light out when they'd entered the forest, but between the tree canopy and the mist, very little light reached the windows of the rover. Payton sat beside her, leaning into her lap to peer out the window with her.

Mattias and his wife, Asha, sat opposite them across a narrow aisle in the back of the rover. Mattias had mostly recovered from the effects of the stun blast Varik had delivered, but his eyelids looked heavy. He was obviously still weak from the experience. Smelled like urine, too, but Asha didn't seem to mind. She was cradling his head in her lap and running her fingers through his hair.

Aria looked away. Samos lay across the row of seats in front of theirs, a supply crate wedged into the aisle to form a makeshift bed. He was also a convenient roadblock to guard against Aria or

Mattias trying something to wrest control of the rover away from Varik.

Not that they could hope to succeed. Markus and Elisa sat right behind Varik, facing the back, with their weapons aimed.

Every now and then Aria would send a glare their way. Whatever Varik was up to, they were complicit in it. It seemed obvious that Varik had brought the cruise ship to Vitaria, but the how and why of it remained unanswered.

Time dragged on in silence. Aria passed that time contemplating the facts. Varik had somehow brought them here. Using everything she had learned about him so far, she tried to figure out what might be motivating his behavior, but her mind came up blank. Whatever Varik was up to, it was too convoluted for her to grasp.

"We're here," Varik said quietly.

Everyone rocked forward in their seats as he applied the brakes. Samos groaned.

"I don't see anything," Mattias said.

"You will." The rover came to a complete stop, and Varik turned to regard them over his shoulder. "Masks on."

They all pulled their masks up over their faces. Aria helped Payton with hers, adjusting the straps and activating the suction seal.

"Everyone ready?" Varik asked, his voice now amplified and distorted by the mask.

"Wait," Aria said. She half-stood from her seat to check that Samos had his mask on.

He did. His eyes were half-lidded with pain, but he was still awake enough to keep up with what was going on around them.

"Ready," Aria confirmed.

Varik's door swung open, and a sullen gray mist swirled into the rover like a living thing.

Payton looked up at her with wide eyes and grabbed Aria's hand in a tight little fist. A flutter of trepidation surged in Aria's stomach, followed by a loud growl and the burn of acid, reminding her just how long it had been since she'd eaten anything.

Markus got up and stood hunch-backed in the aisle. He gestured with his stolen rifle to an empty row of seats between them that was flanked by two doors.

"Everybody out. Come on! Let's go!"

Samos sat up, his crinkled face waxy and pale. He swung his legs over the side of the storage crate in the aisle, and winced as he tested his weight on his broken ankle. He began gripping the backs of chairs to use them as crutches.

"Let me help you," Aria said. She squeezed in beside him and wrapped his arm over her shoulders to help him down the aisle.

"Thank you," he breathed as they hobbled along together.

"Come on old man," Markus said. "Pick up the pace."

Aria's gaze snapped up from watching their feet. "He can't! But if you're in such a damn hurry, you could help him."

"Yeah? So you can take advantage of my inattention and steal this?" Markus patted his rifle and shook his head. "I don't think so."

Aria frowned. Supposedly Varik had forced them all to go see these alien overlords together for their own good. So why did it feel like they were his hostages and he was delivering them to his masters like chattel?

Something was very wrong here.

Aria watched Markus and Elisa the entire way to the exit, looking for exactly what Markus had indicated: a moment of inattention.

But that moment never came. Markus remained wide-eyed and vigilant. His *consort*, likewise. And the closest they ever came to each other was two feet. Two guns tracked them independently as they eased down a set of three steps to the ground. A third weapon aimed up at them from outside. Varik waited just beyond the open door with his stun pistol at the ready.

Aria helped Samos down, and they emerged between two of the rover's eight over-sized wheels. Payton jumped down behind them. The top of each wheel rose several inches over her head, and she was tall for her age at four foot one.

Aria turned a glare on Varik. "So where is this depot?"

Varik pointed to a shadowy rock face some twenty feet away. The rover's headlights were barely enough to illuminate it through the murk, but Aria did notice something out of place—a square doorway carved into the base of the rocks.

"It's inside the mountain?" Aria asked.

"That's right," Varik replied.

Mattias and Asha climbed down behind Aria, brushing her gently aside. Varik backed up to make room and to keep all of them covered with his weapon. He waved the barrel toward the doors in the base of the mountain. "We'd better move. The longer we're out here, the more likely something comes along and eats us before we can get inside."

Aria shuffled forward with Payton, reluctantly taking the lead. Boots hit dirt with tandem *thumps*, and Aria glanced over her shoulder to see that it was Markus and Elisa. They took up positions flanking Varik. Samos was leaning against one of the rover's wheels. She wondered if she should go back and help him, but Mattias and Asha each wrapped one of Samos's arms over their shoulders, and the three of them began hobbling along together.

Aria started forward again. She wished Liam would hurry up. How long had it been since she'd asked him to come rescue her? An hour? Two?

"You gave my husband *these* coordinates? Or the coordinates to the clearing where we landed?" Aria asked, suddenly worried that it had been a trick.

"These coordinates," Varik replied. "They can figure out where to land for themselves."

But that didn't ease her worries. Ice trickled through her veins. If getting Liam and Buck here was part of Varik's plan, then maybe it would be better if they didn't come. This had to be a trap. Aria tried to place a silent comms call to her husband, but he was out of range. Hopefully she'd be able to contact him and warn him before he got this far. Then again, maybe he and Buck would be expecting a trap. Maybe they'd come prepared.

Aria came within five feet of the doors to the alien facility and stopped, peering up at them and chewing her lower lip nervously.

"Now what?" Mattias prompted. "You have the code or something? I don't see a control panel."

"Now, we wait," Varik said.

"For how long?" Aria asked.

"Not long."

A faint crimson gleam caught Aria's eyes, drawing her gaze up to a point some four feet above the doors—a rocky overhang. In the shadows of that jutting piece of rock was a glossy black eye with a faint crimson pupil. A camera. Someone, or some*thing*, was watching them.

The doors began rumbling open.

"See?" Varik said.

Aria peered into the ever-widening gap, but it was even darker inside the depot than it was out in the forest.

"What's in there?" Aria asked.

"Get in and you'll find out," Varik replied.

"No way," Mattias said. "For all we know there's a bottomless pit on the other side of those doors. Why don't *you* go first?"

"Because I don't trust you enough to have you at my back," Varik said. "And because I have the guns. Now get in. We're wasting time."

"Or else what? You'll stun me again and drag me in?"

"Would you prefer that?" Varik asked.

Silence answered him.

"*I'll* go first," Aria said. "Stay here, Payton."
She took a step toward the open doors.

"No!" Payton grabbed her arm and hauled back on it with all her strength.

"Payton! Let go of me, please."

She shook her head emphatically.

Varik sighed. "You have three seconds before I start stunning people."

"I'm just going to have a look," Aria insisted, still speaking to Payton. "I'll be okay."

"No," Payton said again, in a shrinking voice.

"One—" Varik began.

Aria snapped a glare at him. "I'm going!"

"Two," he replied.

She yanked her arm free of Payton's grasp and turned toward the open doors. They were fully-open now, but it was pitch black inside. Aria pressed forward, blinking furiously and squinting in an attempt to get her eyes to adjust to the gloom, but the darkness was absolute.

"You remember this?" Aria asked as she reached the threshold. Cold air drifted out, laced with sharp chemical smells. Aseptic.

"I don't remember anything, remember?" Varik chided. But his voice held a note of grim amusement that put Aria on edge as if he were finally admitting that that was a lie.

"I can't see anything from here. I'm going to have to go in," Aria said.

"Mom, *no!*"

"I have a better idea," Varik said. "Why don't you all go in before I *really* lose my patience."

"Fuck you," Mattias said.

Varik rounded on him with a snarl, his pistol held out at arm's length.

"Don't," Asha put in and stepped in front of her husband.

Varik hesitated.

A sharp warble drew all of their attention to the darkness on the other side of the doors. A shadow appeared, walking toward them, and two bright points of light blazed to life—eyes gleaming in the dark. A second shadow joined the first, and two more eyes.

Aria worked some moisture into her mouth. "Hello?" she called out in a trembling voice. "Is someone there?"

Another warble. Followed by a voice—a human, female voice: "Is it really you?"

"Calla?" Varik replied.

Aria blinked in shock, backpedaling as two bipedal figures gradually emerged from the shadows: one, a human woman with long dark hair, wearing an air filter mask over her mouth and nose—the other a bipedal alien in a suit of matte black armor.

CHAPTER 37

The alien looked similar to a Vitari, but far from the same. It stood upright rather than hunched, and it had to be at least seven feet tall instead of just two or three. It had broad shoulders, a thick chest, and muscular arms and legs—a far cry from the small, furry, winged creatures that she knew. It was covered in colorful fur like a Vitari, but bristly and much less vibrant: in this case, a dark pewter that peeked between the joints in its suit of armor.

Just then, a pair of bony, hairless white arms flared out behind the creature's back where a Vitari's wings would have been.

Aria blinked in shock. *It has* four *arms?* she wondered. The creature raised one of the bony limbs vertically in front of it—a Vitari greeting—and then warbled something that she recognized from their language. It translated roughly to: *I am friend.*

An audible, vaguely human version of that followed from a pair of vertical speaker grilles set in the alien's chest plate. The alien had to have some kind of translator integrated into its armor.

Aria slowly shook her head, unable to make sense of what was happening. She looked to the human woman and raised her eyebrows in question. Someone brushed past her in a blur. It was Varik. He ran straight up to the young woman and folded her into a crushing hug, lifting her off the ground and spinning her around.

"I've waited so long to see you again, Calla!" Varik said, his voice muffled by the woman's long, dark hair. "You have no idea how much I've missed you!"

A long-lost lover? Aria wondered. *So much for having amnesia.*

The woman looked uncomfortable. Her eyes darted around, taking in Aria and the others. "I missed you, too, Dad...."

"*Dad!* She's your *daughter?*" Aria blurted.

Calla's gaze found hers. The woman's eyes were the same vibrant shade of blue as Varik's and Markus's.

Varik put her down and turned to Aria from the entrance of the facility. "That's right."

"How?" Aria asked.

"I thought you couldn't remember anything from your time here..." Mattias said.

"I couldn't. Not at first. The memories only came back later—after the media storm surrounding my return had fully cooled, and people lost interest in my story."

"Well isn't that convenient," Mattias said.

"You wouldn't say that if you knew *why* I was made to forget," Varik replied.

Mattias's gaze flicked to the alien standing beside Varik. "So tell us."

Aria backed away from the entrance of the depot until she was standing beside Payton once more. A tiny hand darted into hers, and they both held on tight.

"What is he?" Aria asked, her eyes on the alien.

"How do you know it's a he?" Mattias said.

"The color of its fur. Blue, green, and black are exclusive to Vitari males. Red, yellow, and brown are female."

"That *thing* is a *Vitari?*" Mattias exclaimed.

"Or a genetic relative of theirs." Aria looked to Calla for confirmation.

"A third life cycle, actually," she said.

"They have *three?*"

"No, they have four. When they reach about sixty Earth years old, they metamorphose for a third time, and at about a hundred and twenty, they do it for a fourth and final time."

"Wha..." Words failed her. But it made sense that she didn't know about those extra life cycles. Varik had only returned to Earth thirty years ago, not enough time for any of his Vitari livestock to reach sixty, let alone a hundred and twenty.

Aria looked to Varik. "What is all of this about?"

"Come inside, and I'll explain everything," Varik said.

"How about you explain now," Mattias said.

"I agree," Samos croaked, leaning heavily on Asha. Quiet as usual, she simply bobbed her head.

The Vitari warbled once more. The translation came a moment later: *"Is she the one we've been waiting for?"* Aria noticed that his eyes were on her as he said that.

Calla looked to the alien and nodded quickly. "Yes, she is." Looking back to Aria, she said, "You'd better come inside. Kratok is getting impatient."

Fear and confusion made Aria's head spin. "You've been waiting for *me?* What for?"

"You haven't figured it out?" Varik asked. "They're harvesting their own children for vitalics and your research team is the only one out of countless thousands spread across two galaxies that have even come close to creating a synthetic version."

"Wait, wait, wait." Aria pressed a hand to her forehead, struggling to catch up with the implications of what he'd just said. "So you admit it now? You're the one who brought us here?"

"Who do you think subsidized your vacation?"

Aria's jaw dropped as that piece fell into place. Suddenly the impossibly good deal her husband had found for their vacation made perfect sense.

"*She's* the reason we're here?" Mattias roared.

"Yes."

"People died! *Innocent* people! If this was all about her and whatever research she's been conducting, then why not just abduct *her*. Why drag all of us into it?"

Calla's face paled. "People died? How... how many?"

"The harvesters attacked our ship when we arrived," Varik explained.

"Oh, no..." Calla looked to Kratok. "Why would you attack his ship?"

The Vitari trilled and warbled at length. Aria waited for the translation.

"*A war fleet preceded your arrival. The harvesters were there to defend us from a subsequent attack. We called them off and returned them to their original programming as soon as we realized our mistake. Unfortunately, they continued attacking because everyone on the ship was tainted with our blood.*"

— 303 —

Calla's expression changed from confused to shocked as she stared at Varik. "You've been harvesting them?"

"How do you think I've stayed so young?"

"I thought maybe you were using vitalics on *yourself*. I never imagined that you were mass-producing them for commercial use."

"I had to raise money for the research somehow," Varik said.

Calla shook her head.

"Why should they care if *I* exploited them? They exploit themselves! Besides, they sent me back with eggs for a reason."

The Vitari trilled quietly. *"We have the right to exploit. You do not. Your assignment was clear."* The alien unfolded one of the bone-white arms on its back to brush Varik's cheek with three long fingers. Sharp claws drew thin lines of blood.

Varik stood his ground, but the intensity of the Vitari's gaze sent a chill down Aria's spine.

Calla stepped between them. "Well, his methods obviously worked."

The Vitari looked at her with those blazing green eyes, and then away. It rocked its head from side to side and warbled something else.

"The deaths of your researchers were unfortunate. If we had known to expect you, we would have withdrawn the harvesters from the gate before you arrived."

"You *weren't* expecting us?" Aria asked. That seemed to fly in the face of everything that she'd witnessed in the last ten minutes.

"They were, but you're early," Calla explained.

Varik shook his head. "My handler wasn't due to return for another three years. I couldn't wait that long to see my daughter again. It's already been thirty years!"

Someone snorted, and Aria noticed Markus shaking his head and scowling. She wondered what his problem was, and then abruptly, she understood. He was the son who'd grown up without a father, a father who'd recently threatened to stun him if he didn't toe the line. And here that same father was desperate to see his daughter, and showing her all of the dedication and love that Markus had never received.

"At the risk of repeating myself, why are *we* here?" Mattias asked. He looked to the Vitari. "Send us home. You did it with Varik, right?"

Calla's blue eyes flew wide, and she gave her head an imperceptible shake.

But Mattias missed it and barreled on blithely, "We can't help you with your research. We'd just be a burden."

"Please," Asha added. "We just want to go home."

Kratok cocked his head and trilled a question. *"Why are you here if you cannot help?"*

Mattias blew out a breath. "That's what I'm saying!" He looked the Vitari in the eyes again. "We can't help you. I wish we could, but we don't know the first thing about—"

A flash of light dazzled Aria's eyes and suddenly the Vitari was gone. Calla screamed and Varik looked away grimacing.

Aria heard something squelch, then gurgle behind her. She slowly turned to see that the Vitari was now standing in front of Mattias and Asha. Markus and Elisa were backing away, their faces twisted with revulsion. Samos lay on the ground beside Asha, sobbing into the dirt. He'd fallen over, possibly in his hurry to get away from the alien.

Aria couldn't see past the Vitari's broad back, but she could hear just fine—another gurgle, followed by a wet sucking sound. A horrible sinking feeling overcame her.

"What is he doing, Mommy?"

Remembering that her daughter was there, Aria clapped both hands over Payton's eyes. "Don't look."

Just in time.

The Vitari turned to face them with both of the bony white arms on its back drenched in blood all the way up to the first of two elbows. Both hands and sets of three fingers were wrapped around glistening red lumps of flesh. Mattias and Asha crumpled and fell at Kratok's feet, their faces frozen in horror and agony, their chests gaping open where their hearts should have been. Kratok dropped their hearts on the ground with a sickening *plop,* and then looked to Samos and warbled something else. *"Is he also useless?"*

Calla ran over to the alien, and grabbed one of its other two arms, the thick muscular ones that dangled beside its torso. She shook her head. "No. We need him."

"He's part of my research team," Aria added, somehow finding her voice even though her mouth was sandpaper-dry. The Vitari looked at her, green eyes widening as it cocked its head back and forth. "Everyone from the ship is part of my research team," she added.

The Vitari tossed its head a few times, and made a trilling sound, baring a set of sharp, triangular white teeth as it did so. It brushed by her, back through the doors into darkness.

That trilling sound echoed back to Aria's ears as the creature went inside, but no translation followed. She looked to Calla in confusion. "What did he say?"

"Nothing. He's laughing."

"Laughing?"

"He *knows* you were lying," Calla whispered. "He can read your mind."

"He can *what?*"

Payton wriggled free of her grasp and peeked around her hands. She sucked in a quick breath at the sight of Mattias and Asha lying face down on the ground. "Are they dead?"

Aria didn't know what to say, so she pretended that she hadn't heard. Her eyes still on Calla, she whispered, "You lied, too. About Samos."

"I know how to get away with it. You don't."

More trilling echoed out of the darkness.

"We have to go." Calla grabbed her arm and tugged her toward the open doors of the facility. "Please. The faster you show us your research, the faster we can all go home."

Aria allowed herself to be dragged, then remembered Samos. "He needs help," Aria said, nodding to him.

Even as she said that Markus walked over. Leaving his rifle to dangle by its shoulder strap, he hauled the old man up by his arm. Samos was still shaking with sobs.

"It killed them!"

"Yeah. Better watch what you say, unless you want to be next," Markus replied.

Payton looked up at Aria with big eyes, then to the dark, featureless void that they were headed into.

"What's in there, Mommy?"

"I don't know," Aria said.

"I don't want to go," Payton said. "It's dark."

"Don't worry," Calla put in. "The lights will come on as soon as we shut the doors. We keep them off because they attract animals."

Aria glanced over her shoulder at the hazy white bloom of the rover's headlights, barely enough to illuminate the ground they were walking on. "If that's the case, we should go back and turn those lights off." Aria began tugging back the other way, resisting Calla's grip. She had an ulterior motive besides turning off the headlights.

"There's no time," Calla said and tugged harder.

The headlights disappeared, and everything plunged into a featureless gray haze. "Done. Remote access," Varik explained.

Aria's heart sank. She'd been hoping to make a run for it.

They crossed the threshold into the mountain, and even the swirling grays of the mist disappeared as complete and utter darkness swallowed every drop of light.

CHAPTER 38

"We're getting close to the coordinates," Buck said, his voice hoarse from all the yelling he'd done.

"Can you check the comms?" Liam asked.

"Why?"

"To see if there are any messages from the cruise ship. I want to know if Niko is okay."

"Sure."

Liam waited in anxious silence, torn between fear for his son and fear for his wife and daughter. Everything was spiraling out of his control. He sucked in a sour breath and held it, distracting himself with the view. A wavy carpet of treetops scrolled by beneath the lifeboat, gilded in the light of the giant planet that Vitaria orbited. It was almost fully risen now, a massive yellow, white, and brown orb that was bright enough to blot out any hint of stars.

"No messages from the *Dream*. No answer either," Buck said.

That hit Liam like a bucket of ice water. He let out the breath he was holding in a rush. "What do you mean there's no answer?"

"I mean, I'm hailing them, but they're not replying."

A dozen worst-case scenarios flashed through Liam's head in an instant. "Maybe there's something wrong with our comms."

"Nope. Not that. And I'm not getting an answering ping from the *Dream*. That could mean one of two things. Either their comms are offline, or we're out of range. My bet is on the latter. We're on the dark side of the planet right now."

"So?" Liam prompted.

"So, from the *Dream's* perspective, the day-side of Vitaria is facing it. The planet has rotated away since then, which means we no longer have a line of sight with them. Technically we're in range, but there's a whole planet in the way of our signals."

"So they're probably fine."

"Yeah."

"How do we reach them?"

"Wait for daybreak or launch a comm beacon into orbit."

"A beacon?"

"Like a satellite. We can use it to relay signals around the planet."

"Do it."

"Hang on..." A loud *clunk* sounded, followed by a hissing roar somewhere above their heads. Liam looked up but saw nothing through the ceiling.

"Did it work?"

"It's not instant."

"I meant—"

"Give it a few minutes."

"Sure..." Liam began tapping his foot impatiently.

Buck glared over his shoulder. "Stop that." His eyes were still red from crying. His wife's body lay on the couch behind them. Her skin red and crusted with blood, magenta eyes staring at the ceiling, hands curled into fists. She'd died fighting.

Sometime later, the trees fell away, and a sparkling lake appeared. Jutting crystals gleamed in the golden night. Mountains rose in the distance, painting a dark, jagged line against the horizon.

They flew across the lake, aiming for a field on the other side. Liam glimpsed another Lifeboat already landed there. "Is that..."

"Varik's? Looks like it," Buck said as he set them down in the field beside the other lifeboat. Liam's heart beat hard against his sternum, excitement and anxiety whipping his blood into a frenzy at the thought of seeing Aria and Payton again.

"Are they still on board?" Liam asked.

"No life signs."

"But Varik said—"

"Fuck Varik." Buck swiveled the pilot's chair around, his yellow eyes narrowed to angry slits. "We can't trust him. For all we know, he's leading us to our deaths just like one of his Vitari herds."

"But where did they go?"

"The coordinates he sent are farther on—through the trees." Buck swiveled halfway back to the front and pointed out the windows. "We'll have to take the rover."

"What rover?"

"You'll see." The former Marine unbuckled and stood up. His gaze found his wife's face, lingered, and drifted out of focus.

Liam grimaced, then glanced over his shoulder to the bedroom. "I could put a sheet over her..."

"No!" Buck thundered, and Liam flinched. "No," he said again, more quietly this time. He dragged his eyes away. "Come."

They walked through the living room to the airlock.

"Wait, what about the comm beacon you sent up?" Liam asked.

Buck's stride faltered, and he hesitated.

"Can you try again to contact Niko before we go?"

Buck frowned.

"Please."

"Give me a second."

Liam waited, watching as a remote ARL interface flickered over Buck's yellow eyes.

"I'm getting a ping now. We've made contact."

Liam's heart soared. "And? What did they say?"

"No, I mean we've made contact with the *Dream*. There's still no one answering."

"But that doesn't make any sense! I told him to stay in the armory!"

Buck sighed, his hands flexing restlessly on the grip and handguard of his rifle. "And I'm sure he did. They're probably not monitoring the comms. Remember the bridge is wiped out. Your bot has full systems access, but that doesn't mean he's actively checking them."

"So you're saying the phone is ringing, but no one is around to hear it?"

Buck shrugged. "Something like that. Are you coming with me or staying here?"

Liam considered that. He couldn't do anything from here, and Nikolai was probably fine. The harvesters couldn't get to him in the armory. Aria and Payton, on the other hand... Aria had called him for help. He couldn't leave her at Varik's mercy—not to mention the mercy of whatever aliens he was taking them to meet.

"Let's go."

Buck waved the airlock doors, and they stepped over the pile of dead bodies piled inside. "Whatever happens, you leave Varik to me, got it?"

Liam didn't agree with Buck's plans for revenge, but he didn't want to argue with an angry, armed mercenary, so he nodded along and said, "Got it."

"Good."

* * *

"Try calling them again," Nikolai said.

"I left a message, remember?" Jules replied. "They'll get back to us when they can."

"Well, then leave another," Nikolai insisted. "They need to know what we saw."

"Very well..." Jules replied.

Several minutes passed, but the bot still hadn't said anything.

"Well?"

"I'm sorry. They're still not answering, Master Nikolai."

His heart sank. "Well, it was worth a try."

"Yes. I'll leave another message for them."

"Do you think..." Nikolai trailed off.

Jules cocked his head to one side.

"What if something happened to them?"

The bot flashed a sympathetic smile. "Buck knows how to take care of himself."

"Yeah, but what about my dad?"

"I'm sure he'll keep your father safe, too."

"Then why aren't they answering? They should have gotten our message by now."

"They might be away from the lifeboat, exploring on foot."

"What if we sent a probe?"

"A probe?" Jules asked.

"Yeah, like the one you used to explore the nebula. We could send another one down to the planet. Buzz around them and see what's up. Maybe we could use it to get their attention somehow."

"Perhaps..." Jules said slowly.

"So? Let's do it!"

"It will take some time to configure and lay in a course."

"How long?"

"An hour. Maybe more."

"Better than nothing!"

"Of course. I'll get started right away."

Nikolai grabbed a bottle of water beside him, took a sip, and then tucked into a half-finished hamburger MRE—one of many that Jules had gone out to get for him a few hours ago. As he thought about that, Nikolai stopped eating and looked at Jules. "Thanks for hanging around here with me."

"It is my duty to serve the passengers of this ship, Master Nikolai."

"You mean you can't decide what to do for yourself?"

"Robotic assistants have some degree of autonomy, but no, we cannot completely stray from our directives."

"Oh. Well, thanks anyway."

"You are welcome."

CHAPTER 39

Aria's heart leapt as the doors shut behind them with an echoing *boom*. Bright lights switched on, and the darkness fled to reveal that they were standing in a short corridor with scuffed gray walls. Metal grating rattled underfoot. A chime sounded, the lights dimmed, and then an acrid mist blasted them from all sides. It stung Aria's eyes and exposed skin.

"Owww!" Payton complained.

Before Aria could say anything about it, the spray vanished, replaced by a blast of choking heat. Their clothes and skin dried in seconds, and a second set of doors parted in front of them, revealing a vast underground chamber filled with dozens of large, bulky vehicles.

Cargo ships? Aria wondered. The familiar spiky, shimmering shapes of harvesters darted between them. Periodic flashes of light accompanied the harvesters as they teleported in and out.

"You can take your masks off now," Calla said. "The air is safe to breathe in here." She turned around, and Aria saw that her mask was dangling from her neck. Calla offered a brittle smile that was probably meant to be reassuring.

Aria took her mask off and sucked in an experimental breath. No ill effects. She took off Payton's mask next.

Kratok waved a bone-white hand over his shoulder, indicating that they should follow him. Calla went first. Varik, Markus, and Elisa tagged along, all three holding their weapons at the ready. Aria was surprised that the Vitari had allowed them to keep the weapons. Was it because they were trusted allies? Or because resistance was futile?

They crossed the threshold of the inner doors and into the hangar. A buzz of activity reached their ears: the metallic rumble of harvesters rolling across the floor, pneumatic hissing as containers in the sides of transports opened and shut with folding doors. Crackling flashes of light as the harvesters came and went.

It was some kind of a depot, just as Varik had said.

Aria looked away and saw Kratok heading for a door on the left side of the hangar. Markus helped Samos hobble along, while Varik and Calla followed the alien more closely. Elisa hung back with Aria and Payton.

"You knew about all of this?" Aria asked the other woman.

"Yes."

Aria glared at her.

"You don't understand. Varik had no choice."

"And what about you?"

"I came because Markus did."

"So, you're just the dog attached to his leash?"

"It's not like that."

"Then what *is* it like?"

"I can't—"

"Elisa!" Markus boomed. "Get over here, *now.*"

Elisa shot a worried look at the rest of their party, busy walking on without them, now twenty feet away. "We'd better catch up. The Vitari aren't known for their patience."

Elisa left at a brisk pace, leaving Aria to wonder what she had been about to say. What was the nature of her relationship with Markus? What did he have over her, and why had she come if she'd known what she was getting into?

Aria ran to catch up, pulling Payton along by her hand. The door in the side of the hangar opened before the Vitari even reached it, and a long, transparent catwalk appeared, gleaming like a sheet of ice high above some type of blue and purple vegetation. *An indoor garden?*

Aria reached the catwalk and started across it with the others. Her head spun with vertigo as she looked down and saw the *garden* for what it really was: a vast indoor forest. Bald patches revealed lumpy structures clinging to black tree branches. Colorful avian Vitari perched around them. Others flitted about, colorful specks darting between the treetops.

The catwalk shivered as they went. It crossed at least two kilometers, supported by unseen means. The railings were made of the same transparent material, and no seams disrupted their view. They were walking on air.

"Wow..." Payton said. "This must be what it's like to be a bird."

Aria just nodded, amazed that her daughter could still experience wonder in spite of their circumstances. *The resilience of a child...*

Dead ahead, on the other side of the catwalk, a wall of windows soared, some illuminated, others dark. Thousands of them. It was the unbroken wall of an artificial trench with an alien jungle in the middle. Glancing back the way they'd come, she noticed much the same thing on the other side. The trench walls soared at least thirty floors above the tree canopy. Her mind boggled at the sheer scale of the complex. *How many researchers are working down here?* she wondered. The forest stretched away endlessly to both sides, and the trees rose to greet a dark turquoise sky at either end—artificial, of course, but all the more impressive for it. To the right, more transparent catwalks shimmered like strands of gossamer, jutting crystals gleamed blue, yellow, and green and a fiery red sun peeked over the trees, just now setting. Directly above, scudding clouds shone cobalt and crimson in the fading light. It was a self-contained biome, cut off from the rest of the planet—possibly to protect the Vitari from their predators. Here their only predators were the beings peering down on them from their skyscraper walls.

Aria wondered who they were about to meet on the other side. More stage three Vitari? Or maybe even stage fours. She still couldn't believe that they had *four* life cycles. What would a stage four Vitari even look like? She couldn't begin to guess.

Everyone walked in silence, either in shock or in fear of what they were walking toward. Varik and Calla had obviously already seen all of this before, but flickers of awe registered on Markus's and Elisa's faces.

Several minutes later they came to another door at the end of the catwalk. It slid open, and they emerged inside of a large room filled with rows of tables. People in white tunics sat at those tables, spooning colorful foods from trays. They were all humans of varying ages—men, women, and even a few children. *How long have these people been here?* Aria wondered. Varik's story came to mind. He'd spent twenty-nine years here, and evidently, he'd had a daughter with one of the other captives.

Eyes converged on Aria's group from all sides.

Kratok turned to them and warbled at length. The translation followed: *"Eat. When you are done, the director will take you to your rooms, and you may rest. Tomorrow you work and share your progress."* Kratok nodded to Calla and then swept by them, back the way they'd come.

Aria saw people lining up with trays along the far wall. Dispensers oozed different colored pastes onto their plates. Her gaze darted around the dining hall, and she realized that the food was *all* like that—different colors of mush, like someone had simply added various food colorings to mashed potatoes and called it a day. A whiff of something appetizing reached her nose, and her stomach grumbled painfully.

Maybe it would taste better than it looked.

"Let's go," Varik said, and led the way to the food dispensers.

Aria looked around for Kratok and glimpsed him striding back down the catwalk. The door slid shut behind him with an ominous *thud,* and she wondered if there was any way to open it, or if they were now locked inside this place. Prisoners of the Vitari.

A chime sounded, and the message icon at the top of Aria's field of view began blinking. She focused on it, and a line of text appeared at the bottom of her ARLs:

New message from Liam.

Read message, Aria thought.

It popped up, unobtrusively at the bottom of her field of view.

Aria, it's Liam. We found your rover. And two dead bodies. Are you okay? What happened? There's a door of some kind in the base of the cliffs. Our scanners say you're somewhere inside the mountain. Did you go through the door? Should we try to get in?

CHAPTER 40

Aria shuffled into line behind the others. She pretended to be distracted by their surroundings as she mentally composed a text-based reply to Liam via her Neuralink. She couldn't be sure how much of what she said next could be intercepted and monitored, or if it would even matter now that Liam had announced his location in his own message. Hopefully the Vitari wouldn't be able to decrypt their comms.

Don't come in. We're fine, but I think we're prisoners here. It's the Vitari, Liam. Varik was working for them all along. They have two life cycles we never even knew about, and they're smarter and stronger than anyone could have guessed. They're harvesting vitalics from their own people, and the reason we're here is because they want my research. The facility inside the mountain is some kind of lab. I'm supposed to share my data with them tomorrow.

Stay close, but don't let them find you. Varik says they'll send us home if we succeed in creating synthetic vitalics, but that could take weeks... or months. I hope you can last until then.

Don't reply. They understand our language, and I don't know if they can also hack our comms.

Aria sent the message. No reply came, but she took that as a good sign.

Markus came over with a stack of trays and passed them around. They had compartments for food, so there was no need for plates. The line shuffled forward. Aria got one serving of each color of mush for herself and Payton. The dispensers seemed to be motion activated. She grabbed a pair of over-sized spoons at the end of the line, filled opaque white cups from a row of water dispensers and placed them on their trays.

"It doesn't look very tasty," Payton said as Aria passed one of the trays to her.

"No, but it smells good, doesn't it?"

Payton's head bobbed agreeably. "Yeah."

"It probably tastes just as good as it smells," Aria added.

They followed Varik to one of the many available tables. The dining hall could have easily seated two hundred, but only about thirty people were present. Aria wondered about that as she slid into an empty seat with Payton. Maybe this wasn't an actual meal time, or maybe there used to be a lot more people here. Her mind flashed back to the way Kratok had brutally killed Mattias and Asha once he realized that they wouldn't be useful to him. She shuddered and pushed those thoughts aside.

Staring at the colors of mush in the different sections of her tray, Aria used her spoon to test the yellow one. It tasted sweet and savory, almost like corn.

"Not bad," Markus said, trying a spoonful of red mush. "Tastes like spaghetti."

Aria dug in with more enthusiasm and encouraged her daughter to do the same. Payton tried some of the white mush and made an appreciative sound. "It tastes like vanilla pudding!"

"See?"

Aria tried that one next. Payton was right. The texture could have been better, but the flavors were okay.

Her reservations mostly settled, Aria dug in enthusiastically, barely taking a break for air. It had been too long since she'd eaten. When nothing but colorful smears remained on her tray, she looked up and sighed. Samos sat opposite her, his head down, slowly spooning mush into his mouth. The others were also still eating, occasionally looking up from their plates to trade glances, but no one talked. It was as if they had already been briefed and had all of the answers that they needed.

Good for them, Aria thought. She still had plenty of questions. "Who are all of these people?" she asked, her eyes settling on Varik.

He looked at her. "Researchers. I thought we explained that already."

"Fine, but where did they come from? How did they get here? You said your expedition left, and you were the only one to go inside one of the depots."

"These people were already here when I arrived. Some of them, anyway." He nodded to his daughter. She smiled tightly back. "Others, like Calla, were born afterward."

"Okay, so the ones who were already here, how did they end up here?"

"How many people in a given year do you think disappear in the Union, never to be heard from again?"

"I don't know..." Aria trailed off. "A hundred?"

Varik shook his head. "Try thousands. There's always a good excuse—organized crime, the Guild, human trafficking, jealous lovers, suspected homicides... even wild animals in the colonies get blamed. If you were one of the ones taken, magically teleported away when nobody was looking, what reasons do you think your loved ones and the authorities would invent for your disappearance? They did it with me all those years ago. I was one of the crew aboard a gate layer ship that went through an uncharted wormhole and never came home."

"But you did go home," Aria said.

"The Vitari *sent* me home because I made a deal with them."

Aria glanced at his daughter. "You obviously had people you cared about here. A daughter... a wife? You were willing to leave them behind?"

Varik winced. She'd struck a nerve.

Calla answered. "They killed my mom because her research team failed one too many times."

Aria's mouth ran dry. "That's what happens here? They kill people for failure?"

"Among other reasons," Varik replied. "Trying to escape is another."

"So that's when you made your deal to go home—after your wife died?"

"We weren't married, but yes. I'd planned to take Calla with me, but they wouldn't let me. They said if we both left, we might just run away and hide, and then I'd never keep my end of the bargain." Varik smirked. "As if it's possible to hide from the Vitari."

"What deal did you make?" Aria asked.

"You don't know? I thought you would have figured that out by now."

"For argument's sake, let's say I haven't," Aria replied.

"I told them that I could get the results they were looking for, but only if they sent me home. I needed to be able to draw on all of humanity, not just a randomly selected subset. I convinced them to send me back so that I could put together a team of people who weren't working with an ax over their heads, people motivated by greed, or even more noble goals like your own. And I was right. It worked."

Aria frowned. "My research isn't complete."

Calla looked to Varik suddenly, alarm registering in her blue eyes. "She's not finished?"

Aria smiled thinly. "Your father didn't tell you?"

Calla glanced at her, then back to Varik. "What were you thinking? You came here early, brought a whole cruise ship full of innocent people with you, and for what? If her research turns out to be a dead end, they'll kill us all."

"Relax," Varik said with a dismissive wave. "She's close enough."

"We've been *close* before!" Calla rose halfway out of her chair, hands planted on the table. "Mom was close!"

Aria noticed people watching them from the other tables, no longer minding their own business. She wondered why they hadn't greeted Varik upon his return. Didn't they remember him? Or were these people all children who'd grown up *after* he'd left? Even so, they should have been more interested in the arrival of a group of strangers. Unless strangers coming in was a daily affair... Varik's words came back to her: *how many people disappear, never to be heard from again...?*

"Sit down, Calla," Varik said.

She shook her head. "No. Tell me you have a plan. Tell me you didn't come here just to get all of us killed."

"*She* is my plan." Varik pointed to Aria. "She will succeed, and when she does, we're all going home."

Aria felt a heavy weight settle on her shoulders. Everything was riding on her. "How do you even know that I have my research with me?" she asked.

"It's in a DNA drive in your left foot. A red pinprick trapped beneath the skin that anyone else would just assume is a broken blood vessel."

"How do you know that?"

"I have my sources."

"Fine, but it might not be enough. That research is the work of a brilliant *team,* not just me.

What made you think I could finish it on my own?"

"Don't worry, you'll find the people here are all equally as brilliant as your colleagues back home." He looked at Calla. "Some of them even more so."

Payton looked up from pushing green mush around on her tray. "Can I ask something?"

Varik nodded. "Of course."

"Why bring all of us here if all you needed was my mommy's research?"

"You never answered that question," Calla added before Varik could reply. "Why *did* you bring so many people with you?"

Varik grimaced. "I'm truly sorry for that. If I'd felt there was any other way..."

"There was," Aria said. "You're the wealthiest man alive. You could have abducted me and hired a ship to take us here. Or you could have taken one of your own ships. Either way, you'd be risking only two lives instead of thousands."

Varik's expression went from resolute to confused. His brow furrowed and eyes drifted out of focus as if he were genuinely baffled by his own behavior.

That transformation gave Aria pause, and suddenly she wondered if Varik was all right in the head.

"Well?" Aria prompted.

"I..."

"Dad?" Calla asked.

But he was gone, staring into empty space and lost in thought. Markus and Elisa wore similar, distant looks on their faces.

Aria frowned. "What's wrong with them?"

Samos looked up from his tray, his bushy eyebrows raised.

Calla snapped her fingers in front of Varik's face. "Hey! Dad! Are you there?"

He started, and his eyes focused, a confident smile wiping away the confusion. "I'm sorry. What were we talking about? I seem to have had a senior moment."

Calla's expression darkened. "A senior... they were asking you why—"

Samos reached out and laid a hand over Calla's. "Sometimes it's easy to forget your father's age because he doesn't *look* old, but as the saying goes, appearances can be deceiving."

Calla frowned. "It's easy to forget his age because he's *not* old. Not in the senescent sense."

"His cells might not be old, but his mind is. His neural connections are."

"His chronological age is only sixty-five," Calla argued. "Besides, he wasn't the only—"

Samos's grip tightened, his knuckles turning white. "Ow, let me go," Calla said, and yanked her hand away from his.

"Sorry," Samos replied, smiling tightly. "Muscle spasm. I must be dehydrated." He made a show of looking around. "So, if this is a Vitari research facility, then I guess they must be monitoring us from somewhere, right?" He looked back to Calla, and the wrinkles around his rheumy brown eyes cinched them to pointed slits.

"They have people on the upper levels, yes. They're always watching."

"That's what I thought."

A quiet understanding passed between them, but Calla still looked confused. Aria understood just fine: don't say too much, they're listening. But what was he afraid the Vitari might hear if they pressed Varik too hard for answers? And what did Varik's, Markus's, and Elisa's *senior moment* have to do with anything? For the first time, Aria began to wonder who Samos was and why he would take an interstellar cruise all by himself.

"There is something about all of this that I don't get," Aria said, changing the topic. "If the Vitari are so technologically advanced, why don't they develop synthetic vitalics on their own? Why go to the trouble of abducting us to work on the project?"

"They did try—" Calla said. "—are still trying. But all of their biggest breakthroughs have come from other species."

"Other species... as in plural?" Aria looked to Varik, suddenly remembering something that he'd said. "You mentioned that there are thousands of other research teams. Spread across *two* galaxies."

Varik inclined his head to her. "That's right. The Andromeda Galaxy, where we are now, and the Milky Way."

"And there are other aliens here?" Aria's mind boggled at that. Back home, people were still hoping to make *first* contact.

Calla nodded.

"In this facility?"

"Not in this depot, no. But there are hundreds of others just like it, each of them designed to cater to a different species' needs."

Aria tried to imagine making contact with all of those aliens, seeing the sheer variety of life from her own galaxy and the Andromeda. She shook her head incredulously and forced herself to focus. "Back to my question—if the Vitari are more advanced than all of the different species that they've put to work on this project, then they shouldn't need us."

"It's not about technology," Calla explained. "One species might favor certain approaches and blind themselves to others. Each of them brings their own unique biological and technological perspective to the project. It's a shotgun approach that ensures we explore every possible avenue and leave no stone unturned. Meanwhile, the Vitari have taken up residence around this system's black hole to accelerate things further. Time passes more slowly for them due to its gravity, so they don't have to wait as long for results."

Aria wasn't sure she'd heard correctly. "Did you say there's a black hole in this system?"

"Yes."

"They built a Dyson sphere around it," Varik added.

"Why..." The situation much worse than Aria had thought. Even if the Union sent ships looking for them, there was no way anyone could rescue them with harvesters guarding the gate and an alien megastructure lurking nearby. How many Vitari called this corner of the galaxy home? There had to be hundreds of trillions of them in a space station that was large enough to even partially encompass a black hole.

"Why go to the trouble?" Calla suggested, guessing at what Aria had been about to ask.

She nodded.

"Because the stage fours are all dying. They've reached the end of their long lives. Some of them are over ten thousand years old, and synthetic vitalics are supposed to be more effective than the natural ones."

"That's it?" Aria said. "They're just railing against the hands of time like everyone else? I thought maybe it was because they find the thought of harvesting their own children to be reprehensible."

"It's different for them," Calla said. "Each life cycle is like a whole new species, and they're separated from the reproductive life cycle by three stages. They don't raise their kids, or even remember laying the eggs back when they were amphibious stage one's."

"We should go," Varik said, pushing out his chair and standing up with his tray. He nodded to Aria. "You're going to need your sleep to think clearly tomorrow, and we need to impress the Vitari." He looked to Calla. "Director?"

She stood up with her tray as well.

"*You're* the one in charge here?" Aria asked.

She nodded. "I am."

Varik smiled proudly. "Yes, she is."

The rest of them stood up. Samos was last with his broken ankle, forced to wait for Markus to help him up.

"We should get that leg seen to," Calla commented, seeming to notice how much he was struggling with the pain. "A couple doses of vitalics and you'll be back on your feet."

Samos hesitated. "No, thank you."

"Why not?" Aria asked. Her ethical concerns over using vitalics had vanished now that she knew what the Vitari grew into.

Markus smirked. "I thought you objected to using vitalics."

"I did, but when the exploited become the exploiters and the underdogs the tyrants, their sympathizers are made to feel like fools."

Samos shrugged. "I've held out this long, why give in now?"

"So that you can walk?" Calla suggested.

"It'll heal."

"Well, we should at least put a cast on it."

"That, I'll accept," Samos said.

"What about you three?" Aria's gaze flicked between Varik, Markus, and Elisa.

"What about us?" Varik asked.

"Aren't you due for another dose soon?"

"Soon, but not yet," Varik replied.

"And all of the evacuees?" Aria asked. "What about them?"

"Buck already warned them about using vitalics," Varik said.

"I meant, what happens when they start going into withdrawal?"

"They won't die right away. You'll have some time to finish your research before we have to worry about that," Varik said.

Aria was incredulous. "We're *close* to a breakthrough, but that could still mean months of work. Vitalics withdrawals only take a couple weeks to kill a person."

"Then that's your deadline," Varik said.

Aria began to object, but he cut her off with a wave.

"Don't worry. I have faith in you. Calla, would you please lead the way to our quarters?"

"Of course."

They fed their dirty trays, cups, and spoons into a slot in the wall beside the exit. Calla stepped up to the door. It swished open to reveal a long, glossy white corridor lined with doors but no windows. Aria spared a parting glance at the windows of the dining hall and the view beyond— blue and purple treetops now gleaming gold in the artificial twilight. Avian Vitari flitted to and fro. The transparent catwalks crossing the chasm were nearly invisible in the dim light.

But just then an avian Vitari smacked into one of them with a loud *thump* and a flash of light. The creature fell, lifeless and tumbling.

Aria blinked in shock. The stage threes and fours who'd designed this place should have made those bridges more visible. Their sheer disregard for members of their own species shocked her. If that was how the Vitari treated their own, how much less would the lives of other species be worth to them?

CHAPTER 41

"**I** don't like this," Buck said as he stared fixedly out the windshield of the rover. Their headlights pooled on the mist, making the world look like it was stuffed with cotton. "If they're prisoners, what are we waiting around here for? We should bust them out."

"We won't do them any good by getting captured ourselves," Liam replied.

"I'll give you that, but let's say things go bad in there—what are we supposed to do about it? If we don't do anything, our tactical situation will be the same now as later, except that later we might not have time to waste, and right now we do."

"So what do you suggest we do with that time?" Liam asked.

Buck grabbed the rover's steering wheel. "Find another way in. If there is one," he said. He began reversing, backing slowly away from the base of the mountain where they'd found the doors.

"What if there isn't another way in?" Liam asked.

"Then we come back here. We don't lose anything by doing a bit of recon."

Buck drove along the base of the mountains, using a sensor overlay that shaded their surroundings in a blue wire-frame, even through the mist. They drove on in silence for at least ten minutes, sticking close to the cliffs. Then a wall of red came flickering between the trees.

"Shit," Buck muttered. He slammed on the brakes, and the rover skidded to a stop.

Liam recognized the lifeform from its colored silhouette: six legs, two forearms, and a massive triangular head with pincers.

"It's only forty meters away," Liam breathed, noticing the range beside the blip.

"Damn close," Buck agreed.

"How did it get that close without us seeing it?"

"It was probably hiding around the curve of the mountains," Buck said.

The muffled thunder of heavy footsteps pounding the ground rumbled through the rover. The sound competed with the roar of warm air blasting out of the vents inside the rover. Mist swirled under their headlights.

Range to the spider creature dropped to thirty meters. Then twenty-five. Trees branches cracked, footsteps boomed, and the monster appeared dead ahead, standing between two giant trees, and staring right at them.

"It sees us!" Liam said, his voice rising with alarm. "Buck..."

"We should give it some space." He twisted around in his seat, about to start backing up—

The creature didn't charge them. It reared up onto hind legs, then back down—

Boom!

A smaller red blip lay at its feet, struggling to get up—six legs pawing at the sky like a beetle on its back. The spider dipped its head and ended the creature's struggle.

Liam grabbed Buck's arm. "Wait. Kill the lights."

"What?"

"Just do it!"

Buck turned off the headlights, and they watched in silence as a shaded red spider the size of a dinosaur fed on its prey.

"Our rover looks a lot like that beetle thing," Buck said. "No reason to think we won't be next."

"Except we don't smell like food, and if we're not moving, we don't look like it either."

"Yeah, maybe. For now."

"What would you rather do?" Liam asked. "You want to drive away? Then you'll really get its attention."

Buck glared at him. "Maybe I want to get its attention."

Liam stared back at him, trying to get a read on the mercenary. Was he planning to throw his life away the first chance he got? "You have your daughter to think about. And there's Varik. He still needs to be brought to justice—after we find a way home."

Buck snorted and looked away. "Justice would be if Varik had died and Ace had lived. All I have left is revenge."

"You want revenge? Get us out of this and get us home, but leave Varik behind in this hell."

Buck cracked a brittle smile, his eyes glittering in the dark. "That's actually not a bad idea."

CHAPTER 42

Their quarters turned out to be an apartment with enough space for all of them to share. The furnishings were sparse but somewhat familiar. A glossy white table with chairs, and a brown couch in the shape of a U, facing a long wall of windows that looked out over the forest canopy. The treetops gleamed golden in the light of a simulated moon. No, not a moon, Aria realized. It was the giant rocky planet that Vitaria orbited.

Calla led them to an adjacent room with no door and twelve single beds inside. The beds were plain white rectangles sitting on the gray floor, without even the simple luxury of sheets or pillows. Markus helped Samos to lie down on the bed nearest the door. From the way it conformed to his shape, Aria guessed that the beds might at least be comfortable.

"This is where we're sleeping?" Payton asked, her nose wrinkling at the thought as she looked around.

Overhead bars of light ran along exposed metal beams, casting a harsh white light through the sparsely furnished room, while a softer golden glow pooled on the floor by the windows, spilling in from the artificial sky.

"You'll get used to it," Calla said. "There's fresh clothing in the closet." She pointed to an open set of shelves on the wall running beside the door. The 'closet' had nine columns of four square compartments each.

Aria went to check one of them. She withdrew a soft white tunic like the one Calla wore and held it up to her chest. It unfurled almost to her ankles, and the sleeves dangled by her knees. The tunic was long enough to wear by itself even though Calla wore pants under hers. It had obviously been made for someone two or three feet taller than Aria.

"The previous wearer was a Martian," Calla explained. "You can make whatever adjustments you need to tomorrow."

"The previous wearer?" Aria asked, holding the garment up in front of her with a frown. "What happened to him?"

Calla just looked at her.

"Never mind... can't you just print something in my size?" Aria asked.

"We could, but we don't like to waste. For tonight you can just roll up the sleeves."

"I'd rather use it as a blanket," Aria replied.

"That, too."

"I'm sorry to interrupt," Samos said through gritted teeth. "But do you have anything for pain? I'm not sure... if I can sleep like this."

Calla looked at him. "We should actually fix your ankle. I'll call down to medical. They'll send someone up for you soon."

"No vitalics," he insisted.

"We'll just put it in a cast and do something for the pain," Calla assured him.

Samos nodded. "Thank you."

"Where's the bathroom?" Payton asked.

"Right over there." Calla pointed to another open doorway in the wall at the foot of the beds. It was dark inside, which explained how Aria had missed seeing it when she came in.

"No door?" she asked.

Calla shook her head. "The Vitari have no concept of privacy. They can't reproduce beyond their amphibious life cycle, so they have none of our hang-ups about nudity."

Aria looked around. "I guess that explains the communal living situation."

"Yes... I apologize for the change of topic, but my father mentioned the DNA drive you have in your foot. Would you mind if I extracted it tonight so that we can get a head start on things? It will take some time to decrypt the data."

Aria hesitated. "You'll need my help."

Calla acknowledged that with a nod. "We have coffee. Or something like it, anyway."

Aria thought about it. Her whole body ached with exhaustion, but she was just as eager as Calla to get started with the research. The sooner they finished, the sooner everyone could go home— assuming the Vitari could be trusted to hold up their end of the bargain and assuming her research actually panned out. She glanced down at Payton and felt a sharp pang of terror at what might happen if she failed.

Varik cleared his throat. "We've all had a very long day, Calla."

Grateful for the distraction, Aria wondered how long the day had actually been. Ten hours? Fifteen? A quick query to her ARLs revealed that they'd boarded the cruise over nineteen hours ago. They'd gone almost an entire day without a proper night's sleep. And it didn't help that they'd landed in the middle of Vitaria's day, a fact which had thoroughly confused their circadian rhythms.

Calla and Varik stared at one another, and something unspoken passed between them. Calla's brow furrowed as if she were confused. Aria wondered if they were communicating silently over their Neuralinks.

"I guess I *should* let you get some sleep," Calla said slowly.

Varik nodded and took in the others with a sweeping glance. "Tomorrow is soon enough to start the work."

"If you need anything, I'm just down the hall in the apartment next to yours."

"We'll be fine," Varik replied.

Calla spared a glance at Samos. "The medics will come to get you soon."

He nodded but gave no reply. Probably in too much pain to speak. His foot and broken ankle had swollen to twice their usual size.

Calla walked out, and Aria stared after her as she left, wondering why Varik had dismissed her so abruptly. Why didn't he want them to get a head start on her research?

Payton began tugging on her sleeve to get her attention. "Can we put our beds together, too?" She pointed to where Markus and Elisa were doing just that. They'd picked the two beds farthest from the door, and were busy pushing them both up against the room's picture windows, putting as much space between them and the others as possible. Aria shivered at the thought of sleeping next to a hundred-foot drop. Each to their own, she supposed.

"Of course we can, sweetheart," Aria said. "But not next to the windows."

"But I wanted to—"

"No."

CHAPTER 43

Liam stared out the windshield of the rover into the swirling gray mist.

"We should go back to the lifeboat," Buck said.

"Not yet. Aria told me to stay close in case they need us."

"I don't think distance is our problem. We need a plan. Unless you'd like to go back to those doors and knock. Maybe if you ask nicely, they'll let us in rather than rip our hearts out like they did with those other two."

Liam cringed at the reminder. He wondered what had happened to provoke the attack. According to Aria, the aliens were actually Vitari—sort of. They were stage threes. An image of the helpless, puppy-faced bird creatures that Liam knew as Vitari flashed through his mind, and he struggled to reconcile that with something that could rip people's hearts straight out of their chests.

"It's hard to believe the Vitari are in charge of this place," Liam said. "If they're the ones who built the harvesters and sent Varik home, then they must be incredibly advanced."

"This planet is like one big free-range farm for their own kind. Makes your stomach churn, doesn't it?"

"Yes. Very troubling." Liam reclined his chair as far as it would go and folded his hands over his chest, waiting for sleep to come.

Buck stared at him. "Getting comfortable?"

"You have a better idea?"

"Yes, we go back to the lifeboat."

"That spider might still be out there. You really want to risk attracting its attention? We should wait for morning. They're probably nocturnal."

Buck snorted. "The days are only eight hours long on Vitaria. I doubt they go to sleep every four hours."

"How do you know the days are only eight hours?"

"Scan data from the flight down. This moon is spinning fast, and that's to say nothing of its orbit around its planet. When we get around to the dark side of it, we'll see a second night that's much darker than this one."

"How long does Vitaria take to complete an orbit around the planet?"

"Sixteen hours, but last I checked the day side of the planet was fully visible so we might have a whole eight hours before the real night begins. If the creatures here have any kind of circadian rhythms, that's your best bet for what regulates them. Eight-hour cycles between utter darkness and daylight."

"Then this is day-time, and the spiders are diurnal," Liam said. "That means we should wait until the real night falls."

"Except that the spiders live in this forest, and it's almost always dark in here. That means they might not care about day and night."

Liam's eyes pinched to slits. "So what's your point?"

"My point is, this is an alien planet with alien creatures that we know nothing about. For all we know they never sleep."

"Vitari do."

"They micro-sleep for half-hour stretches," Buck replied. "I rest my case. There's no point waiting around here."

"If we leave, we'll lose contact with Aria and the others," Liam said. "Her comms won't reach all the way to the lifeboat."

"So that's what you're afraid of," Buck said.

"She told me to stay close."

"She also said that their research project could take *weeks*. How long do you expect us to wait around here?"

Liam hesitated. *As long as it takes,* he thought, but Buck was right. They needed a real plan, and waiting around here wasn't going to help.

"Fine. Take us back."

Buck nodded and flicked on the headlights. A glossy black rock appeared in front of them.

Then it moved.

A pair of giant eyes blazed to life, gleaming like black pearls in a massive triangular head.

Buck cursed and snapped the lights off. A flickering red overlay appeared belatedly on the windshield, as if the rover's sensors had only just noticed the spider sleeping there.

Liam watched it, waiting for it to lunge or rise to its feet. It stared at them for a few minutes, then slowly tucked its triangular head back into the crook of its legs and went back to sleep.

Liam let out a breath. "I guess they *do* sleep, after all."

"You're awfully smug for someone who's stuck in the same rover as me."

Liam folded his hands over his chest again and let his eyes drift shut. "You can take the first watch."

"Smug and cheeky. That's a real winning combination you have there."

"Thank you."

* * *

"That is Lifeboat 312," Jules said. "I am sorry."

"But..." Nikolai's eyes filled with tears, and he shook his head. "It can't be!" The lifeboat had been torn open and shredded, the interior exposed to the toxic atmosphere.

"They may have survived, but there's no telling where they might be now. That explains why they didn't respond on the comms."

"We have to send another lifeboat down to rescue them!" Nikolai wiped his eyes furiously on his sleeves.

"We could... if we knew where they were," Jules said. "Besides, it looks like there's already another lifeboat next to theirs, and *it* hasn't been damaged. Not yet, anyway. It is possible that they are with your mother and the others. Regardless, they will have to be the ones to make contact with us. There is nothing more we can do for them."

Nikolai leaned his head back against the shelves. His skull connected to them with a hollow *thunk*. He shut his stinging eyes and rocked his head from side to side. His family was missing or dead, and here he was, trapped in a closet.

"I just want to go home."

"I know," Jules said. "But we have to hold onto hope. Perhaps your mother will succeed."

Nikolai cracked his eyes open to blurry, confused slits. "Succeed with what?"

Jules hesitated. "She was going with Varik to meet the aliens so that they could ask for help getting home."

"Oh yeah. I forgot about that."

Jules nodded. "As I said, I am sure that she will succeed. Don't worry. Everything is going to be all right."

* * *

Aria woke up under a tunic-blanket, her body curled around Payton, hugging her close. They were both still wearing their environment suits from the day before.

A reasonable approximation of sunlight streamed through the windows, bathing them in a golden light. Aria groaned. Her head felt thick, her body still weighted with sleep. It seemed like she'd only slept for a few hours. Payton was still lights out, her face buried in the tunic.

At the foot of Aria and Payton's combined bed, Markus and Elisa were both sitting up, their backs propped against the wall. Markus checked the charge on his rifle. Elisa had her pistol balanced in her lap, but she was less vigilant, admiring the sunrise from her perch beside the windows.

Again, Aria wondered why the Vitari would allow them to keep their weapons. This time she decided to ask about it.

Jasper T. Scott

"If we're prisoners, then why did they let you keep your weapons?"

Markus looked up, but it was his father who answered: "You wouldn't wonder about that if you'd ever tried to shoot a Vitari." Varik emerged from the bathroom on a cloud of steam, dressed in a clean white tunic and matching pants. His hair was wet and slicked away from his forehead. There was a bulky triangle in one of his pockets that might have been the pistol he'd used to stun Marshall and the other Marine.

Aria's thoughts veered off as she remembered the lieutenant. She hoped Marshall was okay.

"Have *you* tried to shoot one of them before?" Samos asked in a phlegmy voice.

Aria noticed that his foot and ankle were encased in a white hexagonal frame that ran all the way up his leg. She'd seen casts like that before. Designed to redistribute the person's weight so that they could still walk even with the cast.

"Not me, but I've seen someone else try. That armor you saw them wearing is shielded with some kind of force field. Nothing short of a plasma grenade will get through it."

"Energy shields don't exist," Samos said.

"Not in the Union they don't," Varik said.

Markus sighted along the barrel of his rifle at an imaginary target just a few feet to Aria's left. "Well, I didn't see Kratok wearing a helmet."

"Watch where you aim that thing," Aria said, glaring over her feet at him.

Varik nodded to his son. "You're right. Assuming you're a crack shot, you might be able to kill one of them. But then they'll teleport in here with an army and make you wish you'd shot yourself instead."

Markus lowered his rifle with a frown.

Varik looked to Aria. "Are you hungry?"

Her stomach growled at the mention of food. "Yes, actually."

"We should get some breakfast and get started with our day. There's time for you and Payton to shower and get changed first."

Aria peeled back the over-sized tunic that they'd slept under and shook her head. "I'd rather get to work first. We can wash up later. Or tonight."

"Straight to business. I've always admired that about you, Aria. With an attitude like that, we'll be out of here in no time."

A few minutes later, they were all back in the dining hall, sharing a quiet breakfast of white and yellow pastes with a few dozen others. Calla brought her tray over to join them as soon as they sat down.

"Sleep well?" she asked.

"No." Aria shook her head. "Not long enough, anyway."

"Because it wasn't," Varik said. "We only slept for four hours."

"*Four* hours? But the sun is up! It was setting when we came in here."

"The sun is simulated," Varik reminded her. "Besides, this isn't Earth, and the day/night cycle being simulated isn't ours." By way of example, Varik pointed out the windows to the blue and purple treetops below. Colorful specks flitted from tree to tree.

"Here, maybe this will help." Calla passed her a steaming white cup with a dark brown beverage inside. The smell was vaguely enticing. Aria raised it to her nose and gave an experimental sniff.

"What is it?" Payton asked.

Aria glanced at her and shook her head. "I'm not sure." She looked to Calla for an explanation.

"It's our version of coffee. Rich with antioxidants and natural stimulants. Give it a try."

Aria hesitated. "There aren't any vitalics in it, are there?" It occurred to her that the Vitari might be lacing the food or beverages here with vitalic serum to keep their prisoners dependent on them.

"No," Calla replied.

"How do you know? Your father spent twenty-nine years here without having aged a day, right?"

Calla nodded slowly, looking suddenly nervous. Her eyes flicked to Varik, and he shook his head.

"What aren't you telling me?"

"The only vitalics we get are for research and medical use. We're not supposed to use them regularly on ourselves... and there are consequences if anyone tries."

Aria looked to Varik. "So that's what you did? You began using the research samples on yourself?"

Varik smiled tightly. "What's it to you?"

"I'm trying to understand why no one here tries to escape. If everyone were addicted to vitalics, that would answer the mystery."

"No one tries to escape because they can't," Calla said. "There's only one way in or out, and all of the bridges crossing the chasm are electrified." She pointed to one of those transparent bridges, shining like a strand of gold in the rising sun.

Aria remembered last night seeing one of the avian Vitari flying too high and hitting that bridge only to get shocked unconscious and tumble lifelessly to the trees below. The stage two Vitari were prisoners here just as much as the researchers studying them.

"The door on the other end is also locked," Varik said as he scooped a spoonful of white paste into his mouth.

"Anyway, where would we go?" Calla asked. "The whole planet is teeming with harvesters, and whatever they see, the Vitari see. We're in the Andromeda Galaxy, millions of light-years from Earth, and the jump gate on this end is disabled since the jump core was removed." Calla looked to Varik. "I'm actually surprised my father found a way to get here at all. You need a jump core with a thousand times the standard energy output to get this far in a single jump. The only gate with that much power is the one he used to get here the first time, and it's part of a classified expeditionary branch of the navy—hardly the kind of jump gate that a cruise ship would have access to."

Aria frowned. That didn't make any sense. "We went through the Earth gate at L1."

Calla's eyebrows shot up, and she looked to Varik. "The Union upgraded a public access gate to jump between galaxies?"

Varik shrugged. "Being the richest man in the Union has its perks. You can donate pretty much anything you want and no one gets suspicious— that includes experimental jump cores."

"So, there's a chance someone might follow us here, after all?" Aria asked.

Varik waved the question away. "Doubtful. And it wouldn't do us any good if they did. The Vitari could wipe out the Union's entire fleet without even breaking a sweat.

"Anyway... Calla, you mentioned last night that you'd like to start decrypting Aria's research. We should probably do that once we've finished breakfast. And while the data is decrypting, maybe we can give everyone a tour."

Calla looked to Aria. "How much data do you have?"

"A few terabytes."

Calla blew out a breath. "That will take *hours* to decrypt."

"Hence the tour," Varik said. "I thought maybe we could start with a walk through the forest."

Calla's eyebrows shot up, then drew together. "A tour of the facility might be more productive."

"The forest first. There's nothing like a brisk walk to wake up in the morning. The sun slanting through the leaves, mist sparkling. And that sweet, citrus fragrance... Let's start the day out right, shall we?"

Calla's eyes darted around the table, taking in the others as if to ask their opinions. Markus's and Elisa's expressions were neutral.

Aria looked to Samos. "How well can you walk?"

He shrugged. "Well enough. It doesn't hurt if that's what you mean."

"Good, it's settled then," Varik said. "We'll go just as soon as you get the decryption started."

Calla nodded slowly, looking bewildered.

Aria was also confused, but she felt the vaguest stirrings of hope. Varik, Markus, and Elisa had been acting strange ever since they'd arrived—Samos, too—and Aria was beginning to think that there might be a reason for it. Too many things weren't adding up. Why divert a whole cruise ship just to deliver one person to the Vitari? What was that faraway look Aria had seen in Varik's, Markus's, and Elisa's eyes? Why had he changed topics so suddenly when Calla had mentioned the power requirements to jump to another galaxy? And now for some strange reason he wanted them all to go out for a walk and smell the roses—or alien pollens, in this case. And exactly how had he gotten the upper hand on two former Marines even after they'd tied him up?

Something was definitely going on. Aria looked at Varik. His blue eyes were bright and unblinking. "Something on your mind, Mrs. Price?"

She shook her head. "No. Just thinking about my research."

Varik nodded slowly. "You'll be getting back to it soon."

CHAPTER 44

After breakfast, Aria, Payton, and the others went up one floor to the research center where Calla had her office. The corridors were all the same with glossy white walls, beveled gray floors, and bright overhead lights. Colleagues greeted Calla as she strode by. She nodded back, but never stopped for introductions. Aria followed her, and they passed more picture windows with a view to the trees below.

In Calla's office, Aria helped her extract the DNA drive in her foot and get the decryption started. The process would take more than four hours.

"Plenty of time for a walk," Varik said as he led the way back to the elevators. They stopped at their room to get their air filter masks, and Markus and Elisa grabbed their guns.

Aria stared at them. "Expecting trouble?"

Markus shrugged. "Who knows? It's an alien forest. Could be anything out there."

An indoor *forest*, Aria thought but didn't say.

They went back to the elevators and rode straight down to the ground floor. The doors opened, and they walked out into a shifting world of glittering white mist. Sunlight streamed down through the tree canopy. The familiar smells of vanilla and fresh lemons cleared the fog in Aria's brain and brightened her mood.

"Wow," Payton said, perking right up. Until now she'd been a zombie trailing by Aria's side.

Varik led the way. Their collective footsteps crunched through fallen leaves and branches, falling into a steady rhythm.

Tree trunks scrolled by, black pillars holding up a ceiling of luminous purple and blue leaves. Bars of sunlight slanted down, painting the mist with iridescent rainbows. Dew drops glittered like diamonds on the glossy black tree trunks.

"Where are we going?" Samos asked after a while.

"Do we need to have a destination?" Varik asked. "Just enjoy the scenery."

Payton's head swiveled from side to side, up and down, taking it all in. Aria smiled, the aches and tension leaving her body as she let the beauty of nature wash over her. The freshness of the air cleared her lungs and made her feel alive. If they could bottle the fragrance of this world—without the toxic composition of the air—they'd have a rival for vitalics back home.

Home.

The only way they were getting back was with the Vitari's help, and for that Aria had to finish her research successfully. Failure would mean certain death for all of them.

That doused her spirits with a wash of anger. Her family's lives were at stake, too. Not to mention all of the other passengers. None of them had to be here, but Varik had brought them along anyway. He'd unilaterally risked all of their lives on the scant hope that Aria's research would reach a successful conclusion before they died of Vitalics withdrawals, or before the Vitari ran out of patience with her. It was unconscionable, and he had yet to provide a satisfactory explanation.

Aria trailed the group with Payton, but now she picked up the pace, determined to confront Varik.

She strode by Samos, hauling Payton along beside her. He glanced at them, then away. Payton had to break into a jog just to keep up.

"Mom, I can't walk that fast," she complained.

Aria ignored her. They reached Markus and Elisa. Markus flinched, and his rifle swung toward them.

Aria batted it away. "Hey! Watch it!"

He recoiled, expecting her to try to steal the weapon, but she just walked right past him to where Varik and Calla were walking side by side, speaking in hushed tones.

"Varik," Aria called out as they drew near. She was breathing hard, her heart pounding. Varik stopped and turned with eyebrows raised.

"Yes?"

Calla turned as well. Her eyes and expression were wary but brighter than Aria remembered, and there was a fire in her eyes where there'd been a dullness before.

Aria stopped in front of Varik. She thrust her chin out and crossed her arms over her chest. "We deserve answers."

"Ask, but make it quick."

"Why drag so many people into this? When Calla asked you last night, you completely zoned out and pretended not to know the reasons for your own actions."

"Because I didn't know the reasons," Varik said. "I had to alter my memories before leaving Earth, to shunt certain details into digital storage in my Neuralink. It was the only way to be sure the Vitari wouldn't read my thoughts to discover what we really came here to do."

That revelation sliced through her like a laser bolt. She'd been right; there was something more going on. "What did we come here to do?" she whispered.

"To rescue Calla."

"Not just me," Calla insisted. "There are others here, too. I won't leave without them."

Varik glanced at her, looking like he wanted to object.

Aria decided not to address the extreme selfishness of risking so many lives just to rescue his daughter. Instead, she raised another obvious concern: "I thought you said there's no way to escape?"

"There is *one* way, but I couldn't talk about that where the Vitari might hear us. Which is why I wanted to take all of you on a walk here this morning. The facility is monitored, but the forest is not."

"What about my research?"

Varik shook his head. "A sham. I've been falsifying the results for years."

Aria struggled to absorb the implications of that. Her life's work was a lie? She'd poured years of sweat and blood into Vitatech, thinking she'd been on the verge of a breakthrough.

"So... you brought my family and me here for *nothing?* And what about all of those other people? You *still* haven't answered my question."

"Not for nothing. Listen carefully because there's no time for me to say this twice."

The others had gathered around, none of them looked surprised by what they were hearing. They had to be in on it. Even Samos.

"There are surprisingly few differences between a colony ship and a cruise ship. They both have thousands of people on board. Plenty of supplies. Enough transports to get everyone to the surface of a planet. If you have to be stranded far from civilized space and start over somewhere new, you could do a lot worse than using a cruise ship to get there."

Aria's confusion doubled. She shook her head, speechless. "Why would you need to start over..."

"Because we're not going home."

"We're *not?*" Aria's voice became a high-pitched shriek. "What are you talking about? Where are we going?"

Varik spread his hands. "Somewhere the Vitari can't find us. And that means it has to be beyond Union Space. They've infiltrated the Union too deeply for us to go back to our lives like nothing happened."

Markus and Elisa nodded along with him. Samos looked resolute, his jaw set. Calla was the only one registering any hint of surprise. Aria pinned Markus with her gaze.

"You knew about this?"

"In a manner of speaking. We had to compartmentalize our memories, too, but yes, we were a part of my father's plan. He knew we wouldn't be safe if we stayed in the Union and he broke his end of the bargain with the Vitari. So here we are—" He turned to glare at Calla. "Hope you appreciate it, sis. This shit show is all for your benefit."

"Well, *I* sure as hell don't appreciate it!" Aria roared. "Neither do any of my family or any of the other unwitting colonists you dragged along with you." Aria glared daggers at Varik. "Why not use an *actual* colony ship? You're rich enough to have commissioned one. At least the people who signed up for it would have been half-prepared for what was to follow."

"If all of the passengers knew the real setup, then the Vitari would have figured out my plan long before we had a chance to execute it. They're telepaths, remember?"

"Well..." Raw fury pumped air in and out of Aria's chest. "You did all of this just to save your daughter?"

"What would you do to save yours?" Varik countered, his eyes flicking to Payton.

"It's not just about me," Calla said. "We're going to save the others here, too."

Varik's mouth curved into a frown. "Against my better judgment. We'll have to act fast to get everyone out before the Vitari realize what we're doing."

"How?" Aria asked.

Varik withdrew a flat, palm-sized silver disc from his pocket. "With this. It's a teleporter, like the harvesters use."

Aria's mouth opened and shut a few times, gulping air, but no sound came out. "It works?"

"How did you think I got the drop on Lieutenant Marshall?"

Aria glanced at Samos. "You don't look surprised."

"I'm the engineer who designed the device, among other things."

Aria looked back to Varik. "What about your *colonists?*" She all but spat the word at him. "They all evacuated to the surface."

"That was unfortunate," Varik said. "But we came prepared. The lifeboats are equipped with larger versions of the same tech. We'll recall them as soon as we return to the *Starlit Dream,* and then we'll jump out, and the Vitari will never know where we went."

"That's how you got here?" Calla asked. "You *teleported* here?"

Jasper T. Scott

"Of course. Otherwise, I'd have needed to hijack the jump gate to change our destination from Aquarius." Varik shook his head. "Too complicated. Besides, gate jumps can be tracked. We're not going to escape the Vitari like that."

"The *Starlit Dream* is fitted with experimental teleportation technology?" Aria asked. "How did you manage that?"

"Because I rebuilt her from the ground up." Varik nodded to Samos. "And he was the lead engineer." He pressed something on the silver disc in his hand, and it became a rainbow-edged circle of glass, shimmering and translucent just like the harvesters. "Excuse me, I'll be right back."

A flash of light tore through the misty forest, and Varik vanished. A few seconds later, another flash dazzled Aria's eyes as he returned, toting a big black bag. He unzipped it to reveal dozens of silver discs just like the one in his hand.

"Everybody take one and hide it in a pocket. They're all locked onto mine, so when I teleport back to the *Dream*, so will you."

Aria took two halting steps to reach Varik and grabbed transporters for Payton and herself. Markus, Elisa, and Samos each took one, and then Varik passed another to Calla. She stared at the device, turning it over and over in her hands.

"What about the others?" she asked.

Varik hefted the bag. "There's another forty transporters in here. That should be enough for the rest of your team."

"But there are hundreds of other people between the other research teams!"

Varik's mouth formed a grim line. "We can't save everyone. There isn't enough time. It's bad enough that you convinced me to go back and rescue your team. Can you imagine trying to find a way to discreetly distribute hundreds of transporters? The Vitari would figure out what we're up to long before you could finish."

"That's still a problem," Samos pointed out. "How are we going to pass these out? You said the facility is monitored."

"But the forest isn't," Varik replied. "We leave the bag here and go for another stroll, this time with the entire team."

"And you don't think that will raise suspicions?"

"It might, but hopefully we'll be long gone before the Vitari think to send someone into the forest to look for us."

A sudden concern stabbed through Aria. "What about Liam and Buck?"

Varik scowled. "Yes... I've been wondering where they are. I told them to pick up Marshall and her men and then come here, but since they haven't arrived yet, they're probably plotting something stupid."

Aria shook her head.

"You know something?"

"They're waiting outside. Liam contacted me last night from their rover."

"Why didn't you say so earlier? Tell them to get in here! I told them to meet us here for a reason."

"They might be better off going back to their lifeboat," Markus said. "That way they'll teleport back to the *Dream* with the others when you recall the suites."

Varik nodded quickly. "Good point." He looked to Aria. "You'd better contact him now, Mrs. Price, unless you were hoping to fulfill the *to death do us part* clause of your wedding vows."

"Be careful what you tell him," Calla added. "They might be monitoring our comms."

"The encryption should give us enough time to get away," Samos said.

"All the same," Calla replied.

Aria nodded quickly, already placing a call to Liam and praying that it would work.

Error. Contact not in range.

She touched her right ear, found the comms unit missing. "I left my comms in our room!"

"We don't have time for this," Varik growled.

"Here, use mine," Calla said, removing the hook-shaped device and handing it to Aria.

She nodded her thanks, slipped the device over her ear, and placed the call again.

Calling Liam Price...

"It's ringing!" Aria said.

But the call just rang and rang... Aria's pulse pounded in her ears, faster with every passing second. She could feel Varik's eyes on her, his impatience a palpable force stretching her nerves to the point of snapping.

Come on, Liam, answer your damn comms!

CHAPTER 45

Liam awoke to the sound of an insistent trilling in his ear. His eyes cracked to blurry slits. Pale shafts of sunlight had illuminated the misty forest to a gloomy gray. Buck snored beside him, his head resting against the driver's side door, laser rifle balanced in his lap.

Liam wondered why Buck wasn't awake and keeping watch, but then he remembered Buck shaking him awake and telling him that it was his turn. Apparently he'd fallen asleep on the job.

The flashing comms icon at the top of Liam's ARLs caught his eye. He focused on it and saw that the call was from Aria. That woke him up in a hurry. Yanking the lever to straighten his chair, Liam sat up and rubbed the sleep from his eyes with the balls of his fists as he accepted the call. "Aria?"

"Lia—!" Her urgent voice died in static. *Krssshhh...*

"Aria, I can't hear you. What did you say?"

Krshhhh... "—the lifeboat."

Liam cupped his hand over his ear, as if he could somehow shield the comms unit from whatever interference was blocking the signal. "What about the lifeboat?"

Krsshhhhh...

"Aria!"

Buck's head turned, his yellow eyes already sharp and alert. "What's wrong?"

"I can't hear her."

"She's using verbal comms this time?"

"Yes."

"Then she must be somewhere that's safe to talk."

"What good is that if I can't get a clear signal?"

Static hissed in Liam's ear, broken here and there by an unintelligible syllable or two of speech. But then even that tenuous connection vanished, and an error flashed on Liam's ARLs—

Connection lost.

"I lost her. Shit."

"Did you hear anything?"

"No, just something about the lifeboat. She sounded worried."

"Well, you could hear her last night," Buck said. "We could try driving back to the entrance of the facility and see if that works."

"Do it."

Buck punched the ignition and grabbed the rover's steering wheel. He left the headlights off this time but activated the sensor overlays. "Keep an eye out for spiders."

Liam nodded, already scanning the forest as Buck hit the gas and executed a sharp U-turn. Black tree trunks came marching out of the mist like soldiers, an endless parade that blurred away to either side and vanished in the rear view. Red-shaded blips flickered into range—still several kilometers away, but growing closer by the second. None of them looked like spiders, though, and nothing big enough to threaten the rover.

"Keep an eye on the display, too." Buck spared a hand from the wheel to point to a holoscreen between their seats.

It was a 2D display with an icon of the rover in the center. Red dots of varying sizes surrounded it.

"Shit!" Buck cried.

The rover swerved, throwing Liam into the door. He braced himself on the dash and looked up just in time to see the rover going airborne, flying over a slanted rock.

They hung in the air for a sickening second and then dropped, coming down hard on the driver's side. Liam's shoulder slammed into Buck's, and the mercenary's head smacked into the side window with a loud *crack*. Stabbing echoes of the impact rippled down Liam's spine. Buck slammed on the brakes, and the rover skidded in a loose carpet of leaves and sticks, heading straight for a tree.

"Look out!" Liam said. But they may as well have been gliding on ice. He threw up his hands just before the tree stopped them with a deafening crunch of crumpling metal. Liam's head snapped forward and his seatbelt dug into his shoulder like a blade. His head whipped back and slammed into the headrest. He sat staring in shock, his ears ringing.

The windshield was starred with a constellation of cracks. Mist and toxic air poured in steadily. Buck and Liam hurriedly pulled their filter masks up and activated the seals.

The front of the rover was crumpled up like a tin can.

Liam looked at Buck. A sharp pain erupted in his neck as he turned his head. The left side of Buck's head streamed with blood where it had hit his side window.

"Are you okay?" Liam asked, his voice sounding soft and small to his ringing ears.

Buck blinked stupidly at him until a rivulet of blood ran down his cheek and pooled on the edge of his mask. He gingerly touched the wound, and his fingers came away crimson.

"Just a scratch," he said. His hands back on the wheel, he shifted into reverse and tried to back away from the tree. A terrible crunching sound came from the ruined front end of the rover. They began inching backward. Buck turned the wheel and shifted into drive. The rover lurched forward, then stopped suddenly.

"Damn it!"

Buck tried turning the wheel, pumping the accelerator, the brakes—but nothing worked.

"It looks like she died on us. We're going to have to go out on foot."

Liam shook his head, his eyes on the sensor display between them. "I don't know if that's a good idea."

"Why not?"

Liam nodded to the display. A big contact had just appeared, big enough to be one of those giant spiders. Somehow it had evaded detection. It was only three hundred meters away and getting closer by the second. Maybe thirty seconds out. Maybe less.

Liam pointed to the display. "I think we might have attracted something with all that noise," he whispered.

"Shit," Buck replied.

Liam's comms began ringing again. It was Aria. "Hello?" he answered.

"Liam. Can you hear me now?"

"Yes! What—"

"I can't explain right now, but you need to get back to your lifeboat as fast as you can."

Liam blinked. "What? Why?"

"I just told you that I can't—"

"Right. Sorry. It might take us a little while to get there."

"You don't have a little while!" Aria screamed.

Taken aback, Liam paused to process the urgency in his wife's voice. "I understand," he said quietly. "But listen, we've wrecked our rover, and we're a twenty-minute drive from the lifeboat. That's probably an hour on foot, but something's coming after us. Something big. We might have to hide in here until it goes away."

A rush of static came through Liam's comms.

"Can you get to the depot?" Aria asked.

"Probably, yeah. Would that be better?"

Silence answered, but the comms picked up muffled voices arguing on the other end. "He can't!" Aria said. "They crashed it. No, I know! Fine—Liam, are you still there?"

"Listening."

"Varik says not to come here. He says you have one hour to get to your lifeboat."

"That's it? What if we need more time?"

"Just go, Liam!"

"Okay, we're on our way," Liam replied, already unbuckling his seatbelt.

He looked at Buck. "She says we have one hour to get to the lifeboat."

"We can't." Buck gestured emphatically to the sensor display.

Liam wasn't keen on going for a walk with giant spiders chasing them, but it didn't sound like they had much of a choice. "We'll get there as soon as we can, Aria."

"Good." It sounded like she was running—or walking fast. "One more thing, Liam. Did you and Buck pick up Marshall and her team?"

Liam hesitated. "What was left of them... They're all dead."

"What?!"

"By the time we found them they were already halfway to the next lifeboat, and under attack by some kind of..." Buck shot him a furious look, and Liam trailed off with a puzzled frown.

"Some kind of...?" More voices crowded in on Aria's end of the comms, shouting at her. "Okay!" she shouted back. "Liam, I have to go, and so do you. I love you. Please hurry. It's very important."

"I will," Liam replied. "Love you, too." He ended the call and looked to Buck for an explanation.

The other man's hand wrapped around his throat, squeezing off his windpipe. "Who the fuck said you could warn him?"

"Warn who?" Liam croaked.

"Varik."

"I didn't tell him anything!"

"But you told your wife, and she'll tell him." Buck shoved him away with a sneer.

Liam gasped and coughed, massaging his aching throat. Dark spots danced briefly across his eyes. "We have to go," he rasped.

"Too late," Buck whispered. He leaned toward his window and peered up at something. A giant triangular head hovered down beside them with pincers snapping restlessly. Black eyes the size of Liam's head stared unblinkingly at them. The spider's chitinous beak of a mouth parted and revealed a jagged row of black teeth coated in sticky threads of bright green saliva.

CHAPTER 46

Varik led them at a brisk pace through the forest. Payton struggled to keep up, but Aria pulled her along by her hand.

"They need more time," Aria insisted.

Varik shook his head. "They've got an hour. The longer we wait, the higher the chance that the Vitari could discover what we're up to, and then no one is getting out of here."

"Can't you just teleport to Liam's location and give him and Buck a pair of transporters?"

"It doesn't work like that. I have to program the destination coordinates ahead of time, or else have a signal to lock onto. I can't just go anywhere."

"But you did! You teleported out of the forest and then back."

"The device logs its previous location so that you can return to wherever you were previously. And I jumped to a pre-programed destination aboard the *Starlit Dream*."

Aria struggled to think of another way. "What if you teleport back to our lifeboat. They must have landed theirs close by."

"How would that help?" Markus asked from behind her.

"He's right. Even if they did land close by, Liam still has to get back there, so the outcome is the same."

Up ahead, a gray wall of steel emerged from the mist. The side of the chasm. "We're entering the surveillance zone. No more talking about our plans," Varik said. "Don't even think about them. And if you run into a Vitari, blank your mind, or think about something else. As far as any of us are concerned, our only plan for escape is to finish the research."

Heads bobbed quietly. Everyone understood the stakes.

Aria wasn't happy it, and she definitely wasn't on board with going to some distant corner of the galaxy to start a colony, but for now, they needed Varik's help. Once they were safely away, she'd happily lead a mutiny against him and fly back to the nearest Union system.

They rode the elevator back up to the research level above the dining hall and their sleeping quarters. Varik and Calla left them in her office to monitor the decryption of Aria's research data. She went to sit in the chair at Calla's desk with Payton while Markus and Elisa stood by the door, their weapons held casually at the ready.

"Is Daddy okay?" Payton asked from Aria's lap.

She nodded. "Of course he is, sweetheart."

"I miss him."

Aria absently stroked her daughter's hair. "Me, too, Paytie."

* * *

The spider glared at them through Buck's side window. Liam held himself so still that his entire body ached with tension. Buck did the same. Neither one of them spoke, but their breathing was painfully loud, rasping in and out of their masks.

The spider held its forelegs up close to its body like a praying mantis. Giant black hands sagged from its wrists and fingers the size of Liam's arms curled into loose fists.

Buck contacted him silently over their Neuralinks: *It knows we're in here.*

Then what is it waiting for?

For us to make the first move.

Maybe we should. We can't wait here forever. Aria said —

You want to get out? Go ahead.

Liam grimaced, torn between his wife's baffling plea that they return to the lifeboat, and the more imminent threat of the monster outside. He took a long, slow breath and forced his racing thoughts to slow down. A few minutes wouldn't make a difference one way or the other. They could afford to wait a little while.

After what seemed like an eternity, the spider raised its head, and the ground shook as it turned and began walking away. Liam sagged as he let out a deep breath. The tension left his muscles.

Buck looked to him, his eyes gleaming like knives. "Now we can leave," he whispered. His hand flexed on the grip of his laser rifle.

Liam nodded and reached into the aisle between their seats to retrieve his own rifle. Both plasma pistols were still holstered to his thighs.

"We'll have to move like ghosts," Buck whispered. "If you need to say something, you say it over silent comms. You copy?"

Liam nodded. "Copy."

Buck swung his door open. Mist swirled in to join the light haze already pooling inside the rover. The mercenary climbed out and swept the forest with his rifle, then waved over his shoulder.

All clear, he said over their Neuralinks.

Liam cracked his door and slipped out. He activated the optical enhancers still stuck to his temples. The gloomy forest became suddenly bright, but unfortunately, the enhancers did nothing to clear the mist. Buck cut a path to the right, walking swiftly. Liam followed him as quietly as he could. Trees swirled out of the gloom as they went. Liam remembered to activate the handheld scanner in his pocket and a host of red-shaded creatures that he couldn't see popped into existence. Thankfully, no giant spiders. Not yet.

How far to the lifeboat? Liam asked, even as he targeted it on his scanner. A green diamond appeared, dead ahead.

Ten klicks.

How long will it take us to walk that far? Liam queried his scanner for an ETA.

Buck broke into a run, his footsteps drawing muted thunder from the spongy ground.

What happened to being quiet? Liam asked as he struggled to keep up.

Your wife said we have an hour. We're not going to make it if we don't hustle.

He was right. The ETA beside the green diamond that marked the lifeboat's location was busy scrolling down from one hundred minutes. After just a few seconds the clock registered their increased pace and dropped down to forty-seven minutes, but could they really keep running for forty-seven minutes straight?

Liam added a timer, counting down from fifty-five minutes to mark Aria's arbitrary one-hour deadline. He figured it had to have been at least five minutes since he'd talked to her.

As Liam ran, the weight of his rifle on the shoulder strap chafed his shoulders, and the pistols slapping his thighs made his legs numb. His chest burned and muscles ached, but he pushed through it, determined not to waste time by slowing down or asking for a break.

He distracted himself from his body's increasingly insistent demands for rest by studying the shaded red creatures flowing by around them. Most were too small or far away to be a threat, but some were the size of bears or even elephants, and much closer than Liam would have liked. He glanced over his shoulder, saw one of the bear-sized lifeforms trailing just a hundred meters behind them; then a hundred and two, a hundred and five... Good. It wasn't following them.

Dark spots swam across Liam's eyes, and his feet began to drag. Buck drifted farther and farther into the mist, and then he disappeared entirely. Liam glanced at the ETA—thirty-four minutes. The timer next to it was counting down from thirty-nine. Their margin for error was shrinking fast.

Liam cursed under his breath and forced himself to pick up the pace again. Buck came swirling briefly out of the gloom, then vanished once more.

Liam's legs were shaking, his heart hammering, and his lungs burning so fiercely that he couldn't think straight. Then his foot caught on something and he went flying. He landed hard on his hands and knees, rolling with his momentum and fetched up against a tree. For a second, he just lay there, gasping for air, and staring up at the cottony gray world.

Wait up! Liam said over their Neuralinks.

Hurried footfalls came thumping toward him, and a dark figure cut a hole in the mist. *We need to keep moving,* Buck said. He held out a hand. Liam grabbed it, and Buck yanked him to his feet with enough force to make his shoulder pop.

He stood leaning against the tree beside him and rubbing his throbbing shoulder. His whole body shuddered for air, sweat coursing through his hair and making his clothes stick to him. Two minutes trickled away before he was even half ready to go on.

"Time to move," Buck whispered. "Try to keep up this time." Before Liam could reply, he turned and ran, vanishing into the mist once more.

Liam sucked in a deep breath and tore after him. His heart, lungs, and legs were back to screaming at him within seconds. Darkness clouded his vision, but he gritted his teeth and pushed through it. His middle-aged spread and a thousand other bits wobbled and jiggled as he ran, a painful reminder that he'd shunned exercise and healthy eating for far too long.

As they ran, Liam kept glancing at the two clocks on his ARLs. The ETA and the timer crept closer and closer until both were ticking down in tandem. The clocks hit ten minutes.

Almost there, Buck said.

Liam nodded but sent no reply. He needed every ounce of his focus just to stay conscious and to keep churning his weary legs. The clocks reached five minutes.

Contact right!

Liam blinked and shook his head, surfacing from a dreamlike daze. He saw something dart in front of them from between two trees, but it wasn't a spider or even one of the bear-sized creatures he'd seen lurking around them.

This was much worse.

Shimmering tentacle-arms swayed restlessly as the monster pivoted on the spot. Then came a rumble of thunder as the harvester began rolling toward them.

"Weapons free!" Buck cried, and opened fire with a dazzling stream of emerald lasers.

Liam brought his own rifle up and added a second stream of fire. The harvester came within a few feet of Buck and then lunged, its tentacles snapping straight like spears in an attempt to impale him.

Buck dived to one side, rolled out of the way, and came up firing. A loud *pop* sounded, and then the harvester's translucent, shimmering armor went dark. It collapsed at Buck's feet with a clatter of limbs and a hiss of escaping air that sounded almost like a sigh.

Buck jumped up and waved Liam over. "We have to move! There could be more of them."

They sprinted the last kilometer to the lifeboat. Exhausted as he was, that should have been impossible for Liam, but adrenaline infused him with new life.

The trees thinned out, and the mist parted to reveal a clearing of sunlit purple grass. Beyond it, the crimson lake sparkled, and two familiar gray spacecraft hunched in the middle distance.

"We made it!" Liam gasped, half-expecting the lifeboats to vanish like a mirage.

They burst out of the forest and into the clearing, flying down a gentle slope. A cool wind blew off the lake, roaring in Liam's ears.

He checked the ETA and timer. Both were flashing at 00:00.

"Which lifeboat is ours?" Liam asked.

"That one!" Buck pointed to the more distant of the two, on the left.

Liam drew on a hidden reserve of strength to pull even with Buck and then pass him. Buck caught up a second later. "Finally, you stopped dragging your feet!"

Liam would have offered a scathing retort if he'd had the breath to spare, but darkness was closing in, cinching his eyes down to narrow tunnels.

And then a flash of light tore through his retinas, stealing what was left of the world.

CHAPTER 47

Aria was sitting at Calla's desk when it happened. One minute she was telling Markus to stop pacing, and the next she was blinded by an abrupt flash of light and blinking stars from her eyes.

But they wouldn't go away. They were *real* stars. Somehow, inexplicably, she found herself sitting in front of the three-story-high windows in one of the shopping centers aboard the *Starlit Dream.*

"How..." She pushed off the cold deck and rose to her feet amidst a rising swell of louder exclamations that swallowed hers. Aria turned to see a group of thirty or more people standing behind her. Payton stood right beside her, tugging on her arm.

"Where's dad?" she asked.

Aria's heart slammed in her chest as she scanned the faces of strangers for one she might recognize. "Liam?" she tried.

"Everyone, settle down!" Varik yelled to be heard above the rising commotion.

Someone screamed, and then everyone did. The crowd sprang back from the windows with several people pointing in alarm. Some turned to flee, tripping over each other in their hurry to escape.

Bright flashes of light were stuttering across the void. Shimmering, tentacled machines swarmed around them. Two slammed into the windows right in front of her with horrifying *thunks*. Aria flinched and cried out.

She grabbed Payton and backpedaled from the windows. Tentacles scraped soundlessly over the glass.

"There's nothing to be afraid of!" Varik said. "The windows are too thick to break without heavy weapons, and they won't risk that. They want us alive."

"But they can teleport through!" one woman shrieked.

"I've activated a quantum interference field that scrambles the ability to teleport. Nothing is teleporting on or off this ship."

Aria's eyes narrowed to laser beams. "What about my husband?"

Varik's eyes met hers for an instant before roving on to address the clamoring crowd. "We'll be jumping away any second now, and they won't be able to follow us."

Aria went back to scanning the faces in the shopping center. Then she realized that if he'd made it to his lifeboat, he would have been teleported back to one of the ring decks.

Clinging to that brittle hope, Aria tried calling Liam over the comms.

Calling Liam Price...

"Aria?" he answered.

"Liam! Where are you?"

"In the clearing where we landed."

Aria's blood ran cold. "You didn't make it?"

* * *

Liam skidded to a stop, still blinded by the staccato flashes of light tearing through the clearing. When it ended, a line of harvesters appeared, cutting them off from the lifeboat. Both he and Buck snapped their rifles up, but there was no way they could gun all of the harvesters down.

"Shit," Buck muttered. "So much for the harvesters only hunting people with vitalics in their blood."

The comms icon at the top of Liam's ARLs began flashing. He answered it.

"Aria?"

"Liam! Where are you?"

"In the clearing where we landed."

"You didn't make it?"

"We're still working on that."

"The lifeboats are still on the surface? They didn't teleport out?"

"Teleport out...?" Liam shook his head. "What are you talking about?"

He heard Aria arguing with someone on the other end, then: "Liam, there's still time, but you need to hurry! Get on board now! Varik hasn't recalled the lifeboats yet."

Liam's mind swirled with confusion. He stared hard at the line of machines between them and the lifeboats.

"We'll do our best. Have to go. I love you." Liam ended the call before it could distract him further.

"What did she say?" Buck asked.

"Something about the lifeboats teleporting."

"To where? How?"

"I don't know! Somewhere safe, I guess."

Strangely, the harvesters weren't charging. It was if they knew Liam and Buck were short on time and all they had to do was wait.

Thunder rumbled, and the ground shook. Liam glanced up at a clear green sky, then turned to look behind him. The sound was coming from there, but he couldn't see anything except shifting gray walls of mist and the black trunks of hundred-meter-tall trees.

The sound quickly rose in volume and pitch, like an approaching stampede.

"What is that?" Buck asked in a tight voice, his cheek pressed to his rifle stock, eyes sighting down the scope.

Liam shook his head. "I don't—"

Before he could finish, a red-shaded army came flickering through the trees and poured into the clearing. Baby six-legged spiders, thousands of them.

Buck tore his eyes away from the harvesters long enough to look for himself. "Great! We're caught in the middle!"

Liam glanced to the right. Varik's lifeboat was closer than theirs, and less heavily guarded. The wall of harvesters was thinner there.

Liam pointed to it. "That one's closer!"

"Still suicide!" Buck replied.

"We have to try!"

Liam sprinted for it. The harvesters reacted instantly, rolling toward Varik's lifeboat to cut him off. Liam glanced at the approaching spiders to his right, just seconds away.

Liam kept running, looking for a gap between the tentacled machines. The thunder of stampeding spiders became a crescendo in his ears. Too close, too close...

"See you on the other side!" Buck said.

Flashes of light dazzled Liam's eyes, and then the harvesters appeared between them and the approaching spiders. Both sets of enemies tore into each other. Metal tentacles grappled with chitinous pincers and legs, drawing agonized shrieks from the arachnids. The shimmering harvesters vanished, swept under a carpet of black chitin.

"They're trying to protect us!" Liam said. "Why would they do that?"

"Don't know, don't care," Buck said.

More flashes of light dazzled to Liam's right, and the gap he was looking for appeared.

"There!" He pointed to it.

They crossed the remaining distance in a flash, just seconds from reaching the bottom of the landing ramp.

A flash of light dazzled Liam's eyes, and a harvester appeared at the top of the ramp.

Buck opened fire. Liam did the same, neither of them slowing down. The harvester rocketed down the ramp. Dozens of laser bolts slammed into the machine. They reached the bottom of the ramp at the same time as its shield failed with a loud *pop!* It collapsed in a twitching heap, blocking the way.

Jasper T. Scott

Buck darted around and pulled himself up onto the ramp behind it. Liam did the same.

The ramp skipped under their boots as they bounded the rest of the way up to the airlock. Buck waved to open the doors, but nothing happened.

"We're in trouble!"

Liam's heart seized in his chest. He tried to open the doors with his Neuralink. A virtual control box appeared on his ARLs.

Unlock.

He focused on the word, and a pleasant chime sounded. Liam waved the door open, and this time it worked. They darted inside, and Buck waved the door shut behind them. It sealed with a *thump,* sweeping away the sounds of battle.

Liam's ears were ringing. It took him a second to realize that it was an incoming call. He answered.

"Liam, please tell me you're on board!" Aria said before he could say anything.

"Yes! We made it to—" A rush of static roared over the comms before he could finish, and he wondered if he'd lost her. "Aria?"

Blinding light consumed the airlock, and Liam's guts clenched. He whirled around, blinking furiously to clear his eyes, fearing the worst. But there weren't any harvesters in the airlock with them.

Buck stood frozen and staring off into space. An ARL overlay flickered rapidly over his eyes. He'd chosen now of all times to connect to the lifeboat's network.

"What are you doing?" Liam asked even as another flash of light tore through the airlock. This time Liam was sure that he'd feel the searing heat of a harvester's tentacles stabbing through him, but the airlock remained empty. Buck cycled the inner doors. Crimson lights flashed, followed by a warning beep, and an automated voice: "Decontamination commencing."

Moments later, the inner doors parted, and they stumbled into a luxury suite. The picture windows on the far side of the living room revealed a bright band of stars.

"We're in space!" Liam said. He could hardly believe it. He'd expected something like this from what little Aria had explained over the comms, but it was still a shock to be on the surface of a planet one second and then drifting through space the next. But where were they in space, and how did that help? Wouldn't the Vitari simply follow them?

Liam's comms began trilling once more.

"Aria?"

"We made it!" she said. He could hear a crowd cheering on the other end. "I'll see you soon," she added with an audible smile. "Find Nikolai and come and find us. We're on deck forty-seven. Some kind of shopping complex."

Liam struggled to catch up. "We're back on the *Dream?*"

"Yes! Varik had a plan. He saved us."

"How did he..."

"It's a long story. I'll explain everything when you get here."

"Where are we?"

"I don't know. Somewhere safe. Back in our galaxy. The *Dream teleported* here." Aria's voice dropped to a whisper. "Varik has this crazy idea to start some kind of colony on an uncharted planet. He thinks the Vitari will find us if we go back to the Union. We're going to have to convince him to let us go home."

Liam's brow tensed. "We'll talk about that when I get there."

"Yes," Aria agreed. "Where's Nikolai? We should find a way to get him and Jules here, too."

"Not yet. We don't know if there are still harvesters on board, and they'll be drawn to the vitalics in his blood. For now, he's safer in the armory with Jules."

"Okay. I'll contact him to let him know what's going on. Just get here as fast as you can."

"We will. See you soon." Liam ended the call and looked to Buck. "We're back on the *Starlit Dream*."

Buck's brow furrowed, but Liam waved the question away before he could ask.

"I don't know how. Aria said it was Varik. He had some kind of plan. She says he saved us."

Buck scowled. "You mean he saved us after dragging us into trouble in the first place, getting hundreds of people killed in the process. Yeah, he's a real fucking hero."

"I'm sorry about your wife, Buck. I don't think Varik meant for her to die."

"You think I give a shit?"

"I get it, but we need to keep our heads cool for now. They're on deck forty-seven. We'll get more answers once we meet them there."

Buck nodded gravely and checked the charge on his rifle. "Oh, I'm going to get plenty of answers."

Liam's hand tightened on the grip of his own rifle. The barrel strayed casually into line with Buck's feet. "You can't kill him."

"Can't I?" Buck shifted his rifle to a one-handed grip. "Who's going to stop me? You?"

"We need him. We're not home yet. You want to see your daughter again?"

Buck's eyes sharpened. "Explain."

"This ship teleported to get us away from Vitaria, but we're not in Union Space, and Varik has no intention of taking us back there. So unless you know how to operate that drive system and use it to get us back to Earth, we're going to have to convince Varik to do it for us. We need him alive for that."

"Fine," Buck said. "We make him fly us home, and *then* I kill him."

Stuttering bursts of light stole through the corner of Liam's eyes from the direction of the windows, interrupting their argument. He turned to see thousands of blocky gray shapes crowding the stars where before there had been nothing but empty space. Engines glowed bright red as the ships turned toward the *Dream*. It was an entire fleet.

"Are those..."

Buck nodded slowly. "Looks like the Vitari followed us here."

CHAPTER 48

"You said we were safe!" Aria cried, but she could barely hear her own voice over everyone's screaming.

Varik stared out the windows in shock. "They can't have followed us!" he said, ignoring everyone's demands for answers. "It's impossible to track teleportations..."

"There must be some way," Markus replied.

"They're going to kill us all," Calla muttered.

Varik rounded on Samos. "You!"—he aimed a finger at his lead engineer—"How did they do it?"

"How the hell should I know?" Samos replied. "You said it. It's not possible. Not without..."

"Without *what?*" Varik crossed the distance between them in a handful of strides. He grabbed Samos by his white tunic and hauled him up onto tiptoes. The engineer winced as his weight shifted in a way that his cast wasn't designed to compensate for.

"They had to have someone on board helping them," Samos said.

"A spy?"

The engineer nodded. "They could follow us if someone on board were watching the nav and used the comms to broadcast the coordinates to our destination just before we jumped."

"If that's true, then there will be a record of the message in the comms log," Varik said. He released Samos, and the man almost fell over.

"Not if they erased the logs," Samos replied.

But Varik was already checking. Bright images flickered over his eyes as he used his ARLs to scan the comms log.

"There's no sign of... wait, what—" Varik's face turned ashen.

"What's wrong?" Aria asked.

"Someone's trying to lock me out of the ship!"

The shopping center plunged into darkness, and then snapped into pale relief as the lights returned at a fraction of their usual strength. People screamed.

Payton clutched Aria's leg. "What's happening?" she cried.

Aria wrapped an arm around Payton's shoulders in place of a reply. "Varik?" she asked, deferring the question to him. "What's going on?"

"I had to shut everything down to keep whoever it is from locking me out. We'll have to manually reset it all from the engineering deck."

Aria blinked. "But artificial gravity is still online."

"What about the quantum interference field?" Calla asked.

As if on cue, a stuttering storm of teleportations flashed through the shopping center. Terrified faces flashed bright, then dark, then bright, over and over on repeat.

Thump!

Aria jumped with fright. But the harvesters were bouncing off the windows, spinning away in the vacuum, only to jet back up to the glass and begin hammering at it with their tentacles. None of them had managed to teleport *through* the glass, and the fleet in the background wasn't opening fire on them. Not yet.

"All critical systems are still online," Varik explained. "Elevators, trams, gravity, life support, and the interference field. They're all on the same power grid." He fixed them with a grim look. "But the jump drive is offline, along with the comms and everything else."

Markus gestured wildly to the harvesters busy scratching and knocking on the windows. "So we're stuck here with a Vitari fleet bearing down on us?"

"They won't shoot. They want to capture us, not kill us. They still think Aria's research is worth something."

"And what do they think is going to happen when they break those windows?" Markus asked. "They'll capture us, find out that we lied to them, and then they'll kill us. Game over."

"The windows are thick. We have time."

"Time for what?"

"To get down to engineering and manually reset everything so that we can jump away again."

"That's going to take forever!"

"We're wasting time," Calla said.

"Let's go," Varik agreed. He turned and began striding toward a pair of massive doors at the other end of the shopping center. Calla's research team was already fleeing through those doors, not content to wait for the harvesters to break in.

Aria took one look at the milling mass of harvesters trying to claw their way through the glass, and then grabbed Payton's hand and hurried after Varik. At least they had guns. She wouldn't stand a chance staying here by herself.

"What about the spy?" Aria asked. "Won't they just broadcast our destination again before we jump?"

"No," Varik replied. "I can lock them out during the reboot by restricting access."

They joined a group of stragglers waiting for the elevators outside the shopping center. One of the elevators opened with a down arrow signaling where it was headed. Varik pushed through the crowd and led them inside.

"Who could be working for them? Who had access to the ship's systems?"

"All of the crew had access," Varik replied as the elevator doors slid shut.

"Then at least one of them survived," Aria concluded. "They have human agents?"

Varik smirked. "How do you think they abduct people for their research? It doesn't take much to make a puppet out of a man—you just have to threaten what he loves."

"You would know," Aria said.

"Touché."

The elevator opened, and they stepped out into a curving corridor. Varik set a brisk pace. Payton had to run to keep up.

"Whoever the spy is, it won't matter once we've jumped again," Calla said. "Comms are limited to light speed. It's not like they can tell the Vitari where we are after we've left. They'll receive the message hundreds or thousands of years too late."

Varik nodded but said nothing. His silence was telling. What else, besides communicating their location to reinforcements, could a Vitari spy do to cause trouble for them?

* * *

Fifteen minutes earlier...

Nikolai dreamed that his whole family was back together and having a picnic at the xenopark in downtown Philadelphia. Exotic plants from all around the Union flourished behind glass walls in carefully controlled environments. The ones native to the park's default biome swayed to artificial breezes and sparkled in simulated alien light. The default biome was Proxima B—a red star that blazed from a deep blue sky projected on the domed ceiling. Fan-shaped yellow Blade Ferns, red Balloon Flowers, and flute-like opalescent stalks that Nikolai couldn't name were the primary examples of vegetation growing in the park. The 'grass' where they'd spread their picnic blanket was whiter than any snow and smelled vaguely like cinnamon.

Nikolai sat eating a turkey sandwich and sipping grape juice while Payton crawled on the grass with a soother in her mouth. Their parents were chatting about who-knew-what as they snacked on squares of cheese and sipped red wine.

"Can we come back tomorrow?" Nikolai was surprised to hear the tenor of his own voice, a preteen squeak that could just as easily have been his sister's.

"Sure," his father said, then flashed a crooked smile and touched his wine glass to Nikolai's grape juice box. "Happy seventh birthday, little man."

"Hey, wait for me," his mother chimed in as she toasted her glass with Nikolai's juice box, too.

Payton crawled over and placed a tiny palm on Nikolai's hand as if to express the same sentiment. They all laughed.

"Sorry, Paytie," their dad said, still chuckling. "We didn't mean to leave you out."

Time seemed to freeze for a second, and then Liam's parents' faces contorted in agony as a blinding flash tore through the scene. A blast of searing heat swept through and melted his family like wax.

Nikolai woke up screaming, his eyes aching from the glare. It took a moment to ground himself in reality and remember where he was. His head was resting in Jules' lap, and he was lying on the cold metal deck, rather than a sun-warmed picnic blanket. His subconsciousness had conjured the perfect memory for a wish-fulfillment scenario in which his family was back together again—except for that last part with the explosion.

"Something is wrong," Jules said.

"Wrong?"

"That flash of light."

"You saw it, too? I thought that was just a part of my dream."

"It was not."

Nikolai sat up and turned to see Jules staring off into space, his attention drawn inward, and colorful ARL overlays flickering over his eyes.

"We're not in the Vitari System anymore," Jules said.

"We're not?" Dread stabbed through Nikolai. "But my family was on Vitaria! Where are we?"

"Somewhere in the Milky Way."

"How is that possible?"

"I do not know."

"Someone took us through the gate?"

"No, we were far from the jump gate."

Before Nikolai could ask anything else, the comms icon at the top of his ARLs began flashing, and a trilling sound reverberated inside his head.

"Hello?" he answered audibly, not even bothering to check who it was. He wasn't wearing an actual comms piece, so a simulated version of his voice would be relayed to the caller's comms or Neuralink.

"Niko! It's Mom. I'm on deck forty-seven."

"Mom? How did you—"

"Long story. I'll explain everything later. For now, I just wanted you to know that we're all safe.

Your father is on board, too, and Paytie's with me. Everyone is fine."

Nikolai sat up in a hurry. "That's great! Should I go meet you?"

"No, your father thinks it's too dangerous. Stay where you are for now. We'll come get you once we're sure it's safe."

"Okay..."

"I love you, Niko, and I'll see you as soon as I can, okay?"

"Love you, too, Mom."

The call ended there, and Nikolai found himself staring at Jules in disbelief.

"What did she say?" the bot asked quietly.

Nikolai explained.

"That is... remarkable," Jules said.

"It's a miracle," Nikolai agreed. He'd just been dreaming that his family was back together again, and then somehow it had happened. What were the odds?

"I didn't see them coming on the ship's sensors," Jules said.

"You must have missed them."

"Yes, perhaps..."

"I'm going to see if I can reach my dad. Maybe he can explain why we couldn't contact him when he was on the planet."

Jules' bushy eyebrows drifted up. "Does it matter? He's safe now."

"Back home he's always nagging me about answering my comms when *he* calls, and this time he's the one who wasn't picking up."

"Aha, so you'd like to stick it to him."

Nikolai shrugged. "Something like that." As he placed the call to his father, he peripherally noticed Jules standing up and walking over to the weapons rack. He frowned at that, but his dad answered before he could ask what Jules was up to.

"Hello?"

"Dad! I've been trying to reach you for hours!"

"You have?"

"Yes! Don't you check your comms?"

"I could say the same thing. We were trying to reach you, too."

"What?" Nikolai shook his head. "But... I never got any messages."

Jules turned from the weapons rack, something metallic glinting in his hand; then the armory plunged into darkness. The lights came back a second later but at a fraction of their original brightness.

"Dad?" Nikolai tried. "Hello?" No answer. He looked to Jules. The bot had a pistol in his hand, directed casually at the floor. "What happened to the comms? And what are you doing with that?"

"The ship just suffered a global systems shutdown. It appears to have been deliberate."

"Someone pulled the plug? Why would they do that?"

"There's more. Before the shutdown, I noticed something on the *Dream's* sensors. A fleet of ships materialized around us, and there are harvesters everywhere. The aliens followed us here. I suspect whoever shut down the ship's systems may have done so in order to help them capture us."

Nikolai jumped to his feet. "We have to do something! Is there a way to turn everything back on?"

"We will have to get down to engineering to manually reboot the power grid. But it will be dangerous, and that is why I have the gun."

"But you're a bot. You aren't allowed to use weapons, right?"

Jules smiled and shook his head. "I may have mislead you on that score. I'm not your average robot."

Nikolai frowned. "Okay, well I'm getting a gun, too," he said as he hurried over to the weapons rack. He reached for a rifle as long as he was tall, but Jules shook his head. "The recoil would knock you off your feet. Besides, you need something that will still let you crawl out through the ducts." Jules passed him a plasma pistol instead.

It was heavier than it looked. Nikolai turned it sideways and aimed one-handed at an imaginary enemy by the doors. Maybe not so imaginary—there were probably still harvesters waiting out there.

"No, like this," Jules said and demonstrated holding his own pistol in a two-handed grip at shoulder-height.

Nikolai tried that posture. "Got it. Let's go!" Nikolai sprang toward the supply crate stacked under the opening of the ducts.

"I am sorry for this, Master Nikolai."

"Sorry for—"

A searing blast of heat stole the words from his lips with an agonized gasp, and death came for him as an implacable sheet of darkness that slammed his eyes shut like twin guillotines.

CHAPTER 49

The lights died and then came back at half strength. "What happened?" Liam asked.

"Global systems shutdown," Buck replied. "I can't access anything. Someone powered us down."

Liam glanced to the windows and saw dozens of rectangular gray warships catching the light of the system's sun until they gleamed like silver pendants. "Who would power down the ship with an alien fleet bearing down on us?"

"Someone who's working with them. Like Varik."

"Why would he help us escape and then help them capture us? That doesn't make any sense."

"Don't ask me."

"Can't we just turn the systems back on?"

"Not without a manual reset. Same as we did before. We'll need to get back down to engineering for that, and I suggest we hurry."

And they did. Back inside the airlock, Buck cycled the doors and leaned out with his rifle.

Clear. Stay close, he thought over their Neuralinks. Liam kept his rifle in a two-handed grip, ready to fire at a moment's notice.

They followed the curve of the ring deck around the ship to the nearest spoke leading to the central column of the ship. The doors were shut. Buck waved them open, and they ran through. The deck and the trams were littered with dead bodies, but that wasn't what caught Liam's eye.

Shimmering harvesters clamored outside the transparent corridor, hammering on the windows and chipping out flecks of armored glass that glittered like ice chips in the void.

"Why aren't they teleporting in here?" Liam asked.

"Good question," Buck replied.

They ran down the corridor as fast as they could, but it was a long way to the other end—hence the trams. They were almost to the doors on the other side when a whistling gust of wind began shoving them back the way they'd come. Liam's body quickly grew lighter. He felt like he was walking into a hurricane.

"They've broken through!" Buck yelled to be heard over the wind. "Hurry! We have to get to the doors!"

Liam's ears popped. Every step was like walking up the side of a mountain. He was physically incapable of hurrying. Glancing back, he saw the shimmering tentacles of a harvester punching repeatedly through the ceiling barely fifty feet from where they were. When it broke a hole big enough to climb through, they'd be sucked out in an instant.

Liam strained against the tug of the escaping atmosphere. Buck reached the doors first and waved to open them, but nothing happened.

"The air pressure's too low!" he said. "We'll have to crank the doors manually!"

Liam felt himself drifting backward. He braced his feet and glanced around frantically for something to hold onto. Seeing an access panel in the wall, he ripped it open and dug his fingers in.

Buck did the same with the access panel for the manual crank beside the doors. He folded the handle out and began turning it. The doors cracked open, and the wind blasting through the corridor intensified.

Liam's grip was slipping. The fine edge of the metal panel he was holding onto dug into his palms. "I can't hold on much longer!" His voice sounded high and reedy to his ears in the thinning air. Dark spots danced across his vision.

"Almost there!" Buck said.

The doors made a gap wide enough for them to squeeze through sideways. Buck grabbed the edge of the nearest one and began pulling himself through.

A spike of fear shot through Liam. "Wait!"

Buck turned, eyebrows raised.

"I can't reach the doors from here!"

Buck grimaced. "You'll have to jump!" He braced himself in the opening and held out a hand. "Grab my hand, and I'll pull you through!"

Liam judged the distance. Imagined himself falling short and tumbling backward...

"Hurry! When the harvesters break in, it'll be too late!"

Liam shut his eyes, whispered his *I love yous* to his wife and kids, and then lunged with all of his strength. He used the access panel for extra leverage, and the metal edge sliced through his palm. He flew forward about four feet and slapped Buck's hand with his. The mercenary's fingers grazed his, and then they lost contact.

There came a sickening moment of weightlessness. "Buck!" Liam screamed as he drifted off his feet and began flying backward.

The mercenary released his grip on the doors and used the wind blasting through them to shoot forward. He grabbed Liam's ankle just before he could drift out of reach.

"Got you," he grunted.

He was holding on by his legs, both knees braced against the other side of the doors. His whole body shook from the strain of trying to pull Liam through.

"Shit, you're a heavy bastard, aren't you?"

Liam didn't have the strength for a reply.

Buck hauled him through and shoved him to one side of the gap while rolling away to the other. They both lay there pinned against the doors and gasping for breath.

They were inside a short corridor full of elevators with another set of doors at the end. Those doors were jammed open with a tangle of dead bodies, and an open concourse lay beyond that with restaurants inside.

"We have to get these doors shut!" Buck yelled into the river of air roaring between them.

Liam nodded. "Sure! How do we do that?"

Before Buck could answer, the gusting wind tripled in force and Liam's ears popped with the sudden loss of pressure. Buck screamed, but his voice was swallowed by the sound. He pointed wildly to something next to Liam.

Liam turned his head to see an access panel with black and yellow hazard lines around it and bright red lettering that read:

Manual Door Crank. Emergency Use Only.

He strained to reach it. The escaping air had plastered him to the doors, but he managed to roll toward the access panel. He yanked it open and folded out the crank. Began turning it...

And then a familiar metallic thunder came rumbling through the cyclone. Liam glanced over his shoulder to see a dozen shimmering tentacles suddenly appear in the gap between the doors. He struggled to turn the crank faster, hoping to cut off the harvester's limbs, but the crank stalled and began turning the other way. It was prying the doors open.

CHAPTER 50

The elevator doors parted. Markus and Elisa snapped their weapons up, expecting trouble, but there were no harvesters in sight. Aria stepped out behind the others, holding Payton's hand tight in a sweaty grip.

A long curving corridor stretched ahead of them, scuffed gray floors gleaming in the low lights. High ceilings, exposed pipes to the right, windows to the left.

"Give me that," Varik said, and grabbed Markus's laser rifle.

"Hey—"

"Do *you* know the way?"

Markus hesitated.

"I'm not taking the lead without a weapon," Varik explained. Waving over his shoulder, he said, "Let's go!" and ran ahead. Everyone hurried to keep up. Aria was surprised that Samos could match a running pace with his broken ankle. His cast may as well have been a bionic leg.

Overhead lights flashed by as they followed the curve of the corridor around the ship.

A shimmering silhouette swept into view through the windows to the left. A stray harvester drifting in space.

"Do you think it sees us?" Payton whispered in a trembling voice.

Aria's eyes tracked the metal monster. "I don't know. I hope not."

A broad set of doors appeared to their right, and Varik skidded to a stop. "This is it." He stepped up to the control panel and opened the doors.

A cavernous space appeared with catwalks crossing to a cylindrical column in the center. That column glowed with a pulsing crimson light.

"The reactor core," Samos breathed. "Have you ever seen a more beautiful thing in your life?"

Varik raced down the catwalk to the core, his boots drawing echoing clangs. Aria and the others hesitated. Four catwalks crossed to the core from as many entrances around the circumference of the chamber. A set of metal stairs dropped away to their right to a lower level of catwalks two stories down. Control panels and holoscreens ran around the base of the reactor on their level and the one below.

Aria peered over the railing with Payton, Samos, and Elisa while Markus and Calla followed Varik. At least ten levels of catwalks spiraled around the pulsing crimson core, dropping ever deeper into the ship. She pushed back from the railing, her head spinning.

"How far down does it go?" she asked. An echo of her voice bounced back to her ears.

"Twenty-five floors," Samos replied.

"Wow..." Payton breathed. When she heard her own echo, she added, "Echo!"

Echo, echo, echo...!

"Cool!"

"We'd better keep moving," Elisa whispered, glancing back nervously. She still held a plasma pistol, but it was shaking visibly in her hands.

"You want to give that to me?" Aria asked.

Elisa hesitated, her lilac eyes widening at the suggestion.

"We're all on the same side now, right?" Aria went on. "If a harvester comes in here, do you want to be the one standing in front of it, firing until the last possible second? Or would you rather give that responsibility to me?"

Elisa's expression wavered uncertainly. She began to hand the weapon over.

But Markus ran over and snatched it away before she could. "I don't think so," he said with a sharp look at his *consort*.

"You don't trust me?" Aria asked. "*I'm* not the one who's been keeping secrets and abducting people."

Markus snorted. "I don't trust my own father, so how the hell am I going to trust you?" He turned and went back to stand with Varik and his sister.

Aria looked to Elisa. "Does he always treat you like that?"

"Like what?"

"Like an idiot who can't make decisions for herself."

"No, he—"

"Who decided that you were going with Varik on this trip?"

"Markus did, but I agreed with his choice."

"Did you? Or were you afraid of what he might do if you decided to stay behind?"

"It's not like that."

"What does he have over you?" Aria whispered. "You're not his slave."

Elisa chewed her lower lip, looked hesitant, then leaned in and whispered back, "I'm not human."

"What do you mean you're not human? I don't understand. You're a bot?"

Elisa nodded quickly.

"But you're bleeding and your nose is broken."

"Luxury models like me have simulated flesh for added realism. My nanites will repair the damage in a day or two."

Aria grimaced. "And you're his..."

"Consort." Elisa nodded.

"So you *are* a slave."

She shook her head. "I have full autonomy, but... I owe Markus and Varik."

Aria glanced back to Markus and his father. Samos was there with them, too, busy operating one of the control stations arrayed around the core.

"We join them," Elisa whispered. "They have the guns."

Aria nodded and the three of them hurried over to join the others.

"How long?" Aria asked.

"Twenty minutes," Varik said.

"Can't you speed things up?"

Samos shot her a look of wounded pride. "Other ships would take half an hour or more for a manual restart."

Aria glanced back to the doors they'd come through a moment ago. "Can anything get in here while we're waiting?"

"Not a harvester," Varik replied. "Only someone who has the access codes, and that's a short list."

"But the spy would have the codes," Aria suggested.

"Yes."

"I thought shutting down the systems would lock them out?"

Varik shook his head. "I didn't have time to change or revoke any access codes before I shut down the systems, but I'll do that from here once the system reboots."

Aria stared hard at the doors. "So someone could be joining us in here soon."

"I'd count on it. If there is a spy on board, then they'll know that the only way to keep me from locking them out is to get down here and do what I'm doing. Here," Varik passed the laser rifle he'd taken from Markus to her. The butt of it smacked into her shoulder. "I heard you arguing with Markus. You want to watch our backs? Get on it."

Aria stared at the weapon in shock. Markus glared at her as if it were her fault that Varik was undercutting his authority. She grabbed the weapon and checked the charge.

The number 101 glowed on a slanted display at the top of the stock. A hundred and one shots before the weapon would be depleted. Hopefully she wouldn't need to fire any of them. Aria rounded the core to the nearest catwalk and took a knee beside the railings, using them for partial cover. She sighted down the barrel, trying to remember everything that her grandfather had taught her about shooting.

"What should *I* do?" a small voice asked. Payton stepped into view, almost in front of the rifle.

"Stay behind me," Aria snapped. "And stay down."

Payton's eyes flashed with hurt, but she did as she was told, crouching behind her.

Minutes passed with Aria's heart counting out the seconds. Her legs began to cramp. She was about to stand up when she heard something: *swish.* Doors opening. Her eyes darted around to the three entrances that she could see. All of them remained shut. Then she looked behind her. There was one more entrance that she couldn't see. Booted feet thundered along on a catwalk.

"Someone's coming!" Varik warned. "Take care of it, Price!"

Aria burst out of cover, almost tripping over her daughter.

Payton looked like a cornered mouse. "Where do I hide?"

"There!" Aria hissed. She pointed to a recessed alcove between two control stations. "Go!"

Payton scuttled away, and Aria ran around the reactor core with her laser rifle tucked into her shoulder and her cheek bouncing against the stock.

CHAPTER 51

"**Y**ou have to shut the doors!" Buck screamed.

"I'm trying!" Liam cried through gritted teeth. He panted hard in the thin air as he inched the crank around, stealing back precious centimeters from the harvester prying the doors open.

Buck rolled toward the whistling rush of air streaming between them. A screaming torrent of lasers flashed through the darkened corridor as he opened fire. The machine screeched and flailed, scrabbling to hold onto the doors and swipe at him with its tentacles at the same time.

One of its limbs caught Buck in the arm and sliced it open. He screamed but kept on pumping emerald fire into the monster anyway.

The harvester lunged, spearing him through one shoulder. Buck screamed even louder and delivered a solid kick to the machine's bulbous torso. It vanished with a fading screech. Blood streamed in crimson rivulets from his doubly-wounded arm, getting caught in the wind and wiggling out the doors like grotesque party streamers.

"Get them shut!" Buck said as he went back to firing his rifle into the gap.

Liam didn't need to be told twice. He cranked the handle around furiously. And the escaping air whistled with an increasingly higher pitch as the doors ground together. The last whistling gasp slipped out, and then the doors *thunked* shut, and a ringing silence fell.

"Good job! Let's go!" Buck peeled away from the doors and pounded across the deck to the elevators. Liam followed on shaking legs. Spent adrenaline had turned his body to jelly.

One of the elevators dinged open, and they stumbled in. Buck selected their destination, and the elevator fell swiftly into the lower levels.

Liam stared at him in a daze. The mercenary's wounded arm gleamed crimson. Blood dripped from his fingertips in a steady rhythm: *splat, splat splat...*

"You should do something about that," Liam said.

"Just a scratch," Buck replied.

"That's more than a scratch."

"Not important."

Liam decided to shut up.

The elevator stopped, and the doors opened. A long, curving corridor appeared. The outer wall transparent and showing a brilliant view of stars and space. Dozens of harvesters were trying to break in, but none of them had broken a hole yet.

"Clear," Buck whispered. "Push up."

They ran side-by-side, rifles up and swinging. A broad set of doors appeared to the left. Buck skidded to a stop in front of those doors and busied himself with the control panel.

"Can't you just wave them open?"

"Locked," he explained. And then the doors swished open.

"They weren't locked the last time we were here," Liam said.

"Last time the core was empty," Buck whispered. "Someone else beat us here, and they locked the doors to keep us out."

"Who?"

"Probably Varik. Or whoever is working for the Vitari."

"A spy?"

"Yeah."

"Whoever it is, if they locked you out, then how did you get the doors open?"

"Because I still have the access codes that Jules gave us. On me," Buck whispered as he brought his rifle up to his good shoulder and started through the doors.

Liam kept his own rifle at the ready but aimed it to one side of Buck to avoid accidentally shooting him in the back. As they strode down the metal catwalk to the reactor core, Liam scanned the dimly-lit chamber, checking for harvesters.

He didn't see any. That was a good sign. But as they drew near to the core, he heard muffled voices, and Buck slowed to a crawl. Liam's whole body tensed as he steadied his rifle.

"Get ready," Buck whispered.

"For what?" Liam asked.

"The saboteurs beat us here. They're trying to make sure we can't access the ship's systems after they come back online. That means we won't be able to escape the fleet that followed us here."

Approaching footfalls rang on a thin metal walkway running around the core. Liam's finger tensed on the trigger of his rifle as he sighted down the scopes in the direction of the sound.

Swish. The doors behind them parted. Buck whirled around, and Liam began to do the same, reacting to the new threat.

"Eyes front!" Buck snapped.

Too late. A burst of emerald fire screamed past Liam's ear. He dropped to the catwalk, catching a glimpse of the person now sprinting into the reactor room behind them.

"Jules?" Liam asked even as he twisted around to deal with the gunman.

"Liam?!" Aria cried just a split second before he saw her. "Did I hit you? Oh no, please, God..."

Liam pried his cheek off the catwalk, never more grateful to see anyone than he was in that moment. "Hey, beautiful."

She ran to him, her eyes wide with horror as she dropped to her haunches beside him and crushed him into a hug. He buried his face in her sweat-matted hair. A pure explosion of joy rippled through him.

"What are you doing here?" he breathed into her hair.

"Varik came to reset the power grid."

"Is he the one who shut down the power?" Buck asked.

"He had to. Someone was hijacking the ship."

Aria withdrew to an arm's length to regard Buck. Jules walked up behind them, looking grim, but saying nothing.

"You're Marshall's husband?" Aria asked.

Buck stared coldly at her. "Yeah."

Aria laced a hand through Liam's and rose to her feet, pulling him up with her. "I'm so sorry about your wife. She was a good person. She tried to help us. Varik—"

"Did you tell him?" Buck demanded.

Aria blinked. "Tell him about what?"

"My wife."

"No, he never asked."

"Figures. Thank you. I'd like to tell him myself if you don't mind."

"Okay..."

Before either Aria or Liam could say anything else, Buck strode by them, his rifle tracking up as he stalked around the reactor core.

"Shit," Liam muttered. "Buck! Wait!"

"What's wrong?" Aria asked.

"He's going to kill Varik!"

Liam tore his hand free of hers, set his rifle to stun, and brought it up to his shoulder. He aimed it at Buck's back. "Not another step!"

The former Marine stopped and slowly turned. His rifle swung into line with Liam's chest. A blinding muzzle flash was Liam's only warning before a sliver of green light slammed into his shoulder with a screeching report and a breathless burst of searing heat. His rifle dropped from numb fingers as he sagged against the nearest railing, his eyes streaming with tears, lungs huffing the charred stench of his own flesh.

Aria screamed belatedly and brought her own rifle up for a hasty shot—

Missed.

Buck fired back in a stream of emerald fire that tracked bare inches above their heads. Aria dropped to her haunches, sheltering behind a metal railing that wouldn't stop a gust of wind let alone a laser bolt.

But rather than continue firing, Buck vanished around the curve of the reactor core.

"We have to stop him," Liam croaked and struggled to push off the railing with his good arm. A wave of nausea and dizziness almost sent him sprawling through the railings toward the swirling abyss below.

Aria pulled him back. "Careful!" she hissed.

Jules sprinted past them with a sidearm in hand.

"Wait!" Liam called after him. "Where is Nikolai? You were supposed to be looking after him in the armory!"

Jules glanced back, but before he could say anything, a screech of laser fire split the air.

The meatier *crack* of a plasma pistol answered, followed by two more screeching reports. Payton screamed, and Liam's pain-clouded thoughts snapped into focus.

"Payton!" Aria cried.

Liam and Aria tore after Jules, racing around the reactor core to join the fray.

CHAPTER 52

Nikolai woke up blinking furiously, his whole body aching and sparking with shooting pains from tortured nerve-endings. He pried himself off the deck, patted himself down, then scowled up at the opening of the ducts. Jules had stunned him!

Why would he do that? They were supposed to go deal with the spy together! And...

A cold thought slid through his brain. What if Jules was the spy?

Nikolai sifted back through their time together, looking for anything that stood out as odd.

The comms. Jules had been the one using the ship's comms to reach his father and warn him about what they'd seen with the probe. But despite repeated attempts, they hadn't been able to reach his dad. If Jules was working for the aliens, he wouldn't have wanted Nikolai to warn his father about what they'd seen.

Now Jules was on his way to engineering so that he could take control of the ship for himself.

Nikolai spied the plasma pistol he'd had before Jules had stunned him. He sprang off the deck and snatched up the weapon. Stepping up onto the crate below the ducts, he reached for the opening—

But his fingertips grazed empty air. He was too short to reach. He found another crate that he could stack with the first and placed it on top. That made up the missing foot he needed to reach the opening. He cast a lingering glance at the weapons rack. It might be a good idea to get some extra firepower.

Jules was right about sticking to weapons that he could crawl through the ducts with, but he was also smaller than an adult, so he had some room to spare. He tucked his pistol into the waistband of his shorts and grabbed the four-foot-long rifle that Jules had told him not to bother with before—a plasma cannon.

He would drag it through the ducts by the strap if he had to. Jules wasn't the ultimate authority on weaponry. Nikolai knew a lot about guns from his VR games. The recoil was simulated, but still an important element. Take the wrong fighting stance, and your character could get knocked off his feet, smack his head into a wall and be immortalized on the idiots' roster for most humiliating deaths. He knew how to brace for the recoil. Besides, Jules was a traitor, so why should he listen to him?

Climbing up onto the crates, he pushed the rifle in ahead of him and then grabbed the rim of the opening and pulled himself up. Soon he was army-crawling through the ducts with one arm hooked through the rifle's shoulder strap and dragging it along behind him.

Exhaustion came quicker than Nikolai expected. He took a short break and listened to the distant sound of thumps and thunks ringing through the ship. Where was that coming from? Then came a whistling roar, followed by a gust of wind and ringing silence. More thumping and thunking—closer now.

"What *is* that?" Nikolai whispered to himself.

The opening at the other end of the duct system loomed dead ahead. Nikolai started forward again, dragging himself toward the exit. As he went, the mysterious hammering sounds grew louder and more insistent. At the end of the ducts, he pulled himself halfway out and twisted around to get his feet under him before dropping down. The rifle fell out behind him and smacked him in the side of the head. Stars exploded behind his eyes as he crumpled to the deck. Stunned, he lay there for several seconds, gasping against the sharp, throbbing pain in his skull. He touched the area and felt a lump growing but no blood. Ignoring the pain and an intense wash of dizziness, Nikolai staggered to his feet. He held his rifle in a two-handed grip and scanned the corridor.

Metallic thunder rumbled in the distance, quickly growing louder. Nikolai turned to look just as a shimmering, tentacled ball rolled into view at the end of the corridor where he was standing.

His heart slamming in his chest, Nikolai hauled the rifle up and braced it against his left hip. Flicking off the safety, he set his feet in a wide stance and held his breath to steady his aim—just like firing a plasma cannon in one of his VR games back home. He waited for the harvester to reach the cannon's optimum kill zone—point-blank, twenty feet out—and then pulled the trigger.

A searing flash of heat tore from the barrel with a sound like worlds colliding, and Nikolai flew backward off his feet. He did a backward somersault, bending his neck at a painful angle and popping the vertebrae before his knees came down and smacked the deck. His cheek lay pressed against the scalding barrel of the cannon and triggered a fresh spurt of adrenaline that launched him back to his feet.

Up ahead the harvester was slumped and thrashing in a puddle of molten metal. A thousand char-blackened and glowing orange bits littered the deck around it.

"Hell yeah!" Nikolai crowed.

Taking a deep, calming breath, he hoisted his weapon up and ran down the corridor.

* * *

Elisa screamed in a convincing expression of human agony. Payton cried out again, and Aria sped ahead of her husband. Just a few steps ahead of them, Jules had his pistol up and tracking. Aria frowned at that. Bots weren't supposed to be able to use guns.

Aria rounded the reactor. Markus and Elisa scrolled into view, both clinging to railings and gasping from the pain of multiple laser burns. Then she saw Varik, swaying on his feet with a plasma pistol pressed to the side of his head. Calla and Samos stood a few feet away, looking on with Payton clutched protectively in front of their legs. Buck stood behind Varik with his back to the core, shielded by the trillionaire. A rifle peeked around Varik's hip, tracking Aria's approach.

She collided with the railing running around the core, bounced off, and aimed her own rifle at Buck. Liam was right behind her, and Jules came to an unnaturally fast stop, anchored by his mag boots.

"Let him go, or I'll shoot!" Aria shouted.

Jasper T. Scott

"Shoot who?" Buck laughed darkly. "You won't hit *me*."

Buck's rifle swept away from her and into line with Payton. "How about this, you three drop your weapons, or *I'll* shoot."

"Have you lost your mind?" Liam screamed. "This isn't the way to honor your wife's memory! And it won't bring her back. Think about your daughter!"

"What do you think I'm doing?"

Aria took a moment to catch her breath and assess the situation. Varik was gritting his teeth against the pain of various low-powered laser burns on his legs and arms. One hand was black as charcoal and dangling limply from his wrist. Buck wasn't trying to kill him; he was trying to make him suffer.

"She wasn't supposed to die!" Varik ground out. "I told you to go pick her up!"

"Well, I guess shit happens when you betray people," Buck said. He smacked Varik in the mouth with the butt of his pistol.

Varik screamed and spat a glob of blood and a tooth out on the walkway. He almost fell to his knees, which would have given Aria a clear shot, but Buck let his rifle dangle by the strap so that he could hold Varik up. With his free hand, he aimed his plasma pistol at Payton.

"Well? What's it going to be?" Buck prompted. "Drop your weapons, and no one else gets hurt."

"What are you going to do to Varik if we drop our guns?" Aria asked.

Buck shrugged. "What do you care?"

"We need him to get home."

"Likewise," Buck replied. "Why do you think he's still alive?"

"I'm not helping you do anything without guarantees," Varik mumbled.

"You want to lose the rest of your teeth?" Buck asked.

Varik cringed.

It would have been easy to throw down their guns and let Varik get what was coming to him, but this wasn't the way to bring him to justice.

"Don't listen to him," Jules whispered. "This isn't about revenge. He's trying to take over the ship. He wants the aliens to capture us. He is a spy."

Buck snorted. "That's a joke! You're the one who had full access to the ship all this time. If anyone is working for the Vitari, it's you."

Footsteps quietly rang out behind them, and Aria spun around to see who it was.

"Niko?" Liam asked.

He slowed to a stop. "Mom? Dad? What are you doing here?" Then he appeared to notice what was going on, and he heaved his back to bring a massive rifle up to his hip. "Don't trust him!"

"Who?" Aria asked.

"Jules! He's the spy! He stunned me!"

Before Aria could even blink, Jules grabbed Liam and dragged him back against the reactor. The bot used him as a shield and held his pistol to Liam's head.

Buck chuckled. "Quite the party we have going here."

As if on cue, a roar of metallic thunder reached their ears, quickly rising in pitch and volume. What sounded like a hundred different harvesters began clattering and hammering on the nearest set of doors. Then the thunder rolled on and stopped at the next set, adding to the racket. Soon all four entrances on their level were echoing with the same destructive vibrations, like a band of psychotic drummers just hammering away.

CHAPTER 53

"It won't be long before they break in here," Varik groaned, his voice all but drowned out by the incessant hammering of the harvesters.

Aria's eyes skipped around the reactor room, imagining the tangled horde of machines behind those four sets of doors.

"Shut up," Buck snapped.

Aria's gaze landed on him. He was no longer aiming his pistol at Payton. It was aimed at Liam instead as if he planned to shoot through her husband to get at Jules.

"How long until the systems finish rebooting?" Buck asked Varik.

"Not long. Five minutes, maybe less."

"Good. Give me the access codes," Buck said.

"Of course," Varik nodded agreeably, but there was a secret fire in his eyes. He glanced at Aria, his expression grim, his mouth and chin bloody from a freshly-split lip. The beginnings of a smug grin were twitching in one corner of his mouth. He had something up his sleeve.

"What makes you think I'm a spy?" Jules asked in a reasonable voice.

Aria dragged her eyes away from Varik with a scowl. "To start with, you're pointing a gun at my husband's head."

"Because your son was about to shoot me."

"You're not even supposed to be able to use a weapon!" Aria said. "That's proof that you're not an ordinary bot."

"I never said that I was," Jules replied.

"Look, if you're not a spy, just let me go," Liam panted. The pain of the pencil-sized hole that Buck had burned through his shoulder was obviously catching up with him.

"I won't shoot you," Nikolai said in a reasonable voice, but his posture and the giant rifle in his arms said otherwise. "I just want to talk."

"You are lying," Jules replied.

"What is this about?" Aria demanded, looking to Nikolai now. "He stunned you? Why?"

"I don't know."

"To keep him safe!" Jules said. "He wanted to play the hero and come down here with me. It was too dangerous to let him leave the armory, and I didn't trust him not to follow me if I left him alone."

"Bullshit!" Nikolai screamed. "Besides, stunning me isn't all you did! You were manning the comms when we tried to contact my father. Twice you said you left him a message, but he never got any of them."

Liam nodded along with that. "We also tried to contact Nikolai, but no one replied."

Aria shook her head, confused. "Why wouldn't he want you to contact your father?"

"Because we found out that the Union lost an entire fleet at Vitaria. It was there, just drifting through the nebula. And then we saw something that Jules called a Dyson Sphere that the aliens built around a black hole. He didn't want me to warn Dad about that stuff."

"Nikolai, think about what you're saying," Jules said. "Why would warning your father even matter? How could that possibly interfere with the aliens' agenda? He wasn't in a position to do anything to thwart them whether he realized how big of a threat they really are or not."

The lights in the reactor room swelled to their full brightness.

"Time's up," Buck said. "The systems are online. Give me the access codes. Now."

Varik looked to Aria once more, his expression pained. "I'm sorry."

And suddenly she understood the smug curve of his lips.

"No!" she screamed even as a blinding flash of light consumed her. She blinked rapidly against the glare to find herself standing in a familiar setting: the living room aboard Varik's lifeboat. The picture windows looked out on a scrolling wall of metal. Crimson engines flared into view as an alien starship cruised by at point-blank range.

And then another flash of light tore through her retinas, and she was left staring into empty, star-studded space. The magenta eye of an unknown star glared back at her. They'd just jumped to another star system.

Aria looked away from the windows to scan the room. Samos, Calla, and Payton were sitting on the deck behind the couch looking pale with shock, but otherwise unharmed. That was more than Markus, Elisa, and Varik could say. They lay gasping on the deck, struggling with the pain of their injuries. But there was no sign of Liam, Nikolai, Buck or Jules.

Calla was the first to recover. She ran over to her father and dropped to her haunches beside him. "Dad, where are your vitalics?" she asked.

"What did you *do?*" Aria screamed. "Send me back!"

Varik's gaze slid away from Calla to meet hers, his blue eyes narrowed to cloudy slits.

"Are we safe?" Markus interrupted between agonized gasps.

"Yes and no," Varik replied. "The Vitari won't be able to follow us. We're too far away for anyone to tell them where we went, and the harvesters can't jump between star systems on their own, but—"

"But?" Aria demanded.

"But they can still kill us, and there's plenty of them on board. We need to evacuate the ship and use the lifeboats to jump to the next closest star before they find us."

"The lifeboats can jump away on their own?" Calla asked.

"Yes, but we'll only get one chance, and we won't be able to go far. If there aren't any habitable planets in that star system..."

"We'll have to risk it," Samos decided. "Anything is better than staying here with a horde of harvesters hunting us for the rest of our natural lives."

Payton pried herself away from the old engineer and ran to her mother. She locked her arms around Aria's legs and sobbed. "Where's Daddy and Niko?"

Aria jerked her chin to Varik once more and aimed her rifle at his head. "I'm not going anywhere without my husband and son."

"They might already be dead."

"So might you if you keep wasting my time."

"I'll have to drop the interference field again to be able to teleport you back there. If harvesters take advantage of that to get to me, there'll be no one to teleport you back here."

"Then teach me how to use the transporters."

"It would take too long."

"Fine, then I'll risk it. You owe me that much. You saved your family at the expense of mine and countless others. Now you need to start making that right."

Varik winced. "It wasn't supposed to go like this. I was supposed to take you to meet the Vitari on your own, and then we were supposed to teleport back here with Calla and escape."

"Do you think I give a shit about your intentions? You're wasting time! Send me back before someone else dies because of you!"

Varik hesitated.

"Do it, Dad," Calla said. She wiped away a tear that slid down her cheek.

"Send me, too," Elisa added despite looking like something dragged off a battlefield after the smoke cleared. "I can help her."

Markus shot an angry look at her. "Your place is with me, by *my* side as my consort."

"And I will return to your side. Let me go."

"Forget it," Markus said.

"Overruled," Varik replied. "Markus, Samos, give your transporters to Mrs. Price. She'll need extras for her husband and son."

Aria nodded her thanks as she went to retrieve the silver discs from each of them.

"What about Buck and Jules?" Aria asked.

Varik shook his head. "Buck is determined to murder me, and Jules is a possible spy." He looked to Elisa. "If you get the chance, take them out."

She nodded back. "Understood."

CHAPTER 54

"**F**uck!" Buck shouted. He punched the reactor with the hand holding his pistol.

"What just happened?" Nikolai asked in a small voice.

"They teleported away, that's what happened!" Buck roared.

Liam felt Jules' grip on him easing, and the bot's pistol stopped driving a hole into the side of his head. Jules shoved him away and stepped out from behind him to aim his gun at Buck. "Drop your weap—"

Buck riddled him with a deafening tirade of emerald lasers. A molten orange hole appeared in Jules' chest, and the bot collapsed to his knees with a blank expression on his face. The arm holding his pistol twitched and groaned as he struggled to bring the weapon into line with Buck. Sparks shot out of Jules' chest.

The bot's head slowly turned. "Don't t-t-trust—"

A *crack* sounded, and a ball of white hot plasma melted Jules' face off. He fell over facedown with a ringing *clunk.*

The thunder of harvesters raging against the doors sounded distant to Liam's ringing ears. For a moment, he was frozen, unsure of what to do or think.

Nikolai's plasma cannon tracked over from Jules to Buck. "What if Jules was telling the truth?" he asked. "How do we know *you* aren't the spy?"

Buck made an irritated noise in the back of his throat. "We don't have time for this!"

Liam watched as though in slow motion as Buck's laser rifle tracked into line with his son.

"No!" Liam dived for Jules' pistol.

Buck fired, and Nikolai cried out. An ear-splitting *boom* popped split the air, and a giant ball of plasma *whooshed* over him with a scalding wash of heat. Liam grabbed the pistol with his good arm, and rolled over, searching for his target—

Just in time for Buck to land on top of him. He grabbed both of Liam's wrists and smashed the hand holding Jules' gun into the metal grating over and over until the pistol fell from numb fingers. Buck kicked it away, and leapt back off him, aiming his rifle at Liam's chest.

Clutching his battered hand, Liam rolled over to check on his son. Nikolai lay against the railings, looking dazed. The plasma cannon rested in his lap, the barrel still smoking. One of his legs was blackened and oozing from a laser burn.

Liam saw the barrel of the cannon twitch up as Nikolai struggled to aim it.

"Don't even think about it, kid," Buck said. "That cannon takes a second to shoot. I'll see it coming, and you'll miss. Lasers, on the other hand, fire instantly, and I could shoot you with my eyes shut."

Nikolai's expression crumbled, and the cannon clunked against the deck. He burst into tears. "My leg feels like it's on fire!"

Rage boiled inside of Liam. "We'll get you fixed up. Don't worry."

He rounded on Buck to see the former Marine slowly shaking his head. He had his rifle trained on Liam and his pistol aimed at Nikolai. "If those harvesters break in here, you won't be getting him anywhere. His blood is already flooded with vitalics, remember? He's a target."

Just then, a flash of light blinded Liam, and he lay blinking against the glare.

A familiar voice said, "Drop your weapons, Buck."

"Aria?" Liam's vision cleared enough that he could see her standing by the railing, right where she'd disappeared a few minutes ago. She had a rifle aimed at Buck's chest. And she wasn't the only one who'd returned. Elisa was back, too, standing off to one side of Buck, but unfortunately unarmed.

"You're outnumbered," Aria said.

"I still like my odds," he replied.

"Why are you doing this?" Aria demanded. "For your wife? It's not our fault that she's dead."

Buck's eyes flashed and he glared at her. "I still have a score to settle with Varik for that, but no, this isn't about Ace. This is about Maddy."

"Maddy?"

Realization dawned, but Nikolai was the first to say it. "You *are* the spy! You're the reason I couldn't contact my dad! You were ignoring Jules' messages."

"I needed to reach the Vitari and convince them to let my daughter go. I didn't need you scaring your father off before we could get there. If he'd thought you were in any danger, he might have insisted we go back up to the *Dream* instead of heading for one of the depots."

Liam realized he probably would have done exactly that.

"They have your daughter?" Aria asked.

"Yes."

"But if you needed to get to the Vitari because they have your daughter, then why did Marshall try to stop Varik from taking us to meet them?"

"She didn't know," Buck said. "They didn't get to her, only me. Years ago they threatened to kill Maddy if I didn't agree to spy on Varik for them, to make sure that he kept his end of their bargain. As far as my wife ever knew and as far as her parents know as they tuck Maddy in tonight, she's never been in any kind of danger."

"She's on Earth?" Liam asked.

"Yes, but she's being watched, and if I don't get you and Varik back to Vitaria soon, they'll kill her."

Liam grimaced. "You and Varik are two sides of the same piece of shit. Saving your daughters at everyone else's expense."

Buck's yellow eyes blazed at him. "You're telling me *you* wouldn't? What if it was *your* daughter?"

Liam began to fire back with a nasty retort, but it died on his lips. What *would* he do? Would he put other people in danger to keep Paytie safe?

Aria was equally quiet.

Before either of them could answer that question, a sharp whistling noise stole their attention. Liam tracked the sound to a single shimmering tentacle sticking through the nearest set of doors. It withdrew and revealed a sucking black hole that whipped the air inside the reactor chamber to a frenzy.

"They're almost through!" Buck screamed to be heard above the tumult of harvesters bashing the doors and the rising roar of escaping air. "They must have decompressed the access corridor on this level! If we don't get out of here, we're going to get sucked out!" Buck jerked his chin to Aria. "You first! We're going down to the next level. You're taking me to see Varik."

"He shot Niko in the leg," Liam said. "He'll never make it."

"You did what?" Aria cried.

"I'll shoot you, too, if you don't start moving," Buck said. "Now let's go!"

"I'm not going anywhere without my family!" Aria replied.

Liam struggled to his feet, gasping as he accidentally put too much weight on his injured shoulder.

"I can carry Niko," Aria said.

"Drop your rifle and kick it over the side," Buck replied.

"Wait," Aria said.

"I just told you we can't—"

"Listen to me!" Aria snapped. Buck flinched. "Even if you take me back to Vitaria, it won't matter. They'll just kill us all anyway."

Buck's brow scrunched into angry furrows. "What are you talking about?"

"The research was a sham! Varik financed it, and he has been manipulating the results, pretending to make breakthroughs."

Buck's expression darkened. "That is disappointing."

"There's another way. I'll take you to Varik, and together we can convince him to take us home. You can go get your daughter before the Vitari get to her, and then everybody wins."

Buck appeared to consider that. He gave in with a nod. "Fine."

"Let me get Niko," Aria said. Not waiting for permission, she ran to their son's side. She gasped when she saw his leg. "Come on. I'll carry you."

"Your rifle!" Buck called after her, but she wasn't listening. Not like she could use it with Niko in her arms, anyway. The two of them lingered, speaking in hushed tones. Something silvery passed between them, there and gone in an instant, but Buck didn't appear to notice it. His gaze was elsewhere, locked on Elisa. All this time, she had been quietly inching around behind him.

"You! Over here, where I can see you."

Buck had to have his eyes everywhere at once. Something was bound to slip. Liam noticed Jules' pistol, lying half a dozen feet away. Too far to reach. Aria hurried back carrying Niko.

"Everybody stays ahead of me," Buck ordered.

Aria nodded and walked ahead. So did Elisa. Liam struggled to his feet and hurried to keep up. Aria stopped and waited for him, already looking winded from the strain of carrying their son.

Buck watched them with flinty eyes and two different weapons. He left his rifle to dangle and cupped a hand to one ear while he kept them covered with his pistol. "You hear that?"

Harvesters hammering away. Wind whipping by them. Their hair and clothes stirring wildly.

"If you don't run for it right now, we're not going to make it."

Aria ignored him. "Liam. I need you to carry Niko for a minute."

"I can't—my shoulder is—"

Aria silenced him with a sharp look. "Just for a minute!" she ground out.

"I'll try."

Aria set their son down on one leg and steadied him.

"What is this, musical kids?" Buck demanded. "Throw the fucking rifle over the side *now,* or I'll shoot your husband in the back."

"Fine."

Liam held Niko up as Aria ducked out of her rifle's strap. "Elisa now would be a good time to..." Aria trailed off, but Elisa seemed to catch her meaning.

Before Liam even realized what was happening, Elisa ran at Buck, screaming at the top of her lungs. Both of his weapons tracked her, and he fired them in unison. But Aria fired her rifle, too. Elisa crashed into the metal catwalk with a smoking hole in her hip and a molten orange patch on her chest. But Aria's shot also struck its target. Buck screamed and dropped his pistol to clutch a laser-blackened thigh.

Taking advantage of his reaction, Aria ran at him. "That was for Niko," she said. And then she smashed him in the face with the butt of her rifle. "And that's for my husband."

Blood spurted from Buck's nose, and his head snapped back. Aria kicked his pistol away before he could recover, and Liam rushed in to wrestle with him for his rifle.

Aria pressed the barrel of her weapon against the side of Buck's head, ending the struggle. Liam took his rifle and slung it over his good shoulder.

"You've wasted too much time," Buck said in a nasal voice. His lips parted in a bloody smile, and he nodded to the damaged doors where their air was busy raging out into space.

Liam stepped out of Buck's reach, glancing at the doors as he did so. There were a dozen different shimmering tentacles hooked into various holes in the doors and busy prying them open.

"They'll be through any second now."

"And we'll be long gone," Aria replied, smiling wickedly back at him.

Buck's brow furrowed, and then a light of understanding dawned. "You're going to teleport out."

Aria withdrew a silver disc from a zippered pocket in her environment suit. She handed it to Liam. "Put this in your pocket and watch Buck," she said as she hurried over to Elisa's side.

Liam nodded and briefly studied the device before slipping it into his pocket. Keeping an eye on Buck, he risked a glance at Aria to see her kneeling beside Elisa and shaking her by her shoulders. "Elisa?"

No response.

Aria shook her again. Harder this time.

"She took a plasma blast to the chest," Buck said. "She's dead."

"Elisa!" Aria tried again. "Damn it!"

Aria locked eyes with Liam. "We're in trouble."

Buck laughed.

"Why?" Liam asked.

"Elisa was supposed to tell Varik when to teleport us out of here!"

"Can't you just tell him yourself?"

"No, because the ship is on lockdown! Only Varik has access to any of the systems. He gave Elisa the codes before he sent us here, but we didn't count on her getting disabled!"

"Disabled?" Liam echoed.

"She's a bot! Come on, we have to run!" Aria turned and pointed with her rifle to the stairs leading down the level of catwalks below theirs. "Go!"

Liam didn't need to be told twice. He left Buck's rifle to dangle by the strap and ran over to where Niko was leaning heavily on the railings. He wrapped an arm around his son's waist, and they began hobbling toward the stairs.

They didn't make it five steps before the wind whipping through the reactor room became a hurricane. Liam's ears popped painfully, and the wind staggered him into the railings. Then his ears popped for a second time, and an even stronger gust slapped him in the back, pushing both him and Niko clear over the railings. His stomach dropped, and he screamed as he fell, arms flailing for something to hold onto. His good arm hooked through the lowest rung of the railing, and a sharp pain lanced through his shoulder as he jerked to a stop. The rotating column of air whipping around the reactor core buoyed him up, making it easier to hold on, but he also had Nikolai's weight to contend with.

His son clung to him with both arms wrapped around his waist. Their combined weight threatened to tear Liam's arm out of its socket. His eyes darted around. He saw that Aria had lost both of her weapons in her scramble to grab the railings, and Elisa's body was dragging across the catwalk, sliding toward a twenty-five story drop into the bowels of the ship.

Buck was pinned against the railings just a few feet from Liam, laughing like a madman. Elisa's body slammed belatedly into a post and wrapped around it like a car about a tree.

"Looks like we're going down together, fuckers!" Buck cried. "I'll see you all in hell!"

If Liam could have spared a hand to grab the rifle now choking him as it fluttered at the end of its strap, he would have shot Buck in the head.

"My hands are slipping!" Aria screamed.

Liam could barely hear her over the roar of escaping air. "Hold on!" he cried.

"For what?!" Buck scoffed. "We're all dead anyway."

The air grew dizzyingly thin, and black polka dots crowded in on Liam's vision. He could feel his arm weakening, already numb from holding several hundred pounds against the shearing force of the evacuating air.

"I'm not going to make it!" Aria yelled. "I love you both!"

"Don't you dare let go!" Liam screamed back.

CHAPTER 55

Aria's fingers slipped precious centimeters with every passing second. She struggled to flex her hands on the railing, to reel herself back in, but her numb, aching fingers refused to respond. Her strength was a dwindling resource, and the cyclone of air tearing past her was only getting stronger. She glanced back in the direction of the escaping air and saw a gap in the doors wide enough for a human to slip through. Harvesters' tentacles poked through a dozen different holes, steadily prying the doors apart. The wider the gap, the stronger the winds sucking her toward it. It wouldn't be long now...

Glancing back to the front, Aria used her last ounce of strength to hold on just a few seconds longer. Long enough to say goodbye.

"I'm not going to make it!" Aria yelled. "I love you both!"

"Don't you dare let go!" Liam roared.

"Why both of you let go?" Buck said. "You can suffocate with me or crack your skulls together at the exit! You choose!"

Aria's eyes found the back of the former Marine's head and glared, suddenly wondering how Marshall could be so different from the piece of shit she'd married. Rage against Buck gave her that last little boost to hold on a few seconds more.

And that was all she needed.

The deafening roar of escaping air faded to a ringing silence, and Aria felt herself falling. No longer buoyed by the cyclone like a human flag, she now dangled from the railings with her feet above the abyss. Liam and Nikolai dangled beside her.

"Niko, get over the railing!" Liam said. He hurriedly clambered up his father's back and reached for the top rung.

Aria wondered what had stopped the escaping air. Maybe something had been sucked into the gap. But if that was the case, this might only be a temporary reprieve. Either way, she didn't have time to look. Her fingers were still slipping.

Gritting her teeth, she curled her tortured hands, trying to get a better grip, but that only resulted in a painful spasm from her left hand, and it slid clear off the bar.

"Damn it!" she gasped, now dangling by just one hand. "I'm going to fall!"

A strong hand gripped her wrist and pulled her up. She saw that it was Buck. Confusion swirled as he pulled her over the railing. She touched the catwalk on shaking legs, and Buck limped over to help Liam next. But before he grabbed Liam's hands, he snatched the rifle from around his neck.

"Hey!" Nikolai cried.

Buck swept the rifle into line with him. "You want me to help your father up or not? Back away. Now."

"Do it," Liam said in a strained voice.

Nikolai subsided with a glare, and Buck reached over to pull Liam up. Aria was too shocked from her near brush with death to be outraged by Buck's possible ulterior motives for helping them. They were alive. And for now, that was all that mattered.

But *how* were they alive? She twisted around to look at the doors that had been sucking all of their air out a moment ago.

The harvesters had stopped hammering to get in, and the entrance that they'd cracked open was now shimmering with some kind of force field.

As she watched, a pair of giant bipeds in full-body suits of matte black armor stepped through.

An extra pair of skinny arms arced out from their backs, also armored, and holding some type of weapons.

The Vitari had arrived.

A pair of harvesters rolled through after them, taking up guard positions to either side of the doors, and then the Vitari stalked down the catwalk, their footsteps booming as they went.

"Tell them you surrender," Buck whispered as he sidled up to Aria with the laser rifle he'd taken back from Liam. He went on, "Promise to take us back to Vitaria and finish your research."

"I can't," Aria whispered back. "They're telepaths. They'll know that I'm lying." She glanced at Buck. If he was shocked to hear that the Vitari could read minds, he didn't show it.

"They're not lies if you believe them. You know your research better than Varik. Maybe there's something real in there. Or maybe he was lying about falsifying results."

"Maybe..." Aria replied, willing herself to believe it. The Vitari stalked up to them, each holding a pair of black weapons in the shape of an H. Two weapon barrels stuck out from the front of each weapon, and vicious black daggers stuck out the backs.

Aria swallowed thickly as the Vitari approached. She lifted her chin to keep her eyes level with the gleaming black eyelets in their helmets. Liam helped Nikolai hobble over to her. They came to stand beside her, and Liam laced his fingers through hers. A united front against the enemy. She swayed on her feet, blinking dark spots from her eyes. The air around the reactor was desperately thin, but she was determined to stay conscious long enough to see this through.

The nearest of the two Vitari stopped just a few feet away from Aria and warbled something in a deep voice that was muffled and distorted by its helmet. The translation thundered out from vertical speakers in the alien's chest plate.

"Where is Varik?" The Vitari's two weapons angled down on her while the other one kept Liam and Nikolai covered. Both of their thicker more muscular sets of arms dangled beside their torsos, empty-handed.

Aria shifted her weight from one foot to the other and cleared her throat. "I don't know where he is."

One of those muscular arms shot out and seized Aria by her neck, hauling her up onto tiptoes. The world grew. She was dimly aware of Liam and Nikolai battling the Vitari's arm, punching it and prying at its fingers as her windpipe collapsed and her thoughts drifted off into oblivion.

She woke up a few seconds later lying on the catwalk, coughing and gasping for air. Liam hovered over her, his expression twisted with fear.

More warbling came from the aliens. *"Do not lie to us again. Where is Varik?"*

Despite Aria's best efforts to keep her mind blank, her thoughts flashed back to the lifeboat where she'd last seen Varik. The two Vitari looked at each other, then back to her.

"Take us there. Now."

Aria nodded, and Liam helped her to her feet. They turned and walked slowly toward the stairs leading down to the level below theirs. Buck kept them covered with his rifle as he walked beside the two Vitari. They seemed to already know that he was on their side. *Of course, they knew,* Aria thought. They were telepaths.

Nikolai hobbled along, gripping the railing beside him for support. Liam gave him a shoulder to lean on as well. They passed what was left of Elisa, still wrapped around the railings. One of her arms was stretched out behind her at an impossible angle, her hand splayed against the catwalk.

Aria winced as she stepped over Elisa's arm, but Buck kicked it out of the way.

"Hey! Have some respect!" Aria snapped.

"Fuck you."

Aria looked back at Elisa. The bot's arm now dangled over the side with the rest of her, swinging like a pendulum in a lingering updraft.

But there shouldn't have been an updraft. It took a moment for Aria to realize that Elisa's arm wasn't swinging—it was twitching. The Vitari walked by her without noticing a thing. Adrenaline raced through Aria's veins and left her entire body shaking. Elisa wasn't dead. If she could wake up and tell Varik to teleport them back out—

Both Vitari suddenly stopped and turned to look at Elisa. Aria's blood ran cold. Had they just read her thoughts?

"Is something wrong?" Buck asked.

One of the two warbled a reply, and their weapons swung out of line with Aria and into line with Elisa's back.

"What do you mean she's not dead?" Buck asked, his attention wavering for a crucial second.

Aria lunged for his rifle. Before Buck could stop her, she managed to drag the barrel into line with the nearest Vitari and pull the trigger. A stream of emerald fire leapt out, drawing brilliant flashes of light from the alien's armor.

"Hey!" Buck threw her off.

Not having seen that Aria was the one who'd shot it, The Vitari spun around and sliced off Buck's arm with the bladed-end of one of its weapons. Both the rifle and his arm fell to the catwalk with a ringing clatter.

Buck belatedly screamed and clutched the river of blood that gushed from his arm, desperately trying to staunch the flow.

"It was her!" Buck cried. "Fuck! It was her, damn it!"

Both Vitari turned to her. Their weapons leapt toward her, the blades on the backs of them flashing darkly. Aria cringed, her eyes involuntarily squeezing shut in anticipation of those blades slicing through her.

Liam screamed, and Aria's eyes snapped open to see blood gushing from her husband's side as he crumpled to his knees in front of her.

"No!" Aria cried.

A blinding light sucked all the life and color out of the scene, but it was back in all of its gory detail just an instant later. Aria's vision cleared to see that she was now standing in Varik's living room. Liam lay gasping at her feet and clutching his side. Blood bubbled steadily between his fingers.

"Dad!" Nikolai limped over and fell down beside him.

Aria dropped to her knees and replaced Liam's blood-slicked hands with hers. "Somebody help me! I need something to stop the bleeding!" she cried.

But Markus was busy screaming about Elisa's condition, and Samos was frozen in shock, staring in horror at the river of blood streaming toward him from Liam's side. Varik was over by the windows, seated at the manual controls, and Nikolai was just a kid.

"Daddy?"

Speaking of kids.

Aria looked up to see Payton clambering out of an armchair to come and see what was wrong.

Calla dropped into view and checked Liam's pulse.

"I can't stop it!" Aria cried through a haze of tears.

"He needs vitalics," Calla said. "Varik!" She looked at her father. "Where do you keep them?"

"Under the fridge! Pull up the carpet. There's a smuggler's compartment."

Calla sprang up and away. Aria stared after her, willing the other woman to hurry.

Liam's hands fumbled blindly, batting the air. His green eyes were wide and unseeing, his breathing shallow and too fast.

"Don't you die on me, Liam! Don't you dare leave me!"

One of his hands found hers, slid around her wrist and squeezed. Another found Nikolai's shoulder. Their son burst into tears at that.

Payton backed away slowly, her jaw slack and cheeks pale, shaking her head in denial, her eyes dry as a bone.

Liam's mouth was opening and closing soundlessly, blood slicking his lips as he struggled to say something.

"Save your strength," Aria said, smiling brokenly at him. "You're going to be okay." But she was a medical researcher. She knew enough about the human body to know when it could and couldn't be fixed. "I love you," she added in a whisper.

Liam's eyes wandered sightlessly for a few seconds before locking with hers. His mouth opened wide, and he coughed up a clot of blood. His last breath escaped his lips as a gurgling sigh, and the warm stream of blood seeping through Aria's hands abruptly ceased. An animal cry escaped her lips, and she collapsed on top of him, sobbing so hard that her chest felt like it would explode.

Liam was dead, and no amount of vitalics could bring him back.

CHAPTER 56

Footsteps hammered the deck, approaching fast. Calla dropped down beside them, her voice a breathless whisper, "Is he..."

"You're too late," Aria said. She peeled her cheek off Liam's now motionless chest.

Varik made a frustrated noise and leapt out of the flight control station. He ran over and all but shoved Aria aside. "Move!"

She recoiled from Varik, outrage and confusion battling for control of her emotions. He snapped his fingers at Calla.

"Did you find my vitalics?"

She nodded slowly and lifted a silver case off the deck. He snatched it away from her and opened the top half to reveal syringes in one side and vials of serum in the other, but the serum was thick and silvery, not thin and clear like vitalics.

"What is that?" Aria asked in a hoarse whisper.

"Synthetic vitalics," Varik replied.

"Synthetic..." Aria shook her head. "All this time you—"

He cut her off with a wave of his hand. "It's not what you think."

He jammed a syringe into the vial and withdrew the contents with the plunger. Throwing the empty vial aside, he stuck the needle straight through Liam's eye and depressed the plunger.

"If you believe in a god, you'd better start praying to him," Varik said.

Aria didn't, but she wiped her eyes and did just that.

Markus wandered over, looking furious. Elisa clung to his arm, her chest a molten ruin and her hip a blackened mess.

"Is he going to be one of us now?" Elisa asked quietly.

Aria did a double take. "One of *us?*"

"Maybe," Varik replied, already reaching for a second syringe. "But I don't know if we were fast enough."

Hope and horror rose up inside of Aria in equal portions. "What are you doing to him?"

Varik glanced at her as he jammed a second syringe into Liam's other eye and depressed the plunger. "You want your husband back?"

"That wasn't the question!"

Varik ignored her and withdrew a third vial from the case. This time he unscrewed the cap and poured the viscus silver fluid out over Liam's wounded side. The wound fizzed and sizzled.

Aria watched with wary suspicion crawling down her spine.

"Come on, Dad," Nikolai pleaded, either oblivious to what was really happening or not caring about the consequences. Payton crawled over from the living room, her cheeks now streaked with tears.

Varik poured out two more vials with more fizzing and sizzling as the mysterious substance seeped into Liam's veins.

"We'll know if it worked in a few seconds," Varik said.

And then the impossible happened. Liam blinked and sucked in a rattling breath.

"Liam!" Aria pulled him into a crushing hug even as his body convulsed with hacking coughs. Blood splattered across her back and the deck behind her. Nikolai and Payton crashed into them next, making it a group hug.

"What happened?" Liam groaned.

Before anyone could answer, a flash of light tore through the windows behind them.

"We're in trouble!" Markus said. "The harvesters are coming out after us!"

Aria withdrew from Liam to see what was going on.

Varik leapt up and ran to the flight controls. He landed in the pilot's seat with a *whuff* of escaping air from the cushion. It was only then that Aria noticed the *Starlit Dream* drifting away on a rear view display projected over the right side of the windows. Hundreds of other lifeboats were streaking away with them. Varik had evacuated them for the second time, but it might not be enough. Shimmering pinpricks of light were streaking out after them. Hundreds of harvesters.

Another burst of light dazzled their eyes as one of those pinpricks teleported. A nearby lifeboat illuminated with a reciprocal flash as the harvester reappeared inside of it.

"We have to jump out before one of those things teleports in here!" Markus said.

"I'm working on it!" Varik snapped.

"Wait," Aria said. "There are Vitari are on board the cruise ship. If we leave them there, can't they use it to find us?"

Varik shot a worried look over his shoulder. "Vitari? You saw them?"

"Two of them," Elisa confirmed.

Varik tore his gaze away. "The ship is on lock down. Only my codes will provide access to its systems, and the Vitari don't have those codes."

"What if you're wrong? What if they find a way?" Aria pressed. "How many stars are in range of the lifeboats? What kind of radius would the Vitari have to search to find us?"

"Fifty-one star systems in range. A radius of ten light years," Varik replied.

"They could search all of those systems in just a few hours!" Markus said.

"*If* they can get control of the *Dream*," Varik replied.

"But that's just a matter of time," Calla said.

"You want to stay here and die faster?" Varik demanded.

"Can't you self-destruct the ship?" Aria asked.

Varik barked a laugh. "This isn't Star Trek."

"Then what are you waiting for?" she countered. "Jump us out of here already!"

"I need to conduct a spectral analysis of the stars around us to learn more about them. We can't risk jumping to one that's inhospitable to life."

"We don't have time for a spectral analysis!" Markus cried. "You've got fifty stars to choose from, just pick one!"

Varik rounded on him from the control station. "I already did!" He jabbed a finger at the bright magenta star blazing in the upper left corner of the picture windows. "*That* is the star I picked! The one I scouted and rigorously vetted. Do you know how many others I had to rule out because they would never support a human colony? There might not be another system like it within *fifty* light years, let alone ten!"

Another flash of light tore through the void as another harvester teleported.

"Just jump!" Calla screamed. "The next one lifeboat they board could be ours!"

And it was.

A blinding wash of light suffused the deck, and everyone screamed. Aria held her family close, half-expecting a harvester to impale them all before their eyes even recovered enough to see it coming.

But as the glare faded, she saw that it wasn't the flash of a teleportation that had blinded her. It was an explosion.

The *Starlit Dream* was cracking apart in molten chunks.

"Did *you* do that?" Aria asked into the stunned silence that followed.

Varik slowly shook his head.

"It was Buck," Liam said. "He must have found a way to destabilize the core."

"Impossible," Samos put in. "He would have had to shoot it with a rocket launcher."

"What about a plasma cannon?" Nikolai asked. "It didn't fly out with the atmosphere. It got stuck on the railings."

Varik sagged in his chair with a shuddering sigh. "It doesn't matter how. All that's left is to be thankful. Buck just saved us all. He's a hero."

"And a spy for the Vitari," Liam said. "He admitted it."

Varik just looked at him. "Obviously not a very willing spy."

Aria stared at her husband. How was he *alive?* She reached out and grazed Liam's hand with hers. "Are you..."

"Am I what?" Liam's eyebrows scrunched together.

"Liam, you died."

His brow furrowed in confusion. "No, I didn't."

"Yes, you did. Varik brought you back with..." She trailed off, wondering what *synthetic vitalics* really were. "What did you do to him?"

"You're welcome," Varik said without turning from the lifeboat's controls.

"Welcome for what?"

Varik spun his chair around to face her. "He's one of us now."

"One of you? What does that mean?"

"Purely biological beings cannot live forever. It's impossible. Eventually everything breaks. Why do you think I returned home after twenty-nine years and yet somehow I looked the same age as when I had left? It wasn't because I had used biological vitalics on myself. Calla's mother and I invented a synthetic version and we used it on ourselves, becoming the first of a new race of humans — cyborgs with an ever-expanding colony of micro machines coursing through our blood. They make constant repairs as our biological cells wear out. The result is a slow blending of man and machine and true immortality, but it comes at a price. I am more machine now than man, and eventually your husband will be, too."

"But..."

"That doesn't mean he will be any different or any less alive. We're not copying his mind and putting it in a mechanical body. We tried that with models like Jules, but it raised too many existential questions. No, instead we replace neurons that die with synthetic versions that integrate seamlessly with the biological ones. We patch blood vessels with bio-adaptive plastics, clean arteries by dissolving excess fat, and replace lost cartilage. We strengthen brittle bones with aluminum frames, and so on. The process is slow and insidious, and there will be no discernible differences in his personality. His body, however, will become gradually stronger and younger-looking as time goes by."

"That sounds... almost too good to be true," Aria said.

"It works," Elisa put in. "You asked what Markus has over me. It's that he and his father saved my life. I'll never stop owing them for that."

Aria couldn't help but notice a smooth, silver chassis peeking out of the char-blackened hole in her shirt where Buck's plasma bolt had struck her in the chest.

"Owing them your life doesn't them the right to treat you like a slave," Aria said.

"I'll be the first to admit that I am somewhat co-dependent," Elisa replied. "But I am not a slave."

"She and I have an unconventional relationship," Markus agreed. "I've also used synthetic vitalics, if that makes feel better."

Aria frowned. "What about Jules?"

"He was an experimental case," Varik said. "A brain data transfer to an entirely mechanical body. He retained his memories and personality, but one could argue that he was never really alive, or at best, that he was just a digital and mechanical copy of the original man."

"Buck killed him..." Liam said slowly.

"And saved us," Varik added. "A complex man if ever there was one."

"He would have killed you, too," Liam said.

Varik smirked. "He would have tried. Now, if you'll excuse me, there is one last matter to attend to..." He turned away from them, back to the windows and the flight controls.

Aria waited to see what he was talking about. Yet another burst of light stabbed through her eyes and left them streaming with tears. She wiped the tears away to see that the stars had been replaced by a rippling cerulean lake with crystal clear shores. A dome of bright, purple-blue sky soared overhead. Grassy green plains full of colorful flowers rolled out in all directions, and hundreds of other lifeboats sat hunching in the field, looking like identical lakeside estates.

White-capped mountains soared in the distance and leafy green trees swayed between them and the far side of the lake. A swarm of bright red avian creatures flitted low over the water. Schools of fish leapt up to greet them, their scales sparkling like diamonds in the magenta sun.

A herd of white-furred ball-shaped animals slugged along through the grass nearby.

Varik spun away from the windows with a smile twitching on his swollen, blood-crusted lips. "Welcome to Arcadia," he said.

CHAPTER 57

—One Week Later—

Aria stared into a crackling bonfire, inhaling the sweet citrus smell of the air, and listening to the wind sighing through the trees. Arcadia was everything that Earth once had been and more.

There no predators, no prey. Every animal a delight to meet, every plant a delicious delicacy full of nutritious sustenance. The air was fresh and clean in a way that Earth's once might have been. Stunning vistas lay over every hill and in every valley. There were endless wonders around every corner, boundless oceans and crystal rivers with water so clean and pure that you could drink it without even the need for a filter. From the flowering, sun-soaked fields and the sighing forests, to the luminous cave systems below, everything on Arcadia was awe-inspiring.

Aria had only been there a week and she was already calling it home. Everyone else was, too. She glanced around the fire, everyone's faces lit up and smiling as they nibbled on roasted vegetables and shared the days' discoveries with each other. Markus, Elisa, Varik and Calla were sitting two places down from Aria and Liam. The kids were playing hide and seek close by—within the perimeter of the camp, just in case. Curious white-furred *Puffers* sat cooing contentedly and warming themselves by the fire. Their blue eyes gleamed in the firelight. They were by far the friendliest of all the creatures they'd met so far. Aria petted one that sat within reach and it leaned into her hand, begging to be scratched. She obliged. They were like a cross between cats and dogs, but with a rudimentary language and the intelligence of a human toddler.

Liam wrapped an arm around Aria's shoulders and pulled her close. "What are you thinking about?" he whispered.

"How lucky we are to be here. Alive and well."

"Not all of us," Liam replied.

Aria observed a moment of silence for the dead. "No." The ones around this fire pit were lucky. The happy ones. They hadn't lost anyone that they loved, nor had they left lives and people behind that they would like to return to. They were the ones that Varik had chosen and brought to this world ahead of time—members of his chosen ruling class. Cyborgs like him, Markus, Elisa, and now Liam. They were immortal, but the price they paid for their immortality was their ever-diminishing humanity. Varik was the first, a victim of his own creation. He and his dead wife were the masterminds behind it, and the only ones who'd actually come close to creating what the Vitari claimed they wanted. How could Varik have known that fusing artificial and biological life was anathema to the Vitari culture?

Aria didn't share their views. Her husband was *alive*, every part of him aesthetically and functionally the same—better even. He could outlive her by many thousands of years if she didn't undergo the same treatment before she died.

Of course, there were still ways to die as a cyborg. Elisa had come close, but her nanites had pulled her back from the brink.

As for Varik, he'd escaped justice so far, but the jury was out on whether or not that would last. Aria was on the fence about it. He'd saved Liam's life, but he'd also dragged them all into this mess in the first place. If Arcadia weren't such a paradise, a literal Garden of Eden, she would have been angrier with him.

But plenty of others were angry. To say that Varik's reluctant colonists were restless was an understatement. Were it not for the fact that Varik had an army of cyborgs already living here and sitting on a cache of weapons and supplies, the discontented masses might have risen up and formed an old-fashioned lynch mob. As it was, Varik couldn't go anywhere in the settlement without his bodyguards present.

Aria's eyes roved around the bonfire. She counted eleven armed guards standing around the perimeter of the fire, four of whom stood right behind Varik and Calla.

Varik's fear of the people might have driven him to become the despot of a police state if he'd had the aspiration to rule, but Arcadia already had a *Peacekeeper.* That was the ironic title given to their elected president, as if Varik had anticipated that humans and cyborgs would be at each other's throats. But he'd created that situation with his constitution which stated that only cyborgs could be elected to rule. Humans could vote, but that wasn't good enough to keep people happy. Those laws set up a precarious balance between cyborgs and humans, so much so that Aria had wondered why Varik would drag so many flesh and blood humans into his plans. But of course he'd had an explanation ready for that—

"They can breed, whereas we become sterile very quickly," Varik had told her. And then he'd gone on to explain that he couldn't create cyborgs from scratch, not without a biological framework and consciousness to build upon. He needed humans

for that, something like the Vitari with their various life cycles.

The sound of children squealing and hurried footfalls reached Aria's ears. She turned to see Nikolai and Payton come running into the circle with a group of other children.

"Look what we found!" Payton said, and held up a dazzling ball of light.

"What is it?" Aria asked, holding out her hand to receive the object.

Payton gave it to her. It was cool and soft to the touch, about the size of a coconut. Tiny blue specks swirled inside of it, like snowflakes in a snow globe.

Varik walked over, pebbles crunching under foot. Two of his bodyguards trailed along behind him, their eyes and weapons tracking warily through the darkness. "That—" Varik began, nodding to the glowing sphere. "—is Arcadia's most curious lifeform. I call them *Crystal Balls*, because if you stare into them long enough you'll see something."

"Like what?" Payton asked.

"Visions. Hallucinations, really. Some say it's the future, but that's a stretch. Where would the mechanism for that lie? Their skin oozes hallucinogenic compounds, so that provides a more logical explanation."

"They also emit tachyons," someone else said. He stepped out of the shadows and into the ring of stones around the bonfire. It was Samos.

"Tachyons?" Payton asked.

Aria couldn't tear her eyes away from the glowing ball. There were shapes forming inside of it. Images resolving...

"Faster-than-light particles," Samos explained.

"*Theoretical* particles," Markus added from where he and Elisa sat.

"You have yet to prove that they exist," Varik added.

"I've seen their effects," Samos replied. "Faster-than-light particles punch holes in the fabric of space-time. They tunnel through it, making their own wormholes. There are millions of them popping in and out of existence around those spheres with every passing microsecond."

"Fascinating..." Aria said slowly, but she wasn't really listening anymore. She was staring into the glowing sphere in her hands, watching a young boy run through a sprinkler in front of a sprawling log cabin. A man and a woman with familiar faces sat on the porch, smiling and slowly swinging on a rope bench. The boy tripped and fell, then giggled and got back up.

"Be careful, Jules!" the woman said in a familiar voice.

"I will, Grandma," Jules shouted back.

And then a familiar man walked into the scene, holding hands with a young woman. It looked like Nikolai, all grown up. He broke ranks with the young woman and ran up behind the boy to sweep him off the grass. He tickled the child mercilessly. Jules giggled and screamed. "Stooop! I give up! Daaaad!"

The woman swinging on the front porch stood up. "Come on in, you three. Payton has been keeping dinner warm for the past hour!"

"Sorry, Mom," Nikolai replied. He waited for his wife to catch up, and then they hurried the rest of the way to the cabin.

The man on the rope bench stood up then, too, and Aria saw that it was Liam. He looked younger and more vital than he had in years. She recognized herself, too, but barely — she looked like she had in her twenties. Aria opened the front door, and everyone walked inside.

With that, the scene faded to a featureless white glow, and Aria looked up, her eyes still dazzled by light. For a moment, it was impossible to see more than silhouettes standing around her.

"What did you see?" Samos whispered.

A warm blast of Arcadia's citrusy air blew in, bringing with it the fragrant wood smoke from the bonfire. Aria sucked in a deep breath, and her eyes slid shut as she savored the smells and the crackling warmth of the fire.

"Well?" Varik prompted.

"Darling?" Liam asked.

She cracked her eyes open and turned to Liam with a smile. She would tell him later, in private. What she'd seen was too special to be dissected and dismissed by a skeptic like Varik. Saying nothing to either of them, she looked up at Arcadia's twin moons—one a verdant green sliver, the other a blazing golden eye.

In a new world filled with uncertainty and rife with possible conflicts, the future loomed suddenly bright before her. That *hallucination,* as Varik had called it, had been too specific, too real to be a mere product of her imagination. Whatever the science behind it, Samos was right: they really *could* see the future in those spheres, and the future was just as bright as they were.

GET MY NEXT BOOK FOR FREE

<u>A Time for Revenge (Working Title)</u>
(Coming September 2019)

Get a FREE digital copy if you <u>post an honest review of this book on Amazon</u> and <u>send it to me here.</u>
(http://files.jaspertscott.com/revenge.htm)

Thank you in advance for your feedback! Your reviews help more than you know, and I always read your feedback and use your comments to help me improve my work.

KEEP IN TOUCH

SUBSCRIBE to my Mailing List and get two FREE Books!

http://files.jaspertscott.com/mailinglist.html

Follow me on Twitter:
@JasperTscott

Look me up on Facebook:
Jasper T. Scott

Check out my website:
www.JasperTscott.com

Or send me an e-mail:
JasperTscott@gmail.com

OTHER BOOKS BY JASPER SCOTT

Suggested reading order

<u>Scott Standalones</u>
No sequels, no cliffhangers
Under Darkness
Into the Unknown
A Time for Revenge

<u>Rogue Star</u>
Rogue Star: Frozen Earth
Rogue Star (Book 2): New Worlds

<u>Broken Worlds</u>
Broken Worlds: The Awakening (Book 1)
Broken Worlds: The Revenants (Book 2)
Broken Worlds: Civil War (Book 3)

<u>New Frontiers Series (Standalone Prequels to Dark Space)</u>
Excelsior (Book 1)
Mindscape (Book 2)
Exodus (Book 3)

Dark Space Series

Dark Space
Dark Space 2: The Invisible War
Dark Space 3: Origin
Dark Space 4: Revenge
Dark Space 5: Avilon
Dark Space 6: Armageddon

Dark Space Universe Series (Standalone Sequels to Dark Space)

Dark Space Universe (Book 1)
Dark Space Universe: The Enemy Within (Book 2)
Dark Space Universe: The Last Stand (Book 3)

ABOUT THE AUTHOR

Jasper Scott is the USA Today best-selling author of 19 sci-fi novels with 16300+ total reviews on Amazon and an average of 4.4 stars out of 5.0.

With over a million books sold, Jasper's work has been translated into various languages and published around the world. Join the author's mailing list to get two FREE books: https://files.jaspertscott.com/mailinglist.html

Jasper writes fast-paced books with unexpected twists and flawed characters. His latest project is a series of unrelated standalone sci-fi novels; no sequels and no cliffhangers, with two novels currently published, and four more planned to the end of 2019. Previous works include four other best-selling series, among others, his breakout success--Dark Space, a 9-book-long, USA Today Best-selling epic with more than 12,000 reviews on Amazon.

Jasper was born and raised in Canada by South African parents, with a British cultural heritage on his mother's side and German on his father's, to which he has now added Latin culture with his wonderful wife. He now lives in an exotic locale with his wife, their two kids, and two Chihuahuas.

Made in the USA
Columbia, SC
26 June 2020